The Archangel...MICHAEL

The Archangel *Michael*
A Sanction Mate Series
Book #1

S0-BRP-241

ISBN-13: 978-1500406981
ISBN-10: 1500406988

The Archangel...MICHAEL

Thanks,

My sincerest thanks to Emma Brock and Angelia Smith, for their continued support.

I am most grateful to God, for my 'redemption' and for allowing me literary privilege with the 'written' word.

Thank you to all of my readers who embrace my imagination.

DISCLAIMER

There is no scripture, or later discovered scroll, to support this fictional story. It is a figment of this author's imagination. A mere hypothesis meant for the reader's reading enjoyment only.

The Archangel...MICHAEL

"Male and Female, created He them…"
Genesis 5:2

When God created the heavens and earth, He gave all of creation a mate.

To the man, he gave the woman
To the stallion, the filly
To the bull, he gave the cow
To the alpha, the dam
To the tom, he gave the molly
To the cock, the hen
To the drone, he gave the queen
To the stamen, the pistil

Every living creature was given a mate...except the angels!

Or were they? Ask his Chief Archangel and Most Powerful Emissary…

The Archangel...MICHAEL

THE
ARCHANGEL

A Sanction Mate
Book #1

A Novel by

E J Brock

PROLOGUE

Verenda leaned her head against the cyclone fence, and grabbed her chest. The house was less than a block away; but she couldn't make it. She was struggling to catch her breath. She told herself if she breathed with every step, she could make those last few steps.

It took her fifteen minutes to calm her nerves. Then she stood up, held her head high, and made her way to the house…

~

She unlocked the door with unsteady hands. "Are you home, Francis?" she called out to her foster mother. She got no response. Then she saw a note on the table by the door: *"Gone out of town, will be back in two weeks. There is enough food in the fridge."*

Good! No one was home to stop her…

~

She walked into the bathroom and looked in the mirror. Unless it was lying to her, her reflection said she wasn't *ugly*. She wasn't even just an average looking girl. With the exception of her swollen eyes, she was beautiful. She looked like her mother would've looked, had she not been a drug addict. She even had her mother's beauty mark, just above her lip.

She was fair skinned, like her father. He was a Louisiana Frenchman, a Créole. From the pictures she'd seen of him he was a good looking man. That was before he took that first shot of heroin, on a dare. She couldn't remember a day when her parents weren't strung out.

Her experience with them was the only reason she hadn't turned to drugs. Drugs made you do things that you might not otherwise do. Like rape your six year old daughter.

She thought about the day the state took her from her parents. They placed her in a home where she had a bed, and clean clothes. She even had enough food to eat, and foster siblings.

She thought life would be better with her new parents, but it wasn't. Yet again a grownup, who was supposed to take care of her, attacked and brutalized her.

Like before, the state showed up a minute too late. They placed her in another home, and once again she was raped.

By the time she was fifteen she had no self-esteem. She was so desperate to be loved, she let the boys at school use her. One after the other treated her body like it was their rite of passage. They all said *you hot, baby'*, but none of them said the words she longed to hear. That is until Smith Walker came along...

He said them over and over again, *"I love you, Verenda. I love you, girl!"* But it was a lie. He was the biggest user of them all; and she was the biggest fool.

He walked away from her and never looked back, after she provoked his real girlfriend, Leevearne. He didn't call and he acted like she didn't exist, at school. Everyone knew about the fight, and they all were laughing at her.

She changed schools, but it didn't help. Her new classmates knew what had happened. They taunted her, too.

Everywhere she went she heard her classmates making fun of her. They called her stupid, and laughed at her. They said she picked a fight she knew she couldn't win. They left notes in her locker asking her what made her think a stank ho' was worthy of a decent boy. They told her she better not get on the school bus, or they'd finish her off.

They were right; what made her think Smittie could love her? The realization that he didn't love her kept her in constant turmoil. She couldn't face another day, in the life of Verenda Strong. Nobody loved her. Nobody even liked her. Like a pinup doll, she'd been used and abused from the time she was six years old.

Why was she holding on to a life that had no promise of a brighter future?

As she looked in the mirror clarity set in, and her breathing relaxed. For the first time in her life she felt the semblance of peace.

She wiped the tears from her eyes. "Not anymore," she said to her reflection. "It stops today."

She turned and walked into the kitchen.

~

Verenda fell out of the chair, onto the kitchen floor. She felt peace for the first time in her life.

Sammael was holding her soul. "Are you ready to go?"

"Yes. Where am I going?" she asked. She hadn't thought about that before she made the decision to end her life. She sure hoped it wasn't Hell.

Before Sammael could respond he heard Michael's thunderous shout.

"SAMMAEL!!"

Sammael frowned. *"What is wrong, Michael?"*

Michael appeared in front of him. The room reeked of gas. He opened the window and created a windstorm. Then he stared at Sammael. "Give her soul to me!" he shouted.

"Why?"

"She is my *mate!*"

Sammael was the Archangel of death, and had been around almost as long as Michael. He had never *heard* of such a thing. If he gave this soul to Michael, he would most certainly fall. He stepped back and shook his head. "No, brother! I must transport her to her destination," he replied and vanished.

~

Rage and Guilt appeared on the scene, after hearing Michael's shout. They knew something was getting ready to jump off. Both had always wanted to embody him, and bring him over to their side. Now was a *perfect* time. They reached out to touch him, but recoiled! He embraced their persona with fervor, before they even laid a finger on him.

They tried to shake themselves free, but he had a firm grip on them. He was molting the flesh off their bones, virtually consuming them. They shouted, "HELP!!"

~

Michael reached into Sammael's trace, and yanked him back. When he landed, Michael grabbed him by the throat. "I said give her to me!" he shouted. "Or I will destroy you, Sammael!"

~

Verenda wasn't surprised of her awareness, but she

was surprised over the ensuing battle. "Why are you fighting over me?" she asked. "I just want to be left alone."

"Release her, Sammael," Michael barked again. "I will take care of her!" Then he froze Sammael in place, and snatched her.

Sammael knew he couldn't defeat Michael, no one could. But he couldn't allow Michael to have this soul. Father would destroy him before he let him fall. "NO!" he shouted.

Help appeared on the scene, but stood at a distance. He saw that Guilt and Rage were *trapped* in Michael. He sent a shout out to three spirits that could handle Michael.

~

Michael was immediately consumed by Peace, Ease and Calm. He released Rage and Guilt, and they got the hell out of there. He looked at Sammael, and calmly said, "Her soul stays with me."

Sammael heard the Master's gentle voice. *"Michael is correct, that soul is his mate."*

"Did I make a mistake?" Sammael asked. He had never done that before. In ancient times the Son had called back three souls, including Lazareth; but it was not because he made a mistake. It was because the Son had compassion on their grieving loved ones.

"No. Michael did."

He did not understand, but he was not in the habit of questioning the Master. *"Your will be done,"* he replied and vanished.

~

Michael sighed. The Master was right, the mistake

was his. He had watched over everyone's mate, but his own. He spent eons upholding the promise he made to his Watchers. What about the promise he made to her?

He placed her soul back in her body, and lifted her off the floor. She was so young, barely sixteen. What had happened to cause her to want to end it all? Did she not remember the promise she made to him? He'd promised he would come for her, when the time was right. She'd promised she would wait.

He eased into her mind. His eyes twirled, the residue of Guilt and Rage began to take hold, and he cried gray tears. They had tortured his mate. Her parents, her foster-parents *and* her classmates! All of them had used his mate for their sinister pleasure. They drove her to this! And they would pay!

He carried her to her bedroom and placed her on the bed. Then he pulled the covers up over her. He wouldn't let her wake up yet, because he needed to do something. He sent a shout out. *"Slumber. I need you, brother."*

Slumber appeared in the room. Michael didn't have to explain anything to him. All of the Heavenly hosts were witnessing what was going on. All of them were disturbed by Michael's revelation, that this soul was his mate. "At your service," Slumber replied.

"Keep her asleep until I return," Michael commanded, and vanished.

~

"Come to me, Reap!" Michael shouted.

Like Sammael, Reap was neither good nor evil. He wasn't proactive, or malicious; and he never attacked at will. They called Sammael the Angel of Death, but that was a misnomer. Sammael reacted to the *actions* of Reaper aka Death. Reap reacted to the *actions* of Sow.

He appeared on the plain that belonged to Michael. It was neither Heaven nor Hell, Paradise or earth. It wasn't even the place of invisibility. This place was dark and dank, and reserved for the most heinous offender. "What's up, Michael?" he asked, even though he knew.

"I have a job for you," Michael replied.

"I'm sure you do."

Michael smirked. "Are you up to it?"

"I can get it started, but can't stay here forever."

"I need some of your men, then."

"I will give you my best apprentices," Reap assured him.

"Very well," Michael replied. Then he stood up. He was dressed in the ancient regalia, battle axe and all. He wasn't going to use them, it was for effect.

"I will return." He vanished.

~

He reappeared and dropped Verenda's pathetic parents, and foster fathers, at Reap's feet. He was going to summon every perverted spirit, in the universe, to assist Reap.

Just as he was about to call out to them he heard the Master's gentle voice. *"Do not go too far, Michael."*

"Yes, Father," he replied. Too far also meant do not *touch* those mannish boys.

~

"Where am I?" Carmella Young asked.

"Where you will spend eternity for what you have done to your daughter," Michael replied. His eyes twirled with residual rage, and they gasped.

"Verenda?" Damon Young asked.

They were so pathetic; they no longer remembered what they'd done. They knew they were in prison for child abuse and molestation, but they didn't believe it. Their memory loss didn't deter Michael. He burrowed remembrance in their mind's eye.

Their eyes watered. They remembered it all now. "It was the drugs, man," Damon insisted. "It was the drugs."

Her foster father, Roy, could claim no such reason. He jumped when Michael's gaze fell upon him. "I am looking forward to hearing your screams, for all eternity."

"Someone will eventually hear us!" Roy threatened.

Reap laughed. "Not on this plain." Then he struck him with ten times the force he'd hit Verenda.

Roy screamed.

"Music to my ears," Michael said and vanished.

~

When he returned to Verenda's room she was still sleeping. "Release her, Slumber, and then you may leave."

~

"What happened?" Verenda asked.

"You tried to take your life," Michael replied.

"You should have let me. I just want to be left alone."

A tear dropped from Michael's eye. "I am sorry I let you down."

Verenda reached up and wiped his tear. It was gray. He was crying for *her*. No one had ever done that before. "Don't cry. I'm glad you brought me back. What is your name?"

"I am the Archangel, Michael. I will take care of you, from now on."

Verenda started crying. She wrapped her arms around his neck, and sobbed, "God sent me an angel."

~

Chapter I

Lucifer had setup residence in the cave next to where Samjaza was pinned to the wall. For the moment, it was his new throne room, and he was none too pleased.

Seraphiel had pinned Samjaza to the wall below that old tree he called Eunice. It was done as a statement. *You were beneath my mother!* Now here he was stuck beneath that same damn tree!

Infirmity, Divination, Lust, Lethargy, Anxiety, Doom, Gossip, Spite, Hostility, Confusion, Burden, Liar and Python were with him. There were also a dozen minor demons present.

He was having a mega tantrum. "First that damn Seraphiel sicced Orion on me. Then the bastard destroyed my throne room-"

"Not to mention he made you eat dirt," one of the minor demons said, and laughed.

"Don't forget the pitchforks," another said, and laughed. "That was priceless."

"Quiet!" Lucifer demanded.

Seraphiel had made him look like a pathetic fool. He was going to get him back, but right now he had a bigger issue. "Michael has publically embraced his 'sanctioned' mate!"

"Michael has a *woman?*"

"Isn't that what I just said?" Lucifer replied.

"That means he's fallen, like the rest of us, right?"

"DIDN'T I SAY HIS SANCTIONED MATE?" Lucifer screamed.

"Sanctioned. Sanctioned. Ooooh *Sanctioned!*" the

demon replied. "By whom?"

"Who do you *think?*" Lucifer snapped.

"But that's not fair."

"When have you ever known Him to be? But I am not going to take this standing up!"

One of demons laughed. "You mean lying down, don't you?"

Lucifer shot a fireball at him. Then he looked at everyone else standing around. "Anybody else got jokes?"

They all shook their heads.

"That puppet had his master marry him, and his mate-"

"He got married?" Apathy asked. "As in 'I do' married?"

"Do you know of another kind?" Lucifer snapped.

"Is that why she has that glow?" Gossip asked.

"It's a shield, ain't it?" Python asked.

"Yeah!" Lucifer replied. "That puppet gave it to her."

"It's not going to be as easy to get to her as it was Eve," Python informed him. "If that is your intensions," he added.

"DON'T YOU THINK I KNOW THAT!!" Lucifer shouted. He was furious! He'd been trying for years to get to her again, but couldn't. That glow was a shield to keep him, and his imps, away from her.

He thought he had her years ago, when she killed herself. He'd sent several of his most powerful agents to attack her mind. Anxiety, Hopelessness, Despair *and* Pressure!

Like a chain gang they worked in tandem; and

chiseled away at her. Anxiety took her breath away. Hopelessness and Despair gripped her mind. Then Pressure leaned up against her heart. They worked on her day and night. And when she tried to sleep Restlessness took over. But she was human and Sleep always momentarily defeated that spirit.

But Nightmare was always waiting on the other side of her eyelids. Night after night she dreamt about Smith Walker. She saw him laughing

at her, bragging about how he'd used her. Shouting, in front of the entire student body, *'What would make a boy like me settle for a tramp like you, Verenda Strong?'*

Nightmare shouted in her dreams, over and over, *'Nobody's ever gonna want you, Verenda! You are a tramp, and you stink!'*

It was working! But it was taking too long. He called on two more of his most powerful agents and told them what to do, in her waking hours.

Paranoia and Liar sprang into action. Every which way she turned she thought people were whispering about her. Liar told her mind the things they were saying. *"Nobody wants her around, why don't she suck dirt and die; and make everybody happy?"*

"She stunk up the bathroom!"

"Her breath stinks too!"

"Did you know she had sex with her mother, and father?"

"Let's beat her up after school."

"No! She might have some nasty disease."

"This whole lunchroom stinks."

"Did you smell it when she got on the bus, this

morning? I thought I'd throw up my breakfast."

His agents attacked her mind on every front, even when she started eating lunch outside in the courtyard. They compelled other students to stare at her, or go back inside. Then Liar put words in her thoughts, again.

"That's all we need is for her to stink up the outside air too!"

"She smells like a wet dog, on her period."

"I think she has lice, too."

"Her locker was next to mine, but I had the principal move me, because she has crabs."

"Smith said he always made her take a shower, and wash her ass, first."

"He said he used her to get experience, so he'd know what to do when he and Leevearne got married."

"He better get a shot first. No telling what Verenda Strong gave him."

"That's why Leevearne won't take him back!"

His agents grinded and grinded, and didn't let up until she surrendered. They all stood around her, in her bathroom and encouraged her to do what she needed to do.

Then they followed her into the kitchen and made sure she followed through. They wanted to leave once the gas was on, but he commanded them to stay put; until it was over.

The moment Sammael took possession of her soul he'd jumped up, and danced. He told his agents to come home. They were going to celebrate their victory. They all needed this one.

He'd been so busy celebrating and gloating he didn't realize Michael had intercepted the Transporter. That puppet had swooped down and reigned supreme over Sammael's authority. His master backed him up.

He'd been soooo close. If he could've had a do over he would've told them to strike a match. Not even Michael could bring back a crispy body.

Now he couldn't get to her physically, but he wasn't about to give up. He looked at Python and smirked. "But I've still got options."

"Keep in mind Michael is *not* Seraphiel, Lucifer," Confusion added. "He will not suffer you to mess with his woman, again."

"Michael is a puppet on his master's string. I can do whatever I want, and he'll do n.o.t.h.i.n.g!"

"Keep thinking that," Burden warned. "Michael will bring you to bear, if you force him."

"You saw what he did to her parents, didn't you?" Confusion asked.

"Yes, I did," Lucifer replied. "But he never touched me, *did* he? And he knew I was behind everything that had happened to her."

~

At first it had offended him that Michael *hadn't* come after him, or his agents. He'd set the stage for a battle, and escape from this dungeon; but Michael didn't give him a moment's thought. It was like Michael was saying he was insignificant, and not worth the trouble. That Puppet focused all of his attention on her parents, and foster fathers. Once he got them settled he focused his attention on *her*.

Then he realized what was happening, and he used that knowledge over and over again. He looked at his gang and smiled. "That puppet was told to keep his hands off me!"

"That may be so, but he still won't let you near her," Python replied.

"Why would I get near her, when I have you guys?"

"The truth of the matter is you can't get near her," Liar said.

"I can't believe you spoke truth, Liar," Burden replied. "That's not like you."

"You damn sure did," Lucifer added. That gave him a thought. He was going to get even with Michael, and Seraphiel. But for right now, Michael was his priority. That puppet was getting ready to go on his honeymoon, and there was no better time to strike.

Confusion looked at the smile on his face. "You have a plan, don't you?"

"Why, yes I do," he replied. He needed to work it out in his head first, before sharing it with his agents. "Leave me," he demanded.

They all exited the dungeon.

~

Chapter II

Verenda had just finished her meeting with most of the Walkers' children. They'd arrived on schedule at 8:00 this morning. In spite of the confusion, a couple of weeks ago, they were excited to get started.

She didn't know how these lovely children could be related to those nosey people, at the estate. They had a genuine desire to do more than sit around the estate, and act like they were aristocrats. They understood what their parents didn't. They were going to be on earth until Jesus returned. They knew there was a lot to be done. They understood that the harvest was plentiful. There were millions of Watchers that needed to find their 'spirit' mates. A few thousand right here in Indiana.

She broke the meetings down based on their specific talents. She was getting ready to meet with Howard, Henry and Faith to discuss the floor plans.

~

"Come on in the conference room," she instructed them.

Ditto looked around the room. It was nice, but not as nicely decorated as Brock's. He was going to change that. Verenda and her staff deserved as nice of a meeting place as the estate.

Faith hugged Verenda. "I'm so happy for you," she told her. "You know I met you over five thousand years ago."

Verenda returned the hug. "I heard you say that. But I don't have the gift of remembrance, like you do, child."

"You were the only one I would talk to," Faith replied and laughed. "I was mad because I wanted to go with Arakiel right then and there, but couldn't. I wouldn't talk with any of my cousins." She didn't tell her what else she knew. Now was not the time. She didn't know if it would ever be.

Again, Verenda had the urge to hold her hand, Smittie's hand. In her mind she was holding *his* hand and telling him...good bye. The memory of her relationship with Smittie had slipped away, along with the pain. "But you ended up happy, in the end, Faith."

Faith smiled. "Yes, I did."

"Come on let me see what you have for me," she said, and took her seat.

She was impressed with their plans for Georgia House. "I won't know the place, when I get back."

"My cousin, Lara, wanted to come, but we told her she couldn't," Ditto told her.

She looked under eyed at them. "Not even while I'm gone."

"We know. We've told them all that," Henry replied.

"But I think you should reconsider," Faith added.

"Why?"

"She is the school teacher, at the estate. She suggested that the children come to school there."

Verenda frowned. "I have a lot of children here."

"And you and Vicky have been home schooling all of them. Vicky is leaving. How are you going to do that alone?"

"Maria has been very helpful," Verenda replied.

"We know. But Lara, Jodi, Shelby and Smooth are all accredited teachers. They can offer so much more."

"Let me talk with their mothers about that," Verenda replied. It would make sense, plus the children could play outside at the Estate; they couldn't at Georgia House. "What does Seraphiel say?"

"He's all for it if you are willing," Ditto replied.

"He'd teleport them over every day and back home after school," Henry added.

"Plus, they could concentrate on their studies, and not be distracted by all of the hammering and reconstruction," Faith added.

"That's true," Verenda agreed. "But my littlest ones haven't been exposed to the paranormal yet. I thought they might be too young."

"I don't think they are. Our children have adapted to it just fine," Ditto assured her.

"Nevertheless, I'd like to be with them when they first learn," she replied. "Plus, their mothers will flip a lid. They always do."

"They've never seen Michael?" Henry asked. "You don't get more paranormal than him."

Verenda laughed. She liked Henry, because he reminded her of her Michael. "You have something in common with my Michael, Henry."

"What?"

"You both have *beautiful* eyes," she replied. She knew he was self-conscious about them. In Henry's case that was the trick of the enemy. It made him resent what God blessed him with, because of the elicit attention they drew. "Just like you cover yours with contacts, my

Michael has not wanted to frighten the children with his."

"Yes, ma'am," he replied. "I guess we do have that in common." He felt a calm come over him about them.

"Why don't we table the subject of their training, until Michael and I get back," she suggested.

"That's a good idea," Henry replied.

"Faith, your blueprints are wonderful. The only change I would recommend is that you leave the windows the way they are."

"Okay. Is that because no one can see in?" Faith asked.

Verenda nodded.

"When the sun goes down they can see in, Verenda. They see the guards sitting at the desk. We saw them the night we came here. My windows are custom designed with special film. It will darken the inside, no matter what the sun is doing."

"Really?"

Faith nodded. "We know how important it is that no one sees who's staying here. Those windows will allow us to utilize all of that empty space on the ground floor."

"I like that," Verenda replied. "There is a lot of space down there."

"Look at this," Ditto instructed. "This is what we had planned for that area."

"Impressive," she replied. She really liked everything they planned to do to her house.

~

After her meeting with them, she met with Nantan and Addison. They came armed with computers. Some of them were for the young 'spirit' mates, and looked more like toys.

"The computers for the tweens don't have access to the internet, do they?" she asked.

Addison shook his head. "No. We didn't want them on social networks, for fear they'd draw the wrong type of friends."

"That's good, because that was my main concern."

"They do however have access to the website I set up for Watchers and their families," Nantan added.

Verenda frowned. "You setup a Watcher Network?"

"Yes, ma'am. The tweens and young adults are able to communicate with others like them," he informed her. "There are a lot of young people, all across the world, utilizing that site. They get to meet other young adults outside their immediate network. Not only that but Addison and I have encrypted the network so that there is no language barrier."

"That ingenious, Nantan."

"They don't feel so closed off, anymore. They even visit each other."

"Really?"

Nantan laughed. "Their Watcher fathers, or uncles, transport them back and forth. It has also helped a lot of Watchers find their lost relatives."

"I am really impressed," Verenda replied. And she was. She was a grown woman and she felt closed off. She knew her young people did too.

~

She spent the bulk of the day meeting with each group. She'd been apprehensive about leaving her children, but she wasn't now. Donnell and Desiree were going to move into the House until she got back. That was a tremendous load off of her mind.

She took them on a tour to meet all of the little 'spirit' mates, and their mothers. Vicki had agreed to stay on to supervise the group, while she was gone; and to be a familiar face to the children.

~

"Where are you and Grandpa Michael going?" Aurellia asked.

"On our honeymoon, hon," she replied.

Aurellia blushed. This was soooo weird. She couldn't believe her grandfather, the Archangel, had a *wife*. "I know that, but where?"

Verenda heard Aurellia's thoughts and laughed. "My Michael won't tell me."

"He's surprising you?" Symphony asked. "That's so romantic."

Verenda smiled. Michael called Symphony the keeper of his heart. He had a fondness for that girl, because of what she'd been through.

He'd wanted her to stay with Symphony, like she'd done with Desiree, but she refused. At the time she still held great animosity towards Smith. If he'd shown up at the hospital she would have cut him. Michael understood and agreed to stay.

He sat with her day in and day out and protected her, until her 'spirit' mate was *ready* to accept her. Ram thought Michael was in love with her, but he was way off base. But there *was* one...

~

She knew her Michael. He cared for all of the 'spirit' mates. However there was one that he favored even more than Symphony. That 'spirit' mate's life had mirrored hers. If they'd paid attention they would have realized it during their trip to Brock's island.

She and Michael had sat in the park and listened to their interactions. The tone in Michael's voice, towards Symphony, that day, had been harsh. *"Confession is good for the soul, keeper of my heart. But you are not finished. Finish it!"* The family had felt his harshness, but they did not know why.

He *loved* the 'spirit' mate that Symphony had offended. He loved that 'spirit' mate so much that he gave her power *over* her Watcher. And even now he sometimes sat, for hours, and listened to her hum her supplication.

"I know you will have a good time," Hope said, and hugged her. "I am so happy for you."

Verenda smiled. Yeah, Michael loved Hope, the most. He said she reminded him of Hannah, in the Bible. She took responsibility for her hardships, just like Hannah had. Hannah said *'it might be something I'm doing, that makes her treat me this way, Lord.'* Hope sings *'Give me a clean heart.'*

In fact he loved Hope so much, that he directed the social worker's steps when they placed Jon and Jas in the orphanage. Those little boys were abandoned in Illinois, *not* Indiana. By right they should have been placed in Illinois. But, he wanted to give Hope a reason to hold on, until Chaz found her. The boys arrived on her lost baby's birthday, and she embraced and loved them.

Michael even pushed Floyd to intervene, on her

behalf. Then he troubled Chaziel's spirit about the urgency of getting out in the sun. When Chaz found Hope, Michael was standing in front of her. He would've never allowed a single bullet to touch that sweet young lady. He'd been so focused on Hope; he plum forgot that Robyn was there, too.

He said Hope, above *all* others, was the epitome of a perfect wife, and mother. She'd threatened to cut him, because he said that included her too.

She hugged Hope and actually felt the goodness radiating off of her. "Thank you, hon."

~

They all gathered around her. She looked at every one of them and smiled. "You young men and women are all special to me. The way you have chipped in to help my little ones," she said and grabbed her heart. Then her eyes teared. "You give me hope."

Then she cleared her throat. "I will get Michael to open a link, between all of us. That way you can contact me, in case of an emergency."

"I will do no such thing, Verenda," Michael said. "If they have an emergency they can call Seraphiel, and his team."

They all turned around and looked at him. He had *luggage* in both hands. And he was much shorter. Aurellia smiled. "Hi, Grandpa. Why do you have that luggage?"

Michael's eyes twirled. "Verenda is making me travel by airplane."

"Why?" Deuce asked.

"My first husband took me all over the world," Verenda replied. Then she laughed. "But that poor man hated to fly. He said he'd done enough flying in the military. Either we drove or went by cruise ship. I've never been on an airplane."

"I don't blame your husband," Kwanita replied.

Aurellia trembled. "You trust flying?"

Verenda knew what had happened to Aurellia's and Kwanita's parents. Both had died in plane crashes. It was insensitive to laugh. "I'm sorry," she replied. "But I'll be with Michael. I'll be fine."

Aurellia hugged her. "Bring me a souvenir back."

"How are you guys getting to the airport?" Ditto asked.

"I'm driving them," Akibeel replied.

"In what? That little toy car of yours?" Ditto asked.

They all laughed. Akibeel liked little sports cars. They couldn't imagine Michael being able to fit in one.

"No," Akibeel said and laughed. "In that stretch limo, out front."

~

"What about your eyes, Michael?" Henry asked. He knew Michael would be gawked at, just like he was. With eyes like his little children would be afraid of him.

Michael's eyes twirled and then turned a solid but light hazel brown. They were the same color as Akibeel's. Then he smiled. "They will be fine."

"Give me a minute, hon," Verenda said. "I need to go back to the room for a second."

"I will load the car," Michael replied.

~

When she got to her room she sat at her desk. She'd thought about what Brock had said to Leevearne all night.

It gave her an idea.
　　　She sent a shout out…

~

Chapter III

Smittie was walking the grounds with his brothers, Brown, Ev and Smooth. Smooth had been in the ICU with his wife, day in and day out. They all thought he needed a break.

They were discussing where to put the future golf course, when he heard...

"Smith."

"Verenda?"

"It's me."

He didn't know how to respond, or what to say. Donnell had astutely called him out. He'd only stopped seeing her because he got caught. He often wondered how long it could've lasted. But, Donnell was wrong about him being a ho', and her being a *notch*. He'd loved her back then, he loved her now. More than he was willing to admit. Brock was right, if *could* stop loving her, he would.

Verenda knew he was struggling with what to say. *"You couldn't really say what you needed to say, with all of those nosey folks in the room; could you?"*

He laughed. She was still a breath of fresh air. Even as a teenager she called people nosey for getting all up in her business. *"True that."*

"Now is the time. It's just you and me."

"I never meant to hurt you, Verenda. Walking away from you was the hardest thing I've ever done, barring none."

"I know that now. And I'm sorry for the harsh words Donnell said to you."

Smith chuckled. *"He did go in, didn't he? But, he*

didn't lie. I would have held on to you until the rapture. I selfishly wanted my cake and pie."

"And as insecure as I was I would have settled for that."

"What?"

"You walked away without another word. If you had come back and told me you wanted to see both of us I would have settled for that. I would have settled for the crumbs, Smittie, but you never came back."

"You deserved more than that, Verenda."

"I didn't know that back then. You were all I had. I would've gladly been the other woman, just to be with you," she replied, and her eyes watered. *"I would have settled for stolen moments, with you...forever."*

That made his eyes water. He walked away from the other men, and rested his back against a tree. He couldn't believe she said that. For the first time since he walked away from her, he was glad he had. Not for his selfish benefit, but for hers. *"Did Cappy make you happy?"*

"He did, and I still miss him. I didn't love him, at first. He just filled the void in my life. Over time I learned to love him, because he was so good to me. He helped me like myself, and showed me how to live. Our marriage was simplistic. I didn't know how much I loved him, until he died. He knew how I felt about you, but I hope he knew that I loved him, too," she replied. That was one of her biggest fears; that he'd died without knowing.

"I'm sure he knew, Verenda," he assured her. *"You give yourself over completely. That's what made me love you; and I'm sure that's what made him love you, too."*

"But, he wasn't you, Smith. Not in or out of bed."

Damn his selfish ass if that didn't make him feel *real* good! He actually smiled. He wondered how he matched up against Michael, but didn't dare ask.

"I can see you smiling, Mr. Walker," she said, and laughed.

He cracked up laughing. *"Sorry."* That was what he missed the most about her. It wasn't just the sex, even though that was delicious. It was her sense of humor. She always made him laugh, and feel good about himself. He hadn't realized how tragic her life was, because she showed no signs of abuse. She always smiled, and was a delight.

He hadn't taken the rumors of her sleeping around seriously, because he hadn't witnessed it. Jocks always boasted about their conquests. Nine out of ten times they were lying, to boost their reps.

She felt his spirit easing. *"It's time to release whatever you feel for me, Smith."*

"You know what I feel for you, Verenda. It's what I've felt since the day we met," he confessed. He remembered that day, like it was yesterday. He'd wanted to kill his schoolmates for what they did to her. He would have too, but she'd needed medical attention. He did get the instigator the next day, though. *"Releasing those feelings is easier said than done."*

"I imagine it is. I'll always feel something for you, too. They are still precious memories, but I let you go months ago."

"I know. I am happy that you have found someone who can be all that you need," he replied. *"I'm happy that*

you found someone that made you forget about me."

"You have that someone too, Smith. Regardless of how Leevearne feels about me, she is a lovely woman. She has given you over forty years of devotion. She has given you three beautiful daughters, and four handsome grandsons. I could've never done that. You cling to me because it ended so abruptly. It ended before you were ready to let go," she told him.

"I would have never been ready to let you go," he replied honestly. *"A thousand years from now I'll still love you, Verenda."*

"But not enough."

"No. Not enough."

"You made the right decision. Leevearne has always been your future. And Michael has always been mine."

"I'm sorry for the pain I caused you," he told her. *"I wish..."* He didn't finish because he didn't know what he wished. He'd be lying if he said he wished he'd never touched her. He still cherished every moment they'd shared. He be lying, even more, if he said he wished he loved her more than Leevearne. Leevearne was his life partner, lover and friend.

What he really wished is what he'd always wished. That he could be *two* people. He wished he could split himself like Brock. He wished that he could freely love both women; and both of his beings could feel the love from both of them. He wished...

"I wish you well, Verenda. Be happy."

"I am happy. Michael is everything I ever hoped for. My mind, body, and soul are committed; and deeply

in love with him."

"I'm happy for you," he replied. *"You got the top of the food chain."*

She laughed. *"I got the cream of the crop."*

"No, you didn't," he replied. *"Michael did."*

"How sweet, Smith."

"Does he know you are talking with me?" he asked and then thought about it. *"How are you talking to me?"*

"I didn't specifically tell him, but I'm sure he knows. Michael gave me a link to you, the night you were shot; thirty-five years ago. I just never used it."

"I'm glad you didn't. It probably would have scared the bejesus out of me," he replied and laughed.

She laughed too. She still loved the sound of his voice. *"Then it's a good thing I didn't reach out to you."*

"Now that you've reached out he won't come hurt me, will he?" he asked, and laughed. *"I'm pretty sure he hits harder than Cappy."*

"My Michael isn't the jealous type."

"You could've fooled me," he replied. Michael had put the fear of God in him, when they were in Desiree's room. Not only had Michael reminded him of his thoughts, he showed him what he'd do to him. It wasn't pretty.

Verenda laughed out loud. Smittie's voice sounded nervous. *"My husband can be intimidating."*

Smith laughed, but then he got serious. He knew this was his one and only chance to say everything he needed to say. *"I'm sorry I drove you to suicide."*

"You didn't do that," she assured him. *"I was under attack by Lucifer's imps."*

"Don't make excuses for me, Verenda. I was the straw that broke your will to live. Donnell was right; I pushed you over the edge," he said and his eyes watered. *"I was just like all of those other bastards. I made you think you were unlovable. But as you see that wasn't true, because..."* He sighed and grabbed his chest. *"As hard as I try, I can't stop loving you."*

Verenda's eyes watered. She'd spent a lifetime yearning to hear those words again, from *him!* Now that he finally said them they had no effect on her. Before she could speak, he did.

"I wouldn't have been able to live with myself, if you'd died. I would have grieved myself to death, Verenda."

"I know, Smith," she replied. That had been one of the things Michael told her, when he rescued her soul. He'd said more than her life hung in the balance. *"You know what I wish?"* she asked.

"What's that?"

"I wish that you and Leevearne and Michael and I could be friends."

"You are too damn fine, girl," he replied and laughed out loud. *"Leevearne would skin me alive, if I even suggested it. You got all these women hatin' on you."*

Verenda laughed. That was the truth. She'd heard the women say they didn't like how young she looked. They didn't want to look young, but they didn't want her to either. *"Listen, I have to go. Michael is waiting."*

Smittie didn't want to end the conversation. She eased his spirit like no one else could. She was right. There was so much he needed to say to her, that he couldn't say with that crowd.

He started another conversation. *"Do you think Donnell will ever forgive me?"*

"In time," she replied. *"Just don't push him. He doesn't like to be pushed."*

"Okay," he replied. *"Will you?"*

"I forgave you months ago, Smittie," she answered. Then she said, *"But Donnell and I aren't the problem. It's you not being able to forgive yourself."*

"That's true."

"You'll never be able to move on, until you do. That's why I reached out to you. I wanted you to know I'm happy, and I harbor no bad feelings towards you. I want you to forgive yourself. I need you to forgive yourself. Don't let the spirit of Guilt hold a rein on you, Smittie. We are going to live a long time. Kick that bastard to the curb. If not for yourself, then do that for me."

"I'll try," he replied.

"I really do have to go, Smith. Take care."

"You too, Verenda," he replied. Then he boldly said, *"Think about me sometime."*

"I always do," she replied, and broke the link.

He smiled. He couldn't believe a personal conversation with her made him feel this good. She regulated his mind, and eased his soul. He felt like his victim had exonerated him.

But, he also felt something *else*. Verenda was the mother of his children. That didn't make a damn bit of *sense*. Leevearne was the mother of *all* of his children. Verenda couldn't have had his child, and not told him. Her womb had been barren since she was thirteen.

But, the feeling was so real, he couldn't shake it.

~

Verenda watched him smile. She'd just given him what he needed. He needed to know that everything was okay, between them. He needed to know that she was alright, emotionally. He'd be able to let go now, and for that she was grateful.

But something clinched *her* heart. It was so powerful; it filled her with momentary grief...

~

When she walked back to the mezzanine Michael was sitting at the table, with the Walker children. He looked up at her, and his eyes twirled. "You ready?" he asked.

"Let's go, hon," she replied. Yeah, she ended up with the cream of the crop, alright.

~

The Walker children bid them farewell, and watched them walk out the door. Maria went with Akibeel to see them off. All of them wanted to go, but they needed to stay and handle the children.

"That is *soooo* weird," Aurellia said again.

"Looks like Michael has more than a girlfriend," Sam said.

They all laughed.

~

Chapter IV

When they arrived at the airport Akibeel unloaded their luggage. Then he and Maria bid them a safe trip. "Enjoy your honeymoon," Maria said and hugged Verenda.

"Hug my babies for me," Verenda replied. She needed this time away, but she wanted *their* children with them. She was disappointed that neither Donnell and Desiree, nor Seraphiel and Jodi had come to see them off. They hadn't even stopped by the House.

~

She knew the flight number, but not the destination. There was a flight board with all the details, but she couldn't see theirs. That sneak had blinded her to the information on the board. She looked up at him. "I'm gon cut you."

Michael laughed. "I told you it was a surprise, Ruby."

People were staring at them, like they were a freak show. Man, she hated nosey people. Some were so busy gawking at them they didn't notice their children were acting up. She almost told Michael to just teleport them to the destination.

Michael laughed. *"They are staring at you, Ruby."*

"I know," she replied. *"Why are they looking so hard?"* She didn't know it would be this crowded. It was way too many people, for her liking.

"Because you are a vision of loveliness," he replied.

She looked down at herself. She had on black jeans, a red vest and a black blazer. The only jewelry she had on was her wedding ring, the ruby with the angel wings. She'd worn three inch heels, so that she'd look close to Michael's height.

He could be whatever height he chose to be. At present he was only six feet eight, but still much taller than her. *"What's so lovely about what I'm wearing?"*

"Not the clothes. The woman," he replied. Then he wrapped his arm around her waist, and kissed her temple. *"My wife."*

She sighed and caressed his midriff. She loved how his stomach bunched every time she caressed it. To the Watchers he came off as aloof, cold even; but he wasn't. There was a multitude of spirits that didn't come near her husband. Affection wasn't one of them. No one had any idea how romantic he could be, but her. *"Where are we going, Michael?"*

"On our honeymoon," he replied.

"Don't make me cut you."

He laughed and kissed her temple again, but didn't answer.

~

Michael had secured all of the seats in first class. He didn't want gawking eyes, and unsolicited conversations, ruining Ruby's first flight.

When the engines roared, and the plane took off down the runway, she smiled. Then she leaned over him to watch the ground get smaller, and smaller. "This is exciting," she proclaimed.

He stroked his hand up and down her back. "I could have done this without the machinery, Ruby," he said and laughed.

"You are such a dud," she replied.

He gently tugged her hair, and made her look at him. His eyes twirled. "You did not say that last night," he replied and arrogantly chuckled. "If I am not mistaken, you distinctively said-"

She wrapped her arms around his neck, and cut him off with a kiss. He was still laughing, in her head. He wrapped one arm around her waist and bunched her hair in his other hand; and spoke to her mind, *"Stud!!"*

"I said magnificent stallion!"

Kissing each other was so intense, neither of them were laughing, anymore.

~

Once they were in the air, he leaned over and whispered in her ear, "How was your conversation with Smith Walker?"

The tone in his voice made her jump. She turned toward him, his face was stoic. Michael was not the jealous type, but she could see he didn't like it. "I needed to ease his spirit, Michael."

"Did you?"

"Did I what? Need to ease his spirit, or ease it?"

"Both."

"Yes, I needed to, and I think I did, Michael. Are you *jealous?"*

He smirked. For a minute his eyes twirled, and then turned back hazel. He had not liked her saying she would have settled for Smittie's seconds. His *crumbs*. When he snatched her parents out of time, he was tempted to snatch Smittie too. The only reason he didn't was because the Master wouldn't allow it. He reminded him that Smith

Walker had to survive, for Arakiel, and one other. He had no idea, at the time, that it was for Akibeel as well. He reminded him of something else, too.

But, he imagined that was why he *let* Smith get wounded thirty-five years ago. He could have redirected that bullet, just like he'd *directed* Floyd's. Unfortunately Smittie pushed Clyde into the path of the bullet that should have missed him.

He repented for that because he had not meant for Clyde to be hurt. Plus, Smittie was a decent man. He was a good husband, and father. And more importantly, he loved Verenda. He *always* had.

He wasn't jealous of Smittie, but he did not understand why Ruby wanted to ease the man's spirit. She didn't know, like he did, that it was just a temporary relief.

"Amused mostly," he replied.

"Why?"

"Your words were comforting to him; but it was a waste of your time. He will never stop loving you, Ruby."

She didn't want to talk about Smith. They were on their way to their honeymoon. She rubbed his thigh. "Neither will you," she replied.

He leaned over, stroked the beauty mark just above her lip, and kissed her. Then he said, "That is how I know *he* won't." That wasn't the truth.

She stroked his cheek, and smiled. He was the epitome of male perfection. He claimed no specific race, but he was dark, and exotic; with a strong jawline. His coal black hair mirrored hers; like they were woven by the same mulberry silkworm. Those hazel eyes looked good on him, but she *loved* the twirling ones. She loved *everything* about her husband.

It was fitting that none of those malevolent spirits would approach him. After all the evil that had plagued her life she needed a peaceful marriage. She needed Michael.

If those nosey Walker women got to know her they might like her; because she wasn't a threat to any of them. On the other hand they probably still wouldn't like her, because those queens thrived on drama. The only thing she thrived on was her Michael.

She was always under attack by Lucifer's imps. They knew she was Michael's mate, long before she did. They'd tried to destroy her years ago, when Michael wasn't watching. Now they've taken up residency at the peripheral of her mind, and were continuously trying to beset her. But, they couldn't get a stronghold, not anymore, because her husband kept them at bay.

He kept her calm, with his sense of humor. Everything about him calmed her, except his touch. For her to be the first woman he'd ever made love to, he sure knew what he was doing.

She stroked her thumb across his cheek. "You are the only one I *need* to love me, Michael. You are the only one I *love*."

"It took you long enough," he replied, and pulled away.

"I-" She started but stopped. Why had he pulled away?

"Excuse me," the stewardess said. "Is there anything I can get you?"

Oh, he sensed her coming. He was still getting used

to being able to openly display affections. She was too. After Seraphiel's total meltdown, and the family's freak out, they both were skittish.

But this was perfect. He'd leaned his head back and closed his eyes. It was her chance to get some answers. "Can you tell me where we are going?" she whispered.

"I'm sorry, ma'am. We were instructed that it was a surprise."

Michael chuckled. "Nice try, Ruby."

"I'm gon cut you."

He, and the stewardess, laughed.

"Would you bring us a carafe of chilled wine?"

"Yes, sir," the stewardess replied.

Verenda leaned into the aisle, and watched her walk away. When the stewardess opened the curtain she frowned. She turned back around, and looked at Michael. "This airplane is empty!"

He chuckled. "Nosey."

~

When the wine came Michael toasted his bride. "Thank you for finally coming to your senses, and accepting your destiny." He tapped his glass against hers, and his eyes twirled. "Me."

She smiled. "Thank you for your patience, hon."

She didn't know why it took her so long to embrace their union. Of course she was afraid that it was forbidden, but it was more than that. She was afraid for the spirit of Love to encompass him. She knew it would be intense and resolute. She foolishly didn't realize that it already had encompassed him.

He stood in the wings and patiently waited on her to

notice him, as more than just an angel. He even performed the marriage ceremony between her and *another* man. He waited until after her husband died, before he told her that *he* was her destiny. Then he stood on the sidelines and let her lament over Smittie, for years. If Smittie and Leevearne hadn't come to Desiree's room that day, he'd still be patiently waiting.

She didn't understand that kind of love. She tried to fight Leevearne for Smittie, even though she didn't know how to fight. But she did now, and she would cut anybody who tried to take her Michael.

He told Seraphiel that she still had the option to walk away from him. What a crock! She could no more walk away from him, than she could her own feet.

Michael chuckled. "You think too much, Ruby," he said. Then he leaned over and asked, "Would you fight for me, woman?"

"I'd slice and dice Lucifer, himself," she replied.

He laughed. "You could probably take that weasel too."

~

He wrapped his arm around her, and she leaned back against his chest. Then he raised the leg rest, to support their legs. He gently stroked his hand up and down her stomach, while they talked about her kicking Lucifer's rear. "Would you cut him?" he asked.

"Would you let me?"

"I would," he replied and squeezed her stomach. "But, I do not think the Master would like that."

"Then I'll sic Seraphiel on him, again."

They both laughed. It was a moot thought, because

Lucifer couldn't get near her; and he couldn't hurt Michael.

His hand was stirring a powerful and luscious desire in her, him too. That was the advantage of being married to him; everything was magnified to the nth degree.

She tilted her head back, looked up at him and smiled. "You ever heard of the Mile High Club?"

He chuckled and rubbed his thumb under her breast. "Behave, woman. The pilots are just on the other side of that door."

She crawled across his lap, and straddled him. "You can take their hearing, can't you? There is no one else on the plane but us, and the stewardess." She wrapped her arms around his neck, and nibbled his sexy bottom lip. "Distract them, Michael," she demanded, with her sultry voice. Then she unbuttoned her vest, and smiled wickedly. "You know you want to."

He moaned. Women by design were irresistible temptresses. Because of his loyalty to the Master He put an extra effort in her design. He caressed her hips and perused her ample cleavage. "Do not tempt me." And he was tempted.

He held the spirit of Desire at bay, for years; because she was not ready. Once she was, he allowed that spirit in him. It grew beyond its own imagination. Evil spirits were afraid of him, but, Love, Passion, Affection and Desire embraced him to the *utmost*.

They setup permanent residency in him, and *refused* to leave. They even refused to help other Archangels, who like him had sanctioned mates; because they were not as powerful as he. Those spirits opened the floodgates, and sent billions of their helpers to assist humans, and Watchers, alike.

"We cannot. We are about to land, Ruby," he protested, but kept stroking her hips.

She leaned over and looked out the window. Then she sat back up and ran her fingers through his hair. "We're nowhere near the ground."

When she leaned over her breast rubbed against his chest. He moaned. He wanted to resist her wiles, while in flight, but Desire wouldn't let him wait. He reached out and caressed her girls, and they responded immediately. "We are close," he protested...weakly.

She heard the heaviness in his voice. He wanted her as bad as she wanted him. His mouth was protesting, but his hands were sending another message. She shivered and sighed, "You are so bad." Then she pulled the cups of her bra back. "My girls miss you," she whispered.

He snapped his seat back, as far as it would go. Then he raised his knees, and trapped her in place. He leaned down and moaned, as he greedily accepted her luscious invitation.

Verenda felt the swell in his groin and shivered. She'd been celibate since her first husband died, and she hadn't missed sex. She told those who asked that she'd had enough sex to last a lifetime. And she believed that; until she accepted Michael in her bed a few months ago. He gave a whole new meaning to the phrase 'making love'. Her man's touch drove her crazy, and she bemoaned all the wasted years. She could've experienced love at this magnitude, years ago.

She felt like every cell in her body was getting to

know Michael, in the biblical sense. She ran her trembling fingers through his hair, and moaned. His tongue felt like a hot sensual nettle, stamping his brand on her skin. And it hurt, so good. *"Michael,"* she whispered, and rocked her pelvis against his.

He vanquished her bra, but left her outerwear on. They really didn't have much time, but he couldn't help himself. He'd waited longer than Time for her. Now that he had her, he couldn't resist his amply fashioned wife. He scooted further down in the seat and pulled her hips closer.

They were about to run out of time, but that just intensified Desire. Like an exhibitionist, the *possibility* of getting caught was stimulating and intoxicating, to that spirit. He caressed the nape of her neck and turned them both sideways, toward the window. He cupped her breast, and gazed into her eyes. *"Do you know what you do to me, Ruby?"* he said to her mind. *"I cannot control Desire."*

She moaned. *"Don't try, Michael."* Whatever spirit embodied him also embodied her. Desire had a grip on her, too. She scooted her hips closer to his ever growing groin, because her womb was weeping. *"Remove my pants, Michael, yours too."*

As tempted as he was, he wasn't about to do that. They really *didn't* have enough time. But he was struggling against Desire. He stroked her womb, through her pants. The friction caused both of them to quiver. *"What are you going to do, if we get caught?"* he asked.

The pilot came over the speaker, before she could answer. "We will be landing in five minutes. Thank you for flying Air Seraphiel."

~

Verenda went stark still. She looked up at Michael and then at the cockpit door. She scrambled off his lap, and repositioned her clothes. She was flustered, and her face was beet red. "I'm gon' cut you!"

Michael howled. He'd never seen her move so fast. He stretched his legs out and crossed them at the ankles. "I told you to behave."

"Put my bra back on me," she whispered.

"Nope," he replied and kept laughing. "It looks sexy."

"I'm gon' die of shame, Michael." She had never in her life gone braless, she was too top heavy.

"You will not die until the Rapture, Ruby."

"I'm too old for this foolishness! Now put my bra back on me!" she demanded. She was trying to keep from laughing. He had a *warped* sense of humor.

"Foolishness? You wanted to join the Mile High Club," he replied, and roared.

"I didn't know Seraphiel was in the cockpit!" she complained. "I can't let him see me like this."

"Like what?" He reached over and tweaked her breast. Then he ran his finger across her nipple. "They are still standing in attention," he said and leaned down and kissed them.

He hadn't lied, and it wasn't just her nipples. The whole of her breasts were swollen, and her nipples were about to pop. They were tingling and aching for him to finish the job. His touching them, just now, had not helped. A blind man would be able to see them, even though her jacket was closed. Every cell in her body was pleading for him not to stop. "Please," she whispered and pouted her lip. "Don't make me beg, Michael."

"I told you not to tempt me. This is what happens when you do," he replied and laughed.

"Alright," she said and laughed. "I'm not going to be the only one embarrassed." She reached over and stroked his groin.

Michael jumped and lifted her hand. He crossed his legs higher up, to hide his excitement. He forced Desire all the way down, and materialized her bra. Then he leaned over and kissed her. "Next time do not tempt me."

She laughed. Nobody knew his playful side, but her. "I'm gon get you," she replied.

"You already have, Ruby," he replied. Then he leaned back, closed his eyes. "You already have."

Just as the cockpit door opened he spoke to her mind, *"Your clothes look presentable, but your hair is ruffled."*

She gasped and grabbed her head.

~

Chapter V

Brock *and* Donnell walked through the cockpit door. They immediately noticed how flushed Verenda was. Her face, neck and chest were just as red as the jewels she wore. That white glow she normally had was red and orange fiery streaks. That, along with the condition of her hair, was telling signs that they'd interrupted hers and Michael's tryst. She was desperately trying to get her hair back in order.

Michael was sitting with his legs crossed, and his eyes closed, looking all innocent. But they were men, and knew *why* his legs were crossed. Their lips quivered, as they tried to keep from laughing.

"I hope you enjoyed the flight, Ms. Verenda," Donnell said.

"What?" she asked, but refused to look up at him. *Donnell too!* Not only was she embarrassed, she was confused. She shook her head and mumbled, in her mind, *Don't understand. What are Donnell and Brock doing on this plane? Why are they here, Jesus? Michael play too dang much! I'm gon' cut him!*

Never once did she suspect Seraphiel owned an airplane. Why would he need one, anyway? She kept her head down, because her face was on fire. *"What in the world are Donnell and Brock doing flying this plane, Michael?"*

Michael was cracking up, in her head. *"I own a fleet of private jets. They are mostly used for shuffling the little ones to the cities where they will meet their 'spirit' mates,"* he informed her.

That made sense to her. In the past neither the young 'spirit' mates, nor their mothers, knew what they were. It was up to the Watchers to tell them their destinies. *"But why are Donnell and Seraphiel on this plane?"*

"You wanted an airplane ride, so I gave you one. Seraphiel and Donnell were our pilots."

She kept her head down, but saw that her chest was returning to its natural color. "Where exactly are we?" she asked for the umpteenth time.

"Let's go and see," he replied, and handed her a glass of wine. "But comb your hair first."

She blushed and her chest turned red again.

Brock and Donnell laughed.

~

When she finally stood up she saw all of her little 'spirit' mates sitting in the back of the airplane, with their mothers. They were all smiling and waving at her. She blushed, deeper. This plane wasn't empty; she just couldn't see or hear anybody. Lord she hoped they hadn't heard her, and Michael. She looked at Michael, with tight lips, and rolled her eyes. *"I'm gon' cut you, Michael."*

He cracked up.

Along with them were all of the Ultimate Watchers, and their mates. They were all smiles. They all lifted their wine glasses and toasted her. Every single one of them had sneaky, Chester the cat, grins on their faces.

She blushed so deeply, she looked like Hellboy. She knew damn well those nosey Ultimate Watchers were listening. *"Could they hear us, Michael?"*

He chuckled. *"No."*

"Could they see us?"

He stood up and wrapped one arm around her. He felt how tense she really was. *"No, Ruby. I would not dishonor you in any manner."*

She visibly relaxed. *"I'm still gon' cut you."*

She looked back at everybody, lifted her glass, and put on a faux smile.

Then she thought about it. Why were all of them on the plane? She didn't want this crowd with her, on her honeymoon. *"Why are they here, Michael?"*

"To see us off," he replied. *"I thought it would be nice for the little ones to enjoy a plane ride, too."*

~

Desiree was the first one to stand up. She walked into Verenda's open arms. "You didn't think I wouldn't give you a proper sendoff, did you?"

Verenda hugged Desiree, and her eyes ran. She didn't mind Desiree being here, this was her baby. She could let all the other 'spirit' mates go, just so long as she got to keep this one. "This is the best wedding present ever," she said and kissed her cheek.

Then she turned around and hugged Donnell. "I didn't know you could fly a plane."

"We can't. We just kept it in the air," he replied.

Verenda laughed and then she hugged Brock. "I was disappointed that you didn't come see us off," she admitted. She was still concerned about his acceptance of hers and Michael's relationship. She didn't know how he would accept their being married.

"I wouldn't have missed it for the world. Michael told me you wanted to fly on an airplane, so I offered to help. It was only fitting that Donnell be my co-pilot. It's my way of saying I'm sorry, Verenda," he replied. He leaned down and kissed her cheek. "Congratulations. And welcome to the family."

Jodi walked up and hugged her. "I am sorry for my mother and aunts," she said. "But my sisters, cousins and I love you." Then she hugged her again. "I am glad that you are back in my life."

"Me too, hon," Verenda replied and hugged her.

"Brock and I would be honored if you'd recognize our children as your grandchildren, too."

Verenda started bawling, like a baby. She was squeezing Jodi so tight, she was choking her. All of their children were Michael's grandchildren. She never thought they'd want her to play a pivotal role in their children's lives; especially knowing how SnowAnna felt about her. She was too emotional to speak; she just kept crying.

Desiree got in on the hug. "Back in the day it was just the three of us, remember?" she reminded them. "Both of you took care of me, when I was too weak to take care of myself," she added and her eyes watered too.

"We sure did," Jodi replied. That was when they both met Verenda. "And Verenda gave me my first car."

"We've come full circle," Verenda choked out, and the tears started again.

They were a hot mess.

Just as they were about to settle down Verenda looked up and saw Ester and Dena walking up the aisle. "Oh Lord," she whispered and started crying, all over again. Her entire family had come to see her off.

"Hush now, child," Ester said. Then she hugged her

and kissed her cheek. "Everything worked out just fine." She'd always known that Michael loved Verenda. She just didn't know the nature of that love.

Dena hugged her too. "Zeek and I are so happy for you, Verenda." Verenda was like a sister to her. Both of them were in their late sixties, but looked thirty-five. She'd been horrified when she heard the things the Walker women said about her sister. Her and Ester, both, had wanted Zeek to teleport them to the estate, but he refused.

~

Verenda finally pulled away and wiped her eyes. "Thank you for coming," she told them. Then she looked at Jodi and Brock. "When we get back home may I meet my grandchildren?"

"Yes," Jodi replied and wiped her eyes. "Hannah and Elizabeth can't wait."

Verenda looked at Michael, and then at Donnell and Brock. "Will someone please tell me where we are?"

They laughed and looked at Michael. He smiled. "We are in Chicago, Ruby."

"What?"

"Where we are going no airplane can go," he informed her.

"So all of this was-"

"To give you your plane ride," he replied and winked.

She loved her man, she always had. Everyone on this plane knew they were in love, and married. It was time to stop hiding their affection for each other. Discretion could go to Hell. She walked into his open arms.

With everyone watching, Michael leaned down, stroked her cheek and passionately kissed her. "We are on Satariel's and Adabiel's property. Sarah and Gabriella have prepared a luncheon for us."

"Wait," she said and frowned. "My children don't know what you guys are. How did you get them on the airplane?"

"Ditto and his crew drove them over as soon as you guys left," Brock informed her. "They were already on the plane when you and Michael boarded."

"He and everybody else are waiting just outside the plane," Desiree informed her. She was so grateful that they liked her mother, even Smittie's daughters.

Donnell told her that the Walker brothers wanted to come, because they really liked Michael; especially Floyd. But, they were scared of the backlash from their wives. They did, however, volunteer to watch all of the grandchildren, so that their sons and daughters could participate.

Donnell also told her that Leevearne was upset that her three daughters were coming. But Smith told her it was time to let it go. He told her that Verenda had never been a threat to their marriage.

Then Donnell told her something Michael had shared with him; and it blew her mind. It blew his, too. She wondered if Smith and Verenda knew. Probably not.

~

"Lara, Amanda, Charity and their husbands are out there too," Jodi informed her. "We *all* wanted to see you and Michael off."

Donnell wanted to be the one to escort Verenda off

the plane. He reached for her hand. "Let's go."

~

When they exited the plane, Aurellia and Deuce were standing on the tarmac. Aurellia ran up to greet her. "We fooled you, didn't we, Grandma?"

"Yes, you did, granddaughter," Verenda replied and hugged her, and Deuce.

Adam and Mordiree were next in line. He hugged her, and kissed her cheek. "You are the *sexiest* grandmother I've ever seen."

Verenda's eyes watered again. She thought Jodi just meant their four babies. This meant more to her than anyone would ever know. Aurellia and Adam accepted her, not just as Michael's wife, but as their grandmother. They wanted to be in her life, regardless of what SnowAnna thought about her.

She sheltered her little 'spirit' mates and then let them go. But these children would always stay close. Michael had given her a family she could *keep*.

~

Akibeel, Maria, Doc and Kwanita were next. "We want you to be our children's grandmother too," Kwanita told her.

"And ours," Maria added.

Akibeel hugged her. "Whenever we decide to have some," he stipulated.

~

One by one each couple hugged her, and apologized for their mothers' behavior. They all told her they loved her, and wanted to be a part of her life. It meant so much to her for them to take the time, even Smittie's three daughters.

Candace, Celia and Celina tipped her over the edge, and she sobbed. All three of them collectively hugged her and Candace said, "We know how you feel. We didn't have anybody that loved us, either."

By the time she finished crying she looked Goth, again. But it wasn't over...

~

Brock's and Doc's teams appeared, with their spouses. And the hugs and well wishes started all over again.

Next were all of the Ultimate Watchers and their wives. One of their wives had played the role of stewardess.

Like always, Nate had jokes. He stood at arm's length and shook her hand. "I would hug you but that jolly - pretending he's not black - giant over there might hurt me."

Michael cracked up. He claimed no race, because he wasn't. Unlike the Watchers, he had no race that was dearest to his heart; they all were. His skin tone was the same it had been since he was called into existence, exotic.

For the first time, in five thousand years, he felt like one of the boys. None of them were bowing to him, or treating him like he was a deity. "What happened, your marbles shrink again, boy?" he responded to Nate's joke.

The Watchers roared.

"No," Nate replied, and looked Michael up and down. He wasn't the giant anymore. He was the same height as he was. He met him eye to eye and then let his eyes peruse to Michael's groin and back. "But proportionately speaking, apparently yours did," he replied and flipped Michael the bird.

The Watchers screamed. "Damn Nate!" Brock said and cried.

Michael laughed and extended his fist...Nate met it half way. "That was a good one, boy."

~

Gabriella hugged Verenda. "Please forgive me, Verenda. I am sorry for my behavior. I fell in line with those women and judged you, when I'd never even met you. I know better than that. I couldn't see how wrong that was, until MeiLi attacked my granddaughter. I hope we can be friends."

Verenda hugged her. "I'm sure we can," she replied. But she was just being polite. They could *never* be friends, or even close acquaintances.

She could accept Gabriella's apology, because she knew she truly meant it. That wasn't the reason they couldn't be friends.

They couldn't be friends because Gabriella was the type to hold your secret, until she got mad at you. She was like chaff, controlled by the wind. If Adabiel hadn't shut her down she would have hurt all of these young couples; including her own daughters.

Gabriella reminded her of the girls who'd made fun of her, when she was a teenager. They said things about her, in her presence, without consideration for her feelings. They'd all bullied her, with their mouths, and made her feel worthless. She'd love to see them now, and rub it in their faces. She was sure they'd have the same response, to her, as Leevearne.

If she allowed Gabriella into her inner circle she'd eventually have to slice, and dice her. And although she had no problem cuttin' a sistah, Michael would not be pleased.

Michael chuckled. *"Behave, woman,"* he whispered to her mind.

"I'm just saying."

~

Sarah and Gabriella had laid out a nice spread for their reception brunch. It was outside on a large patio that overlooked a giant maze.

The children were having a ball running through it, and getting lost. She decided she was going to take Seraphiel up on his offer, to take her children to the Estate. They needed to be able to play, in the sunlight. She knew Seraphiel would protect them from those nosey Walker wives.

~

Sarah had a wedding cake with a replica of her and Michael on the top. The cake had white icing, but instead of roses, it had red sugary rubies all over it. The top layer had real rubies. "How did you do this?" Verenda asked her.

"Arakiel did it," Faith answered. "I told him I wanted something special for you, Verenda. Daddy told me that your middle name is Ruby."

"It is. It's also my birthstone," she replied.

"It's our gift to you and Michael. Take a closer look."

Verenda and Michael both examined it closely. It even had her ruby wedding rings, on the statue's hand.

And a ruby crown on her head. It was stunning.

~

She spent a little time with all of her little 'spirit' mates and made them promise to behave, while she was gone. She promised to bring them a gift back, but only if they were good.

~

She also told them about the Watchers. She wanted Akibeel with her, because they liked him. She also wanted Aurellia, because she'd lived the life. "They are special men, and they are here to protect you."

"Can Unc Kibee do magic tricks?" one of the little 'spirit' mates asked.

Akibeel laughed. "Yes, I can. I will show you. Let's play hide and go seek."

~

The children ran in the maze to hide. Verenda laughed at their screams, whenever Akibeel found them and teleported them out of the maze.

They were jumping up and down. "I want to do it again, Unc Kibee!"

~

The teenagers were hanging around Aurellia, because they thought she was their age. They wanted to know what it was like to grow up with a father, who didn't want to kill her. She told them that her father had never hit her; and that in fact she was spoiled.

When she introduced them to Deuce, one said, "Your daddy let you get *married?*"

"He didn't like it at first, but I was grown," she replied.

"Grown? How old are you?" one asked.
"Twenty-four," she replied.
"You look so young."

~

Chapter VI

Michael walked away from the gathering, with the Watchers. He wanted a last minute meeting with them. When they were all seated in the sunroom he perused the crowd. "It has been a long road to get where we are," he said. "You men have been magnanimous. The Master left it up to me to select twenty-one good men to lead the Watchers. I only selected twenty, because the twenty-first wasn't ready to answer my call," he added and looked at Yomiel.

Yomiel smiled.

"Over the last four years, you have more than made up for the lost time," Michael added. "I picked Seraphiel because I had no choice," he said and laughed. "It was that...or kill him."

Brock raised his brows. "What?"

"You did not think the Master would let you side with Lucifer, did you?" Michael asked. It surprised him that Seraphiel had not figured that out. "My orders were clear, *'recruit...or execute'*. And I always follow orders."

Brock was dumbfounded. "WHAT?"

"Damn!" all the Watchers said.

"That's cold, Mike," Nate added.

"I picked the next nineteen born, because you guys were the most powerfully gifted. I picked Yomiel because he was the seed of Samjaza; which made him powerful."

"You gave me something, too," Yomiel injected.

Michael nodded. "Yes, I did. I wanted to make it up to you for frightening you," Michael responded. "Had I known Akibeel hadn't said no to me, he would have also been an Ultimate Watcher."

"What?" Akibeel asked.

Michael nodded. Then he looked at Donnell. "If Donnell hadn't been so hard to get along with he would have been also. His personality was not right, at the time."

Donnell already knew that. He would not have been a good leader, though. He would have been just like Brock...arrogant.

Brock did not know that. "Neither was my personality," he replied.

"True, but you were too powerful. You would not have taken direction from anyone but me."

"True that," Brock replied, and laughed. Back in the day he was too arrogant. He would have crushed anybody who tried to tell him what to do.

"In spite of your long wait for your mates you all remained faithful. I am proud of each and every one of you. Even you, Nate," Michael said and chuckled.

"You should be," Nate replied. "Why didn't you give me more power? You scared me too, man."

Michael laughed. "I have not had an opportunity to speak to you guys since I frightened you, at the House. I apologize for the stress I caused you. I know my son has informed you that Verenda has always been my 'sanctioned' mate. I am giving all of you a chance to ask any questions, you might have."

He knew who would be the first to speak...

~

Donnell leaned back in his chair, and sighed. Michael had shared some important information with him. It was to ease his disdain towards Smith Walker. It didn't help, like Michael thought it would. "How in the world did you let that shit go down, Michael? If you knew about Verenda, all along, how could you let it happen? She tried to kill herself, man. That bastard, Smith Walk-" He stopped because he was getting angry, again.

"How is it that you didn't destroy Smith, and all of those bastards, for what they did to her," Ram asked. He'd killed every single one of the bastards that hurt his woman.

"Watchers react to attacks on their mates by allowing Guilt, Rage and Anger to take control," Michael replied. "I do not have the luxury of being embraced by, or embracing, those spirits."

"What?" Donnell asked. Neither he, nor any of the regular Watchers understood. The Ultimate Watchers did. They all knew what would happen if that ever happened. Or so they thought they did.

"Those spirits want no part of me," he replied.

"Why?" Donnell asked. When he saw Rondell attacking Desiree, he'd embraced those spirits like a *motha*. When those demons attacked the beach, in an attempt to get to her, those spirits were his closest allies. Even now, with Smith, they were standing at the door knocking.

Michael was listening to his thoughts. He wished he *could*. "Even if I were willing to embrace them, they won't accept my invitation."

He thought back to that day over forty years ago. "I felt it the moment Verenda took her last breath. Guilt and Rage made the mistake of reaching for me, and were overpowered by Terror. Then they snatched Overwhelm, into the fray. The four spirits *screamed* for Help. Help was not foolish enough to come near me. If it had been, I would have *helped* myself to Sammael's behind," he told them.

"What?" Ali asked.

"Sammael wasn't aware that we were mates, and he attempted to leave with her spirit."

"Wait a minute! She *succeeded* in killing herself?" Donnell asked. "She actually died?"

Michael nodded. "I snatched Sammael back and ordered him to release her."

"Did he?" Nate asked. "I mean I know he did, because she's here. He probably thought, like we did, that you would fall. I can't imagine he surrendered her spirit without pause."

"You are correct, Nate. He did indeed pause," Michael replied and laughed. "I *froze* him and snatched her, out of his hands."

"And probably scared the crap out of him," Nate replied. His mind wandered back to the day Michael scared him. He actually shivered.

"He was definitely on edge," Michael replied and cracked up. "Just like you guys, he had the order of the 'fall' all wrong."

"How?" Kobabiel asked.

"My wayward brothers didn't fall because they raped the human women. They fell because of their pride, and their refusal to acknowledge the Master. The fall came *first*, and then they raped the women."

They all looked from Michael to Batman and Jehoel. Their father was still an Archangel. Batman smiled. "That's right!"

Michael nodded and kept going. "Anyway Sammael shouted for Father."

"Did Verenda know what was happening to her?" Akibeel asked. When Ram killed him he never lost awareness. But he didn't know if it was different for humans.

"She was very much aware, but she did not understand why I was fighting to keep her. She forgot that we knew each other from the beginning. She forgot her promise to me."

"Did you tell her?" Brock asked.

"Not then. She was only a sixteen year old child," Michael replied. "Anyway, Sammael shouted for Father. Help shouted for three of his closest mates: Calm, Ease and Peace."

"None of those spirits are more powerful than you, Michael. You could have rejected them," Donnell stated. "Why didn't you?"

Brock answered, "If he had, that day would have been disastrous. That day would have been the end of the world."

"Not true," Michael replied. All of the demons, Ultimate Watchers and Archangels thought he'd destroy the world, if possessed by an evil spirit. And that day he would have most definitely tried.

They all thought he was the top of the food chain, even humans. Seraphiel had all but lost his mind, over the prospect of him falling. He understood that though, because he was all they'd ever had. He was their go-to man, their leader. But he was just the messenger.

"I am not the top of the food chain, gentlemen. I

never have been."

Brock frowned. He knew for a fact that Michael was the most powerful Archangel, called into existence. "Who is then?"

Michael was reading his thoughts. "As you accurately thought, I was *called* into existence; therefore I cannot be the top of the chain. That title still belongs to the *caller*. The Creator, Seraphiel. Yahweh. The Alpha and Omega. He would no more let me destroy the world He created, than He would let you side with Lucifer."

Nate was intrigued and leaned forward. Of course Yahweh was the top, how could they forget that. "What would He do to you, Michael?"

Michael smiled at Nate. There were no fun and games in that question. He wasn't preparing for a snappy, or off color, come back. He genuinely wanted to understand. This was the first time any of these men wanted to know Michael, the man. And he liked that.

"If I were ever embraced by those spirits Master would rein me in, and reduce me to nothing more than a dead star."

All the Watchers leaned forward and said, *"What?"*

Michael laughed at the expressions on their faces. "Then He would shoot me across the galaxy into a black hole; as far away from His so loved as possible."

"Does Lucifer know this?" Kobabiel asked.

Michael shook his head. "If he did he would try and convince one of those spirits to sacrifice themselves for the greater good."

They all got nervous. "Damn Michael!" Adabiel shouted. He'd just made a colossal mistake. "Why did you tell us? Lucifer can read our thoughts, man."

"I am aware of that," Michael replied.

"Then why would you *do* that?" Hakael asked.

"He will most assuredly make it his mission to get you cast aside," Zeek said. "Don't you know the outcome of your not being around?"

"Then he will start on Seraphiel, again," Jehoel added.

"You may have just started the end of Time, my friend," Hasdiel told him.

"I'm sorry I asked," Nate added.

Michael looked at all of them. They all, including Seraphiel, were disturbed by his presumed slip of the tongue. They were all wondering if married life had affected him. He shook his head. "First of all, Time will *never* end; you boys know that. Secondly, I am *still* Michael. Lucifer can only read what is available to him. He cannot hear what I do not allow him to hear. He cannot take from your minds what I block."

"What about my father. He took the information about Aurellia," Kobabiel asked. "And *gave* it to Lucifer."

Brock nodded his head.

"I am not omniscient, Kobabiel. And for the most part, I do not snoop. I was not aware that you knew about her, until I saw you on the ground in Aceldama. Otherwise I would have blocked it."

They looked at Kobabiel. "You went to The Field of Blood?" Brock asked.

"I was ashamed, Seraphiel. My father stole my memories. I put your children at risk," he replied. "You should know a portion of your wrath still hovers."

Brock chuckled. "Trust me; I am well aware of that fact." He left it there so that Judas' spirit would forever be undisturbed. Aceldama is Judas' one man penal colony; his isle of Patmos, so to speak. His spirit would remain there until that Great Day of Judgment. Then the Son of God would decide where his final home would be. But, until then, he wasn't allowed visitation from demon or Watcher. Kobabiel and Adabiel were the only two Watchers that could penetrate the shield he'd placed there. Even so, he couldn't believe Kobabiel had gone there. "Did you see him?"

"No, but I wasn't looking either. His spirit was there, though. It tried to get my attention by bleeding through the stones. I ignored the blood and the stench, of that bastard."

Brock and Michael nodded.

~

Arakiel was nervous. After hearing how Faith lost it when he disconnected from her he left their link open. She was hearing what he was hearing, right now. Before he could warn Michael, Michael started talking.

"Your links are still intact, but none of your 'spirit' mates are hearing this conversation. None of them will ever be able to pull it from your memories. Not even your mate, Ali."

They all breathed a sigh of relief.

~

"I shared this information with you guys, because it is time for you gentlemen to stop treating me like I am a deity," he informed them. "Like I've always told you, I am *just* the messenger."

"The minute you started knocking boots all bets were off, Dawg," Nate replied.

The Watchers roared. Donnell was laughing so hard he almost tumbled his chair over. "I told you years ago to go for it, man. Look at all the time you wasted."

Michael laughed. "If I am not mistaken I believe you crudely said, *'You should hit that, man'*." He threw his voice to sound just like Donnell.

"DON!" Zeek shouted. "OH MY GOD! DON!! You didn't! What is wrong with you, breddah!"

Donnell was nodding his head, and wheezing. He was the only one who *never* treated Michael like he was special. Even though he sometimes went too far, Michael appreciated it. "Michael practically *lived* at our house, just to be close to Verenda," he replied. "In my house, I was the alpha. Plus, I was right. I told y'all there was something going on with those two."

"I still can't believe you said that, breddah," Zeek replied.

Donnell hadn't stopped laughing. He squeaked out, "He looked at me like he wanted to hurt me. His eyes twirled in two different directions!" He raised his hands and showed them. "Wax on...wax off!"

Brock was the only one who didn't know what that meant. The other Watchers, and Michael, howled.

~

Michael materialized five bottles of vintage wine, and pure gold chalices. When everyone's glass was full, he raised his. "To the end of an era," he said. He was about to materialize something else, but Brock cut him off.

~

"What?" Brock asked, and frowned. Everyone held their glasses up, but him. He was the only one who truly heard what Michael had just said. *'To the end of an era.'*

"You had to know this day was coming, Seraphiel," Michael replied. "I thought you would be pleased."

"What day?" Nate asked.

"What's going on, Dad?" Akibeel asked.

Brock's heart was racing. He was glaring at Michael. "You are not walking away, Dad. We still need you."

"Walking away? What the hell is he talking about, Michael," Kobabiel asked.

They'd misunderstood what he meant, but they needed to discuss this topic, as well. So he let it ride. He never took his eyes off of Seraphiel. "You are their leader now, son. And you certainly do not *need* me."

"Like Hell!" Brock replied. Even five thousand year old men need their fathers. He was devastated. "How are you going to walk away from your grandchildren, Michael? How are you going to walk away from your sons?" he asked, and his eyes glazed. "How can you walk away from me?"

Michael chuckled. "I could never do that, son. You misunderstood."

"Explain it then," Brock snapped.

"I told you months ago that I would no longer be involved in the day to day. I turned all of that over to you, and your team," he replied. "I told you that I would only answer *your* call. These men look up to you, son. They were all willing to come up against me, and stand with you. Even old scary Nate," he said and laughed. "It is time for you to stop holding back, son. Show yourself. Stop *pretending* you are less than you are."

"I can't believe you, Michael," Brock said. He sounded like a child. He'd had three fathers in his lifetime: Samjaza, H and Michael. Samjaza tried to kill him, and still would if he could. H stood by and let another man attack him, when he was at his weakest. Michael was his only father who hadn't *ever* let him down, not from day one. He felt a sense of woe. He rubbed his face. "So you will only come around if I call for *help?*"

Yomiel was feeling the same trepidation. "What about the 'spirit' mates that haven't been united with their Watchers. What happens to them?"

"They are still my responsibility, Yomiel. I made a promise to every Watcher that chose our side. I am a man of my word," Michael replied.

"So you just don't want to hang with us anymore?" Dan asked.

"That is exactly what I want to do, Denel. I am not your leader. Seraphiel is, and rightly so. I just want to be one of the boys," Michael replied. "Besides, when I said it was the end of an era, you guys misunderstood."

"What era then?" Adam asked.

Michael looked at all the Watchers. They really were the best of the best. "You don't need me as a messenger, anymore." He raised his glass again. "This wine is your first communion," he told them. Then he materialized, in each of their hands, a disc of unleavened bread.

They all slowly smiled. Nate's eyes watered. "To the Son."

"Here...here!" they said in unison and partook of their first remembrance of Christ.

Batman drank his and said, "I can go to the Father for myself!" He had such conviction in his voice everybody else chimed in.

Akibeel laughed and said, "I always did."

Michael laughed. The Master got such pleasure out of Akibeel's prayers. That boy gave thanks for *everything!* "Yeah well, the Master said to tell you that you can stop thanking him for bathroom tissue. He knows you appreciate it."

The Watchers roared.

Akibeel laughed too. "Just so long as He knows," he replied.

The Watchers screamed!!

~

"I do have one favor to ask of you, Seraphiel," Michael said. "And you too, Yomiel."

"What's that?"

"While I am away I would like for Donnell, Akibeel and Batman to stay at the House. The children need to be protected, while I'm gone."

"I planned on staying with them," Brock replied.

Michael shook his head. "The children know and are comfortable with Donnell and Akibeel. I need *Batman,* as a backup."

Brock frowned. Michael was up to something. "Alright," he replied.

Yomiel nodded too.

~

When they walked out on the patio Verenda was

talking with Charity, Faith and Maria. Smith Walker's daughters really liked her, and were monopolizing *all* of her time. All of them could have been her daughters, if...

"Are you ready, Verenda?" Michael asked.

Verenda looked up and smiled, and zoned everyone else out. "Yes, hon," she replied. "Where are we going?"

He wrapped his arms around her and smiled. "Our honeymoon," he replied.

And they vanished.

~

Chapter VII

Verenda had traveled the world over, with her late husband. They were Nomads, always on the go. They traveled to the known sights and the obscure ones, as well. They hiked up the most challenging mountain; and treaded their way through the most dangerous rainforests. He took her to every Island he could think of. They took one cruise, after another. She'd seen it all, with him. He was trying to get as much living in as he could, before he died.

He was poisoned by the country he loved, while serving that country in Vietnam. He was at ground zero when they dropped that damn pesticide on Laos. He knew she'd tried to kill herself and wanted to give her a reason to keep going, without him. He made sure she knew the world was bigger than her little corner, in it.

She'd seen some amazing things, but nothing as astonishing, as this...

~

She was standing on the whitest sandy beach, she'd ever seen. The ocean was so blue and crystal clear, she couldn't tell where it ended and the sky began.

Several large pieces of sun bleached driftwood, that resembled antlers, stretched along the edge of the water. Palm trees sporadically stood on the beach, but leaned towards the ocean. Their trunks were so white they looked like Greek columns.

A flock of Barn Swallows flew overhead. Some landed in search of food, or maybe rest. Others continued on their migration, across the ocean. They all seemed to greet her, in song.

Dozens of newly hatched sea turtles raced along the sand, toward their new homes. She watched as they splashed in the water and swam away. Swimming was as natural to them as breathing was to humans.

She turned and looked up at her husband. "Where are we, Michael?"

"We are home."

"Home?"

He reached for her hand. "C'mon, I'll show you."

~

Michael led her up a path that was bordered by red tipped photinia, shadowed by twenty foot tall sago palms. On both sides of the path beautiful tropical foliage stretched across the terrain. Several large trees had ghost lilies growing in the arc of their trunks. Wild parrots, of various colors, were perched high on the tree branches. Some sang beautiful welcoming songs, while others spoke 'welcome home'.

At the end of the path glass brick pillars stood on each side of ascending stairs; that were made of the same clear brick. On each side of the stairway beautiful bouquets of snapdragons, oriental lilies, lobelia and begonias were overflowing, in glass pots.

She was busy admiring the scene, and hadn't looked to see what was at the top of the stairs. Before she knew it she was standing in front of their home. She frowned, looked up at Michael, and then back at the house. Her eyes watered.

She'd grown up in *squalor*. She never had anything decent, as a child; not even personal hygiene products. She went to school dirty, and smelly. Tattered hand-medowns were all she ever wore. The only shoes she'd ever owned had been shaped by someone else's feet.

By the time she got to high school she'd learned personal hygiene. She also found out that baking soda had many uses, one was as deodorant. She also learned how to iron and make her clothes look presentable. But they were still *used*. She used Vaseline and baby oil to make her shoes shine, but they were scuffed, nonetheless.

Then the day came when Michael found her. The first thing he did was gift her with a wardrobe. He provided all the personal items she needed. He provided *everything* she needed, even someone to help her cope. Ester!

She'd stayed with Ester for two weeks. That old broad had been just what the doctor ordered. She showered her with maternal love and made her feel good about herself.

She returned home the day before her foster mother got back from her trip. The woman saw all of her new clothes and accused her of shoplifting. In the end it made the woman look like she was a good foster mother. No one but her knew it was Michael.

~

She looked back at him but couldn't find her voice. She decided she was going to stop wearing makeup altogether. She knew for sure she looked Goth, yet again. She'd seen the house that Seraphiel owned, through Michael's eyes. It was the most beautiful abode she'd ever seen. Until now...

Her husband and her best friend...

The man who had always supplied her needs...

The one person she could always depend on…
The man she loved more than life…
Had just gifted her with a *glass house!!*

She laid her head on his chest, and sobbed. It had always been…Michael.

~

Michael kissed her cheek, and wiped her tears. Even Goth she was beautiful, and not just to him. Every man that was blessed to gaze upon her thought so; demons, humans, and Archangels, alike. But she was his mate; a gift from the Master.

He thought back to the first time *he* saw her, and his heart clinched. He would have to tell her what happened soon, because Lucifer knew…

But, not right now. He stroked her cheek. "A *crystal palace*, Ruby," he corrected her.

"Crystal?" Her tears tripled. "Palace?"

He nodded. "Shall we go inside?" he asked.

She nodded her head.

He lifted her in his arms, and kissed her. Then he carried his bride across the threshold. Some human traditions just felt right.

~

Verenda was overwhelmed, as she stood in the vestibule; and took it all in. The floors were white marble, with red veins. A large gold circle was in the marble, just beyond the entryway. In the center etched in red crystal were the initials, "M & R".

Two feet ahead a large round beveled glass table, with a white marble pedestal, stood in the middle of the floor. A crystal vase filled with fresh cut white roses, with red tips, sat in the middle of the table.

Beyond the table the opening revealed just how large the house was. She was speechless. She had never seen anything like this, in her life. She never *imagined* anything like this.

The walls were crystal, with red and gold sconces. Dozens of beautiful crystal chandeliers hung from the vaulted crystal ceiling. All she could say was, "Michael."

"The entire first floor is a grand ballroom, Ruby."

On each side of the ballroom six foot wide stairs spiraled upward. They, and the railing, were frosted glass. They ascended to a huge landing, on a second floor. It reminded her of her idea of a stairway to heaven. A beautiful ruby red teardrop chandelier hung in the center of the landing.

"Our living quarters are upstairs," Michael informed her. Then he wrapped his arms around her, and transported her to the landing.

~

The landing, itself, was the formal living area. The sofa, loveseat and chaise lounge were white silk; with red silk throw pillows. The cocktail tables were red marble, with white and gold veins. The walls were crystal blocks, like the path. Off to the left, she could see the dining and kitchen areas. Both rooms were extremely large, and had the same color scheme. She knew the abundance of red was a dedication to her. It represented her name, birthstone and favorite color. "This place is beautiful, Michael."

"Not as beautiful as its owner," he replied.

She looked up at him and smiled. Then she stroked

his beautiful face. "It most certainly is not."

He palmed her hand, and kissed it. "I'm talking about *you,* Ruby."

"I've never seen anything like this," she said. "What island is this?"

Michael's eyes twirled. "We are inside the Bermuda Triangle."

She blinked. "Stop playing. Where are we?"

"Inside the Triangle, Ruby," he replied, and laughed.

She looked under eyed at him. "You bought me a house inside *Devil's* Triangle?"

"No," he replied.

"I didn't *think* so."

"I built you a *home,* inside Devil's Triangle," he replied.

The look on her face was precious. She knew he had a sense of humor but an Archangel living inside... "Nah," she said and shook her head. "Where are we, seriously?"

"Ask Cook," he replied.

"Who is Cook?"

"You'll meet him, and all the staff, later. Let me give you a tour of the house, first."

~

The house was unbelievably spectacular. There were twelve bedrooms; each with a different motif. Two of the bedrooms didn't have crystal walls.

One of those rooms had two twin beds, with Pocahontas bedspreads, and three decked out white baby beds. It had murals of the cartoon characters on the walls. There was even a little table with a tea set on it.

The other bedroom had six decked out baby beds with blue covers, and two car beds. It had a variety of action figures on the mural. It also had an elevated train set, on a mantel that looped along the mural.

Both rooms were stuffed with animals, dolls, action figures, trucks and toys, galore.

Verenda frowned. Michael knew she was barren. He knew more than anything she wanted children. His children. That was her greatest regret. Why would he do this? "Why do we have these children's rooms?"

"We cannot have children, Ruby. But we have a lot of little grandchildren, one or two on the way, and a few grown ones. These two rooms are for the little ones," Michael replied.

"I can't wait to get to know all of them, Michael; especially the little ones."

"You will," he replied. "There are enough rooms for all of our children. Only our children, and grandchildren, will be welcome to *sleep* in our home."

Then he wrapped his arms around her and stroked her hips. "But not today. Today is *ours*. Tomorrow too."

Every cell in her body *burned*, and not just from his touch. It was his gaze...his voice...it was *him!* She wrapped her arms around his neck. "It has always been you, Michael."

"Not always," he replied and passionately kissed her. Then he teleported them to their bedroom.

~

Verenda thought she had seen all of the bedrooms, but she hadn't seen this room. That made thirteen bedrooms. Leave it to him to go for unlucky number thirteen.

It was on a wing of the house, by itself. It wasn't a suite. It was just huge! There was a minibar, on the far side of the room. It held their crystal coffee pot; and their favorite coffee. Crystal coffee cups, wine tumblers and aged wine, were stored on the lower shelves. It was right outside the spacious bathroom.

The tub, counter, toilet and shower were crystal. However, the bathroom walls weren't. They were wall to wall mirrors! Sexy!!

The towel racks were made of rubies. He knew her idiosyncrasy about colored towels. She did not like them!! Every single one of them was 'white', and a silk blend.

Their bed was much larger than a normal king size bed, and as expected it was covered with a ruby red silk bedspread. The bed sat upon a crystal pedestal. There was a light inside the platform that lent a sensual glow. Tall crystal vases, with long stem red roses, sat on the pedestal; and white rose buds were splayed on the bed. The room only had three walls.

There was a large opening where the fourth wall should've been. It opened out to a large patio garden. Driftwood, with glass topped, patio tables were strategically placed. Vases filled with birds of paradise sat on them.

Lounge chairs were shaded by potted palms. Ferns, arctotis African daisies, aster, and black eyed susan, all bordered the banister. Butterflies, in an array of colors, flew over and rested on them.

Crystal bird baths stood along the far end of the patio, amidst potted lilies and wild flowers. Perched on the edges were several pairs of mating lovebirds.

Her little spirit mates weren't the only ones who needed to get out of the House. She had never seen Mother Nature at her finest.

She walked to the edge of the patio, hugged herself and gazed across the horizon. It was an astonishing view of the sun going down, over the ocean. The ocean breeze caressed her cheeks, and wrapped itself in her hair. She had never felt so free.

This place was beautiful, but it wasn't her port from the storm. Michael was. Her eyes crested again, because she was emotionally full.

Michael walked up behind her, and wrapped his arms around her. She leaned her head back on his chest, and sighed. "I love you, hon."

"Then why the tears?" he asked, and kissed the crown of her head. He didn't have to see her face to know she was crying.

"I'm sorry I made you wait for me," she replied and her eyes spilled. "I made you watch me marry another man. I made you listen as I grieved over a teenage crush."

"It was more than a crush, Ruby. Don't undermine what you felt. What you still feel for him."

She turned in his arms. "I don't feel for him what I feel for you, Michael. My feelings for him have never been as strong as they are for you."

He strokes her tears. "I know that, Ruby."

"I'll never be able to watch you pine over another woman. I know you don't feel emotions, but how could you stand by?"

"I have spent an eternity keeping Love at bay,

because *you* were not ready," he replied, and caressed her cheek. "Once you were, I let that spirit in," he replied, and kissed her cheek. "Now Love has taken control of me."

"I'm sorry it took me so long, Michael. I'm sorry I don't remember us."

He lifted her, in his arms, and carried her to bed.

~

He laid her on the bed, and stretched out next to her. Her eyes were still teary, and her heart filled with regret. He caressed her cheek, and wiped her tear with his thumb. *"It is not your fault that you do not remember the promise we made, Ruby,"* he told her. Then he leaned in and kissed her.

"I'm still sorry." Her eyes spilled again. She'd done to him, what she hadn't been able to handle. She changed schools because she couldn't deal with seeing Smith with Leevearne. Yet, she made Michael bear witness... *"Help me remember."*

"Soon," he replied and kissed her again.

"I love this house and I love this island. But more than anything, I love you, Michael," she whispered.

Michael's eyes twirled. Passion, Desire and Love heightened. He vanquished their clothes, and caressed her breast. *"Show me."*

~

Verenda had never been sexually inhibited. As sad as it was, her past indiscretions liberated her. However, what she thought of Smittie's touch was from a teenager's perspective. The best is only the best until better comes along. Then better becomes the best, and what you previously thought was the best becomes inconsequential.

Making love with Michael made her realize that she hadn't had a clue. The way he made love to her was not just the best, it was superlative...

She felt it the moment Desire and Passion took control of him, because it was contagious. They took control of her too, and she was downright *brazen.*

~

She rolled over and straddled him. His flesh felt like hot magma, against hers. She leaned forward and kissed him passionately; and rocked her pelvis against his. They both moaned.

She licked his bottom lip and smiled. *"I can do that,"* she replied to the request, he'd long forgotten about. Then she slowly slid down his massive frame.

~

Michael grabbed two fistfuls of her hair. Her tongue was like the perfected brush stroke of a master artist. It had his nerves tingling and standing on edge. He moaned as his Ruby worked her way downward. His stomach bunched, like it always did when she touched it. But her tongue was more enticing, more intense. It was warm, silky and decadently provocative. Desire was reaching a boiling point.

~

Verenda reached down and gently caressed his boys. She smiled, when he quivered. Then she caressed and methodically stroked his manhood. She chuckled when he and his groin jumped. She was just getting started.

~

Desire, Love and Passion swelled, right along with Michael's groin. They almost blew the top off of his head.

He'd waited longer than, what seemed like, forever for her acceptance. He had allowed Patience to work perfectly in him, until Ruby was ready. But, Patience was gone! Kicked to the curb!

He tried to flip her over, but she wouldn't budge. *"No! I haven't finished showing you,"* she whispered to his mind, and continued her exploration.

His sweat, and natural musk, was an *intoxicating* elixir; that quenched her sexual thirst. Like a feline, her fiery tongue lapped at him, with zeal. She twirled her tongue around his belly button, and nibbled. In his head he roared, but his ears said it was a *screech*. And she wasn't finished.

Michael shouted, "Ruby!"

~

Verenda was sure her Michael couldn't take any more torture. His manhood was throbbing, and so was her womb. Both wanted more. She slowly worked her way back up his quivering frame. He was soaking wet.

~

Michael grabbed her by her waist and pulled her up his sweat slickened body. Her lips were provocatively moist, and swollen; and he devoured them. Then he lifted her higher and leaned her breasts down to his lips.

He held her in place, by her waist, and suckled them. Her weeping womb was pressed against his stomach. They both quivered.

She rested her hands on the sides of his head to balance herself, and her soaked hair fell in his face. Then she bent her legs backward, and stroked his erection between the silky arches of her feet.

Michael screamed in her mind, *"Ruby! Ruby! RUUUBY!!!"* His woman was *t.a.l.e.n.t.e.d!!*

He grabbed her hips and flipped them both over. *"You are driving me crazy, woman,"* he told her and nipped her chin.

"Are you too old to handle me?" she asked and laughed. She loved being able to tease while making love to her Michael.

"Turnabout is fair," he whispered and stroked her quivering thighs. Then he leaned down and suckled her breast, while he tempted her womb. He stroked over and over...just beyond reach.

"Michael, please," she begged. Desire, and at this point Lust, had every pore in her body weeping. Her womb needed to feel something! She scratched her nails down his back. *"Please!"*

"No. I haven't finished showing you," he repeated her words, and chuckled. *"I'm just getting started."*

His hands teased her most sensitive spot, but wouldn't penetrate her womb. His mind was caressing and squeezing her cheeks. His lips were suckling one breast, while his mind suckled the other. With his mind, he nibbled her thighs.

She groaned, and pulled his hair. Then she lifted her hips and made him do what he wasn't ready to do. The minute he stroked her womb it had a major spasm. She screamed, *"Michael!"*

~

Michael didn't let up, he couldn't. He wasn't in control...Desire was. He stroked...and stroked, and the heat was searing. The sweet nectar from her womb was erupting like volcanic lava.

~

Verenda couldn't hold out any longer. Her womb clinched, and she screamed, *"Michael!"*

~

Michael grabbed her thigh, in the cuff of his arm, and turned both of them. He sliced into her womb and landed flat on his back, at the same time. The heat from the union jolted their nerves; and they both momentarily paused.

She braced her arms on his pecs and, while staring in his eyes, slowly whirled her hips.

Michael palmed her cheeks and whispered, *"Rock steady, baby,"* and took control of the sensual strokes.

~

Verenda screamed, *"Michael!"* He was rotating her hips at just the right angle. The thrust of his pulsating erection went so deep; he was hitting spots she didn't know were there. Her arms trembled and she screamed again, *"Michael!"*

His stroke was nothing she'd ever get used to, *or* tired of. It was heaven *and* hell. She was grateful that she wasn't a virgin; otherwise she wouldn't have been able to take all of him. She leaned down and bit his bottom lip, then kissed him. The heat, from his tongue, seared hers. She screamed again, *"Michael!"*

~

Michael groaned and grunted, *"Geez!"* Ruby's warm sleek womb always felt like it was her first time. *"I love you, Ruby!"*

~

She couldn't take anymore. Her womb clinched, and her entire body spasmed. Her toes curled down so far, they cramped! She spastically plopped down, and her chest landed against his. She caressed his head and whimpered, as their soaked skin and hair melded together.

Unlike humans and Watchers, Michael's heart was on the right side of his body. The Watchers had to take their 'spirit' mate's blood, but Michael didn't have to take hers. Instead he gave her his. For a split second their rib cages, and flesh around their hearts, became invisible. They physically became one! Their blood comingled, and their hearts kissed. It was otherworldly! It was too much!

They were both caught up in the flagrant throes of one perpetual orgasm. She couldn't take anymore, and screamed, "Michael, stop!!"

He tried to stop, but Passion and Desire amped up their power over him. They invited Need and Passionate Greed along! He squeezed her cheeks, threw his head back, and roared, "I.....*CAN'T!*"

~

Michael wrapped one arm around her waist and the hand of the other held her head. Her legs were trembling, against his side. His wife was worn out. He kissed her cheek and whispered, "My Ruby."

"Ummmm," she sighed, but couldn't speak. She whispered to his mind, *"Trifecta."*

He chuckled. *"I'm still your stud?"*

"Stallion," she replied. Nobody else would ever measure up to her Michael. He was the most powerful in more ways than one. *"My mind, body and soul belong to you."*

He stroked his hand up and down her back. He told Seraphiel that she still had the option to walk away from him. He didn't know how he'd ever let that happen.

He could always push Love, Desire and Passion out of his being; but Memory was another story.

He hoped that when she found out what happened, it wouldn't matter to her. He needed her to still love and want him.

He kissed her cheek again. *"Promise?"*
"Always."

~

Chapter VIII

Lucifer was foaming at the mouth, like a mad dog. He had instructed Taz and Faust, to keep an eye on Michael, and his wife.

Both of them were human, at one point. While on earth they worshipped him, and had pledged the Oath of Fealty. They, and other humans, called them devil worshipers. He called them *Vassals*. They believed, like he knew, that he'd win in the end. They believed that this dungeon was just a temporary setback. When that Day of Judgment came, he and his followers would finally come up out of this dungeon, and rule Heaven!

However, he was slowly learning never to send insignificant vassals to do what the Fallen could. Although truthfully vassals could leave the underworld, the Fallen couldn't.

"What do you *mean* you lost them?" he shouted.

Taz and Faust were trembling. They knew they were expendable. But it wasn't their fault. They'd done exactly what their master told them to do.

"We never took our eyes off him," Faust said.

Taz nodded. "We even watched them get on an airplane-"

"A what?" Lucifer shouted. "Why would they need to get on an airplane?" He materialized a fireball. They were a waste of his time. What the hell!

The vassals backed up. "It is the truth, My Liege," Taz shouted.

"It was filled with all the Ultimate Watchers, even Seraphiel," Faust added.

"What?"

"They had a bunch of little 'spirit' mates on there, too," Taz replied. "We saw them when they boarded the airplane."

"What the hell is going on up there?" Lucifer asked.

"I heard Seraphiel say that Michael's wife had never flown before. It was a wedding gift to her," Taz replied.

"And you didn't think to notify the PRINCE OF THE AIR!" Lucifer shouted at them. "I could have brought that airplane down!"

"How?" Taz asked. "It was filled with Watchers! Michael was on that plane!!"

"And no doubt distracted!" Lucifer shouted.

The vassals recoiled. That was the truth. They saw Michael and his wife carrying on. That was the one thing they missed about being alive. Sex!!! Especially lascivious sex! They wanted to see Michael and his wife doing it and didn't think to notify Lucifer.

"What happened next?" Lucifer asked.

"They landed the plane on Satariel's property. They were having some kind of celebration there."

"Michael had a meeting with all of the Watchers, including Seraphiel's and Yomiel's teams," Taz informed him.

"You are telling me there were no Watchers on Seraphiel's property?"

They both nodded.

"And..." He materialized a second fireball, in his other hand. "You didn't think to inform me!!" he shouted.

"We thought you were aware of everything that went on at the estate, Master!" Faust shouted.

"We did exactly what you told us to do!" Taz added.

That was the truth. Vassals didn't have enough brain function for initiative. They strictly followed orders. They were his version of Michael...puppets.

He vanquished his fireballs. "What did they talk about, in the meeting?"

"We couldn't hear what they were talking about."

"It evidently had something to do with His Son," Faust added.

"Why?" Lucifer asked.

"Michael produced wine and crackers," Taz replied.

"They all ate and drank, together," Faust added.

"They *what!!*" Lucifer shouted. This was not good. This could only mean one thing. Those Watchers were *forgiven* by their master. He, *and His Son*, would talk to them!!

Unlike Michael, they could see into the future. They would step in and direct those Watchers' path. His job just got that much worse, because it also meant that Holy was in the fray.

Holy blocked him at every turn. Holy worked on the hearts of many humans who would otherwise be *his* disciples. Holy sent Joy and Peace to those humans that *he* tormented. Every time he told those humans to go left, Holy stepped up to correct them. He hated that spirit!

"Then what happened?" he asked his vassals.

"When the meeting was over Michael put his arms around his mate and everything went black."

"Went black?"

Faust nodded. "We haven't been able to see him, or her, since."

"That's not possible!!" Lucifer shouted. He reached out with his mind and searched. And searched. And searched. "Where the hell is he?" he shouted.

"We told you. It's like they stepped out of Time," Taz replied. He was relieved that Lucifer couldn't see them either. He was their master. If he couldn't see Michael and that woman he certainly couldn't expect them to be able to.

Lucifer whipped around and stared at him. "That's a good point." He forgot that Michael had a place where he kept the most heinous offenders. It was out of the realm of Time.

He reached out to see if he was there. He didn't see Michael but he saw a few of Reap's vassals. They were *still* working Michael's woman's parents over. He wished he could go there. He'd release them and make them his servants.

"He's not in his dungeon," he told his vassals.

"Maybe the Seer can tell us where he is," Taz suggested.

That was the last Fallen, in Hell, Lucifer wanted to ask for help. That bastard was arrogant and refused to acknowledge him as superior. He roamed the halls like he was the ruler of Hell. He never came to any of the required meetings. That was because he saw what was going to happen, before it happened. But, he needed him. "Seer!"

~

Seer appeared in the dungeon, at his own leisure. "Yeah," he replied.

"Can you see where Michael is?" Lucifer asked.

"Yeah," Seer replied.

"Tell me, you ass!" Lucifer shouted.

"Ask nicer," Seer replied.

Faust and Taz couldn't believe Seer's arrogance. He was antagonizing their master for the fun of it. He knew their master would take it because Seer could see into the future. Their master needed him.

Lucifer gritted his teeth. "Will you *please* look and tell me where Michael is?"

"Why? The last time I gave you usable intel you got your ass spanked by Seraphiel," Seer reminded him. "Don't think Michael won't handle you in a similar manner."

"Just tell me."

Seer reached out and searched. He laughed out loud. If it were possible for Lucifer to have a stroke this news would certainly give him one. Michael's location was as in your face as it gets.

"Why are you laughing?" Lucifer shouted.

Seer kept laughing. "I'm not sure you want to know," he replied.

"Just tell me," Lucifer demanded.

"He is in the Devil's Triangle," Seer replied and cracked up. Then he clapped his hands. "Oops up side your head!"

The vassals gasped.

Lucifer screamed! That bastard was taunting him. He growled and materialized two fireballs to hit him with.

"You want to fight me?" Seer asked and materialized his own fireballs. "I see you losing this battle, little brother."

Lucifer vanquished his. Seer was a whole lot of things, but a liar he was not. If he said it, it was true. He calmed his rage and said, "Michael had a meeting with all of the Ultimate Watchers. Will you tell me what they talked about in the meeting?"

Seer vanquished his fireballs and nodded. Then he reached backwards in time to see. He'd be able to not only see, but hear the conversation.

The minute he spotted them he screamed. His eyes looked like Michael's, and they were twirling at an alarming rate. Blood was shooting out of them, and his ears. He shouted, "Help! I can't see! I can't hear!"

Lucifer and the vassals jumped and moved as far away from him as they could. They wanted no part of whatever was happening to him.

Seer grabbed his ears. There was a thunderous roaring in them. He shouted again, and again, "I can't hear! I can't see!"

Lucifer had no doubt that Michael had set a trap for Seer. He made sure Seer wouldn't be able to share the information, like he had about Aurellia. He shouted, "Come back to the present!"

Seer could not hear him over the roaring in his ears. He kept shouting, "Help!"

Help did not respond or appear. He remembered the last time Michael went off. He wanted no part of this feud.

Lucifer grabbed Seer, and shook him. "COME BACK TO THE PRESENT!" he shouted.

~

Seer heard Lucifer's shout and returned. He shook his head. "Michael was prepared this time. My eavesdropping days for you are over," he said and walked out of the dungeon. Along with the pain, Michael had stamped an ominous warning on his brain. *'Snoop again and I will permanently remove your sight! Look into the future and I will destroy you, the moment I get there!'*

~

Lucifer looked at his vassals. "Grab a group of friends and go to the Crystal Caves."

"But Master, if Michael did that to the Seer he will destroy us," Faust replied.

"Don't *bother* him," Lucifer replied.

"Then what do you want us to do?" Taz asked.

"Michael is keeping a secret from his wife. One that is sure to destroy that relationship. Find a way to tell her," he instructed.

"What is the secret?" Faust asked.

Lucifer smiled and then revealed it to their minds.

"I can't believe Saint Michael did that to her," Faust said. "That was ruthless. She'll never forgive him for that."

"Oh my! That will definitely do it," Taz added. "You are right. His wife will be hurt, and feel betrayed."

All three of them laughed.

~

Chapter IX

Michael and Verenda walked into the kitchen, hand in hand. They'd missed dinner last night and she was starving. Michael didn't have to eat, but he would while they were on their honeymoon.

The kitchen was as elegant as the rest of the house. The inner walls were a deep red, with swirls of gold and white. The outer wall was clear red crystile bricks, with white grout. The entire wall bowed out.

The cabinets were white, with the same red countertops. She'd never seen red appliances before, but the stove, refrigerator and dishwasher were red. And stunning.

Instead of an island there was a long half-moon shaped peninsula, with four barstools. A white table sat in the deepest bow of the window. It had four, high-back, red silk covered chairs.

Cook was preparing their breakfast, when they walked in. "Good morning, Michael."

"Good morning, Cook," Michael replied. "This is my wife, Verenda."

Verenda smiled. "It's nice to meet you."

~

Cook had been around almost as long as every other Watcher. He wasn't the *son* of a Fallen, but the *grandson*. His *father* was the son, and he'd embraced *his* father's habit of raping human women.

He'd worked for many of the Ultimate Watchers. He was a consummate professional, and knew how to act, but not today. Michael's wife made him dumb it up.

He'd never seen a finer looking woman. For a human, her face had no pores, or blemishes. And it appeared that it never did. That mole above her lip was the sexiest thing he'd ever seen. From the angle she stood, he could see that her hair was in a ponytail, and mirrored Michael's. She was dressed in a black and white spaghetti strap sundress; and it hugged her waist. It came just short of the most perfect ankles he'd ever seen. Even with no makeup, she was absolutely stunning.

He felt like a school boy, who was seeing his teacher for the first time. If only he had a nice shiny apple to give her. He actually blushed.

It took him a minute to compose himself. He coughed. "I assure you, the pleasure is all mine."

~

Michael's eyes twirled. Not from jealousy, but amusement. All men were drawn to his wife, and found her hard to resist. Gay, straight, married, single, preacher, deacon, young, old, Archangel, Watcher and demon, it didn't matter. But none would be foolish enough to approach her in anything but a respectful manner.

He let Cook get away with his behavior today, because it was his first time casting his eyes upon her. But he knew the boundary.

"Where is the staff?"

"They have gone inland to gather more supplies," Cook replied. He saw Michael's eyes twirl, but he wasn't afraid. Michael knew what a jewel he had. Plus, Michael knew after his initial shock, he'd be the utmost professional. He'd also be loyal to her. He and the entire staff would protect her, as if she were their 'spirit' mate.

Michael rubbed Verenda's back. "You will get to meet them when they return," he informed her.

"I look forward to it," she replied. Then she remembered she needed to ask him something. "Cook," she stated.

"Yes, ma'am," he replied.

Michael laughed.

"Where are we?" she asked.

"Why, we are in Devil's Triangle, ma'am," he replied.

Michael cracked up laughing. "I told you."

Verenda rolled her eyes at him. "I'm gon' cut you!"

"Is there a problem?" Cook asked.

"I don't understand why Michael built me a home here," she replied.

Cook looked at Michael and laughed. "Because of the name?" he asked.

Michael nodded.

"I mean face it. It is ironic, isn't it?" she asked.

"Not at all, ma'am," he replied. "It was by design."

"Whose?"

"Michael's and Seraphiel's," he told her. "Seraphiel's island is just across the bay."

She frowned. She'd seen the entire family on that island, but she hadn't realized where it was. She looked up at Michael. "Why would you both do that?"

"Before we took up residence here demons were having a field day with aircrafts and ships. Once they realized we were here all demonic activity ceased," Michael replied.

"But they have to know that you and Seraphiel

rarely come to the island."

"That is true. But, Cook and his brothers are always here. They have homes on this island, but they keep an eye on both islands, Ruby."

She gazed at Cook. "I don't mean to offend you, but I didn't think domestics could fight."

"They can't," Cook replied. Then he smiled. "But Watchers can cook, ma'am."

Michael cracked up. "Every member of my staff is Watcher, Ruby. Their job is to keep demons from attacking anymore airplanes or ships."

She blushed. "Oh. I'm sorry."

"For what? It was a logical assumption."

"They also keep watch on the Crystal caverns, just below us, and the Bermuda Island," Michael informed her.

"Crystal caves?" She'd never heard of that. No wonder this house was all crystal. He had the supplies right here on the island.

"Speaking of which," Cook said, but didn't go any further. The look Michael gave him told him he'd better shut his damn mouth. He'd been with Michael long enough to know when his eyes rapidly twirled he was not happy.

"What?" Verenda asked.

"It would be nice if Michael took you on a site seeing trip. The caverns are an awesome handiwork of the Master."

She looked up at Michael and smiled. "I'd love to see them, hon."

"After breakfast," he replied.

~

Cook had prepared Belgian waffles, topped with powdered sugar, and fresh strawberries, eggs, and Canadian ham. The minute they were seated he served them and quietly disappeared.

~

Normally Verenda ate like a bird, but after last night she was starving. Her stomach actually growled. It hadn't done that since the day Michael rescued her. Those waffles were the best she'd ever had. They were light and fluffy, and to die for. She dug in, like tomorrow wasn't promised.

Michael laughed. "You would not be hungry, would you?"

She shook her knife at him, but couldn't speak; because her mouth was full. She couldn't even speak with her mind, because it was savoring every bite.

He cracked up. "I know, you gon' cut me, right?"

She nodded and kept chewing.

He howled.

~

When they finished breakfast Verenda started to clean the kitchen. As if on cue Cook returned. "Please, ma'am, allow me," he said.

"I can do this, Cook," she replied. Then she smiled. "Breakfast was fantastic."

"Thank you, ma'am, but I would appreciate your allowing me to do *my* job," he replied.

"Okay. I'll let you clean the kitchen, if you stop calling me ma'am," she replied. "Verenda or Ruby will do."

"Verenda will do," Michael corrected. He would

not allow anyone else to call her Ruby.

"Very well," he replied. "Do you have something special you would like for lunch and dinner, Verenda?"

She started to say no, but then thought about it. She loved making love with her Michael. But she needed to eat heartily to have enough energy. She needed to load up on carbs.

"Yes. I'd like pasta and seafood salad, with garlic bread for lunch. Shrimp Primavera, with a red sauce, and garlic bread for dinner."

"Both of those are easy enough," Cook replied. "Can I tempt you with a nice red velvet cake, for dessert?"

Verenda's mouth watered. "Absolutely."

~

Michael chuckled. He knew what she was doing. He spoke to her mind, *"Good choice, seeing how you crashed on me last night."*

She blushed. She hadn't been able to move after they made love, last night. She'd fallen asleep lying on top of him. When she woke up this morning, she was still in the same spot. They made love again in the shower and it was just as intense, but she hadn't been the only one overwhelmed. She looked at him and smirked. *"I heard you screaming a conjunction last night,"* she said and mimicked him, *"I...CAN'T!"* She cracked up laughing, because he hardly ever used conjunctions. *"I took you there, didn't I, hon?"*

His eyes twirled. She had most definitely done that. The only reason Desire wasn't accosting him right now was because of Decorum. Decorum said there was a time and place for everything under the sun. This was not the time, or place, for Desire or Passion to surge. They both yielded. But, Desire and Passion were definitely looking forward to tonight. He was too. "We would like a bottle of wine with dinner, Cook," he instructed.

"Of course," Cook replied. "Tea with lunch?"

"Sweet mint," Verenda replied. "Heavy on the sweet."

Michael chuckled.

~

Chapter X

Lucifer glared at Taz and Faust, all tangled up on the floor. They'd just crash landed in the throne room …head first. He shouted, "Get up!" Once again he'd sent them to do a job, and they came back looking like idiots. "What the hell happened?"

"Michael knew we were in the caves," Faust replied, and wiped at the blood running down his face.

"I told you not to go near that puppet!" Lucifer shouted.

"We didn't," Faust replied. "The minute we got there I felt those eyes on us, but he was nowhere around."

"It was creepy," Taz added and shivered. "They are still twirling under my skin."

"What?"

"It's true, look," he said and opened his shirt. "See!"

The skin on his stomach was protruding and swirling like pinwheels; like Michael's eyes. He rubbed his hand over them, and snatched it back. It burned. "Look at my stomach! We're his lab rats! He's toying with us, Lucifer!"

"What did you call me?" Lucifer shouted. Vassals knew never to address him by name.

Taz took a step back. "I mean my Liege."

"Face it," Faust said. "We are not going to be able to sneak up on that Archangel! Every time we try he lets us know he's watching. That's what he did to Seer. That's what he just did to Taz!!"

"Michael is not omniscient!" Lucifer shouted.

"Yeah well, he damn sure has his eyes on us!" Taz replied.

"We are going to have to find another way to get to his wife," Faust added.

"Michael and his mate are surrounded by water, on every side," Taz pointed out. "Call in Tempest. He is more powerful than we are."

Lucifer smiled. That was an excellent idea!! The Atlantic Ocean was known for traitorous weather. A squall would not seem out of the ordinary. Michael would think it was just Mother Nature.

The mainland of Bermuda, along with Florida would be in jeopardy, as well. Nearby boaters would be in peril. He would have to respond by limiting the amount of devastation, and human tragedy.

That would leave his woman exposed, and would allow Taz and Faust to get to her. They could finally tell her what Michael had done. They could make her see how he wasn't so perfect, after all. They could make her see that he had deceived her, *not* Smith Walker.

She'd be furious and cut all ties with Michael. Because of Michael's deceit she would leave the little 'spirit' mates. He'd have access to them!

He clapped his hands in jubilance. "Oh, this is decadent," he said and clapped his hands again.

"What?" Taz asked.

He told them his new plan; his fail proof new plan. He'd send a host of Resentment's imps with them, to attack her heart, and have Hatred's imps standing in the wings. Because of Michael they couldn't attack her, unless she opened herself up and welcomed them. By the time Taz and Faust got through with her she'd be ripe for them *and* Hostility!!!

This was going to be priceless. "If I was double-jointed I'd pat my own back," he said and smiled.

"That's a good plan, my Liege," Faust told him.

Lucifer stopped smiling. "Screw this one up and it's your ass!"

Faust and Taz bowed.

"Now get out!" Lucifer demanded. Then he called out to Tempest. He needed to make plans.

~

"I like your idea. It has been a minute since I've been allowed to cut loose," Tempest said. "But will you take my advice?"

"Depends," Lucifer replied.

"My work is more effective during the twilight hours, when most humans are asleep. Even Michael periodically sleeps," he said and paused.

"Keep going," Lucifer instructed.

"When demons attack human women they are immobile for hours. Michael is on his honeymoon. I'm willing to bet he is drained dry by nightfall," he replied and laughed. "If you get my drift."

Lucifer smiled. "Go on."

"I can come up and swipe the Florida Straits, with mild winds. The human's weather center won't think I'm a threat, because I won't reach maximum speed on land."

"I want Florida hit hard to distract Michael," Lucifer said.

"Michael won't be distracted if I hit Florida. He has an abundance of Watchers along the Florida Coast. I say let me hit the triangle and create a perfect storm around the island he's holed up on."

"He'll just teleport out!" Lucifer shouted.

"When have you ever known Michael to run? Plus, I assure you he doesn't have his wife sleeping on the ground. He'll want to save that crystal house he built for her."

"He built her a glass house...on an island...in the middle of the ocean?"

"A crystal palace; and it is *huge*."

"You've seen it?"

"I'm wind *and* rain, of course I have," Tempest replied. "My grandsons live on that island with him."

"Your grandsons?" Lucifer asked. "Let me see it."

"Are you sure? I heard what he did to Seer. You sure you want to chance it?"

Lucifer shook his head. "Never mind."

Tempest laughed.

~

After his meeting with Tempest, Lucifer was flying high. He was not afraid of Michael's retaliation because, just like Seraphiel, that puppet could not touch him.

He decided it was worth a try to see this glass house. He reached out again to see if he could see that island. He was able to see the caves. "That's good," he said to himself. Then he tried to see above ground.

He got nothing... "Damn!"

~

Chapter XI

Strolling along the beach with Michael had always been a treat for Verenda. Every year they celebrated the life she lived, because of him.

He always took her to the French Riviera. She thought it was because her late husband died before he could take her. Now she realized that wasn't the reason, at least not in totality…

Michael didn't want to take her anywhere she'd been, with her late husband. He didn't want her mind muddled by *another* ghost of the past. It was bad enough that he had to endure her pining over Smith. He wasn't about to let her romanticize over a ghost he couldn't compete with.

Her husband was not jealous, but he wasn't naive, either. Nostalgia often attacked her when she least expected it. A smell, a scene, a touch, and even a gentle breeze often put her in a melancholy mood. Sometimes the attacks were so severe he had to ease her spirit.

That was why he built her a home in the Bermuda Triangle, Devil's Triangle. Her late husband had not brought her here. It was the one place that he couldn't have *ever* brought her.

She was actually grateful, because she'd never loved anybody like she loved Michael. She didn't want to remember things that would make her feel guilty. Like not loving her late husband, as much as she did Smittie. And not loving Smittie anywhere near as much as she loved her Michael.

She loved this place, because it was hers and

Michael's. If she had her way, none of the Walker brothers, or their wives, would ever be welcome here. She would never visit their estate, and they would never set foot on her island.

This was hers and her Michael's spot, and it was perfect. She wanted to stay here every night, instead of going back to her room at the House.

"We will," Michael replied to her thoughts.

"Really?"

"This is not a vacation spot. This is our *home.*"

Her heart swelled. Michael was forever putting her needs first. He constantly preempted her desires, before she voiced them. That was strange, because he was neither a deity, nor omni anything.

Michael wrapped his arm around her waist. "But I know my wife," he again replied to her thoughts. "You have been cooped up in Georgia House for more years than I planned."

"That was my doing?" In retrospect she didn't know why she put him off for so long. He'd been the one constant in her life, since she was a teenager. He never once let her down.

He squeezed her waist. "You mean that was your stubbornness."

"Yeah," she replied.

"Deborah Dunson will be back in Indiana shortly. I believe she will be good for Georgia House."

"Deborah?"

"Yes. She will be able to replace Vicky."

"I haven't seen her in a hundred years. I thought she was-"

"She was, but not anymore."

"That'll give me a lot of free time with her, and the Walker children, working there."

"I know," Michael replied.

He reached down and picked up a large, red and white, conch shell. He placed it to her ear. "Listen."

At first all she heard was a wind sound. People often mistook it as the sound of the ocean, but it wasn't. Not really. I was actually the reverberating sounds around them. Nature's own surround sound, and the larger the shell the greater the sound.

She pulled it away from her ear. She'd never seen a red seashell before. "This is beautiful, Michael."

He took it and placed it back up to her ear. "Be patient."

She listened again. Then she heard it, over the sound of the wind:

"What took Michael so long to bring his mate to the island?"

"She's stubborn, man. She would not even give the brotha a chance."

"That's cold, man."

~

She pulled the seashell away from her ear, and stared up at Michael. "What?"

He frowned. "What what?" he asked.

"How can I hear a conversation going on in this shell?" she replied. "Cook and the staff are talking about us." Man, she hated nosey people. What was it their business anyway?

"What? What are they saying? Let me hear," he

replied and put the shell up to his ear. "I do not hear anything, Ruby."

She took the shell back and put it up to her ear.

"How she gon play a brotha like that?"

"I don't know. Michael's better than me, though. I would have snatched her and said 'now look...I'm man...you woman! You my woman, you understand! Now come here!'"

"That woman likes to cut people, does she not?"

"Yeah, I see your point. She might've cut that brotha."

Verenda snatched the shell away from her ear. "What? They have a lot of nerve!" she said indignantly. She turned to look up at Michael, but he wasn't beside her anymore.

Michael was walking away from her, backwards. He was a good ten feet away. He smiled. "What did it say that time?"

"You sneak!" she replied and ran toward him. "It said you are doing this!"

He laughed and started to jog, backwards. Then he started having the conversation again:

"That brotha's got some kind of patience."

"Tell me about it! But, I guess that is what love will make you do."

"Do you think she knows how much he loves her? Maybe that's the problem. She doesn't know."

"It might be. That brotha is kinda starch."

"No kinda about it. He is a real stick in the mud. No emotions what-so-ever."

"I know. Poor man, he cannot help it. It is how he

was designed."

Ruby ran down the beach after him. "That's you talking, Michael!"

He kept jogging backwards, and having his conversation.

"It was a catch twenty-two."

"What do you mean?"

"He could not embrace emotions, until she accepted him. She would not accept him, because he was emotionless."

"That's not true!" she shouted. "That's not true, Michael!" She speeded up trying to catch him.

He kept jobbing backwards, and talking.

"I guess it was like hearing a tree trunk say it loves you."

"Trees have more personality than that dude had!"

"That is true."

"Stop it, Michael!" she shouted after him.

"Maybe he should have let her hear his thoughts."

"That would not have worked. Even his thoughts were monotone."

"Then there was nothing he could do to make her see how much he loved her?"

"No. He kept trying to tell her with his eyes."

"How?"

"Every time they twirled it was because emotions were trying to get in."

"Why didn't he just let them in?"

"She was not ready."

"I don't understand that."

"Me either. She knew he had always been there for

her."

"You think she knows how much he loves her now?"
"I hope so."
"Me too."

"I know, Michael!" she shouted and kept trying to catch up with him. It wasn't that he was jogging fast, but his legs were much longer. She'd chased him almost a half of a mile. "I know you love me! Please stop, hon. I can't keep up with you."

"But she doesn't know that she has always loved him too?"

"She forgot."
"Why doesn't he just remind her?"
"I do not know. I would."
"Me too."

"Michael!" Verenda shouted. "Watch out for the tree!"

Michael laughed and jogged right up to it. Then he leaned back and folded his arms. "I knew it was there, Ruby."

When she finally caught up to him she was out of breath. "That was not funny," she complained.

He reached for her hands, and eased her exhaustion. Then he palmed her left cheek, and kissed her right ear. He whispered, "Yes, it was."

"Maybe just a little," she replied. "But I know you love me, Michael. My slothfulness had nothing to do with you. It was me, all along."

"No, it was not. I was boring, and uninspiring," he replied.

"You always inspired me, Michael," she replied.

"Not the way I wanted to," he replied and squeezed her closer to him. "I wanted you to want me, as much as I wanted you. I wanted you to remember that you loved me, not just take my word for it. I wanted you to come to me because you remembered that we chose each other, in heaven; not because I told you we did. I wanted you to remember that you belong to me."

She wrapped her arms around his neck and smiled. She'd been so bad to him. She'd teased him about popping into her suite without giving her warning. She kept saying *'one of these days you are going to see something you're not ready to see.'*

In truth, she was the one that wasn't ready. She hated that she couldn't remember, when they first committed to each other. She looked up in his eyes and whispered, "I'm sorry I don't remember. Tell me how I loved you, in Heaven."

~

He imagined now was as good a time as any. Lucifer had already sent a few of his vassals to the caves. They went back to Hell, with their tails tucked between their legs. Lucifer thought he would not get down in the trenches, because he had never challenged him before. But he was *wrong...*

Nevertheless, he needed to have this conversation with his wife. It was only fair that she knew the truth. It would be better if she heard it from him.

He leaned down and kissed her. "Let's go back to the house," he replied. Then he dispelled all emotion. "We can talk on the terrace."

"Alright," she replied, but she felt a sense of dread.

She heard aloofness return in his voice, accompanied by a chill in the air.

~

Chapter XII

Once they were on the patio, Michael materialized a bottle of wine. He poured them both a glass and sat across the table from her.

Verenda thought that was odd, because the table was a good five feet wide. Why didn't he sit next to her? She felt him shutting down. She wanted to tell him never mind. Whatever it was wasn't important. Not as important as they were.

~

He leaned back in his chair, and rubbed his eyes. When he removed his hands they were light brown, instead of the twirl that she loved. "You were the brightest soul in Heaven, and a joy to everyone who crossed your path. Archangels, and human souls alike, vied to spend just a few minutes near you; including me."

Verenda smiled. "Really?"

"You regaled me the first time I laid eyes on you," he replied. "We spent countless hours together."

She could almost see herself walking around Heaven, with him. She wished she could remember. He must feel like he's married to an amnesiac. Her heart went out to him. "Oh, Michael," she whispered.

"But you were a *nosey* little thing."

She got over it. Now she wanted to cut him. "What?"

He chuckled. "If anything was going on you had to be in the know. You skulked around; hid and listened in on conversations you had no business hearing. I imagine that is why you do not like nosey people."

"Why?"

"Your nosiness got you in trouble. It changed your lot," he replied.

"How?"

Michael shook his head. "You found out that Father was going to expel the Fallen from Heaven. You compelled me to tell you the why, when and where. I could not refuse, because you were such a charming soul. Once I told you, your little nosey butt just had to see it go down."

"What happened? What did I do? Show me, Michael."

Michael opened her mind and let her see.

~

Verenda was amazed at the scene she was witnessing. The Fallen knew God was aware of their plan. They thought He would command Michael, and his army of warriors, to battle with them. Their plan was to preemptively take Michael out *first*.

She was afraid for Michael and told him so. *"There are so many of them. They plan to corner you, and destroy you."*

"Be easy, Verenda. I am aware of their plan, but none of them can defeat me."

"Maybe not one on one, but it's a third of your brothers, Michael."

"A third or all of them, individually or collectively; they cannot defeat me."

"How can you be sure?"

He gazed down at her, and smiled. Then she saw it, through those gorgeous eyes. She fell in love with him, right then and there. In Heaven!!

"You must never tell a soul, Verenda."

"I won't. I promise."

But she and the Fallen were wrong. The Master did not utilize Michael, or give the Fallen a warning. He just softly whispered, *"I am Elohim."*

Then a gust of wind swept throughout Heaven. All of the scheming betrayers hoisted their wings, and drew their weapons. That is all except Araciel. He looked confused, at first. Then he fell face down, in submission, and shouted, *"Bow down, brothers! Bow!"*

The betrayers ignored him, and waited for Lucifer's command. Lucifer shouted a rally cry and they all raised their swords. Then they charged the temple from every angle.

Michael, and his warriors, were standing near the throne; close to the Master. All of the other Archangels were dressed in long white robes, but not Michael. He was dressed in ancient regalia.

All of *their* biceps sported removable gold bracelets, but *not* Michael's. His biceps, and triceps, were banded with spiraling hieroglyphics made of ruby and jasper dust.

The Archangels materialized their swords, and shields, and took a battle stance.

Michael roared a command to his mighty warriors, *"Stand down, brothers. This battle is not ours to fight. It belongs to the Lord."*

All the multitudes of heaven were standing around Him, on His right and on His left. The Seraphim stood above Him, each having six wings. With two of their wings they covered their faces, and with two they covered their feet. Then with two they flew above, and *canopied,* the throne.

The Master was seated upon His throne, and He was high, and lifted up. The train of His glory *filled* the temple. He had the appearance of *jasper* and *ruby.* A rainbow that shone like sparkling emeralds encircled the throne.

The Master gazed upon Michael, and slightly nodded in agreement. Then he softly proclaimed, *'I am Jehovah-Sabbaoth.'*

One of the Seraphim shouted in exhortation, *"The Lord of Hosts"*. The other Seraphim joined him, in joyous refrain, *"Holy, holy, holy, is the Lord of Hosts!"*

~

Verenda palmed her mouth, in awesome wonder. God seemed to be emotionless, as His called into existence sons rebelled. Next to His presence they all, including Michael, looked like insignificant grasshoppers.

Just as Lucifer, and his warriors, got close to the throne the Master softly declared, *"I am El-Shaddai."*

The same Seraphim shouted, *"God Almighty!"*

~

The wind intensified and caught them up. The power of God's might tossed them backward, and cast them out of *His* holy temple.

Then His glory rose up, above the cherubim, and moved to the threshold of the temple. The threshold trembled, and the temple was filled with His vapors. The outer court was consumed with the radiance of His glory. Yet, He had not moved from His seat.

He softly whispered again, *"I am El-OLAM."*

The Seraphim shouted, *"The everlasting God!"*

The multitude of heaven, angels and human souls alike, bowed down; in humble adoration. That is all except Lucifer, and his traitors. They were caught up in His whirlwind.

The Master gently whispered, *"I am JEHOVAH-GMOLAH."*

The Seraphim shouted, *"The God of Recompense."*

Then He blasted them over the balcony of heaven. They shot across the firmament like a meteor shower. They crackled and sizzled like lightning!

Their anguished wails and lamentations were excruciatingly unbearable. All of the human souls, including hers, began to weep for those that had been cast out.

Some of the betrayers held on to the balcony, and pleaded for mercy. Others crashed into each other, disoriented by their sudden discharge.

Lucifer, and some of his followers, tried to ascend above that great city; but there was no *above*. They flew around, and around, trying to find a side entrance; but there was no *side*. The whirlwind caught them up and turned them, in circles. The force entangled their arms, legs and wings together. They looked like run-a-way wheels; in the middle of the air. Big ones, little ones; they all rolled across the galaxy, pushed by the mighty wind of God.

Araciel did not resist his banishment, nor did he try to reenter. He accepted his fate, and just swooped down to earth.

~

Then the Master softly declared, *"They have defiled my throne with all their rage, against me. They have contaminated my throne with all their abominations. Remove them from my heavens, Michael!"*

~

Michael hoisted his wings. They stretched eighteen feet...tip to tip. They were white, with red and jasper tips. The glyphs that served as his armbands began to glow; but his eyes went stark still. Emotionless!

Then he crossed his ancient swords, like an X, at the Master's feet, and slightly bowed his head. *"Thy will be done, Father."*

Then he shouted, *"On my command!"*

Archangels, from every corner of heaven, discarded their robes. They were clothed in nothing but loincloths. They had shield in one hand, and sword in the other! They raised their chests, and spread their legs, in readiness. The muscles in their arms and legs rolled, like boulders, in anticipation. Then they raised their swords, in unison; and waited for Michael's command.

They looked like ancient Spartans.

~

All of heaven heard Michael's declaration, *"Your day of reckoning is at hand, Morning Star!!"*

~

First she heard a flapping sound; that was so great she covered her ears. Then she felt a rushing wind. Heaven was darkened by the wings of Michael's brigade. Thousands of them flapped their wings, and floated overhead; with their ancient swords drawn back, at the ready.

Michael did not float, and he did not fly. And unlike human generals, he did not secure a seat on the sideline. He was front and center, as he *led* his infantry to battle.

Although his wings were extended he did not utilize them. With his warriors floating above and all around him; that big archangel stepped out on the firmament, and *walked* on the air!

~

Power and authority embodied Michael, like a second skin. In all of the years they'd been together, Verenda had never seen her angel in his *ultimate* greatness. She was utterly mesmerized, in body and in spirit, by his pageantry. He! Was! Magnificent!

~

On Michael's command the Archangels charged their fallen brothers. The sparks, from sword kissing sword, sizzled across the cosmos. The Fallen were aiming for Michael's warriors, with deadly intent. Michael's warriors were only defensively blocking their aim.

She saw Gabriel and Raphael in their own battles. The muscles in their legs and arms were unbelievably taunting, and intimidating. She had never noticed that before.

Like all of the other Archangels, they were more animated than Michael. The impact of their fists making contact, with the adversary, sounded like sonic booms. It was deafening!

One of the fallen sliced Gabriel across his back. His back bled a brilliant light. That light shot out like beams, but only pierced the Fallen's *wings*. His torso, arms and legs were not touched! She wondered why?

Raphael had one of the Fallen by the throat. She recognized him. He was Zuzim, the *Seer*, and Kobabiel's father. He was also high on the hierarchy, just below Araciel.

Raphael was about to blind him, but she heard Michael's voice. *"Do not go too far, Raphael,"* he commanded.

Raphael yielded to Michael's authority. He released the Seer, clipped his wings, and kicked him across the universe. She saw the Seer plummet downward, at great speed.

~

Lucifer, Samjaza and Azazel all attacked Michael, from behind. She watched as they tried, over and over again, to stab him. Each time their swords were impeded, by some invisible force. At first, he didn't even acknowledge them. Then he slowly turned around and faced them. They stabbed at his chest, but could not penetrate his flesh. Michael neither smiled nor frowned, when he reached out.

He grabbed Samjaza's left wing, and Azazel's right. Then he yanked outward, and hurled them across the cosmos; in opposite directions. The force of his hurl allowed them to remain airborne, for a moment. Then they dropped down, with great velocity. Their wings were still in Michael's hands!!

Lucifer turned to fly away, but to no avail. Michael didn't grab his wing. He grabbed a handful of Lucifer's locks, and snapped him back against his chest. *"You have created enmity in the family, Morning Star! The onus of this battle is on you, and your pride. You are no longer considered a son of God, or my brother! Was it worth it?"*

Before Lucifer could respond, Michael clipped his wings, and released him. He spiraled downward.

At first she didn't understand why Michael and his fencing team weren't aiming to kill. Then she remembered God's command, *"Remove them from my heavens."*

Michael always followed the Master's commands, to the letter. He never presumed that there was wiggle room, in his orders. The Master said "remove them", and that's what he and his warriors were doing.

One by one they were overpowering the Fallen, by slicing their wings. She watched in awe, as they lost their gravity, and tumbled towards earth.

During their out of control spiral, their swords slipped from their grips. Michael's eyes shot out, and intercepted the weapons. On contact, the blades exploded into tiny brilliant lights. Then they were pinned to the cosmos, like their brothers...the *stars*. They twinkled, in gratitude; grateful to be released from the adversary's bondage.

She sighed when the battle was finally over. All of the archangels discarded their weapons, and ascended back to the Master's throne. All except Michael...

~

She saw him fold his arms, and thousands of eyes shot across the galaxy. They were in a straight line, below the balcony of heaven. She was amazed when she realized what he'd just done. With audacity, he'd just created a *divide* that separated the second and third heavens. What great authority God had given His most faithful servant!

~

Then she heard Michael call out, *"I need a hunter!"*

She watched as a group of stars came forth, and formatted themselves into the shape of a huntsman.

~

"You shall be called Orion!" Michael commanded.

She watched as Michael called out his desires, one after the other. The stars started forming their alliances, according to Michael's specification: "Pegasus, winged horse! Lupus, the wolf! Draco, the dragon! Leo, the lion!" He went on and on, until all his shining warriors were in place.

Then he spoke to the newly formed constellation, *"This is where you take your stance! For all eternity, you will be the first line of defense to the Master's throne!"*

~

Chapter XIII

She jumped, in person and in her vision, when she heard Michael shout her name.

"VERENDA! NOOOO!"

That was the first time she saw him fly. He swept across the cosmos, with urgency. *"What have you done!!"* he shouted at her.

She'd been so busy watching the battle she hadn't paid any attention to her own actions. When she glanced at herself on the balcony, she couldn't believe what she saw.

She jumped out of the vision, and stared at Michael.

~

Michael started talking again. "You, and a few of your friends, decided to run to the balcony to get a bird's eye view. You wanted to see the battle. Several of the betrayers reached for you, and your friends; in hopes of surviving their banishment."

~

Verenda gasped, as the vision came back into view. She and her friends wanted to see the battle. She wanted to see *Michael!*

They were leaning on the balcony, when one of the Fallen grabbed her wrist. His wings were shredded, and he pleaded, *"Help me! Please!"*

On instinct she, and her friends, tried to keep him from slipping off the balcony. Three of them had a hold of his arms, and four were pulling at his leg. They were struggling to hold onto him, because he was so big.

Michael snatched that Fallen from their grip, and

slung him across the sky. Then he shouted, again, *"What have you done, Verenda!"*

That was the first time she'd seen any emotions from that big Archangel. His demeanor changed. He was enraged. He didn't wait for her response. Instead he dove down, in pursuit of that Fallen.

She watched as Michael angrily ripped off both of that Fallen's wings, with his bare hands. He threw them into a black hole. Then he roared, like a wounded bear, and lifted him over his head. With great force he threw that Fallen, like a harpoon, towards the earth. The speed was so great he couldn't stop the spiral, or reposition himself.

She and her friends watched as he plummeted to the earth. All of the other Fallen merely fell to the earth, and crash landed; but the one she'd touched didn't.

He shot straight through the earth's crust, plowed through the mantle, the outer core engulfed him, and the inner core sucked him in. The earth closed up, all around him; and trembled!

From the impact they saw fault lines begin to ripple beneath the earth, and molting volcanoes form; from Michael's rage. Somehow she knew what that scene meant. It was a testament to his displeasure of that Fallen touching *her*.

~

She looked at Michael, and whispered, "Oh my God!"

"That was a Barren," Michael informed her.

"What?" she asked. Her eyes watered. Michael told her years ago that her womb had always been unfruitful, but he didn't tell her why. "I *touched* Barren?"

Michael closed his eyes, and squeezed the bridge of his nose. "I did not know that you had followed me, Ruby. You should not have been on that balcony," he said. He shook his head. "You should not have been there."

He rubbed his face and sighed. "Father was *furious* with you."

"Because I tried to help him?" she asked.

Michael nodded his head. "Yes. Plus, you changed the course of your life."

"How?"

"From that point on you were barren," he replied. "But, Faith and I, did not know at the time, Maria had to be born."

Her heart skipped a beat, and she frowned. "I don't understand, Michael."

"Yes, you do," he replied, in the coldest tone she'd ever heard.

Her eyes crested and she palmed her mouth. "Are you saying those girls were supposed to be *my* children? They were *my* babies!"

He nodded. "Yours *and* Smith Walker's."

"What?"

"Your womb was the intended vessel to nurture Smith Walker's seed. They had to come through him. They had to come down the Walker lineage, Ruby. But, Father always has a ram in the bush."

"Leevearne," she whispered.

Michael nodded.

"But He is God! He could have healed me. Why didn't He?"

He stared at her for a long time. This was the beginning of the end, but she had a right to know. She needed to hear the whole story from him; no matter what. "I asked him not to," he replied, again in a dry tone.

"What? Why would you *do* that, Michael?"

"I wanted you, for myself."

"What?"

"I loved you," Michael replied, in a much softer voice. He shook his head, remorsefully. "Even though Father made us anatomically compatible with humans, we were not allowed to cohabitate with them. That was one of Lucifer's complaints. The Master had given all of creation mates, *except* us. We were otherworldly and much too powerful for procreation. After you touched Barren your condition was perfect for *me*. And I wanted you."

All she heard was he loved her, and he wanted her! Nothing else he said mattered. "You did?" she asked and her tears slid down her cheeks.

Michael felt bad when he saw her crying, but he misunderstood her tears. "I asked Father to give you to me. And because of my faithfulness, He granted my one desire. You were more than willing to accept the change, because of who I was. But, you wanted those young ladies to be born. You picked Leevearne's womb, to replace yours."

She wiped her eyes. "I did?"

Michael nodded. "But Father warned me that you and Smittie would always love each other. Smittie will always love you, because you were Father's *divine* will; for him. You will always love him, for that same reason. Leevearne and I are His second choice. We are the rams in the bush. His *permissive* will."

~

She thought back to her conversation with Smith. He said *'As hard as I try, I can't stop loving you.'* Her heart went out to him, and Leevearne. She felt the sorriest for Leevearne. She had to share a piece of her husband's heart with another woman. She thought about what Leevearne had screamed *'she's trying to take my family!'*

That was ironic, because in actuality she had given Leevearne *her* family. *Her* three beautiful daughters! *Her* four precious grandsons! *Her* soul mate!

She thought about Faith and Maria...and Charity. They'd clung to her, at Satariel's house, like they *knew* she was supposed to be their mother. Like they knew it was her womb that should've been their first home. Maria came to her, day in and day out, and hugged her with familiarity. Sometimes she'd catch her just staring at her, lost in thought.

When she comforted Faith, after her anxiety attack, she'd looked at her and Michael; like she *knew*. She kept shouting at her mother and aunts, *'Verenda and Michael are mates, I saw it!'* Now she wondered exactly what Faith had seen.

She would have given anything to experience motherhood, through her womb. Anything...*except* Michael. She was still solid on that front.

A part of her may still love Smittie, but she wasn't *in love* with him. That space in her heart was occupied by her Archangel, and there was no room at the Inn.

Her love for Michael was so complete, that it drowned out any lingering feelings for Smittie. She didn't care if their union was God's permissive *or* divine will. Both were still *His* will. God is *Sovereign*. He doesn't have to explain Himself, or His will, to anybody.

The minute she had that thought, a scene unfolded, in her mind's eye. She knew Michael wasn't showing it to her, because he wasn't in it. It was *her* memories finally coming back. She was talking with God. She was beseeching Him to give her to Michael.

~

"I love Smittie, but not as much as I love the Archangel, Master."

"The Archangel? Which one?"

"The big one."

"Michael?"

"Yes. Michael."

"Archangels do not have soul mates, Verenda."

"Who made that rule?"

"I did."

"You're God, right?"

"I am."

"All by yourself?"

"Yes."

"Then you can make new rules, and not have to ask permission, right?"

"Yes."

"Please make an exception for me and the Archangel. Please, Father."

"Why would I do that?"

"I have bound my heart to Michael's, here in Heaven. I will never love Smith the way I love him. I will not be a good wife to him, because he will not be enough

for me. Only the Archangel will do."

"What about the children you were supposed to have with Smith?"

"Can I have them with the Archangel?"

"No."

"Why not?"

"Archangels cannot father children."

"Can't you make an exception?"

"No, Verenda."

"Why?"

"I do not have to explain. Is that not what you just told me?"

"Yes, but pleeeeease."

"No."

"Then give the children to my best friend Leevearne. She's upset anyway, because you didn't give her a mate. She really loves Smith. He loves her, too."

"How do you know that?"

"I see the way they look at each other. Leevearne looks at Smith, the way I look at Michael. Plus, Leevearne told me. She said Smith confided in her that he wished she was his, instead of me."

"Are the three of you saying I made a mistake, Verenda?"

"Of course not, Father. That is not possible. I messed up when I tried to help Barren. I should pay for that by remaining barren."

"So you would rather remain barren even though I can heal you?"

"Yes, if it means I can have the Archangel. I really really want him, Father. And Leevearne wants Smith."

"Leevearne's destiny is to be a nun."

"Leevearne doesn't want to be a nun, Master. And I don't blame her! Leevearne is too beautiful to be stuck behind a habit. Teresa would make a much better nun, Father."

"Yes, I know. She is also slated to be one."

"Leevearne will make a better mate for Smith. She will be a good mother for my children, too. No one else will love them, as much as she will. Can I have the Archangel?"

"Michael knows the rules. What if he does not want you?"

"Oh, that Archangel wants me, Father. He just thinks he can't have me."

"Did he tell you that?"

"Not with his mouth. But I see it in his eyes. They twirl every time he sees me coming. That Archangel loves me, too. But, he will never go against you, like the Fallen has."

"I know. He is my most faithful servant."

"He can still be that, and my mate. Please can I have him? Pretty pleeeeease? Pretty, pretty please?"

"Very well. What you have bound, in heaven, I will bind on earth. But only if he asks. Do not tell him to ask, Verenda."

"I won't. Thank you, Father. Can I have my children, too?"

"No, Verenda. Choose now, Michael or your children."

"I choose Michael."

"So be it."

"May I ask you a question?"

"Go ahead."

"You knew all along that I wanted Michael, didn't you?

"I am EL-ROI."

"That is why you did not provide a mate for Leevearne, isn't it?"

"Yes, my child. That is why."

"May I ask you another question?"

"Yes."

"May I tell Leevearne and Smith?"

"Why?"

"They are very unhappy, Father."

"I know. And yes, you may tell them. You may explain it to the children, also."

"Can't I have the children? Please?"

"You cannot have the children, Verenda. They are Smith's seed."

She stomped her feet. *"I don't want Smith!"*

Then she heard God laugh, at her tantrum. WOW!

~

She jumped to another memory...

"You and I are mates, Verenda."

"We are?"

"Father has given us His blessing."

"When do I get my human body?"

"It will be eons from now."

"But what if you find somebody else before then, Michael?"

"I will not. Father has given you to me, as a special dispensation. There shall never be another woman for me.

I love you, and I will patiently wait for you."
　　"I love you, too.　I'll be waiting for you, Michael."
　　　　　　　　　　　~

Chapter XIV

She gazed at Michael, sitting at the other end of the table. He had deliberately put space between them. She hadn't understood why he'd done that at first, but she did now. He was prepared for her to reject him; to blame him. He was waiting on her to accuse him, of ruining her life. He was sitting with his arms folded over his chest, stoically staring at her; devoid of all emotions.

~

She stood up and walked around the table. When she reached him she hiked her dress up, and straddled his lap. Then she ran her fingers up his folded arms, to his massively powerful biceps. The ruby and jasper glyphs were still there.

He told her, years ago, that they had been scribed by the hand of God; and were written in Aramaic: **ישאר דאלמ רתויב קזחה חילשו.**

He said they decreed his position in the hierarchy, and translated to: 'Chief Archangel and Most Powerful Emissary.'

Even his name bore witness to how powerful God had fashioned him. Michael means 'he who is *like* God'. Although he embraces his power, he rejects his name's inference. He has always declared *"I am just the messenger."*

She was not the only human soul that vied for his attention. She was just the only one to get it. She knew even in Heaven, that she was made to love him. She'd always needed the Archangel. She just forgot.

~

She wrapped one arm around his neck, and caressed his cheek, with the other. She stroked her fingers through his sideburns, as she examined his facial features. He was ruggedly handsome, and majestically beautiful. His lips, his nose, his eyes and skin tone were all perfectly formed. They were all designed by the Master's call.

The eyes she didn't like stared back at her, with no emotion. He was prepared to let her go, but that was never going to happen! She gently cupped his chiseled chin...

He didn't look a day older than he did when she asked for him. Only God knows how old he really is. She fell in love with that face the first time she saw him, dressed in his ancient regalia. He was still big and powerful, with an imposing presence.

~

She traced her fingertips through his soft sideburns. She loved the way they merged into his perfectly shaped 'stache and goatee. Even the hairs on his face were perfectly fashioned, yet a razor had never once touched them.

She stroked his 'stache with her thumb, and stopped at the corner of his inviting lips. She looked in his emotionless eyes. It was evident that he didn't have any idea how *much* she loved him.

Her eyes watered at that notion. "I don't care what Smittie and I were supposed to be. I *never* did. I loved you. I wanted *you,* Michael. My mind, body and soul have *always* belonged to..."

~

Michael cut her off with a desperate kiss. He was sure she would be upset with him; maybe even leave him.

They weren't 'spirit' mates. They were only sanctioned mates, as long as both of them agreed to the union. If she had wanted to leave him he would have had no choice but to let her go.

He would have teleported them both back to Georgia House, and wiped her memory of *them*. But he would have never forgotten. He'd already blasted Passion and Desire out of his being, but Memory would have tormented him for all eternity. Love would have lingered, like a sweet fragrance on the wind.

Peace, Joy and Relief, ripped through him; like a tidal wave. He held her face between his clammy palms. "You *still* love me?"

"Sinfully," she forcefully replied.

He hugged her closer to his chest, and caressed the nape of her neck. He could not imagine letting her go. Thank God he did not have to. *"I am sorry, Ruby."*

She pulled away from him. "For loving me?"

He caressed her cheeks and stroked that sexy mole, above her lip. "I will never apologize for that," he replied and kissed her again. "I am sorry I cost you your children."

"No you didn't. I did that," she replied and stroked his cheek.

"What do you mean?"

"I always wanted you *more* than Smith, Michael; even in Heaven," she replied, and kissed him. "It has always been you. I'm sorry I broke my promise to wait for you. I forgot."

"That is not your fault," he replied.

She stroked his lips. "I asked God to give me to

you. He agreed, because He already knew we loved each other."

"What?"

"I remember everything. I *begged* Him to let me have you, instead of Smittie. I wanted you more than Smittie. I still do. I always will. I'm sorry I forgot, hon."

He read her mind. She asked for him, as soon as she realized she was barren. She had asked for him, *before* he asked for her.

He knew that she had recommended Leevearne, but he did *not know* she had turned down the option to be healed. And he did not know that she had recommended Leevearne, *before* he told her God had consented to their union. He had always assumed she had done that after the fact.

She had struck a deal with the Master, in exchange for him. She had chosen him over her soul mate. She had chosen him over *motherhood*. The weight of that knowledge was mind blowing.

He whispered, "You wanted the Archangel."

"The big one," she said, and ran her fingers through his raven hair. "The one with the twirling eyes, and hieroglyphic biceps," she added. "Let me see those dangerous eyes, Michael."

His smiled, and his eyes twirled. He held her cheeks and passionately kissed her. *"My Ruby,"* he whispered to her mind.

She rubbed her groin up against his, and whispered, *"My love for you is endless, and there is no out. Make love to me, Michael."*

"Cook has already prepared lunch. He is on his

way to our room," he replied, while he continued to kiss her. He nibbled her lip and pulled away. "You need to eat."

"I'll eat later. Tell him to give us an hour," she demanded, and started unbuttoning his shirt.

This younger generation liked men with waxed chests. Not her!! She may look thirty-five, but she was old school. Nothing was sexier than a hairy-chested man, especially *her* hairy-chested man. "Maybe two hours," she added.

She kissed his newly exposed flesh, with the opening of each button. By the time she finished unbuttoning the last button, his stomach was spastic. She walked the tips of her fingernails up his stomach, and then slowly scraped them back down. She drew little circles, through the hair on his chest; and then stroked it back in place. The hair was as silky as that on his head. She loved the way it laid against his washboard stomach. It wasn't overly thick, which allowed her a tantalizing view of his rippled eight-pack. It formed a narrow, but dense, line to his groin. As soft as the hair was it looked ruggedly manly, and sexy.

She stared in his eyes while she unsnapped the top button on his pants. She seductively licked, and then sucked, her bottom lip. Then she scraped her fingernails along the base of his stomach. She smiled at the way it bunched, and his groin swelled against her womb. "Tell Cook to go back," she erotically whispered. "I want *you.*"

Desire and Passion slammed into him, like raging bulls; horns and all. After decades of celibacy his wife meant to make up for lost time. He groaned, "It is too late.

He is almost at the door, Ruby."

She leaned in and nibbled his nipple. Then she gently suckled it, as she scraped her nails along his pecs. *"It's our honeymoon,"* she reminded him, and flexed her womb against his groin. The friction was electric. *"Tell him to go back, hon. Pleeeeease!"*

~

Michael moaned and fanned his fingers through her hair. He squeaked, *"coook!!"*

"Yeah?"

"GO BACK!!! GOOOO...BACK, MAN!!"

~

Cook chuckled. *"No problem,"* he replied and vanished.

He took it upon himself to throw up a cone of silence, around the house. Neither he nor any of the staff cared to hear them carrying on.

They'd heard part of their lovemaking, last night. It had been embarrassing. They'd all been preparing dinner when they heard *big bad* Michael squeak. They looked at each other, dropped their utensils, and vanished at the same time.

Clearly his wife was more than just a pretty face. The lucky bastard!

~

Michael didn't want to vanquish her clothes, not this time. He reached down and lifted the hem of her dress. He paused, and stroked his hands up and down her thighs. Her skin was as smooth as silk, and as soft as cotton. He ran his hands up her hips, caressed her cheeks, and groaned. He kissed the crown of her head, and whispered,

"You are a temptress.   You are not wearing any underclothes, Ruby."

"I know," she replied, and kept suckling his nipples.

He wrapped an arm around her waist and lifted her up, against his stomach.   Then he ran his hands up the inside of her thighs.

She quivered and moaned.   Her husband knew her spot.   It was erotic torture.   She arched her back and moaned, *"Michael."*

By the time he eased the dress over her head, they were both at the cliff's edge.   Her breasts were full with desire, like his groin.   Her soft silky skin was glistening, so was his; and not from the sun.

He caressed her delicate waist, and suckled her breast. *"You asked Father for me?"*

His voice was so seductively husky it caused her womb to spasm and weep.   *"I've always loved you, Michael."*

"And I have always loved you."

She fanned her silky hair upward.   Then bowed her back until her head rested on the table.   *"Show me,"* she whispered. *"Now!"*

Michael growled at the exposed view of her exquisite tapestry.   He vanquished his clothes.   Then he grabbed her thighs, in the cuffs of his arms, and lifted her off of him.   He stood up and leaned over her.   His soaked hair fell in her face.   *"My pleasure,"* he whispered, and penetrated her sizzling womb.

They both moaned.

~

Chapter XV

Michael placed their lunch on the patio table. Ruby was starving, again. "I have never seen you eat so much, woman," he said and laughed.

She looked up from her pasta salad and smiled. "I've never exerted this much energy, before." Lord knows that was the God's truth.

He smiled and stole a shrimp, off of her plate. "Neither have I," he said and popped it in his mouth.

"You know what I'd like?" she asked.

"Another round?"

"That too," she replied. He kept her in a perpetual state of need.

"What would you like?"

"I'd like to spend the rest of the afternoon with our grandbabies," she replied. "Do you think Seraphiel and Jodi will let us have them for a few hours?"

~

She'd given up her own children for him. He realized that in all the years she'd overseen the House she'd never held a baby. All of the little 'spirit' mates arrived at a minimum age of six or seven. She needed to hold and care for infants, and toddlers. And he was going to *make* that happen.

"Seraphiel...Jodi."

"Hey. Is anything wrong, Dad," Brock answered.

"Hey, Michael," Jodi replied.

"Nothing is wrong," Michael replied. *"Ruby and I would like to spend a couple of hours with the little ones."*

"All four of them?" Jodi asked.

"Yes, if it is okay with you, and Seraphiel."

The link went silent. He knew they were privately discussing it. He gave them their time, because this was a big deal for them. Their children had never been out of their reach, and the babies were only weeks old.

It wasn't about their children being safe. They both knew he could protect their children, *better* than Seraphiel could. And they knew he would.

In fact Seraphiel knew he would do it seamlessly, without the babies being frightened. Just like he had been handling Lucifer since he arrived on the island.

That gutless wonder had already sent his minions twice, since he and Ruby arrived. And she was none the wiser.

Unlike Seraphiel, when he fought against Lucifer there was no loud hoopla or brouhaha. No one was ever the wiser, except Lucifer and his envoys.

~

Brock finally replied, *"What time do you want them?"*

Verenda's heart leaped. She was sure they would say no, especially about the newborns. Their willingness to share their children with her more than made up for her not having her own. She squeezed Michael's hand. *"In an hour,"* she replied. She needed to get herself together, first. *"Thank you, Jodi,"* she replied.

She knew this had to be hard for Jodi. She had given her children up in Heaven. However, if she'd birthed them, here on earth, it would have been a different story. She would've cut Leevearne, to shreds, and Smittie too; if they even thought about it.

"No. Thank you, Verenda," Jodi replied and then laughed. *"I need some romantic time with my husband, too."*

Verenda looked at Michael and blushed. *"I need a break,"* she replied and laughed.

Brock roared! He still didn't like talking about sex, but the thought of Michael doing *it* tickled his fancy. Once the Master gave him the assurance that their union was sanctioned, he was happy for them. Especially Michael.

When he thought about how long his dad had quietly waited on his mate, it made his wait seem like a blink.

Michael chuckled. *"See you guys soon."*

~

Brock and Jodi appeared in the foyer, an hour later, with their four little ones. Jodi's eye's bucked. Michael's house was wall to wall crystal. She looked up at the domed ceiling, and all she saw was sky.

The gold circle in the floor, with Michael and Verenda's initials in it, was a touch of class. The ballroom added an ambiance of privilege, to the place. The entire place was suited for royalty. "Oh my God!" she exclaimed. "I feel like I've just invaded the Empress' imperial palace."

Brock was also taken aback. He hadn't visited Michael's island, in years. And when he had, it didn't have this house, estate, palace or whatever it was. It certainly was beyond anything he could've imagined.

He reached out with his mind, to get a better view. On top of the sitting area, on the upstairs landing, there was a crystal steeple, with a cross at the top. A steeple!!

He looked up and saw Michael and Verenda coming down the stairs. "Man, how you gon' outdo me? You plopped my-" He paused because Jodi did not know they were sitting over Lucifer's head.

"If I am not mistaken I outdo you in a multitude of arenas, son. You almost lost your mind over that truth, did you not," Michael replied, and chuckled.

Brock could only laugh, because that was damn sure the truth. When he thought Michael had fallen his mind had slipped into the abyss, and refused to come back. However, Michael didn't have to throw it up in his face. He raised his brows. "I got you in one area though, old man," he replied and smirked.

"Think again," Michael replied, and squeezed Verenda's waist. "I got you there, too. Do I not, Ruby?"

"Michael!" she chided. She looked like a walking hot flash.

Michael, Brock and Jodi chuckled.

"We will give you guys a tour," Michael told them.

"You bet your ass you will," Brock replied.

Elizabeth and Hannah ran to them. "Grandpa Michael!" Elizabeth shouted and jumped up in his arms.

"Grandma Vaninda," Hannah said. Then she jumped in Verenda's arms, and kissed her cheek.

"I told you her name is Verenda, Hans," Elizabeth reminded her. "Ver...ren...da!"

"Shut up, Lizzie. You make me *sick*," Hannah replied. Then she kissed Verenda's cheek again. "Sorreee, I forgot. Can I just call you E-li-si?"

"E-li-si?" Verenda asked.

"That means Grandmother, in Cherokee," Jodi

informed her.

Verenda's eyes watered. She'd seen them through Michael's eyes, but that view had not done them justice. They were absolutely beautiful. She hugged Hannah closer to her heart, and kissed her cheek. She was going to spoil the hell out of them. "Yes. You can most certainly call me E-li-si, sweetheart."

Elizabeth leaned over and kissed her cheek. "Me too?" she asked.

Verenda kissed her cheek. "You too, hon," she replied.

When they reached Jodi and Brock, Verenda handed Hannah to Michael and reached for Eunice. When she had her in her arms, her heart swelled. Eunice looked like a tiny little Indian doll. She wanted to keep this one, too. "She's beautiful, Jodi. They all are."

Eunice opened her eyes and looked up at Verenda. *"Hi, E-li-si,"* she said and smiled.

"Hi, hon," Verenda replied through glazed eyes.

Then she reached for Hezekiah with her other arm. When she looked at him she was surprised at how much he looked like the twins, and not Eunice. But he was a fine boy. "Can you talk to E-li-si, too," she asked.

"Hi, E-li-si," he replied and smiled.

She fell in love with their little tiny voices. She looked at Jodi. "Thank you, hon."

"Are you sure you want to keep the babies?" Jodi asked.

"Please don't change your mind," she begged.

"Oh no, I'm not," Jodi assured her. "I'm just saying four little ones are a handful."

"No, they are not," she replied. "C'mon, let me show you their bedroom."

"They have a bedroom?" Jodi asked.

Verenda smiled at Michael. "My Michael thought of everything. There is one for you and Seraphiel, as well."

"Really?" Jodi replied. Her dimples went in deeper than normal.

"We have rooms for all of our children and grandchildren," Verenda replied.

~

They took Brock and Jodi on a tour of the house. Then they showed them *their* bedroom. Jodi loved it. "It will be awesome to lie in bed and look up at the stars, won't it, Brock?"

"This is really nice, Michael." Brock added.

"Let's go see our room," Hannah said and ran down the hall. She already knew where hers and Elizabeth's room was, because she'd snooped.

~

The girls fell in love with their room. They each picked which bed was theirs. Hannah picked the one closest to the window. Elizabeth wanted the one by the door.

"Can we spend the night?" Elizabeth asked.

"Can we?" Hannah echoed.

Jodi shook her head. "No. E-li-si and Grandpa just wanted to visit with you girls, for a while. Daddy and I will be back to get you in a few hours, okay."

Brock noticed that Verenda looked as disappointed as the girls. He knew the only reason Jodi said no was because they hadn't asked. Plus, it was their honeymoon.

If it was anyone else he'd say no, too. But he trusted Michael, because Michael was... Well, Michael was Michael. He'd no more let anything happen to the girls, than he would Verenda; or *him*.

He spoke to Jodi's mind. *"Verenda wants them to stay, Dimples."*

Jodi looked at Verenda. She saw the same thing Brock did. Disappointment. "Did you want them to spend the night, Verenda?"

Verenda pouted her lips. "Yes. Michael will bring them back tomorrow. I promise."

Elizabeth and Hannah were jumping up and down on the bed; and fiercely nodding their heads. "Please, Mommy! Please, Mommy!"

Verenda joined in. "Please, Mommy! Please, Mommy!"

Michael would let Verenda want for nothing. "I will make sure nothing happens to them, Jodi."

"I know that, Michael," Jodi replied. "You are the only person I would *ever* trust my children with, outside of the estate."

"You mean besides me, right?" Brock teased.

Jodi stroked his cheek and smiled. He still gave her a thrill. "You are the only person, other than their daddy."

That was the truth. She didn't even trust her own father to take the girls off the estate. Not if Brock wasn't with him. Doc, Adam and Akibeel could forget about it. It was not going to happen. She'd waited too long to be a mother, to be careless.

"Thank you for saying that," Michael replied.

"You can keep the twins overnight, but not Eunice and Hezekiah. They are too young, still." She was breastfeeding them, and she still wasn't ready to share them. The only reason she agreed to let them visit was because she and Brock were going out. They needed this time, and a babysitter.

Her mother had offered to keep them, but the girls didn't want to stay with her. Brock was right; they hadn't liked how their grandmother had yelled at her. Plus she was still miffed with her mother, and her aunts.

She, Lara and Amanda, had cornered their mother, about Gabriella's revelation. Her mother had admitted all the awful things she, and her aunts, had said about her; and her cousins. Evidently, they did that often.

Lara, always the good big sister, blasted their mother. She pulled a Charity on their mother, and called her by her name. She said, *"Everyone has acknowledged their shortcomings, but you, SnowAnna! Amanda and I apologized to Jodi. Uncle Floyd apologized to Jodi. Daddy apologized. What have you said? Nothing!! You should have been the first person to apologize, instead of making fun of her!"*

Amanda was quiet, and never talked a lot. Her emotions were always displayed in her body language. She'd said three words, *"I'll be damned!"*

She, herself, didn't understand how they could criticize their daughters' hardships. She'd never do that to her girls, and she wouldn't allow anyone else to either.

She would never tell her little cousins what was said, because they'd be as hurt as she was.

~

The girls jumped in Verenda's arms. "Yay!" all three of them shouted.

Brock and Jodi smiled.

Michael was holding Eunice and Hezekiah. They were beautiful babies, and they felt right, in his arms. He looked at Brock. "Thank you for allowing us this time with our grandchildren, Seraphiel."

"Trust me you are helping us out. Your timing was perfect. Jodi and I are going to the theatre with our four oldest children," he replied. "We were trying to figure out what to do with our little ones."

"Where is Abraham?" Michael asked. "Yomiel and Kwanita could have brought him, as well."

"He's with E-du-di and Sharon," Jodi replied. She'd refused E-du-di's offer to keep them, because she didn't trust him either.

"We'll be back in a couple of hours," Brock informed them.

"Take your family dancing too," Verenda told him. "Take all the time you need. The children will be fine." She kissed the girls' cheeks. She was overjoyed. "Take all the time you need."

Jodi kissed the babies, and then opened her arms. "Come kiss Mommy and Daddy good bye."

The girls jumped off the bed and ran to her. "Good bye, Mommy!" they both said, and kissed her.

Brock picked them up and kissed their cheeks. "Behave, okay."

"We will," Hans replied.

"We will," Elizabeth echoed.

Brock put them down. "We will be back soon," he

told Michael. Then he and Jodi vanished.

~

Michael materialized pizza, and they all ate dinner on the patio garden. Hannah and Elizabeth liked their bedrooms, but they loved their E-li-si's bed. "This bed bigger than my daddy's," Hannah said, while jumping up and down on it. "When I get big I want one just like this! Okay, E-li-si?"

"I promise I will make Grandpa get you one, sweetheart," Verenda replied.

Elizabeth was doing flips on the bed. "Me too! And I want lights under my bed, just like these."

"Grandpa will get those for you, too, honey."

Verenda was having the time of her life. She was lying on her stomach blowing raspberries on the bottoms of Eunice's and Hezekiah's feet. They were both giggling. She wanted to keep them.

The twins plopped down on each side of her. "We didn't know Mommy had Eunice in her belly," Hannah told her.

Verenda looked at her, and then at Elizabeth. "You didn't?"

Elizabeth shook her head. "She was playing hide and go seek."

Verenda looked at Eunice and laughed. "What?"

Eunice giggled. *"I hid behind Hezekiah."*

"Oh my. You're going to be a little trickster, aren't you?" Verenda replied and laughed.

Michael was sitting in the recliner watching her with the children. He felt how content her spirit was. *"Any regrets, Ruby?"*

She didn't look up, but shook her head. *"None, hon. I love that you have provided me with these grandchildren. I already love them. But I wouldn't trade you for any one of them."*

"Are you sure?"

She looked up that time. *"The only thing I'm surer of is my love for you. I didn't make a mistake, Michael. I didn't want any children if I couldn't have you. I didn't want any children if they weren't yours."*

"And Charity, Faith and Maria?" he asked.

"I won't lie to you. I am going to have a hard time not wanting to steal them from Leevearne. But they are her children. She nurtured them in her womb, and I am grateful she was willing to do that. But, even if she had not been willing to birth them, I would have still chosen you," she replied. *"No one and nothing is more important to me than you."*

He smiled.

"Besides, Akibeel thinks of you as his father. That affords me a relationship with Maria. You gave me these beautiful grandchildren. That's more than enough. I can't wait to get to know Aurellia and Adam, too. And little Abraham. You brought Desiree to me. Now she is expecting another grandchild. My cup runs over, Michael."

He stood up and sat on the side of the bed. "You girls want to watch cartoons?"

"I like scary movie, Grandpa," Hannah told him.

"Daddy don't want us watching that, Hannah," Elizabeth reminded her.

"He just *mean!*" Hannah complained. "He don't let

me do nothin' I like to do." Her little lips were pouted. She crawled in his lap, and huffed. "He a big *ole* meanie, Grandpa."

Michael roared. Hannah was a character. He was looking forward to spending as much time with them as Seraphiel and Jodi would allow. Not only did it make Ruby happy, it made him happy too.

He'd spent eons watching the Watchers marry and raise their families. None of them knew he was a man in waiting. Now that he had his bride the only thing lacking was children. But Seraphiel's children were more than enough.

"How about this. We'll watch cartoons and eat ice cream."

They both licked their lips. "Yum!"

~

Brock and Jodi returned later than they'd planned. They had taken Verenda up on her idea, and gone dancing. It felt so good to be away from the family, with their older children; they lost track of time.

Brock teleported directly into the girl's bedroom, but the beds were empty. *"Where are you guys?"* he asked.

"We are all in our bedroom. C'mon in," Michael replied.

When they walked in the room, Jodi palmed her mouth. Hannah and Elizabeth had fallen asleep, on Michael's lap, propped up in his arms. Their little arms were around his waist, and their heads were resting on his chest. They looked so sweet and innocent, but her twins were bad!

Eunice and Hezekiah had fallen asleep, lying across Verenda's lap. Her babies looked adorable. Rembrandt couldn't have painted a more endearing family portrait. No doubt she was prejudiced, but Brock had given her some beautiful children.

She was going to ask Faith to draw a portrait of this scene, from her memories. She'd like to ask her Aunt Leevearne to draw it, but she knew that was not going to happen.

"Are you sure you want to keep the girls tonight?" she asked.

"Quite sure," Verenda replied. "They wore themselves out on this bed. They'll sleep through the night. Tomorrow I'm going to take them to play on the beach, before Michael brings them home."

"Okay," Jodi replied and reached for Eunice. She handed her to Brock and picked up Hezekiah. They both bowed their backs, and snorted.

Verenda stood up and hugged them. "Thank you for letting Elizabeth and Hannah sleep over. I hope we can do it again."

Brock leaned over, and kissed her cheek. "Any time," he promised and vanished.

~

Chapter XVI

Verenda was lying back against Michael's chest. The gentle ocean breeze was blowing in from the patio, and it felt wonderful. The lightning bugs were so abundant, on the patio and overhead, they looked like the constellation. Every so often rain drops would land on the patio, sizzle and evaporate. Even though the wind was blowing in none of the rain drops, or lightening bugs, did.

She was going on and on about her visit with the little ones. The elation in her voice made him smile. Over the years she'd housed hundreds of little 'spirit' mates, thousands even. But not only were they older, their protective mothers were there too. Plus, those children were all traumatized and frightened. None of them had *ever* crawled in her bed, like Lizzie and Hans had. Her only parental role was to keep them safe, and remember their birthdays.

He rubbed his arm up and down her stomach. "So, I guess you enjoyed them?" he teased.

"I did. I thought they'd be standoffish towards me, because they didn't know me." That was how all of her little 'spirit' mates were at first. They fearfully clung to their mothers.

Michael laughed. "Those little ones are just as nosey as you were, Ruby. They have always known you."

She looked up at him. "What?"

He chuckled. "They are powerful little girls. They snoop on everybody."

"Does Brock know?"

"Of course. He threatened to let everybody snoop

on them, if they did not stop," he replied and laughed.

"It didn't work?"

"They have inquisitive minds. Brock and Jodi keep them locked up behind the estate walls. They know there is a big world out there, so they see it with their minds."

"Do you think they are watching us now?" Verenda asked. God, she hoped not. She did not want those little ones to see hers and Michael's intimacy. That would be awfully inappropriate.

Michael chuckled. "No. Their innocent minds do not work like that. They heard all the offensive things their other grandmother, and great-aunts, were saying about you. They wanted to see for themselves, so they have been observing you for months."

"What?"

He laughed. "Everybody thinks Hannah is flipped, and she is. However, Elizabeth is the one they are really going to have to watch."

"Why?"

"That little one is sneaky."

"Why do you say that?"

"She is the most powerful of all of Seraphiel's children. Including Adam, Akibeel and Yomiel."

Verenda sat up. Michael had allowed her to see many of their battles with demons. Those young men were formidable. They were only a minute weaker than their father. She looked at the smile on Michael's face. "You are kidding?"

Michael propped his arms behind his head. "Hannah is *physically* as powerful as Elizabeth. But Elizabeth is more powerful than all of them, with her mind. She does not know how to wield all of her powers yet, but she is always testing their limits."

He thought about some of the amazing powers she had already discovered. If the Master, and Seraphiel, would allow him he would definitely make her a Watcher. She was definitely her father's child.

He looked at Verenda, and smiled. "Elizabeth can split herself, just like her father. Except there are no physical ramifications when *she* does it."

"What!"

She heard the pride in Michael's voice, but it was disturbing to her. She knew from experience that little ones get in trouble. They always test the limits. Of course she believed life's lessons have to be learned, but not without close supervision.

Brock and Jodi would think their baby was safely tucked in bed, but she wouldn't be. She'd be wandering who knows where. "God, Michael, she could be doing that right now, and we wouldn't know. You *have* to tell Brock, Michael."

"There is no need to frighten her parents right now. I have been keeping an eye on her from the moment I realized she could do it, Ruby."

He thought about the day Elizabeth appeared at the House. It was the night Hezekiah spanked Adam. She hadn't liked that. She was only seventeen months old, and no one could see her, but him.

~

He reached down and picked Elizabeth up. *"What are you doing here, Little One?"*

"Grandpa Hezekiah hit my baby brother. I want

you to beat him up."

"He did not hurt Adam, Elizabeth. Did your father allow you to come here?"

"He doesn't know I'm here."

That statement had shocked him. Seraphiel always knew when people came and went from his property. That is everyone but *him.*

"How is that possible?"

"I'm here and I'm home too, Grandpa."

He was the most powerful Archangel the Master ever called into existence. Nothing and no one frightened him. But that statement had. She was too young to experience the pain of merging her beings back together. He reached out and checked. Sure enough she was in her bed with her eyes closed. Her grandparents thought she was asleep.

"You can split yourself, Little One?"

"Just like Daddy."

"Promise me you will not do this again. It is too dangerous."

"But I like it, Grandpa."

"Promise me, Elizabeth, or I will tell your parents."

"That will scare Mommy."

"I know it will. It will scare your father too."

"Okay. I won't do it anymore."

"Let me take you home. And behave yourself, Little One. I will be watching."

He watched her merge her beings back together with *no* physical ramifications. He stayed with her all night just to be sure, but *nothing* happened. No nose bleed, no swelling. Nothing!! It was astonishing. In this area, she was stronger than her *father.*

To be on the safe side, he blocked her memory that she could do that. Then he installed a safeguard around it. If she ever tried to reach for it, it would frighten her, and she'd move on.

At the appropriate time he would discuss it with Seraphiel. It would be his decision whether or not to give it back to her. If it were his daughter he would not.

~

He smiled. "She will definitely be formidable."

Verenda scooted to the end of the bed. "I'm going to check on them," she replied.

He reached for her. "They are fine, Ruby."

~

Before she could respond the wind blew so fiercely her skin crawled. It whistled and swirled around the patio, at hurricane speeds. The planters toppled over, and broke. The chairs flew up against the banister, and crash landed.

They both heard the girls scream. She shouted, "Michael!"

He jolted up and swung his legs off the bed. At the same time the girls ran in the room. They were holding hands, screaming and crying.

"Grandpa Michael!" Elizabeth shouted, and ran into his outstretched arms. Then she spoke to his mind, *"Look, Grandpa! Look!"*

"I see, Little One," he replied. Then he rubbed her trembling back. "You are alright, Little One."

"E-li-si!" Hannah screamed, and crawled up Verenda's lap.

"Shh," Verenda said, and rocked her back and forth.

Then she kissed the side of her head. "E-li-si's got you, baby."

Their little faces were soaking wet. They were squeezing Michael's and Verenda's necks, and screaming. They were both hysterical.

~

"MI...CHAEL!!"

"Stay put, Seraphiel," Michael responded, and blocked his access to the island. *"The girls are fine."*

"Why are they crying, then? Why are they afraid? What's happening? Let me in, man!"

"No! Stay put, son." He could not let Seraphiel on the island, because he would trip out. If he were to come, he would invite all of those negative spirits with him. That would expose what was really going on, to Ruby and Hannah. He would never allow that, because they'd be frightened. *"It is just a rain storm,"* he added, and chuckled. *"You really need to expose your children to Mother Nature, boy."*

Brock felt bad. He never let it rain or snow on the estate. His babies had never even heard thunder, until the Fallen attacked Adam. No doubt they associated it with that night. He was ashamed of himself, because he was making his children ignorant. They were just like the people Noah tried to tell it was going to rain. They were like what the hell is rain?

"Hans, Lizzie, are you girls alright?"

"Yes, Daddy," they both cried.

"Do you want Daddy to come and get you?"

"Noooo! Noooo!"

"Do you want Grandpa to bring you home?"

"No, Daddy! No, Daddy!" they both replied.

"Okay. Daddy loves you girls."

"We love you, Daddy."

"Get rid of the rain, Michael!"

"I will do no such thing. They need to know about these things. Now leave us be, Seraphiel," he replied and broke the link.

~

"Can we sleep with you, E-li-si?" Hannah asked. She was still trembling. She didn't want to go home, but she was scared to go back to her bedroom.

"Of course, sweetheart," Verenda replied. This was right up her alley. She rocked Hannah and kissed her temple. "E-li-si gon' cut that mean wind for scaring her babies."

Hannah pointed her finger towards the patio, and shook it. "My E-li-si ain't got no problem cuttin' a brotha."

Michael howled. "I told you they have been watching you," he said and kept laughing.

Verenda laughed and kissed Hannah's cheek. She loved these babies. She looked over at Elizabeth, she'd settled down too. She had her little arm wrapped around Michael's neck, and was laughing. It was obvious she was his baby, and Hannah was hers.

~

Verenda pulled the covers up over the girls; and kissed their cheeks. "Better?" she asked.

"Love you, E-li-si," Hannah replied and snuggled up against her.

Elizabeth smiled at Verenda, but spoke to Michael's

mind, *"I saw that demon, Grandpa. He was bigger than Night Terror."*

"I am sorry, Elizabeth. I forgot how powerful you are. Did Hannah see him too?"

"No. I scared Hannah, when I screamed. I thought he wanted to take us, like Daddy's brothers. I thought he was going to break the glass. I didn't want my sistah to get cut."

"Do not tell her, or your E-li-si. They will be afraid."

"Okay. Can he get in?"

"No, he cannot. He is just being a pest."

"But there is no wall over there, Grandpa."

To keep Verenda and Hannah from knowing what was going on he leaned down, and put his face in front of hers. *"Look in my eyes, Elizabeth,"* he replied.

He let her see the invisible shield he had put up. It was also important that she knew the difference in Mother Nature's rain, and Tempest. Otherwise every time it rained she'd be fearful.

She reached up and held his face, in her tiny hands. "Good night, Grandpa," she voiced. Then she looked in his twirling eyes.

"Sleep well, Little One," he replied, and kissed her forehead.

Then he stood up and walked out on the patio. The wind squealed. Then it howled, whined and moved back out across the ocean.

~

He walked back to the bed, and slid under the covers. Elizabeth snuggled up in his arms. *"Is he gone,*

Grandpa?"

"*Yes, he is gone,*" he replied and kissed the crown of her head. "Sleep well, Little One."

~

Chapter XVII

"DAMMIT!" Lucifer shouted, and stomped his feet. Then he kicked the wall and shouted, "NOT AGAIN!!"

"I tried," Tempest replied. "He cut me off at every turn."

His clothes were shredded and smoldering. His arms were stretched out, like he was walking the plank. His skin was covered with little Michael eyes. It was creepy. Every time he dropped his arm against his side, he felt sharp stabbing pains. He swore Michael was a thorn in his side...*literally*. The only part of him that wasn't affected was the bottom of his feet.

"What happened?" Lucifer asked.

"I started out as little rain drops."

"That was clever," Lucifer replied. "It helped you get close, right?"

"Hell no! That bastard turned me into flying balls of fire. And it hurt! I looked like damn lightning bugs to his woman! Those drops that did get through landed on the patio and it felt like I landed in acid, Lucifer!"

"What?"

"Michael was toying with me, but he was acting like nothing was going on. He was laughing and talking with his woman, and kicking my ass; at the *same* time. Then when I scared Seraphiel's twins-"

"Wait!" Lucifer shouted. "The twins are there?"

"Ain't that what I just said?" Tempest shouted. He was more than a little uneasy. Plus his arms were getting tired.

"Okay, keep going," Lucifer replied. He didn't say

anything about Tempest yelling at him. It was obvious that boy was rattled.

"One of the twins saw through my façade, and knew I was not the elements."

"She saw you?"

"That little one is powerful. I heard Michael tell his woman that she was as powerful as her father. I wanted to see her."

"For true?"

"Do I look like I'm lying?"

"You look like you are scared to death."

"I am! When that child saw my face she beat the shit out of me!"

"What?" Lucifer shouted. "You let a little girl beat you up?"

"She may be little, but she is *p.o.w.e.r.f.u.l.* She slammed my ass into the patio furniture, like I was a feather. I was whipping and whirling, and knocking over planters; trying to catch my balance. All the while, she was tapping my ass!"

Lucifer actually chuckled. "What happened next?"

"She grabbed her sister's hand, and they ran. Keep in mind she was running and beating my ass at the same time! I have not seen anything like her, since Seraphiel!"

"Where did they run to?"

"Where do you think? To Michael's bedroom, man! They jumped in the bed with him, and his woman. They were both screaming and crying."

"What did Michael do?"

"He picked that one up and patted her back. When he did that, he told her she was okay. Then he released me out of her snare."

"Did you run?"

"I COULDN'T! He froze me in place until the little girls were situated. That other little girl couldn't see me, but she pointed her finger anyway; and mocked me."

"Mocked you? How?"

"She said her grandmother was gon *cut* me! And then they all laughed! At me, Lucifer! They laughed at me!"

Lucifer chuckled again. Michael's wife was good with a knife. "What did Michael say?"

"That bastard stepped out on the patio, and folded his arms. He displayed no sign that he was upset, or preparing to do battle. He didn't materialize his battle axe. He didn't call in back up."

"What did he do?"

"With a blank face, he stood there and made me squeal like a damn pig, Lucifer!! ME!! TEMPEST!!"

"What?"

"Then he released me, and I ran back towards the ocean; but he was waiting for me there!"

"What did he do?"

"He called in Holy, that's what!" he shouted.

"What could Holy do in the ocean?"

He whimpered, "He troubled the water, man!"

"What?"

"Didn't you hear me? That spirit moved over the water, and anointed the entire ocean!! I was hovering over the ocean, trying not to touch it. Then Michael blocked my wind tunnels on every side, including the top; with twisters of his own. They burned the shit out of me, man!"

he shouted. "When his twisters died down I thought I could escape. That bastard turned those twisters into tiny little nettles. They attacked me like a band of angry hornets. That bastard made me beg, and scream, for mercy. By the time he finished, I was left looking like I was made of his eyes!"

"You have got to be kidding," Lucifer replied. He did not know Michael could do that.

"LOOK AT ME!! Do I look like I'm kidding! I can't let my arms down!! I am covered in his eyes! I can't even touch myself without feeling like I'm being stabbed, by my own damn skin!! EVEN MY PLUMS ARE COVERED IN HIS EYES!!!" he shouted and then whimpered, "Why would he put them down *there*, Lucifer? Why?"

Lucifer reached out and touched his arm. He snatched his hand back. His fingers and thumb were spurting orange and black blood. "What the hell *was* that?"

"Weren't you listening?" he shouted. "THEY ARE HIS EYES, FOOL!!"

"How were you able to escape?"

"That bastard dipped me in Holy's water."

"No," Lucifer whispered. He knew what was coming next. Tempest could be wind *and* water. He could be water in the wind and create rainstorms, mighty tornadoes and hurricanes. But wind *in the* water...can anybody say whirlpool! *He* actually trembled.

"That bastard turned *me* against *me!* I turned my own damned self every which way but loose! I was inside out, Lucifer!!" he cried.

Lucifer thought back to the Seer. His eyes momentarily looked like Michael's. They had blinded him, plus made his own eyes bleed.

Even Taz had Michael's eyes under his skin. Now this! What was it about his eyes? "How can he be using his eyes as weapons?"

"They *are* weapons!!!" Tempest shouted. He turned around and let Lucifer see his back. "How am I supposed to sit down?"

Lucifer stared at his backside. His shirt and pant legs were in strips, and those eyes were protruding. If he were to sit down he'd cut his own ass to pieces. How ironic that his arms looked like they were being held up, like a puppet.

Even before they were kicked out of Heaven Michael had those eyes. No other Archangel had them, but *Michael*. Why hadn't he used them when they'd fought? It was as though they were the ultimate secret. Why?

He looked at Tempest. "Do you have any suggestions?"

"Yeah," Tempest replied.

"What?"

"Leave him and his woman the hell alone!" he shouted. Then he turned around and walked, wide legged, out the door. He was whimpering with each step, "My plums...my plums."

~

Lucifer started pacing back and forth. He wasn't the type to back down. There had to be a way to get to Michael's woman.

He sat down on his new sorry ass throne chair. "Maybe I just need to settle down and think it through," he said to himself.

The moment he calmed down he had the most devious thought. He was going at it all wrong. He'd been sending the wrong messengers. He knew exactly how to get through.

He'd wait a day or so. Let Michael drop his guards. Then he'd go in for the kill. Besides, who says it has to be at the island. He could reach out to her at any place. It would be better if they weren't on the island, then he could *see* her face when she got the four-one-one.

~

Chapter XVIII

Cook fell in love with the twins. "Oh my," he exclaimed. "These are Seraphiel's daughters?" They were just about the cutest little ones he'd ever seen.

"Yes," Verenda replied. "This is Hannah, and this is Elizabeth."

"I was there the day your mommy and daddy got married," he told the children.

Chef had solicited his help to prepare the food, and serve the guests. He thought it would be best to have Watchers that could cook, instead of domestics. That way they could work as security, in case something jumped off.

He and his entire staff had eagerly jumped at the opportunity; for more than one reason. It had been one of the grandest affairs they'd attended, since Adabiel's daughter's wedding. "You look just like your mommy," he said and smiled.

The girls smiled sheepishly, but didn't say anything. They were holding Michael's and Ruby's hands, really tight. Elizabeth was almost hiding behind Michael. Hannah was taking her cue from Elizabeth. She felt her sister's heart race, and hers raced too.

"What's wrong, Lizzie," she asked.

"Don't go near him, Hans. He bad," she replied.

Verenda didn't think anything of their behavior, because she hadn't previously been around them. She just assumed they were being shy, like the little 'spirit' mates were when they first met someone.

~

Michael knew better. He picked the girls up, and

kissed their cheeks. "They are a little shy this morning, Cook," he said. "We had quite a *storm* last night."

"Is that right?" he replied. Michael and Elizabeth were the only two who noticed Cook's hand tremble. He spoke to Michael's mind. *"I am sorry. After dinner my brothers and I left to hang out with some friends, on the mainland."*

"Ease yourself, Cook," Michael replied. *"I did not require your assistance, handling your grandfather. Unfortunately, Elizabeth saw Tempest's face."*

Cook frowned, and turned his back. It was no wonder the child was afraid. His heart was breaking. *"How is that possible?"* he asked.

"She is Seraphiel's 'first' born."

He gasped. *"He gave her all of himself?"*

"Yes, but he does not yet realize he has done that."

"Oh my, Michael. She's just a little girl!"

"A very powerful little girl."

"Should my brothers and I leave, while you guys are here? I don't want to frighten the child any more than I already have."

"Of course not. They will be spending a lot of time with us, because it pleases my wife. They will need to become familiar with you. Turn back around," he ordered.

Cook turned back around and faced them. He had a slight smile on his face.

Michael spoke to Elizabeth's mind. *"Cook is not the demon you saw last night."*

"He not?"

"That demon was Cook's grandfather. His name is Tempest."

She looked over her shoulder at Cook, and back at Michael. *"He looks like him, Grandpa."*

This was going to be a teachable moment; a moment that Seraphiel should have handled himself. He was so busy shielding, and protecting his children, he hadn't prepared them for the world they lived it. It was paramount that they be able to recognize the difference in good and evil. Watchers all over the world looked like their demon fathers. At some point or another they would experience seeing the fathers. They needed to be able to tell the difference, in a split second, especially Elizabeth. Like her father, she was strong enough to destroy demons *and* Watcher. If not properly trained, Seraphiel will spend a lot of time cleaning up her innocent messes. He'd had that same problem when Seraphiel was just a lad. It appeared history was going to repeat itself, unless he stepped in.

He made up his mind he was going to have a father/son talk with Seraphiel. He needed to do better by his *girls*. He of all people knew age was not a factor. He had been unimaginably powerful at Elizabeth's age. That was why Samjaza continuously tried to kill him. That is why Samjaza failed, every single time.

~

"Look at Cook closely, Elizabeth," he instructed. *"He has his grandfather's face, just like your brothers have your father's face. But look deeper."*

She looked back over her shoulder and stared at him. It took her a minute, but she finally saw the difference. That demon was shadowed by a silhouette of darkness; Cook wasn't. He had a light that only Watchers could see. She wasn't a Watcher, but she was powerful enough to see it. She relaxed. *"He like my daddy,"* she said.

"That is correct. He is a Watcher, like your daddy. You can always tell the difference in Watcher and demon; even if they look alike."

She smiled and kissed Michael's cheek. *"Okay."* Then she looked back at Cook, and smiled. As powerful as she was, she was also sensitive. She knew she'd hurt his feelings. "Do you cook good as Chef?" she asked.

Cook relaxed and laughed. "I cook better than that bird," he replied.

She wiggled out of Michael's arms. "My daddy said Chef is the best cook in the whole world," she added.

"That's because he hasn't eaten my cooking, Little One," he replied.

Elizabeth laughed.

"Don't go near him, Lizzie. You said he bad!" Han warned.

"I was wrong, he not bad," Lizzie replied.

Hannah immediately relaxed, too. She wiggled her way out of Michael's arms. "Can you make chocolate cookie pancakes?"

"It's chocolate *chip* pancakes, Hans," Elizabeth corrected.

"Shut up, Lizzie! You make me sick!" Hannah replied. Then she folded her arms and pouted her lips. "She always correctin' me, E-li-si."

Verenda laughed. She didn't hear the conversation Michael had with Elizabeth, but she knew he had one. And she also knew he would not share it with *her*.

Cook laughed too. "Yes, I *can* make chocolate chip *cookie* pancakes," he said and picked the girls up. "You girls want to help me?"

"Yes! Yes!" they both replied.

"Chef never lets us help," Elizabeth told him.

"He let his daughters help, but not us," Hannah added.

"They our cousins," Elizabeth said.

"But they bigger than us," Hannah added.

~

By the time they finished the kitchen, and their faces, were a mess. Unlike the Watchers, Michael didn't believe in taking shortcuts. At least not in most things. These children needed to practice doing things the human way.

He wet a towel to manually clean their little hands and faces. They were smiling so deeply, flour was trapped in their dimples. "Stop smiling," he commanded.

"I can't, it tickles, Grandpa," Hannah replied and giggled.

Michael chuckled. He was never going to get this done manually. Both girls were holding their cheeks and giggling up a storm. He cleaned their faces with his mind. "Let's eat before the pancakes get cold."

"I made the smiley faces, Grandpa," Hannah informed him.

"I helped," Elizabeth added.

Michael ate a forkful that had the mouth on it. "You forgot their mouths," he teased.

"You ate it, Grandpa!" Elizabeth replied and giggled.

Verenda was enjoying breakfast, with the children. She wasn't eating with as much gusto as she had her previous meals. That was because she hadn't overexerted herself, last night. The girls slept with them and kicked them all night long. It was wonderful!

Her heart raced, because this was the first real sit-down family breakfast she'd ever had. "Breakfast is wonderful, girls. I didn't know you girls could cook."

"Cook said we can help him fix lunch too," Elizabeth replied. "I like cooking."

"Me too, E-li-si," Hannah added. "I can't wait to fix Mommy and Daddy pancakes."

Verenda looked at Michael. *"Seraphiel is going to kill us."*

He laughed. *"I know."*

~

After breakfast, they took the girls down to the beach. They were dressed in cute little pink 'hello kitty' swimsuits. Michael's eyes twirled at Verenda's outfit. She was dressed in a black one piece swimsuit, with openings on each side of her waist. It was covered with a sheer white blouse. It was open in the front and gave him a teasing view of her cleavage. It just did not get any sexier. He whispered, *"Temptress."*

She was looking at him, in that same manner. He had on a black tank top; and black spandex shorts that came halfway down his rippled thighs. That man was magnificently designed. *"Stallion,"* she replied.

Elizabeth pulled on Michael's arm. "We don't know how to swim, Grandpa."

"Yeah, and that's a *lot* of water," Hannah added.

"That's okay, E-li-si and I will teach you," he replied.

"No, we *won't*," Verenda replied. She was frowning and vigorously shaking her head.

Michael saw the expression on her face. It was fear. "Why not, Ruby?"

"E-li-si can't swim, either," she replied.

"You never learned how to swim?"

"No," she replied. Then she showed him a scene in her head.

His eyes twirled. *"You never told me that."*

"It was just another humiliating moment in the life of Verenda Strong."

He nodded, but it was times like these that he wished he could embrace Revenge. He never should have waited for his mate to grow up. *"I am sorry, Ruby."*

"It's okay, hon. That was a long time ago."

"But you are still afraid of water."

"Yes."

"I will teach you how to swim, after I take the children home."

She didn't respond.

~

He smiled down at the girls. "Okay, you girls can play along the edge of the water."

"Okay, Grandpa," Hannah replied.

She and Elizabeth ran towards the water.

"Not too far, girls," Verenda shouted after them.

"Okay!" they both shouted back.

~

Michael stretched out on the sand, next to Verenda.

"Cappy never tried to teach you how to swim?"

"He tried, but I was too afraid," she replied and laughed. "That poor man almost drowned, trying to teach me. I was on his head."

Michael cracked up laughing. He saw the vision in her head. She was choking him and screaming. He was trying to get away from her, but she kept dunking his head.

"That is pitiful, Ruby."

She laid back in the sand, and placed her hand on her stomach. "I'm terrified of the water, Michael."

"I will take that fear, while I am teaching you how to swim. It is a wonderful feeling, Ruby. There are beautiful creatures in the sea."

"I'd rather go see the caves."

He leaned over her and kissed her nose. "Okay, we will go to the caves."

"What time are you going to take the girls home?"

"Are you ready for them to go now?"

"No. I want to keep them," she replied. "They are so cute. Thank you for my grandchildren, Michael."

"They are cute indeed, but I did not much appreciate being kicked all night," Michael replied.

Verenda laughed. "You are so silly."

"Okay, I did not appreciate not being close to you," Michael replied. "I missed your warm body."

"In other words they can't spend another night."

He laughed, but he would deny her nothing. "Do you really want them to?"

She smiled. "No. But I'd like to have all the kids over for dinner before we go back."

"That is fine," he replied.

"Are you in a hurry for them to leave, Michael?"

"No, but I am in a hurry to make mad passionate love to my wife. I can't do that with them here," he replied and kissed her. "This is our *honeymoon*."

He was right. If it rained again tonight, the children would want to sleep with them again. They might want to sleep with them even if it didn't rain. She turned on her side and stroked his face. "I missed you last night, too, hon."

"I will take the girls home, after they get out of the water. Then you and I can spend the remainder of the day together."

"What about having the children over?"

He knew she was *speaking* of their children and grandchildren; that would include Akibeel and *Maria*. But he also knew she *wanted* Charity and Faith, and their children, too. He was going to make that happen for her.

"We can have them over in a couple of days. We can throw a dinner party," he replied and stroked her hair.

Her heart lurched. "That's a wonderful idea, Michael." It would be the first time, in her life, that she had a sit down *dinner,* with family. She never ate dinner with the children at the House, because she was busy serving and cleaning up behind them. At best she nibbled here and there.

"You are going to have a time getting all of this sand out of your hair."

She smiled. He would definitely have to use his powers to get the sand out hers and the children's hair. He just didn't know it yet. Children don't like their hair washed, and they couldn't send them home looking a mess. "You know what I'd like to do, tonight?"

"What's that?"

"Enjoy a cup of coffee and a good movie."

He sighed. "That sounds good."

~

The girls ran up and plopped down on them. "We havin' fun, Grandpa!!" Elizabeth exclaimed. "Can we spend the night again?"

"Please!" Hannah squealed.

Michael's eyes twirled. He growled in Verenda's mind, *"Say something, Ruby!"*

She cracked up laughing. His eyes were twirling so fast, she was getting dizzy. She wanted to let these little ones have their way, but she wouldn't; not this time. Michael's needs and desires were infinitely more important to her.

It had taken her a long time to accept their union. Now that she had, he would always come first.

"You have to go home today," she told them.

They pouted their lips. Hannah folded her arms over her chest. "Why come?"

"Grandpa and I want to prepare a big dinner, for your parents."

"But Cook will do the cooking," Elizabeth replied.

"We can help him," Hannah replied. "He said we can."

"Not this time, sweetheart," Verenda replied. "You have to go home today."

Hannah's eyes started to run. "You don't like us no more, E-li-si?" she said and started crying. Elizabeth was right behind her.

Verenda gasped. Oh my God! What in the world was she going to do? She looked at Michael for help. He seemed to be amused, but didn't say a word. Her husband was going to make her the villain. *"I'm gon' cut you!"*

He chuckled in her mind. Then he tweaked her nipples to give her incentive.

She sat up and pulled both of them in her lap. "E-li-si loves her babies, more than ice cream."

"You do?" Elizabeth asked, and sniffled.

"Of course I do. You girls are much sweeter, and you last longer," she replied and blew a raspberry on their cheeks. "Yum!"

They both giggled and squealed, "E-li-si!"

"But you can't stay tonight. Besides I know your mommy misses you. She'll think you don't love her if you don't come home."

"Okay," Hannah replied. "When can we come back?"

"In two days, with your parents," she promised.

~

Chapter XIX

Verenda looked around in awe. She'd never seen or even heard of caverns. In all the travel she'd done with Cappy he never mentioned them. She wondered if he knew they existed. He probably did, but he knew her. In her state of mind, back then, she would've found one to hide in. No buses, cars, or mean spirited people.

Michael stroked her waist. "You would have become a modern day cavewoman?"

"In a minute," she replied, and glanced back at the scene.

There were bridges and waterways, and crystals galore. It looked like a mini city. But there weren't the accompanying noise, or nosey people. She would've felt like the crystal princess. "It is tranquil down here, Michael."

"Yes, it is," he replied. He stroked her hair and pushed it behind her ear. "You are more than a princess, Ruby. You are my Empress. These caves do not compare to your beauty."

She sighed. "How were they formed?"

"They are a natural underground void; that have formed over the millennia. Some of them formed after Father recreated the earth. Some formed after He flooded the earth, with his wrath. Others formed from human excavation. The crystals, in this cave, are formed from the natural elements indigenous to the soil in this region."

"All of the caverns aren't crystal?"

"No. There are limestone caverns, diamond caverns. Tennessee has the most beautiful ruby cavern."

"I'd like to see that."

"We will," he replied.

It surprised her that he hadn't built them a home in Tennessee. That would have been logical since he loved rubies.

"I do not love rubies," he replied to her thoughts. Then he held her face in the palm of his hand. "I love Ruby..." He stroked her lips with his thumb. "I love *you.*"

She closed her eyes, and leaned her face into his palm. His touch made her heart stutter. He was more romantic than she could've imagined. All the years that they'd been together he'd been restrained, emotionless. They'd spent thousands of hours together, over the last forty or fifty years; but it was a business partnership.

She took care of the little future 'spirit' mates, while he watched over his Watchers. At the end of the day they shared coffee, and maybe a movie.

Once a year he took her out to celebrate and to thank her, but even then he was reserved. She was okay with that because he didn't have the, as he called them, pesky emotions humans did.

He always left before, or around bedtime. And it was always formal: *"Have a good night's rest, Verenda."* Who says that? Have a good night, have a good night's sleep, yeah; but a good night's rest? It was too formal.

Then the day came, when *everything* changed. That was the day Smith and Leevearne, and everybody else, bogarted their way into Desiree's suite.

When she thought back on that day she could've heard the change in the tone of his voice; if she'd been listening.

~

They'd gone back to her room, at the House. The heavy load she'd carried, for way too long, had lifted. She'd been so lighthearted, she was giddy. She even teased him about threatening the Walkers, and Watchers.

He sat there, without a glint of a smile, and stared at her. That was the night she really looked at him, and saw him in a different light. She didn't see the angel, she saw the *man*. And he was hers, for the taking. He'd already told her, years ago, that they were mates. All that was required of her was to open up her heart.

In that moment, reality pierced her heart, like cupid's arrow. She loved Smith Walker, and she always would, but she wasn't *in love* with him. She was *in love* with Michael; and she always had been.

She knew he wasn't ever going to make the first move, because she'd put him off for too long. He'd already told her what they were to each other, and the next move was hers.

She leaned over, stroked his cheek and kissed him. His eyes twirled, but he did not move, or reciprocate. She kissed him again, only that time she used her tongue, and gently nudged his lips apart.

He grabbed her hand and pulled away from her. Then he leaned back, in his chair, and stared at her. She thought he was rejecting her, because she had waited too long. She thought he didn't want her anymore, and her eyes watered.

In a husky voice he commanded, *"Do not start something you are not ready to acknowledge. I have waited patiently for you to accept me, as more than your angel. I will continue to patiently wait, until you are ready. But I will not be teased or toyed with, Verenda."*

She, of all people, knew how *that* felt. She rose from her chair, and sat across his lap. *"I'm sorry I made you wait so long, for me to get it together. It took me over forty years to realize I love you. I was too wrapped up in my pain to see that I always have,"* she replied and kissed him, again. *"I love you, Michael."*

When she kissed him that time he responded. Those spirits that he'd held at bay, Passion and Desire, jumped at the opportunity to embody him. And he allowed them to.

"Ruby," he whispered and stroked her cheek.

That was the first time he called her Ruby. That was the first time she saw him go from eight feet, to six feet six.

It was the first time they made love, and...

~

Michael chuckled. "I take you on a trip through the caves, and your mind wanders."

"You were so patient with me."

"Love suffers long," he replied, and kissed her nose. "And I love you."

She wrapped an arm around his waist. "That's all I need."

"Let's keep moving. There is still much to see."

~

The crystals that hung from the top looked like large icicles. The natural light that sparkles off the water was unbelievable.

"Where is the light coming from?"

"From the opening in the cave, that leads to the ocean. Would you like to see it?"

"That would mean I'd have to get in the water, wouldn't it?"

"Of course. But you will be fine, Ruby."

She stopped. "I'm afraid."

"When have I ever let you down?"

"Never."

"I am not those insensitive boys and girls, who threw you in the pool. I will teach you how to hold your breath underwater, first. It is an amazing experience, even for an Angel. Trust me, alright?"

She nodded because she did trust him.

~

He didn't teleport them to the water, because he wanted her to take the first step. When they reached the bottom of the cave, he stepped in first. "See, it is very shallow on this end," he said and reached for her hand.

She looked down. It barely came above his ankles. She accepted his hand and stepped down. It wasn't cold, like she thought it would be. It felt like a sauna. "I can feel vibrations, Michael."

"That is Hell," he said in a matter of fact tone.

"What?"

He laughed. "I am teasing. What you feel is the earth's electromagnetic waves."

"What's that?"

"Like the human body, the earth is made up of matter."

"Dirt," she replied.

"That and other forms of matter. Matter has a

resonate frequency. That is what you feel, Ruby."

"Why can't I feel it at the House? Or even in the Palace?"

"We are below sea level, so we are closer to the source."

"But-"

"Are you stalling, Ruby?"

She laughed. "Yes."

He cracked up laughing. "I told you I would protect you, woman."

~

With each step they took, she felt the water rising, and she panicked. "Michael!"

"It is not rising, Ruby. The floor beneath us is slanting down. I will not take you too far, I promise."

"Okay," she squeaked.

When they reached the point where the water was below her breasts, he stopped. "You comfortable?"

"No," she replied and nervously laughed.

He kissed her forehead, and eased her spirit. "Hold onto my hands, and bend your knees. Hold your head under the water as long as you feel comfortable."

She trusted Michael implicitly, but more importantly he loved her. He loved her too much to do to her what her schoolmates had done. So, she took a deep breath and dunked her head. And came right back up, fighting!!!

Michael chuckled. "I guess you do not trust me after all," he teased.

"Yes, I do, hon."

"How about we do it together? When we go down, keep your eyes on me, alright?"

"Okay."

They squatted at the same time. Her eyes were squeezed shut, and her cheeks puffed with air. If she expelled that air she'd panic. He could feel her nervousness rising; evidently she realized her mistake. He started talking to her.

"Open your eyes and look at me, Ruby."

Her eyes popped open. Her hair was floating under the weight of the water, but his was still intact. She was holding her breath in her mouth, he was smiling...with his mouth *open.* He wasn't talking to her with his mind. His lips were moving...under water. *"How are you doing that?"*

He smiled wider. He knew curiosity would outweigh her fear, and she would relax. "I am the Archangel, remember?"

"Yeah, but you aren't even swallowing the water, Michael."

"Nothing touches, or enters, my body that I do not allow."

"That goes against the laws of nature."

"I was not fashioned for the natural laws of *this* world."

He had not been born, so he didn't have any of the limitations that humans and Watchers had. He didn't have *any* limitations. He was the first Archangel called into existence, and the most powerful. Just like Samjaza had done with Seraphiel; God stopped short of giving him all that He was.

He had every gift that every demon and Watcher had, and then some; including Seraphiel. Although not omniscient, he could send his peepers forth to handle the adversary. Lucifer, and his cronies, had just found out about that heavily guarded tidbit. Unfortunately, Nate found out about them, eons ago.

He sometimes slept, and ate, but that was his choice. He didn't have to do either, but he enjoyed supping with his wife. He enjoyed doing a lot of things with his wife...

~

Verenda was so intrigued she forgot that she was still underwater. She didn't remember until he stood up, and brought her up with him.

"You held your breath for five minutes, Ruby," Michael informed her.

She took a much needed deep breath, and smiled. Michael had deliberately distracted her. "You did that on purpose."

He wrapped his arm around her and vanished.

~

They appeared in the ocean. She looked around and all she saw was water. She panicked and screamed, "Michael!"

Thank God he wasn't Cappy. She wrapped her arms around his head, and tried to climb up his body. "Michael!"

Michael was laughing so hard, he almost let her go. He had never seen a person as afraid of the water, as she was. She was pulling his hair, and although that was uncomfortable, it was funny. He froze her legs, and eased her spirit, just before she kneed him in the groin. Although he didn't have limitations; a knee to the groin was a knee to the groin.

She felt it the minute her legs went numb. She thought she was paralyzed, from the waist down. "I can't feel my legs, Michael!"

"I know," he replied and laughed. "My groin did not want to be introduced to your knee."

She also felt it when Michael eased her spirit, and her body relaxed. She looked around, at all that water, and then at his smiling face. "I'm gon' cut you!"

He leaned back and became sort of a gondola for her spastic body. "Trust *me*, Ruby."

He still had his arm around her waist. He stroked it up and down her back. His lips were twitching. "I am trying to teach you how to swim, woman."

"Why would you do this?"

"I am more powerful than Fear. I cannot allow him to control my wife, Ruby. If allowed, he will have you fearing all sorts of things."

"Okay," she replied. He was right. Those spirits were always just at the edge of her mind. "So what's next?"

"Lay on top of me," he instructed. Once she did, he lowered himself down in the water. "Now practice your arm strokes. Keep in mind I am under you, so you will not sink."

She followed his instruction. At first she was doing it too fast, but she realized that; and slowed down. When she got that down pat, he spread his legs, and allowed room for hers to move. He unfroze them and said, "Paddle your legs up and down, slowly."

She followed his instruction and actually got very comfortable. He had one more step. He eased his body further down in the water, but made sure she could still feel him.

She almost panicked the minute she realized her head was submerged. He squeezed her waist. "I am still under you, Ruby. When you feel the need to breathe, turn your head from side to side. That will allow you the opportunity to take a breath."

She relaxed, and did what he told her to do. *"How awesome is this, Michael."*

"Indeed." He slowly propelled them through the water. When he felt her get totally comfortable, he eased out from up under her. She didn't realize it, because he left the sensation of his form in place.

After she'd been swimming on her own, for a while, he whispered to her, *"Water is heavier than the human body. If you relax, you will always stay afloat, instead of sinking."*

"If you say so," she replied.

"That is a law of nature, you were designed for. If you do not fight the water, it will hold you up."

"If you say so," she repeated.

"I do not say so. Your body does," he replied.

"What do you mean?" she asked.

"I am not under you. You are swimming on your own, Ruby."

Her eyes popped open, she screamed and sank. Straight down!! Something grabbed her leg. She was screaming and thrashing, trying to get loose. Something else yanked her. She was going down, and farther out into the ocean. Fortunately she had the mindset to speak with her mind. *"Michael!"*

Michael swooped down and caught her. He wrapped his arms around her and transported them to their patio.

~

She was coughing and choking, which he expected. But, she was also crying, and he didn't like that. He sat down with her on his lap. Then he expelled the excess water out of her lungs. "I am sorry," he apologized.

"What was that?" she sobbed.

"It was a riptide and an undertow," he replied stoically. "I thought you were ready to stay above it."

"I was until you told me I was swimming on my own," she replied. "But you are right. I can't let fear control me. I'm willing to try again."

"Not today," he replied and kissed the crown of her head. "Let's get showered, and dressed for dinner."

"Okay."

~

Chapter XX

Lucifer slammed Riptide and Undertow against the throne room wall. "What the hell were you thinking?"

"I did what I do. What's the big deal?" Undertow bragged. He almost had her close enough to wrap seaweed around her ankles, and trap her.

"What's the big deal?" Lucifer shouted, and punched him in the face. "What's the big deal?"

Riptide blocked his next punch, and pushed him away from Undertow. "You've been sending demons after her since you found out they were hitched. Michael opened up a can of whoop-ass on every one of them. They've all come back with a piece of him still attached to their incompetent asses. We saw an opportunity and we took it," he shouted. "Your inept ass should be thanking us."

The demons and imps, standing around the wall, shook their heads. Neither of those minor demons had a clue how much trouble they were in. It wasn't about them doing what they did. It was *who* they did it to!

Lucifer was furious. Not once had he instructed any of his vassals to *touch* Michael's woman. Not once! He would antagonize that puppet all day long, but he'd never let them put their hands on her. Because, he knew what would happen if he did. He materialized two fireballs, set on destroy, and threw them at those idiots.

They both vanished...

"Where did they go?" one demon asked.

"They are on the run?" another replied.

"They probably ran back to the ocean," another

added. "They think Lucifer can't get to them there."

Lucifer smirked. Did they think they could escape his wrath? Hell was his dominion, but he could reach out and touch any demon...anywhere; including the ocean. He would destroy them to avoid a visit from Michael.

He reached out to see where those bastards had run to. He was sure they had abandoned their corporal form. But that didn't matter; he could still snatch them back.

Oh damn! They hadn't run after all...

~

Riptide and Undertow found themselves in a strange place. It was darker than Hell, and more ominous. They were different from most other demons. They didn't live in Hell, they lived in the deep. And like fish, their corporal bodies had gills.

They could visit Hell, because the heat produced enough humidity to momentarily sustain them. But this place afforded them no such consideration. They were flopping around on the floor.

"Where are we?" Riptide asked.

"Michael's private dungeon," Reap replied.

Their punishment would be much greater than the Seer's, or even Tempest. None of those demons had physically touched Michael's woman. "You made his woman struggle to breathe. He insists that you know what that feels like."

"For how long?" Riptide asked.

"As long as it pleases him," Reap replied. "But you must realize he enjoys longsuffering." Then he pointed at the three men, and one woman, on the other side of the room. "They touched his woman too," he informed them, and laughed. "They have been here close to fifty years."

This was too painful. Riptide tried to lose his corporal body, but couldn't. And like all other demons he couldn't die. He was gasping. "I...need...hydration!"

Reap materialized a tumbler of water...and took a big gulp. "This *is* refreshing," he antagonized them.

Undertow was trying to crawl over to Reap. If he could get to him he could take that water.

Reap took another gulp. "It is really hydrating too," he said and looked down at Undertow. "You want some?"

"Please!"

Reap poured a little on the floor, but it immediately evaporated. "Oops!" he said and laughed.

~

Chapter XXI

Michael and Ruby were on the patio, enjoying a romantic dinner. Unlike the Watchers, he did not have cursed eyes. He could see both day and night, but night did not impede his vision. He could still see every organism.

When the sky and the atmosphere are pitch, all of creation emits its own light. From human terminology, one might say all objects were infrared.

Scientists, in their quest for knowledge, have tried to explain why certain nocturnal creatures can see at night. They have come up with all types of theories that are plausible, to the human understanding. None are correct, of course; but at least they were interested. He'd like to see them explain *his* ability. He would not mind being a human experiment, just for the amusement of it.

There was no reason for candles tonight, because he was allowing Ruby to see through his eyes.

~

"Everything looks radioactive, Michael," Ruby complained. "Even these oysters are glowing."

His eyes twirled, and he cracked up laughing. "I was trying to set the mood, by going for a romantic atmosphere."

"Ain't nothing romantic about glowing food, hon," she replied. "You gon' have to give me my perfectly normal vision back."

Michael kept laughing, but returned her eyesight to normal. Then he materialized several candles, so that she could see. "Better?"

"Much. Besides, you don't need to set a mood. You are the mood, hon."

"I thought you women like to be romanced."

She reached over and cupped his chin. "Other women yearn for special moments, from their men; that I get naturally from you. They long for that first glance, and that first touch. The feeling they felt the first time they made love." She stroked her thumb across his lips. "I get that from you, every single time."

He nibbled on her thumb. That was about the sexiest thing he ever heard. Of course, he could not take all of the credit. It was those spirits! They'd helped him in a variety of ways.

"So you are saying these oysters were not really necessary?"

She forked one, with her little skinny fork, and offered it to him. She never understood how they became something people eat. They reminded her of a slug. If it wasn't for the red sauce, with the spicy horseradish, she'd never even attempt to eat them.

Besides, she was a chewer. She liked to use her teeth and tongue when she consumed her daily caloric intake. She had to swallow these oysters whole. They slid down her throat like a piece of un-chewed fat meat, or slime.

"No, we didn't need these oysters," she replied and fed him the one on the fork. "How did they become an aphrodisiac anyway?"

Michael swallowed the oyster, while he listened to her thoughts. She was not impressed with this appetizer, at all! He would have to advise Cook, so he would not serve them again.

"You humans believe the amino acids they embody stimulate sex hormones. And the high content of zinc, in their system, produces testosterone."

She smirked. They must already have an abundance of amino acids and zinc; because they didn't need help in that department. "Whatever. It doesn't work for me, Michael."

He cracked up. Then he vanquished the remaining ones. "Dance with me, while we wait on the main course," he said and reached for her hand.

~

He had heard her terrified thoughts, when Undertow and Riptide grabbed her. It had only been a second, but she thought it was much longer. Near death experiences always seemed longer than they were.

Her life had flashed before her eyes, and she thought she was about to die, again. This time she did not want to go. She wanted to stay here with him. In her panic she forgot that he could catch her soul, and put it back.

What did not make sense to him was that weasel knew he would do just that. So why had he sent someone to kill her? Lucifer and all of his emissaries had to know he would never let Ruby die. They should have factored that into their ploy, *before* they decided to hurt her.

They should have also known he would not let them get away with putting their hands on her. Reap was right; he believed in longsuffering when it came to his Ruby.

~

He started the stereo, with his mind. It was an instrumental of one of Sting's all-time greats. He slowed the tempo down, to a slow jam.

Then he wrapped one arm around her, and palmed the side of her face with the other. "I know that you thought I was not aware, you were caught in that undertow."

"It felt like a hand was around my ankle, Michael. For a minute I thought-"

He cut her off with a full and passionate kiss. Then he twirled her around, and started singing; to her mind. He changed the words, just a bit.

"Every breath you take, and every move you make. Every yoke you break, and even while you pray..."

He leaned down and kissed her. *"I'll be watching you..."*

Verenda's heart leaped. She was experiencing so many first moments, with her Archangel. She had never been sung to before. The angelic sound of his voice caused her to sway. It may have been Sting's lyrics, but it was Luther Vandross' voice.

Michael pulled her closer, and rubbed her back.

"Every time you sway, and every word you say. Every single day, and every night you stay..."

"I'll be watching you."

"Oh, can't you see, you belong to me? How my poor heart aches, with every step you take."

~

He stopped singing, but continued to hum out loud. He squeezed her even tighter, almost desperately; and palmed the nape of her neck. His Ruby! His bride!

He hummed, *"Can't you see, you belong to me?"*

~

Verenda fell in love, all over again. She had no idea that it was possible to love Michael more than she already did. Wrapped in his arms, she actually *felt* how much he loved her. His emotions were over the top, and heightened hers.

~

The stars twinkled, in rhythm, to the beat of the music.

Beautiful love birds perched on the banister, and tweeted in harmony with the Archangel's wordless serenade.

Angels leaned over the balcony and witnessed, in awe, the tenderness of this *mighty* warrior!

~

Cook and his staff quietly placed the main course on the patio table. They turned to leave, but paused. They marveled at the way he held her. And the way she held him, too!

Seraphiel had told them how Michael and his bride zoned everyone, and everything, out. They hadn't had a clue.

Those two were so much in love, it hurt to witness their display.

They quietly vanished.

~

Neither Michael nor Ruby noticed *any* of them. The only thing they noticed was the feel of each other's arms. And the desire their arms invoked.

~

Once again, they never got around to eating dinner. Instead, Michael teleported them to their bed; and they made love until the break of dawn.

~

Chapter XXII

Verenda finally got an opportunity to meet Cook's brothers. Like him, they did not go by a Watcher name.

Cook made the introductions. "These are my brothers, Saul, Zacharias, Jacob, Malachi and Isaac. And this is Michael's wife, Verenda."

"Good to meet all of you young men," Verenda greeted them. Then she looked at Cook. "What is your given name?"

"Gideon," he replied, and smiled. "But Cook will do."

"Okay. Who was your father?"

"Our father was not a Fallen," Saul replied.

Verenda frowned and looked at Michael. "What?"

"These young men are only six of the many grandchildren of the Fallen."

"What?"

"They were born before I made the offer."

She looked back at them. They were all very handsome young men. "I thought Yomiel was the youngest?"

"He is. These young men's father did what Seraphiel refused to do. He followed in his father's footsteps, at a young age. He produced these young men before he himself was fifteen."

"What?"

They all nodded.

"Where is their father?" she asked.

"Adabiel killed him," Jacob answered.

"What?"

"Our father attacked his younger brother, and Adabiel killed him for that attack."

That story sounded familiar to Verenda, but she couldn't put her finger on it. She looked at Michael. "Why do I know that story?"

"Their father's brother is Arakiel, Ruby."

"What?" That makes them Faith's nephews, by marriage. They didn't look like Arakiel, though. "Does Arak know?"

Michael shook his head. "Not yet."

"After all of these years?" she asked. "How could he not?"

"Most of the Watchers do not know that there is a next generation. Nate and Kobabiel were the only ones that knew."

"They never told anyone?"

Michael laughed. That was why Nate was afraid of him. "Nate just recently shared it with Seraphiel. Kobabiel has never told a soul."

She liked these young men; it was evident they were hiding out on this island. "Would the Watchers not accept them?"

"Arakiel was bitter, after their father attacked him. There was not much of his flesh left on his bones, when that demon got through with him. It would not have been the time to introduce the sons of the man that attacked him. Adabiel took Arakiel under his wings, to properly train him. These young men are the same age as Arakiel. At the time, they didn't want to meet him either."

"His brother was that much older than him?" she asked.

"Thirteen years."

"Our father was a bully. He made all of us say no to Michael," Saul added.

Her eyes grew. "You all said *no!*"

"They said no, I said yes," Cook replied. "When my brothers saw that I wasn't afraid of our father they said yes too."

His brothers nodded.

"I figured if our father tried anything Michael would protect us," Cook continued. "None of us knew that Adabiel had already taken care of him."

"I don't understand," she said and frowned.

"I'd already made my rounds with the first generation Nephilim. They were my first priority. Their father had already rejected my offer by the time I got back around to them."

"Oh. So are you ready to meet your uncle now?"

"We've actually seen him. He just does not know who we were," Isaac replied.

She remembered Cook saying they were at Brock's and Jodi's wedding. They looked like each other, but not Arakiel. She could only assume that Arakiel looked like his mother. That would mean they all looked like their father. Certainly Arakiel would have noticed the resemblance. "He saw you and didn't know?"

"We mostly stayed in the kitchen, preparing the food," Isaac replied. "Plus, Arakiel and Brock's team were concentrating on Yomiel's wife."

"She knew all about Watchers, before Yomiel even knew about her."

~

Verenda nodded. She and Michael took a seat at the table. She was halfway through her, much needed, breakfast when another thought crossed her mind.

"How will they ever find their 'spirit' mates? It's not like this island has an abundance of travelers?"

Michael smiled. He was glad that she hadn't said that out loud. If she had, it would have required him to respond in kind. *"When the time is right their paths will cross. Since you and I have taken up permanent residence here, they will be getting out, more often."*

"Will they continue to live here?"

"They are more than welcome to continue to reside here. This is their home, Ruby."

"When are you going to introduce them to Arakiel?"

"Soon."

~

After breakfast Verenda and Michael went over their dinner party plans with Cook. Since this was an island, seafood was in abundance. "I'd like to have a fish fry," she informed Cook.

"With potato salad and-" Cook started, but she cut him off.

"Our children are from Indiana. In Indiana, a fish fry ain't a fish fry, without spaghetti."

"What?"

She laughed. Every region had its own preferred side dish with fish. Some liked french-fries, others coleslaw, or potato salad. Some preferred just potato chips. But, not Indiana. "Spaghetti and a salad," she replied.

Cook looked at Michael. He had never heard of that. "I've been on this island too long, man."

Michael chuckled. Then he spoke to his mind and told him how many were coming. "It would be good if you prepared something that the children will like."

"I hadn't thought about that. How about fish sticks and fries," Verenda suggested.

"I can do that," Cook replied.

Chapter XXIII

Michael was sitting in the recliner, in their bedroom. He was watching Ruby go through her daily ritual of getting dressed. It was a monumental task; that he did not understand. He had been with her for years, and nothing had changed. "Why does it take you so long to get dressed, Ruby?" he impatiently asked.

It took him twenty minutes to shower, comb his hair and get dressed. And another minute to put his socks and shoes on. There, done...ready to go!

It took her twenty minutes to shower, an hour to put her makeup on, and three hours to get dressed. That didn't make any sense to him.

She changed from one outfit to another, a dozen times. She always asked him how she looked, in each outfit. He didn't know why she bothered, because he said *lovely* every time. And every time she would change into something else.

And now that they were intimate, she added underclothing to the decision making. He always made her mad with that answer: *"What difference does it make, Ruby? Nobody is going to see them, but me."*

Then it took her another fifteen minutes to decide which cologne to wear, with the outfit she had finally chosen. Humans didn't understand that natural musk smelled better than anything manufactured. Hers was the sweet smell of jasmine.

What amazed him was at the end of her tedious ritual she always looked the same to him. Perfect!!

~

Verenda was listening to his thoughts. She laughed. Men! They were the biggest liars. Their body language told the tale their mouths were too afraid to. It was their way of keeping the peace.

She'd seen women in outfits they had no business owning, let alone wearing. Their husbands would be dressed to the nines, while they looked like they'd been deceived by their husband; *and* the sales clerk. She always wondered to herself why in the world did he let her leave the house looking like *that*.

She decided to mess with her impatient husband. She walked to the door, and braced her hands on both sides of the doorjamb. "How does this look?" she asked innocently.

~

Michael's eyes twirled, and he growled. His wife was stacked. That lace bra and panty set was red, and hot; just like her. She was plus, but not in size.

He knew from years of providing her clothes, that she wore a woman's size twelve. It was the same size she had worn since the day he rescued her. Not an ounce more, or less.

She didn't have the muscles, or six packs, that the Walker children had. And for that he was grateful. Women's bodies weren't meant to be fine-tuned, by protruding muscles. By design, they were supposed to be soft and curvy. Besides, he had enough muscles for both of them.

"Keep that up and you will have to start your ridiculous ritual all over again."

She laughed and walked back into the dressing

room. "I'll be ready in a minute."

"You have been at it for hours, Ruby. Our guests are going to think something else is going on up here."

That was the truth. She slipped her dress over her head and stared in the mirror. Not formal, but not too casual, either. "Here I come," she replied.

This event was more than dinner with their children. It was a dinner party. And she was the host. She walked to the door. "How about this one?" she asked and twirled around.

She was an angelic vision, with a dab of temptress. That red sleeveless dress hugged all the right curves, and flared at the tail. The cowl neck in the front emphasized her beautiful neck. He was tempted to send everybody home, and call the whole dinner off.

He walked over stroked her waist, and leaned in. "We will be getting rid of our children, as *soon* as dinner is over, Ruby," he whispered and kissed her neck.

She stroked his chest with her fingernails. "Behave," she replied.

~

When they reached the bottom of the stairs Verenda's heart leaped. She didn't know why she even bothered with makeup. She'd promised herself she wasn't going to wear it anymore. Now she was looking Goth again.

ALL of the Walker children, and grandchildren, were in her grand ballroom. Every single one of them.

Her eyes immediately fell on Charity, Faith and Maria. It was harder seeing them than she imagined it would be. She wanted them to be her daughters. She wanted her babies back!! She turned into Michael's chest, and sobbed.

He wrapped one arm around her, and tilted her head up. Everyone watched as he tenderly wiped her tears. Then he leaned down and touched his forehead to hers. *"That is not possible, Ruby. They are Leevearne's daughters. You gave them to her,"* he whispered and stroked her back. *"In exchange for me."*

"I know. Why did you invite them, Michael?"

"They begged to come. They want to be a part of your life. All of these children do," he replied and kissed her forehead. *"Should I cancel the affair?"*

"No. But give me a minute to freshen up." She turned and ran back up the stairs.

~

"Is she okay?" Jodi asked. Verenda looked grief-stricken.

"She is a little emotional that *all* of you thought enough of her to come," Michael replied. "She will be fine."

They assumed he meant because of how their mothers and grandmothers felt about her.

Desiree knew better. She and Donnell both knew what had upset her. No doubt Michael told her. She understood, because she had chosen Donnell over motherhood for over twenty-four years. She rubbed her baby bump. "I'll go see about her," she said and moved toward the stairs.

"NO!" Faith shouted. "Let me." She'd seen the way Verenda looked at her, and her sisters. Verenda knew...and so did *they*. The minute Verenda held her hand at Georgia House it had all come rushing back. She told her sisters what she'd remembered.

"Maria and I will go with you," Charity said and handed her son, Malcolm, to Eugene. "It's our mother…"

Desiree snapped around, and cut her off. "What?"

Michael's eyes twirled. He looked at all three of Smith's daughters. He never took the liberty of snooping on them, but he did this time. In fact he blocked their thoughts from everyone in the ballroom, just in case. His eyes twirled, again. They knew…

Charity finished her sentence, "…that *created* this mess. Verenda needs to know that we love her." She stared back at Michael. "She needs to know that my sisters and I *love* her, and don't harbor *any* resentment."

Michael looked at their husbands. Salvador, Akibeel and Arakiel were slightly nodding their heads. They also knew. He looked back at Charity. "Very well, you three young ladies may go. Everyone else enjoy the wine."

~

Verenda was standing on the patio, looking out across the scape. Her face was streaked with black tears, but she didn't care. She was torn up, inside. She hoped Michael didn't think she had any regrets, because she didn't; at least not about him. She'd never trade him for anybody.

She'd made an informed decision. It was either, or. At that point Smith Walker wasn't even part of the equation. She'd already chosen Michael over him. She'd begged for him, in fact.

The choice was between her children and her

Michael. Those two options were all that were put on the table. If she'd chosen her children, Smith would've been part of the package. She could hear the Master say *'Choose you this day.'*

She chose wisely, but life just never seemed to treat her fairly. She sobbed. *'I'll give you this, but you can't have that!' 'If you want him, give them up!'*

Why couldn't she have it *all?* Why couldn't those girls be hers and Michael's? And if she couldn't have it all, why were they in her house; just beyond her motherly reach.

She wanted to renege on her agreement with the Master. She wanted to scream, *'They are mine! Give me back my children! You can't have them, Leevearne!'*

How was she supposed to go back downstairs and smile at them? How was she supposed to go back to the House, and work side by side with Maria? She couldn't do *either.*

A flock of birds were flying overhead. Out of nowhere, a dove landed on the banister, right next to her. She thought about King David. *"If I had wings of a dove I'd fly away, and be at rest."* She held her face, in her hands, and sobbed.

~

Michael walked up behind her, and wrapped his arms around her waist. *"You do not have wings,"* he whispered and kissed the top of her head. *"You cannot run. You cannot hide, on this patio, Ruby."*

She closed her eyes, and leaned her head back on his chest. She wanted him to ease her spirit, but didn't ask. She knew him well enough to know he wouldn't. She had to work through *these* emotions, because they were cleansing. Her tears were only the first stage of her grief. "I just needed a minute, Michael. I wasn't expecting them to be here," she cried.

"You do not have a minute," he replied. "Several young ladies would like to talk with you. They are in our suite."

She turned in his arms and stroked his cheek. "I would still choose you, Michael. No matter what I am twisted up about, I would still choose you. You know that, don't you?"

"I know," he replied. Then he reached out and cleaned her face. "We were destined to be together."

Her eyes clouded again. "I love you so much, it hurts. I would've never been happy, without you."

He palmed the nape of her neck. "I have always loved *you*, Ruby," he whispered, and passionately kissed her. Then he held her hand, and kissed it. "Your visitors are waiting. I will leave you with them," he said, and vanished.

~

When she walked back into her bedroom, her eyes glazed. She had assumed it was Desiree and Jodi, not her... She paused and shook her head, to retrain her thoughts...not these young ladies. But why had they come to see about her?

She put on a faux smile, but refused to meet them eye to eye. She walked over to the dresser, and started fidgeting. "I am sorry for my emotional instability. I am honored you young ladies came."

Faith was the first to speak. "I told you I met you in

Heaven. The minute you held my hands I remembered *everything.* By your response to us, you remember, *too.*" She took an unsure step toward Verenda, but stopped.

Verenda scowled and her eyes ran, but she didn't speak. She didn't look at her either. Guilt was eating her from the inside out. She folded her arms over her chest, to steady herself.

"You didn't just make the decision you made and forget about us," Faith added. "You sat us down, in Heaven, and we talked about it."

Verenda did not remember that part. That revelation forced her to turn around and momentarily gaze at them. They were such beautiful girls. Her tears flowed...

Faith kept talking. "You promised us that somehow you would find us, and make us a part of your life. But you would *not* be our mother."

Verenda moaned, but she didn't say anything. She couldn't. She felt like she had aborted her children, in Heaven. Her mind went to an old song by Eric Clapton, 'Would you know my name, if I saw you in Heaven?' She cried harder.

"We understand, Verenda," Maria told her. "We don't blame you for choosing Michael, over us. We just want to be a part of your life."

Verenda's tears were running so fast, she couldn't see them. She was sobbing and trembling all over.

Charity walked over and put her arms around her. "Shh," she whispered, and stroked her back. "It's *alright*, Mi celestial Madre."

Verenda let out a gut wrenching sob. Charity had just called her 'her heavenly mother'. "I'm so sorry! I'm so sorry! I'm so sorry!" she sobbed.

She was making all three of them cry. Faith and Maria wrapped their arms around her, too. Their actions only made her cry harder. She was a mess. "I loved Michael *so* much, and God made me *choose*," she sobbed. "I asked Him to let me have you girls, too! I begged Him. But, He said no! I'm so sorry, He said no! He said you were Smittie's seed. He said no!"

"We know," Faith replied. "We know, Verenda."

~

Michael hadn't left the room. He stood in the shadows, just in case his wife needed him. It was apparent to him that she was not going to calm down. The girls' kindness seemed to upset her, even more.

He reached out and calmed her spirit. Then he vanished.

~

Chapter XXIV

Everyone seemed to be enjoying themselves. All of them were in awe of the Palace. None of them could believe they were inside the Devil's Triangle.

Cook was doing an excellent job entertaining them. He piped in the music, and some of the couples were slow dancing. Others had ventured out on the beach, with their children. Some were standing around him, engrossed in conversation.

Cook laughed. "I can't believe Seraphiel never told you guys that his island was just a stone's throw away."

"What?" Henry asked.

Brock laughed. "My bad."

"We spent a week in the Bermuda Triangle, man?" Mark asked. He looked at Arak. "Man, why didn't you tell me?"

The Watchers laughed.

Everyone chimed in. It was a good distraction, because no one was wondering what was going on upstairs.

~

The minute Michael appeared, Arakiel asked, *"How are they?"*

"They are talking," Michael replied.

"This is some heavy crap, Michael."

"It is what it is, Arakiel."

"I've been a little miffed with Smittie, but he can't help himself."

"No, he cannot," Michael replied, and his eyes twirled. *"No more than I can. I need to talk with you."*

"Now?"

"Meet me in the kitchen."

~

Brock wanted to know what was going on. He eased up next to Michael. "Can we talk?"

"Later," Michael replied. "I need to talk with you about something anyway."

"Alright," Brock replied and walked away.

~

Desiree was worried. She pulled Michael off to the side. "What is going on up there? Are they being mean to her?"

"You have known me longer than any human, in this room. Do you think I would allow that, Desiree? Ruby is my wife. She is just as important to me, as you are to Donnell."

She heard the reprimand in his voice. "I'm worried about her, that's all. Can I go up there?"

"No. *Ruby needs to talk to her children.*"

Desiree felt a pinch of jealousy. She wanted them to like her mother, not steal her. *"Her children? What the hell am I?"*

"You are the one she chose, Desiree. They are the ones she forsook. She needs to find peace with the fact that she gave them away, for me. She needs to come to grips with the fact that she forgot them. You cannot help her with that. They can."

That was a fact, but Desiree was still jealous. Verenda would shower those girls, with affection; just like she'd done her. Only with these girls guilt would make Verenda desperately cling to them. She wanted to cry, because she felt like she was losing another mother.

"Ruby will always love you, Desiree. Love abounds. You will have to learn how to share your mother."

He walked away from her, toward the kitchen. Then he thought better about it. "Arakiel," he called out.

Arak was about to walk into the kitchen area. He turned around. "Yeah."

"Come with me," he replied. "Let us step outside."

They walked out the front door.

~

When they reached the walk-way Michael leaned against one of the glass poles. "You are not aware that your brother fathered sons, before he rejected my offer," he blatantly said.

"Adriel had sons?" Arakiel had never heard that before.

"He had six sons, to be exact."

"Why are you telling me this, Michael? And why has it taken you so long, to tell me?"

"You were not ready to hear it."

"Are they in hell, with that bastard?" This brought back unbearable memories. When his brother found out he'd chosen Michael's side, he tried to kill him, and would've; if not for Adabiel. Afterward, Adabiel put all he had into training him, and his brothers.

Then Michael stepped up and trained him on how to strategize. There were none as prolific as him, because he'd learned from the master.

"They are not in hell, Arakiel. They chose our team," Michael replied.

"Where are they? Why have I never crossed their paths?"

"You were just talking with one of them,"

Arak frowned. "Cook?"

"And his brothers are in the kitchen."

"Man, they've been here all of this time?"

"They've lain low, because they were afraid to meet you."

"They are all domestic?"

"None of them are. They are Watchers, Arakiel. This island, Bermuda and the Florida coast is their territory. Your father creates a lot of havoc on these waters."

"Tempest!"

"Yes. Do whatever you want with the information I have provided. I just thought it was time you knew you had family."

Arakiel shook his head. "There have been a lot of revelations here today."

"Indeed."

Michael did not ask him what he was going to do. That was up to him. He could either forge a relationship with them, or brush it under the rug. The choice was his.

~

Arak walked back in the dance hall and stared at Cook. When he got his attention he tilted his head and diverted his eyes towards the kitchen and back.

Cook slightly nodded and exited the room.

~

The six brothers were leaning against the kitchen counter with their arms crossed. They'd wanted to meet their uncle, but thought he would not want to meet them.

Michael had informed Cook that he'd be here. He left it up to them as to whether they were finally ready to meet him. They were.

Arakiel walked in the kitchen carrying his son. Lil Smittie was big for his age, thanks to his parents. He stared at his six nephews. He didn't know how he hadn't seen it before. They all looked just...like...his...father! The bastard!

He extended his hand, and smiled. "I'm Arakiel, your uncle. This is your cousin, Smith."

All of them smiled back, shook his hand; and told him their names.

"Your son is a handsome boy," Jacob said and reached for him. Smith went right to him. "Heavy too!" he added.

"So you guys know how to fight?" Arak asked.

"Michael taught us," Cook replied.

Arak laughed. "I'd say that's a yes!"

They all laughed.

~

They stood around the kitchen getting acquainted. They told Arak how ruthless their father had been to them.

"His friends weren't any better," Isaac told him. "He let them attack us all the time."

Arak got angry. "I'd love to see that bastard now!"

"You and me both," Cook replied. "But I'm glad to finally meet you, Arak."

"I am too. It's good to know I have family, that chose the right side," he told them. "Listen, there are things going on here today. It may take a minute for things to level out. After everything settles down, in a few days, I'd like to introduce you guys to my wife, and team."

"We'd like that," Malachi replied.

~

Chapter XXV

The only reason Verenda wasn't crying was because Michael had eased her spirit. She and *Leevearne's* daughters were sitting on the patio. She wanted to learn as much as she could about them. She brushed her hair behind her ear. "Did you girls have a happy childhood?"

Charity smiled. "We had a very good childhood. I was an only child for a long time. After our parents lost my little brother-"

"Oh God," Verenda sobbed. *Her son.*

Maria saw that she was getting upset and decided to make light. "Then came the zombie," she said and laughed.

Verenda knew what Faith's youth had been like. After she'd had her anxiety attack at the house, Michael told her all about it. Faith of all people knew how she felt. She'd given up a part of her mind, because of her need for Arakiel. She looked at Faith and smiled.

Faith reached for her hand. "The heart wants what the heart wants."

"I wanted you girls too," Verenda replied. "I'll never understand why I couldn't have it all."

"You made sure that since you couldn't be our mother we got a good one," Charity informed her. "Leevearne may be acting out, at the moment, but she was a good mother to all of us."

"She is off the reservation, that's for sure," Maria added. "I still can't believe she was going to slap me. She has never hit me in my life."

"Don't be hard on her," Verenda told them. "She

doesn't remember, but she jumped at the opportunity to be you girls' mother."

"She jumped at the opportunity to be Daddy's soul mate," Faith added. "We were part of the package."

Verenda didn't like their attitude towards Leevearne. That woman had done what she refused to do. "You girls are not being fair to your mother."

"That's not true," Faith replied. "We *were* part of the package. Just like we *weren't* part of Michael's package. The choice in both of your cases was your husbands."

"It is not a slight, Verenda," Charity added. "It is what it is. It wasn't that you didn't want us. You didn't want *Daddy*. You wanted Michael. Momma knew that to get Daddy, she had to take us."

"You girls make it sound cold, and it wasn't. Your mother was excited to know that she was going to have a family. She walked around Heaven smiling for days. She did not want to be a nun."

"A nun?" they all asked.

"That's right. Her lot was to be a nun," Verenda replied and laughed. Leevearne was too sexy to walk around in a nun's bulky robe. Her hair was too thick and gorgeous to be hidden under a habit. "She was upset because she didn't want to be a nun. She loved your father, much more than I did. And even if that meant it was a package, she loved you girls."

"We know that," Faith replied. "And we adore her."

Her sisters nodded.

"But we want to know how we fit in your life?" Maria said.

"We want to be a part of it," Charity added.

"I'd like that more than anything, but not at the cost of your relationship with your mother," Verenda replied. "She already feels like I'm trying to steal her family, and she is right. Not about your father, but I'd love to reclaim you girls. My heart hurts from wanting you to be mine, but that is not going to happen."

"So you won't even be our friend?" Charity asked.

"No. Not until your mother is okay with us having a relationship."

It was their turn to cry, and all of their eyes watered. They could not believe her. They'd seen her tears. They knew how she felt about them. Why would she do this to them? They wanted to get to know her. They wanted to be a part of her life. This was unbelievable.

"You are abandoning us again?" Maria asked.

"Not at all," Verenda replied. She couldn't believe the words that were coming out of her mouth. She wanted to grabbed these girls up and keep them here, in Devil's Triangle, for all eternity. "You girls are important to me, and I'll always wonder what could have been. I want to be a part of your lives. I want to know your children. But I won't be the source of contention between you and your mother; or your father and your mother. They deserve better than that, and you girls know I am right."

"What about us working at Georgia House?" Faith asked. She was going to teach the children art classes.

"There's no need for you girls to ever come back to the House. I have decided to let the children go to school at the estate."

"When did you decide that?" Maria asked.

Verenda smiled. She knew what they were thinking. They thought she'd just decided that, and she was honestly glad that they were wrong. "Before we left Satariel's property," she replied. "I saw how much fun they were having, playing outside. They cannot do that at the House. I planned on discussing it with their mothers. If they agree, which I am sure they will, I plan on asking Akibeel and Donnell to transport them back and forth."

She made a valid point, and they all accepted it. The estate had plenty of space for classrooms. In the end it was about preparing the little 'spirit' mates. However, they still wanted to be a part of her life.

"What if Momma never gets comfortable with you?" Faith asked.

"We'll pray that is not the case," Verenda replied.

Then she stood up. "I have a house full of guests, downstairs. Shall we go?" she asked.

"Before we go down, will you ask Michael to open up a private link between all of us?" Maria asked. "I want to talk with you sometime."

"He has already done that, sweetheart," Verenda replied to all of their minds.

~

The minute they descended the stairs, Hannah and Elizabeth ran toward her.

"E-li-si!" they shouted.

"There are my babies," she replied and picked them up.

They kissed her cheek. "Can we take our cousins to our room?" Hannah asked.

"Pretty please," Elizabeth added.

~

Verenda laughed. The twins wanted to show off to their cousins. Justina and all the other little girls were standing in front of her, waiting on an answer. Michael said only their children and grandchildren were welcome to spend the night. Yeah right! She'd love to hear him tell these girls no to anything. She could envision a slumber party happening here, and she was all for that. "Yes, you may. Just be careful, okay," she replied and sat them back down on the floor.

They all ran toward the stairs. Jon and Jas went right along with them. It was so sweet, the bigger cousins were carrying the smaller ones; even Joy was going with them.

~

Desiree hugged Verenda. "Are you alright?"

"Yes, baby," she replied, and kissed her temple. "Your momma's fine. I just needed a few minutes."

She immediately noticed the looks on Charity's, Faith's and Maria's faces. It was a combination of rejection and jealousy.

Lord, have mercy. She'd spent her life with no children, of her own. Then she fell head over heels for Desiree, and she became her baby. Now she had three other daughters; that she'd turned her back on.

She made up her mind that she was going to find a way for those girls to be in her life. She'd find a way, even if it meant groveling to Leevearne. She could do that easily for the sake of her daughters. When Desiree walked away, she whispered to their minds, *"Introduce me to my grandsons."*

They all perked up.

~

The ballroom was filled with round formally dressed tables. Michael had taken care of everything. He knew how torn she was. He made sure she would not have to make a choice of which daughters to sit with.

Each table had a maximum of six chairs. Most of the couples had a table for themselves, and their children.

The couples who didn't have children, were seated with their siblings. The couples who didn't have siblings, were seated with their closest friends.

That meant Charity, Faith, Maria and their husbands were at a table together. It also meant Desiree and Donnell were at a table with Kwanita and Doc.

She and Michael were at a table with Seraphiel and Jodi, and their four little ones. That was perfect, because no one questioned Michael seating his son next to him.

~

Michael laid his arm across Ruby's lap. *"You feel better?"*

She squeezed his hand. *"I love you, Michael."*

"That is not what I asked. Do not hide your feelings from me."

"No," she replied honestly. *"But can we talk about it later, hon?"*

"Yes," he replied. Then he leaned over and kissed her neck. *"We will work it out together."*

She stroked his chin. She wouldn't give him up for anybody.

~

No one was ready to leave, but Michael gave them

all a feeling of *needing* to leave. They all hugged Verenda and told her they had a good time. Charity, Faith and Maria all hugged her, and whispered to her mind, *"We'll work on Momma."*

Desiree hugged her with desperation. Verenda whispered to her mind, *"No one will replace you in my heart."*

~

Seraphiel and his family were the last to leave. The twins jumped in Verenda's arms. "Can we spend the night?" Elizabeth asked.

"No," Brock answered. "You girls cannot spend the night."

Hannah pouted her lips. "Meanie!"

Michael laughed.

"Don't encourage her, Michael," Brock chided him. He handed Eunice to Aurellia, and reached for the twins. "Behave yourself, Hannah. I said you can't stay. Now tell Grandpa and E-li-si good bye."

She and Elizabeth wrapped an arm around Brock's neck. "Bye," they both said.

"I had a wonderful time, Verenda," Jodi said and hugged her.

"I'm so glad you all came," Verenda replied. She felt immensely blessed.

"We will talk soon, Michael?" Brock asked.

"As soon as we get back, son," Michael replied.

Brock and his family vanished.

~

Michael wrapped his arm around Ruby. "How about coffee?"

"That sounds good, hon."

~

Chapter XXVI

Verenda put on a pot of coffee, and then changed into her nightgown and robe. They decided to sit on the patio, and enjoy the ocean breeze. This day had been emotionally draining for her, and she was glad it was over.

She'd heard Seraphiel say that you don't love with your actual heart, but your brain. If that was true, why was her heart so heavy?

She held her coffee cup with both hands, and gazed across the scape. Her mind was definitely not on the moment, or Michael.

"What would you like to do about those young ladies," Michael asked.

She didn't hear him. She just kept staring across the ocean. In spite of the circumstances, she still felt immensely blessed. She'd abandoned them before they were born; yet they still wanted her in their lives. She would find a way. She had to.

She started to verbalize in her mind what she would say. *"I don't want to steal your children, Leevearne. I just want to be a part of their lives."* She would get down on her knees and beg, if she had to. She'd surrender authority over her life to Leevearne, if she allowed her just a little time.

Michael grunted.

That got her attention. She stroked his arm. "What's wrong, hon?"

"You will not grovel to Leevearne, or anyone else, Ruby."

For a man who didn't embrace negative spirits; his

voice was unbelievably harsh. "I will if it means I can spend time with those girls."

"You are my wife. I thought you understood what that entailed. If demon spirits sense you bowing down, they will see it as a *weakness*; and use it against you."

He was right, just like he had been about swimming. But she had to do something. "I can't abandon them again, Michael."

"I do not intend on letting that happen, but you will not gain access to them by begging. Those young ladies are grown and can befriend whomever they choose. They have the same free will that you *and* Leevearne have, Ruby."

"It's not about free will. It's about maintaining the peace."

"You have never cared what Leevearne thought of you, in the past. You never cared what any of them thought about you."

"I still don't," she replied. She didn't care what anybody thought of her, besides him. Well, maybe Seraphiel, but no one else. However, this wasn't about her. "I'm not concerned with what Leevearne thinks of *me*. My concern is how she will treat her daughters, if they forge a relationship with me. She already feels like I'm trying to take her children."

"That is her issue, not yours."

"It may be her issue but it affects all of us, Michael. You can't tell me it didn't bother you that Floyd did not come see us off."

"It did," he admitted. "I had already spoken with him, so I understand why he did not come."

"It's not right," she replied. "Her hatred for me is like a *virus*. It is spreading and affecting everyone at the estate. I get that she resents me, and I was okay with it; until I found out the truth. She used to love me, Michael. I've got to find a way to make amends."

"You have done nothing to make amends for. You have already apologized for attacking her when you were girls. Your marrying me should have let her know you are not interested in her husband. I do not know what else you can do. Truthfully I think you will be wasting your time and energy."

"Why?"

"Look at how she has responded to you and Smith. Imagine her possessiveness when she finds out about those young ladies."

She laughed out loud, and it was genuine. "She'll probably say *'you can have Smith Walker, but you keep your damn hands off mi hijas!'*"

Michael laughed, too. "You are probably right."

"What am I going to do, Michael?"

His eyes twirled. "I can wipe your memory. I can wipe the girls' memory, too."

She was vigorously shaking her head. "No. No. No."

"It would make it easy on everybody."

"That is true, but I need to remember..." she replied and squeezed his hand "...when I first loved you. I need to remember the promise we made."

She leaned in and stroked his cheek. "I need to remember that God gave us his blessings; not from your lips, but from my memory."

He palmed her hand. "Very well, but trust me, Ruby; everything always works out the way it should."

She nodded. "You know what I'd like to do?"

His eyes twirled.

"Not that," she said and laughed. "Well yeah, that too, but not right now."

"What would you like to do?"

"I'd like to take a walk. I haven't seen the entire island."

He stood up and reached for her hand. "Let's take a walk then."

"I need to put some clothes on first."

His eyes twirled again. "No, you do not. No one is on the island but us."

"What about Cook?"

"He and his brothers are out for the night. They left right after the dinner party."

She thought he would teleport them, but he didn't. He took her literally. They walked down the stairs, and out the door.

~

Deeper in the island, the various paths were lined with orange, lemon, lime, pear, kiwi, fig and even apple trees. The sun hadn't quite gone down yet. Its rays beamed through the glades like hazy *prisms*. She felt like she was walking through the Garden of Eden.

She looked up at him and said, "I can eat everything, but the apples, right."

He laughed. Humans were so amusing. What they did not know they made up, and it became the gospel. In 1470 the artist Hugo Van Der Goes painted a picture of his vision of the Garden of Eden. In the painting Eve was reaching up, and her hand was wrapped around an apple. From that day to this one, humans equated the apple to the forbidden fruit.

That did not make sense to him. If the apple was the forbidden fruit why was it available now? Why the phrase 'an apple a day keeps the doctor away'? Why was apple juice a favorite amongst young mothers, to give their toddlers? And why is the apple pie called 'America's pie'?

A businessman even named his company "Apple". The logo is an apple, and it has a bite out of it. If they truly believed the apple was the forbidden fruit, was that logo representative of them thumbing their noses at the Master? Were they saying they were as smart as Him? If they were, shame on them.

The duality of the human mind was contemptuous, especially in America. They boast of their motto 'in God We Trust'. They put it on their coins, and paper money. They sing in patriotic stanzas "God Bless America. Stand beside her, and guide her." Yet, they willfully *outlawed* prayer in school.

The claim they are one nation, under God, but they are divided by class. They boldly constitute that they hold the truths to be self-evident, that all men are created equal, but prejudices are commonplace.

Their need to commune with the Master is tempered by their fears, of the latest catastrophic event. They test the Master's patience, on every hand. But, the Master loved them, and he did too; especially the one standing in front of him.

~

He reached up and plucked an apple off the tree, and offered it to her. "Taste," he finally replied.

She wrapped her hands around his and bit into the apple. Then she moaned. It was juicy like a peach, grainy like a pear, and as sweet as pineapple. She licked her lips. It tasted like a fruit salad, wrapped inside an apple skin. "It's like nothing I've ever tasted, Michael. Taste it."

"I told you, you were a temptress," he said and took a bite. Then he deviously smiled. Just like in the Garden of Eden he'd taken a bite *after* the woman. The minute he swallowed, he chuckled. "Were your eyes opened?" he asked, and cracked up laughing.

"Ha ha!" she replied, and took another bite. "We've gotta take some of these home."

"This *is* home, Ruby," he replied and leaned against the tree.

She loved this place, and her Michael. She could spend the rest of her life on their island, so long as he was here. Their children could visit. *All of their children.*

He was right; Charity, Faith and Maria were grown women. There was not going to be a custody battle. If they wanted to be in her life, they had every right to be.

She walked up closer to him. "Are we never going back to Indiana?"

"Of course we are," he replied. "I am committed to the little 'spirit' mates, and so are you. But your days of working long hours are over."

"I enjoy the children, but I enjoy our time more," she replied and rubbed up against him. "Especially, when we're alone."

"Now you are just being greedy," he replied and cupped her hips. He was too, though. He loved how she freely gave herself to him even though, more often than not, it was too intense for her. He needed to work on teaching those spirits moderation. But not right now.

His eyes twirled. "Temptress," he added and pulled her closer. With his mind he vanquished her robe. The black, and magenta, laced nightgown gave him a tantalizing glimpse of her smooth tawny cleavage. But a glimpse was not enough.

He pulled the spaghetti straps off her shoulders, and smiled. "Definitely a temptress," he whispered, and wrapped one arm around her. He leaned down and ran his tongue across her neck, and kissed it. *"Sweeter than that apple,"* he whispered to her mind. *"And just as tempting."*

One touch was all it took. Her breathing labored, and she swayed in his arms. She wrapped her arm around his back for support. *"We are outside, Michael. We're going to get caught,"* she replied, but didn't try and stop him.

"We are on our private island," he responded, and kept suckling her neck. Then he vanquished her gown.

"I know, but what if Cook comes back?" she asked.

Michael chuckled and cupped her breast. *"This from a woman who wants to join the Mile High club?"*

Her stomach was bunching, like his always did when she touched him. *"Yes,"* she replied breathlessly.

He ran his hand down her stomach and stroked her. *"Are you sure you want me to stop?"*

"Ooooo," she moaned. Dang if he didn't just hit the right spot. She quivered and her womb clinched. There

was no turning back now. *"You play dirty."*

"It is your fault," he replied, and nibbled her neck. *"You wore that gown to shamelessly entrap those spirits in me, Ruby. I think you love Desire and Passion more than you love me,"* he teased.

"It's a package deal, hon. You need them." She really didn't want to get caught. *"Let's go back inside,"* she suggested.

"No," he replied and kept stroking her. *"No one is here, but us."*

She moaned, but she still wasn't comfortable. She reached down and grabbed his wrist. *"What if someone teleports in, Michael?"* she asked and then trembled.

He leaned down further and suckled her nipple. *"No one will."*

She felt like she imagined Eve felt, in the Garden. Michael was the fruit, and their entire surroundings was the garden. And just like Eve the temptation was too great, for her not to yield to it.

Out of nowhere the thought of getting caught heightened Desire, in her too. That spirit had no filters, and was unashamedly *freakish!!* She reached down and squeezed his groin. *"You going to make love to me leaning against this tree?"* she asked seductively.

"Right here," he replied and continued to tease her womb.

"Then remove your clothes," she replied and scraped her fingernail over the bulge in pants.

He vanquished his clothes. The heat from her hand made him jump and groan. She groaned right along with him.

He leaned further back against the tree and lifted her off the ground. She wrapped her legs around his waist and palmed his cheeks. She kissed him and whispered, *"Stallion,"* as he gently slid into her womb.

Michael held her up by her hips and made the most decadent love to her, against the tree. In the garden!

~

Chapter XXVII

Michael was in the kitchen, meeting with Cook. They were discussing Lucifer's menacing ploys. That weasel had plans on bringing the house down.

He'd put up a cone, so Ruby would not hear what was going on. "No doubt he is planning to ramp up his ploys, in the next few days," he told him.

"No worries. We will keep our eyes open," Cook replied. Then he asked, "Is he not aware of *your* plans, if he keeps acting up?"

"I have given him plenty of warnings." Michael replied. "If he is not aware, he will find out soon enough."

~

Verenda was in their bedroom, absentmindedly packing her suitcases. Their honeymoon was over, and it was time to go back to the House. As much as she loved her little 'spirit' mates, she wasn't ready to go.

She'd thought the Walker women acted like aristocrats, because all they did was sit around the estate. Now that she had her palace she understood them more.

Before the state took her from her parents, they were homeless. They lived from one abandoned house to another.

When she and Cappy were married they lived in an apartment. It was nice, but still an apartment. They didn't need much space, because they traveled three hundred days out of the year.

Michael said Georgia House was her house, but that wasn't true. Georgia House belonged to the 'spirit' mates, both present and future. She was just the house mother.

She had never owned her own home, and she still couldn't believe she did now. A crystal house, to boot! She did not want to go. She wanted to spend her time planting flowers, and working in a rose garden. She wanted to spend her days in shorts, and tee-shirts; making sand hills with her grandchildren.

The more she thought about it, the more depressed she got. She loved her house.

~

Michael walked in the room, and frowned. Suitcases were open on the bed, and bags of shoes were lined up on the platform.

Ruby was in the bathroom, packing her toiletries. He walked to the door and leaned against the doorjamb. "What are you doing, Ruby?"

"Hmm?" she replied.

"Why are you packing?"

"We're leaving today, hon?"

"Only for a few hours," he replied. Then he walked over and stroked her side. "I told you *this* was home."

Her heart leaped. "We're coming back *today?*"

"I told you we are coming back every day, Ruby," he replied and kissed her cheek. "Eventually Deborah Dunson will take over the House on a full time basis. That will leave room for you to not go, if you do not want to."

She leaned her head against his chest and sighed. Michael *had* told her they were coming back every day. She guessed just the thought of leaving, at all, depressed her. "I'll always want to go, but not every day. But, that is too much work for one person."

"With her background, I am sure she can handle it."

"Does she know about 'spirit' mates?"

"Not yet. But she will," he replied.

"How are we going to get her to the House?"

"She is coming to town for your class reunion-"

"What?"

"Your class reunion is coming up. She is coming to town for it. You will get reacquainted with her there."

"I'm not going to no class reunion, Michael! Are you crazy?"

"Yes, you are."

She pulled away from him. "Why would you think I'd want to see any of those people? Deborah was the only friend I ever had. Her experience with them was almost as bad as mine. Why in the world is *she* going?"

She hadn't seen Deborah since they graduated. Both of them were foster children. Deborah's mother died of pneumonia when she was six. Her father died when she was eleven, during open heart surgery.

When she changed schools Deborah did too, because their classmates didn't like her either. Back then there was a stigma associated with being parentless.

It wasn't until she grew up that she realized children picked on parentless children because they were afraid. They knew in their hearts that the same thing could happen to them. So they picked on the ones that reminded them, her in particular, that no one was exempt.

But their town was small and changing schools just gave her a new group of nemesis. They got the same treatment at the new school, because everybody knew everybody.

They were even worse to her. They threatened to

attack her if she got on their bus. She had to walk a mile, to and from school.

~

Deborah was always quiet, and a good person. She got straight A's in school and was extremely religious. Her birth father was a Priest. She had never heard of Priests having wives and children. But Deborah was an Episcopalian.

Deborah never once judged her, but she often told her that her lifestyle was a cry for help. She didn't believe in all that religious crap Deborah spouted.

Where was God when she was being raped, on a nightly basis? Where was He when her foster father beat her to a pulp? Where was He, when that boy threw her into the school swimming pool; and the girl dumped soap and ammonia in behind her? Where was He when the mixture of chlorine and ammonia burned her lungs, and skin?

All those boys and girls had run out the pool area coughing, and left her struggling in the water. Smith Walker had bravely jumped in and saved her...not God! Smith had run, with her in his arms, to the shower stalls. Then he ripped her clothes off, so the burning would stop! He gently flushed her eyes and washed her skin; and wrapped her in a gym towel. He held, and comforted, her until the paramedics arrived.

Then he rode in the ambulance with her, and held her hand the entire time. She had to stay in the hospital overnight, and Smith never left her side.

It was Smith that had saved her life that day, not God! That was the day she first loved him...or so she'd thought.

She didn't believe in God, until the day she killed herself. When she saw all of the angels and demons vying for her soul she knew God was real. But it still begged to question why He had never once helped her.

That was when Michael explained that it wasn't God's fault, but his. He said *he* was the one that was supposed to be keeping an eye on her. He had dropped the ball.

She still remembered the tears that spilled from his eyes, when he apologized. They were a dark *gray*. She'd never seen gray tears before. Somehow in her spirit she understood the color represented his emotions. He was filled with grief. She'd reached up and wiped his eyes and said, *"Don't cry. I'm glad you brought me back."*

He'd held her hand in his and replied, *"I will take care of you, from now on, Verenda. No one will ever hurt you again."*

~

Michael was listening to her thoughts. He spoke to her mind, *"And no one ever has."*

She snapped out of her daydream and looked up at him. He most certainly had taken care of her, from that day to this one. "But, why do you want me to go to that class reunion, Michael? Can't I just invite Deborah to the House?"

"No."

"Why?"

"I have never asked anything of you," he replied. "Other than to take care of the little 'spirit' mates, have I?"

That was the truth. From day one he kept his

promise. He never asked anything of her. He gave her a credit card, with no limit. And just like lottery winners do, when they get that pot of gold, she spent - spent - and spent some more!!

She and Cappy got married on Michael's dime. They even traveled, at Michael's expense. She laid him to rest, with Michael's credit card. Good God, how much more selfish could she have been?

She smiled. "You have never asked me for anything, Michael. I'm sorry."

"For what?"

"For taking you for granted all these years."

He leaned down, kissed her ear and whispered, "You can make it up to me by letting me escort you to your class reunion."

"I don't wanna go," she said, pouted her lips, and stomped her foot. "You just a big ole meanie!"

He was surprised she hadn't said *'I'm gon cut you'*. He cracked up laughing. "I guess Hannah is rubbing off on you."

She laughed. "I guess I'll go. When is it?"

"Thank you," he replied and kissed her again. "In two weeks."

She looked around the bathroom. "I need to put all of these things back where they belong."

"I will help you," he replied and smiled.

Everything, including their clothes was back in its own place.

"Thanks, hon."

He wrapped his arm around her waist and asked, "Did you enjoy our honeymoon?"

She squeezed him. "Yes. And I will enjoy it even more when we get back this evening. I still want you to teach me to swim."

He'd given up on that. It would not be a good idea for her to take a swim, because of those demons. He'd imprisoned the ones who attacked her, but there were millions of Undertows and Riptides. If she learned how to swim she may take it upon herself to swim alone. He couldn't chance that. "I think I will install a swimming pool."

"I'd like that. In a pool I won't have to worry about undercurrents."

He nodded. It pleased him that he did not have to explain why. "Also, my brothers want to know when they can stop by. They want to see the place, and you. We can have a pool gathering."

Her heart leaped. She really liked his brothers. Raphael, Gabriel and Araciel were close to him, but they weren't his inner circle. They were the Archangels right under him, and they had their own circle. Well, Araciel didn't yet, but he would eventually.

Gabriel was over the Nazarites, including James and his brother. Raphael was over the alter-egos, which included Leibada, Nitsuj and Leilazeb. Michael was over the Watchers, and 'spirit' mates. Well, just the 'spirit' mates, now. Seraphiel had been elevated to archangel status, of sort. He was the Ultimate of Ultimate Watchers, and was now over *all* Watchers.

Michael's inner circle was Ariel, Chamuel, Jeremiel, Jophiel, Raguel, and Zadkiel. They each had sanctioned mates, too. But, none of them had claimed their mates.

They, like Michael, had spent years with their women. But like her, their women were holding back on them.

Other than Vicky, they were her closest friends, and she couldn't wait to see them. She knew them in Heaven, but didn't realize it until Michael showed her. They were her friends that had tried to help Barren. One was even closer to her than that, but she hadn't had a clue. Now she looked forward to seeing that one especially.

"Let's plan a soiree for this weekend, Michael."

"Sounds good," he replied. "But you cannot tell them, Ruby. They have to remember on their own."

"You told *me*," she replied.

"That is true, but it is up to their mates to help them remember."

"Did they give up their children too?"

Michael nodded. Then he said, "Are you ready to go to the House?"

She knew that was all he was going to say about it. She never had to ask him what he wanted her to know. If he didn't volunteer the information, she didn't ask. "Yes," she replied and wrapped her arms around his waist. "Oh wait! I forgot to get some seashells. I wanted to give them to the children."

"I have them already," he replied. "They are in our room at the House."

She frowned. "How are we going to explain not having any luggage?"

"No one is at the House."

"What? Where are they?"

"The Walker children have taken them on a field

trip."

"How sweet."

"Let's go," he replied. "I have an appointment with Seraphiel."

"You are going to tell him?"

"Yes," he replied and vanished.

~

Chapter XXVIII

Brock was in the conference room, waiting on Michael to arrive. He assumed this meeting was about what happened with Verenda. He couldn't imagine what had upset her, but her tears had disturbed him.

For Smith's daughters to go upstairs and see about her, only increased the mystery. The way Michael had stared at Charity, Faith and Maria was telling. Had they had a negative thought, and she heard it? Michael always let Verenda hear everything he heard. Of course Verenda was the only one he let hear. He felt it the minute Michael put up the cone to block *him* from hearing their thoughts.

When they returned to the estate he couldn't glean, from their minds, what it was about. He even tried to circumvent Michael's block, by going through those girls' husbands' minds. Once again he was blocked by Michael's rampart. What was he hiding?

It reminded him of how Michael had blocked him from reading Floyd's mind. Something was definitely up.

He wished Michael would hurry up and get there, before he ran himself crazy; with speculation.

~

Michael appeared in the conference room, with his back to Brock; right in front of the coffee pot. He nonchalantly poured himself a cup of coffee. Then he casually walked to the far end of the table, and sat down.

He took a sip of his coffee, and threw up a cone of silence. "Let's talk."

"Okay," Brock replied. Michael looked peculiar. He couldn't put his finger on it, but he was off. "Is this about what happened with Verenda?"

"No," he replied. "But now that you mention it."

~

Brock was flabbergasted. He could not believe what Michael had just told him. That was some *cold* ass, *ruthless* ass, *shit*! He stared at him for the longest time.

His mind automatically went to a song by Johnny Taylor, *'ain't no use in going home. Jody's got your girl and gon.'* It appeared he had a wife name Jodi, *and* a father name Jody! "Man, you *stole* the brotha's woman!"

"You would see it that way, Seraphiel," Michael replied, and chuckled.

Brock grunted. "Ain't no other way to see it." He was thinking it could've just as easily been Jodi that Michael decided *he* wanted. Or any of the Watcher's 'spirit' mates, for that matter. Then what?

Michael was listening to his thoughts. He almost laughed. Seraphiel was tripping, again. They all had beautiful 'spirit' mates, and he had known them all in Heaven; but please...

He cared greatly for Hope, but even she paled, in comparison to Ruby. They all did. Ruby was like fine linen...

"It was not one sided," he informed Brock. "Ruby knew she was supposed to be Smith's mate, but she did not want him. She asked Father for me, *before* I asked for her."

Brock's chin dropped. "What?"

"She did not want him. She still does not. Her only regret is the girls."

Brock furrowed his brows. Verenda's reaction to

Faith and her sisters made sense now. His heart went out to her. "Oh my God, Michael," he replied, and rubbed his face. "Oh my God!"

"Yeah," Michael responded.

"She chose you over them, too? Or did she not know about them, at the time?"

"She knew, and she still chose me."

"And they know, don't they?"

"When Faith came to the House she had a panic attack. Ruby held her hand, to comfort her. The minute Ruby touched her, Faith remembered everything. She told her sisters. They all want to be a part of Ruby's life, but Ruby is worried about Leevearne's reaction."

"That is a problem," Brock replied.

"The problem is Smittie. He has an inkling, too."

"What?"

"He has the feeling that Ruby is his children's mother-"

"What?"

"He knows it is not true, because he was there when all of his children were born. But, he still cannot shake the feeling."

Brock shook his head. "And that is why he can't get over her. He was *supposed* to be with her. Damn!"

"He will always love her, and she him. But he loves Leevearne more, and Ruby loves me more."

"That doesn't bother you, Michael?"

"You said yourself that people have a right to feel what they feel."

Brock chuckled. "I did, but that was just bullshit lip service, man. It was to create peace and settle those people down. I couldn't handle Jodi loving another man. I would kill the bastard."

Michael didn't comment, but he looked guilty. His eyes twirled like they were caught in the wind. He grunted and then he let Brock *see*.

"You didn't?" Brock asked.

Michael grunted again. "Yes, I did. I was tempted to let that bullet hit Smittie's heart, but I repositioned it."

"Damn Michael!" Brock replied and laughed. Michael was more like him than he knew. "Man, you know how the grapevine is on this estate. If one knows, they all know. What are you going to do?"

"The girls will not say anything," Michael replied. "You have already seen that not even you can get through my blockade."

"True that."

Michael crossed his legs. "But I did not come here to talk about Smittie's daughters. I came to talk about *yours*."

Brock's heart hiccupped. "Mine?"

~

Michael waved his hand. The coffee cup floated over to the pot. Once it was refilled it floated back to him. He took a sip and nodded. "Yours. I believe Jodi should be in on this."

"Why?"

"It is about her daughter, as well. She should be a part of any decision that relates to her children."

That was true. He and Jodi never kept secrets where the children were concerned. He sent a shout out. *"Are you busy, Dimples?"*

"Not really," she replied. *"I'm just talking with Aurellia and Deuce. They came to visit Hezekiah and Eunice. What do you need?"*

"Ask them to watch the babies, for a little while. Michael needs you in this meeting, too."

"Really?" That surprised her. She never went to his meetings, that didn't involve all the family. After she pissed Arakiel off during a meeting, years ago, she was banned from any other meetings.

She had been so disruptive Arak shouted at them - her – *'Would everyone please...please let me finish a thought; before jumping in?'*

That was when they realized that, during strategy meetings, even Brock took a backseat to Arakiel. That boy had yelled at Brock *'Shut the damn link down!'* Brock did it too!! Then he put all the women out of the room.

But, now she wondered what Michael wanted with her. Maybe it was about the children spending more time with them. She was more than okay with that.

The girls had come home excited about the time they'd spent with E-li-si. They'd wanted to go right back with Michael. He stared at her and his eyes twirled!! She knew he wanted time with his bride, so she told them they couldn't go. Then she cracked up laughing in his mind.

"What's up, Boo?"

"I don't know. He said he needed to talk to both of us, about the girls. Maybe he wants to set up regular grandpa time."

"Wouldn't that be nice," she replied.

"SnowAnna will have a stroke, if that's what he wants," Brock said and laughed. Jodi, and her sisters,

were giving SnowAnna the cold shoulder. He was thinking about sending the women to his island; and leaving them there until they ironed out their differences. He knew every man at the estate would appreciate that gesture.

"Okay. Give me a minute."

~

Chapter XXIX

"Hey, Michael," Jodi spoke and hugged him.

"Thank you again for allowing me, and Ruby, time with the little ones."

"Anytime," she replied.

"You may not feel that way after this meeting," Michael replied.

She frowned. "Why? They said they had a good time. They didn't want to come home."

"What's going on with our daughters?" Brock asked. His imagination immediately jumped back to that weasel, Lucifer. Had he done something to the girls on the island? Michael had blocked him out for some reason. "What happened to them in the Triangle, Michael?"

"Something happened to them?" Jodi asked. She got nervous and she reached for Brock's hand.

"Nothing happened to your girls. You know I would never allow that."

"Then what is this about?" Brock asked.

"When Samjaza deceived and raped your mother, he had a purpose. It was to create an army to take over Father's throne."

"I know that."

"Samjaza was very focused on obtaining his goal. As you say, you were the first experiment."

"That's true," Brock replied.

"He was watching and saw how powerful you, in the form of his sperm, were. He stopped the flow of his essence just before he gave you all that he was."

"I know that too. What does this have to do with

my daughters, man?"

"You were not watching, son," Michael replied.

"Watching what?"

"Samjaza was using your mother's womb as a lab; you on the other hand were not."

"Of course I wasn't. I was just being conceived."

Michael almost laughed. "Not your mother's womb, son. Jodi's. You did not know at the time that you were just as fertile as Samjaza. You were just making love to your woman, without thought of procreation."

"Oh God!" Jodi replied, and squeezed Brock's hand.

Brock squeezed her hand. That was true. Jodi was pregnant way before either of them planned on her to be. But it wasn't a big deal, because they were mated for life. "So?"

"You should have been paying attention."

"Why?"

"She's a beautiful little girl, but powerful. More powerful than either of you will probably be able to accept."

Jodi grabbed her mouth. "Oh God!" she said again.

Brock trembled. "Who?"

"She was your *first* born, Seraphiel. You gave her *all* that you are."

Brock remembered that he had chided himself about monitoring Adam's powers, but not the girls'. He gripped the table with enough force, the edges snapped. The rumbling in his ears sounded like the buzzing of a swarm of cicadas; being announced by African tribal war drums. He squeaked out..."All?"

"One hundred percent, maybe more." Michael

nodded. "She can reach out and touch somebody with as much power, and force, as you can."

"My baby?" Jodi asked.

"Elizabeth?" Brock added. She was his most kindhearted and easy going child. For the most part, she always behaved herself. Hannah was another story, but Elizabeth?

"Yes," Michael replied. "We were attacked on the island."

"WHAT?" Jodi shouted. "Attacked?"

"WHAT?" Brock echoed, and his eyes turned red. "By who?"

"It wasn't just rain. It was Tempest," Michael calmly replied.

Brock got angry. "Why did you lock me out, man? I knew my daughters were crying for a reason. What the hell's wrong with you?"

"You heard them crying and didn't tell me?" Jodi asked Brock.

Brock didn't respond. He just glared at Michael.

"I locked you out because you would have overreacted; much like you are about to do now. You would have frightened Hannah and Ruby. I was not about to allow that. They thought it was just the storm, but Elizabeth knew better."

"How?" Jodi asked.

"What?"

"She saw through Tempest's façade," Michael replied and laughed. He clapped his hands, and his eyes twirled. "She spanked his...!" He cracked up.

"What?"

"My baby?" Jodi asked again.

Michael let them see for themselves what Elizabeth had done to Tempest.

~

Tempest was in the form of raindrops, and had saturated the window, in their room. Even though she'd never seen rain, she knew he wasn't it. She actually saw his *face* peeking through their window, like a perverted peeping tom. She bitch slapped that bastard, over and over, and knocked him away from the glass.

He tried to run, but she kept kicking his ass, with precision. She was hitting him so hard, *and fast*, he couldn't counterattack, or get away from her. The scene reminded Brock of his fight with his demon brother, Emim. Michael hadn't lied, Elizabeth was just as fast as he was.

She thought her grandpa didn't know the demon was on the island; so she maneuvered him onto her grandpa's patio. She was knocking him around and forcing him to make a noise, so her grandpa would get a clue.

Then she screamed and woke Hannah up. She grabbed her sister's hand and they ran. But, she kept kicking his ass on the patio, so he couldn't escape.

Her tears weren't because she was afraid of Tempest. They were because she was afraid for her sister. If Hannah had seen him, she would have wanted to stand there, and fight it; instead of run to the adults.

She also thought the demon wanted to kidnap her and Hannah, like her daddy's demon brothers had wanted to. She knew her grandpa was more powerful than her father. She knew he would get that demon for trying to take her, and her sister.

She jumped in Michael's arms and screamed *'Look, Grandpa!'* But she still didn't stop beating the hell out of that demon. It was Michael who untangled Tempest from her *wrath!*

Tempest hadn't scared Hannah, Elizabeth's scream had. She was indeed her father's daughter.

~

Brock stared at Michael. He didn't know if he should be upset with him, or not. Michael was justified to not let him in, because he *would* have gone ape crazy, and scared everybody. Not only that, but he would have insisted his children come home. In his heart he knew that would've been wrong too. Nobody could protect his girls, like Michael. Not even him.

Not only that, but he knew demons were always going to be after his girls. Better they experience it while protected by Michael, than wait until they are teenagers. "You didn't know Tempest was on the island, man?"

"Of course I did. Those were not lightning bugs. I was burning him, piece by piece. I just forgot how powerful Elizabeth was," he replied. "And to be truthful she is even more powerful than I thought. I had no idea that she could see the true nature of a disguised demon."

~

Jodi was crying, and her mind was reeling. She thought back to how the twins, as babies, teleported everyone to the preserves to help their father. They had boldly said *'we are our father's daughters.'*

She thought about how they had jumped time, to let her know they were okay; in the future. Hannah had bragged about wanting to drop Elizabeth in Hell. Elizabeth had come back with: *'You tried that. It didn't work out too good for you, did it?'* Hannah had replied: *'You caught me off guard.'* What exactly had Elizabeth *done* to Hannah? And did she do it with her mind?

She thought about what Ali had told Akibeel about him and the demons coming to kidnap the girls: *'Don't get it twisted. Those badass girls would have torn you guys a new one.'*

Aurellia had told her that when Hannah made her and Aurellia invisible, Elizabeth uncloaked them. As far as she knew Brock was the only one able to uncloak a Watcher or demon.

Aurellia had also said Hannah made the bag of popcorn explode all over the room, but Elizabeth cleaned it up with just a thought. She said Elizabeth bragged about being more powerful than Hannah.

Hannah clung to Brock, but Elizabeth was his daughter. His first born. Why hadn't they figured that out?

~

"I have been so afraid for my children," she sobbed. "Lucifer is never going to stop!"

Brock wrapped his arm around her. No doubt this revelation had just reignited her fears, and rightly so. It scared him too. "I'm sorry, Jodi," he said.

"Don't you *dare* apologize to me, Brock," she replied. "For the first time in months I'm *not* afraid!"

He frowned. "What? I'm scared to death, Jodi!"

"Don't you see what just happened?" she asked. "Elizabeth protected herself *and* Hannah. She didn't engage that demon, because she knew it was a *grownup* fight. She was able to keep both of them safe, until she got her grandpa's attention. Don't you see what she did? She pushed that demon in Michael's line of sight!" she said and sobbed again. "She didn't take a risk, Brock. My baby did the *right* thing. She let her grandpa know that they were in danger!"

Brock realized that Jodi had not seen how Elizabeth responded to Night Terror. She'd heard the twins talking but it was so noisy she probably hadn't heard the words. Elizabeth kept assuring Aurellia, *"We'll keep you safe, until Daddy gets here."*

He remembered how animated and vocal Hans had been, while Lizzie was offensively calm. Hannah shouted, *"Watch out for the fire, Lizzie!"* Lizzie's confident response rang, in his ears. *"Don't worry, Hans. I...got...this!"*

His first born was powerful, but she was reasonable, too. She'd held those demons at bay, because she knew the battle wasn't theirs. It was his! And for that he was grateful.

Michael had the right idea to let Jodi witness Elizabeth in action, but still. "She did do the right thing, but I don't want our daughters fighting demons, Jodi."

"I don't either. But demons don't care what we want, do they?" she asked. "They just keep attacking, don't they?"

"I'll always protect them, Jodi."

"I know that, Brock. But they are going to grow up one day. We are not going to be able to shield them forever."

"Yes, I will, Jodi," Brock replied.

"No, you *won't*. You were there when they vanished right out of my arms. You couldn't stop them, and you couldn't trace them. You saw their future selves. They got away from us long enough to get those piercings. They are going to demand their freedom, just like Adam has. I've been so *scared* for them to grow up, because they will *fight* us for their independence. You said yourself that we can't treat our grown children like we do our little ones. One day our little ones will be our grown ones. Then what?"

Everything she said was spot on. He still didn't know how those piercings had happened. He was sure he wouldn't have ever taken his eyes off of his children. Had he gotten complacent, in the future? How in the world had that happened?

Michael heard Brock's thoughts. He hadn't planned on telling them everything, but he might as well. Jodi had taken the news better than he expected; even better than Brock. "I don't know how Hannah was able to get away, but I know how Elizabeth did."

Brock and Jodi both said, "How?"

"When I said Elizabeth is one hundred percent, I meant one hundred percent...*S.e.r.a.p.h.i.e.l.*"

~

Jodi wanted to scream but couldn't, because she was hyperventilating. The sounds coming out of her mouth were short gasps; that were mere hiccups. She was flapping her hands, like they were burning.

Brock had been in a lot of pain when he split himself. He had internal bleeding and went into convulsions. He couldn't walk, talk or see, for weeks. He was the most powerful Watcher in the world, and the pain was still too much. Elizabeth was just a baby! Hers! Her baby would never be able to endure that pain. She was hysterically shouting in her mind, *"Take it! Take it! Take it! Take it!"*

But she wasn't alone…

~

Brock had worried about Adam being able to split himself, but not his daughters. The thought that they could had never once crossed his mind. They weren't Watcher! They were *girls!* What the hell!

This was more terrifying than the possibility of Michael being a Fallen. He couldn't deal with the prospect of his baby experiencing that magnitude of pain.

He was experiencing involuntary contractions in *all* of his muscles. His shoulders were jumping up and down. He was trying to stand up, but neither his arms nor legs would cooperate. His head was bouncing around, like a bobblehead. It looked like he was trying to shake it, in the negative. But his head had a mind of its own and it was trying to nod, in the positive.

Brock was shouting in his mind, *"Hell nawl! Hell nawl!"* But Seraphiel was responding, *"Hell yeah! Hell yeah!"*

He was about to give his own self whiplash.

~

Michael was amused, at their reaction to this revelation. They definitely were not ready to deal with this issue. They both looked like caricatures, or puppets.

First he got his laugh out, and then he wiped their

memories of what he had told them. There was no rush to inform them, because he had already taken Elizabeth's gift. He would try again, at a later date.

~

Brock shook his head. "I can't begin to imagine how they were able to get away from us, Jodi. But now that I am aware that they did, I will make sure it doesn't happen again."

"I think it is important that you give your daughters more exposure. You need to spend time training them, like you did Adam. When Elizabeth saw Cook she was afraid."

"She thought you'd let Tempest in your house?" Brock asked.

Michael nodded.

"I thought I had time, Michael. They are still babies."

"You were just as powerful at their age, Seraphiel. You of all people know age is not an issue," Michael replied. Then he arched his brows. "Neither is gender."

"You're right." Brock nodded. He needed to change his way of thinking. In the past when Watchers had daughters it was no big deal, because they were human. His daughters were the first female Nephilim. He needed to factor that in on his decision making.

Michael was right. It didn't matter that they were just babies. He'd only been a baby the first time he fought his own father. Plus, like him they were cognizant; and even communicated from the womb. In addition, all of his children did what he could *not* do. They protected their mother, by teleporting out of her womb!!!

"I'd like to be involved in their training, Brock," Jodi informed him.

Brock laughed. "So you can beat me up if I'm too hard on them?"

Jodi and Michael laughed. "No, Boo," she replied. "You are their father, and they are Daddy's little girls. I want to make sure you don't hold back. I want to see for myself that my babies will be able to protect themselves. They will be grown before we know it."

Brock smirked. "I am not going to treat them like I treated Adam. They are girls, Jodi."

"Jodi is right, Seraphiel. You have to put all you have into their training," Michael replied.

"I'm not going to beat them up like I did Ad-" he paused and looked sheepishly at Jodi.

"YOU BEAT ADAM UP!!" Jodi shouted.

Michael cracked up laughing. Jodi had her fist balled, and momma wolf was mad. Mothers didn't like anybody hurting their babies, not even their fathers. It was unfortunate that Ruby's mother had been devoid of maternal instinct.

"Answer me, Brock. You beat my baby up?"

Brock sighed and sheepishly replied, "Yeah. See what had hap-"

Jodi popped him in the chest. She had just taken his blood that morning, so she was *strong*. "Bully!" she replied.

Brock wheezed.

Michael rolled. Then he made a suggestion. "Allow me to nurture their talents."

"What?" Jodi asked. If she didn't want Brock to

hurt her babies, she damn sure didn't want Michael to.

"That's a good idea," Brock agreed. "I was too soft on Yomiel, and too hard on Adam. It's evident that I am not a trainer. Michael trained me and not once did I experience a knee in the-" He paused and waited for it...

Jodi punched him again. "You kneed Adam in the groin, Brock!"

"I didn't mean to, Jodi," he replied.

Michael laughed. "He never experienced a busted lip, either."

Brock caught Jodi's fist before she could hit him again. "Thanks a lot, Michael!"

"I can't believe you, Brock!" Jodi complained.

Brock shook his head. He never intended for Jodi to know. He remembered how she'd come to Aurellia's defense, when Dee and her crew came to fight Symphony. His woman would fight for her children, and he loved that about her. "I didn't mean to hurt Adam, Jodi."

She smirked.

Michael kept laughing. He was laughing so hard Jodi and Brock started laughing too.

"Just as I did with Seraphiel, the gifts that are too powerful I will take, for the moment," Michael informed them.

"You held some of Brock's powers back?" Jodi asked.

"It was imperative that I did so. I metered out Seraphiel's more powerful gifts, based on his handling of the weaker ones."

"I wasn't aware of that," Brock replied.

"You thought that I found you sitting on the side of

the road, Seraphiel. But that is not true. I have always monitored your steps. The day Seraphiel proper showed up, for the first time, the Master sent me to you."

Brock's chin dropped. "That was years before I met you."

Michael nodded. Then he said, "I assume the fact that we were under attack has not changed your minds about the children visiting with us."

"Of course not," Jodi replied. "You are still the only person I trust with my girls, besides their father. They love you, and their E-li-si."

"You guys can have them anytime you like, Dad," Brock agreed. He hadn't asked, and Michael hadn't volunteered, but he knew Michael had handled Tempest.

"You are right, son, I did indeed handle him. He will not be a threat to anyone, anytime soon," Michael replied to Brock's thoughts. "Ruby and I would like to have the girls this weekend."

"That's fine," Jodi replied.

Brock nodded. He actually felt good about the girls spending time with Michael. Michael had been a *good* father to him. He knew he'd be no less with the girls. Plus, just like with him, Michael would train them properly. As it stood right now, the only gift *he* wanted them to have was invisibility. Michael would know what to let them keep, and what to withhold. He was grateful that Jodi was onboard. Actually, she was more onboard than he was.

~

Chapter XXX

Verenda went from room to room, inspecting the renovations. Those Walker sons had done an exceptional job. She absolutely loved the computer room. They removed the individual desks and replaced them with long tables. Each table had a desktop computer, for each chair. And as promised the only site available was the Watcher website.

It surprised her that each mother's bedroom had a laptop, as well. Those computers weren't limited to the Watcher website. She needed to discuss that with Nantan.

The game room was her second favorite. It had every game that Nantan had designed; at least the ones that were child friendly. She didn't know that was part of the agreement, but she appreciated it.

The exercise room was equipped with every type of machinery imaginable. Some she'd never even heard of.

The conference room almost mirrored the one at the estate, except it had windows. They replaced her table with a greenish tinted Plexiglas one. They'd added an industrial sized refrigerator, and coffee pot. The pictures they hung were extremely old, and original. No doubt they had come from Seraphiel's collection of fine art.

One picture hanging over the breakfront caught her off guard. It was a profile picture of her and Michael, standing on the stairs, at their palace. She was looking up at him and he was looking down at her, wiping her tears. She knew Faith had drawn it. It made her eyes waters.

They'd redone the mezzanine area too. They'd knocked out walls on both sides, and made it twice as large; and stunning. On both sides of the mezzanine were open bookshelves, sitting in the alcoves.

One side was replete with classic children's books. She saw titles she'd long forgotten about, like a collection of Uncle Ramus books: Br'er Rabbit, Br'er Bear and Br'er Fox. They also had editions of Dick and Jane, Heidi, James and the Giant Peach, and many other titles.

The other side had books for tweens and older teenagers, like Great Expectations, Black Beauty, and Moby Dick. She'd never seen so many books, in her life. There were even modern day vampire and werewolf love stories. They were the ones that made the creatures of the night loveable.

All of the furniture was replaced with heavily cushioned tan leather. The coffee table was lined with bridal magazines. There was nothing subtle about that. It was their intention to get these 'spirit' mates' minds on their future Watchers.

Trees and other plants were everywhere. They even lined the stairs with them. On each side of the stairs they'd replaced the open space with floor to ceiling aquariums. The aquarium hid most of the sitting area upstairs, and the elevator area downstairs. She could only imagine how the little 'spirit' mates responded to those.

~

She made her way downstairs. As promised all of the windows were modernized, with a special tint. The transformation on the first floor was amazing.

What once was a wide open empty space was now filled with sofas, recliners, a coffee station, and plants galore. It didn't look untouchable, but homey; welcoming even.

They'd even updated the guard station. Instead of a plain metal table, they replaced it with a cherry wood round station. Instead of the guards sitting out in the open, they were behind an L shaped glass partition. They'd installed a metal detector and a panic button. It also had a monitoring screen that let them monitor the outside of the building, from all angles.

She'd have to talk with them about that, because the alley was already being monitored by Watchers. She didn't want their actions seen, or caught on camera.

~

Bruce was sitting at the desk. "Hey, Verenda," he spoke. "I didn't know you had made it back."

"Yeah, you were away from your station, when we arrived," she lied. "I was just surveying upstairs. Those children have done a fantastic job, in a week's time. I don't know how I'm going to thank them."

"I know. I've never seen a bunch of young men work so hard. Their pride and focus, on getting it right, should be noted. They didn't slack off, not even for a minute."

"I can tell."

"When they were replacing the windows they brought in a bunch of their friends to stand guard," Bruce informed her.

"Who?" Verenda asked. She did not want those Walker men on her property. That would just create more problems, and make Leevearne resent her even more. "Their fathers?"

"No, ma'am. Hold on, I had them sign in," he

replied and pulled out the log. Then he read off the names, "Chaz, Ram, Arak, Dan, Batman, Ali, Baraq, Adam, Balam and Caim. Donnell and Akibeel came too, and said it was okay for these guys to help."

She breathed a sigh of relief. Of course they would've come. Their wives would've been here, and just as exposed as the children. "That's fine," she assured him. "But why were they needed?"

"Batman practically lived here. He and his father both."

Verenda frowned. She wasn't aware of that, but it made sense.

"And there was a woman that showed up. Her name was Deborah Dunson."

"She was here?"

"Yes, she is a beautiful woman."

"Did she leave her phone number?"

"No. She said that she would see you at the reunion."

She hated that she missed her. That could have been her out from the class reunion.

"Anyway, they ran behind schedule. The fish tanks gave them a headache," he said and laughed. "By the time they started on the windows, the sun was going down. They wanted to have the job complete before you returned."

Verenda looked around and nodded. There were a lot of windows to this building. She could almost see them working in teams to complete the job. "When did they put the windows in?"

"They finished late, last night. They worked

together like a well-oiled machine. I'm telling you, I've never seen anything like it. One of them brought a radio. They were jamming on old school songs," he said and laughed again. "The one they call Ditto had some smooth old school moves. The children were upstairs dancing and having a ball. I even cut a rug."

Verenda laughed.

"Those women cooked nachos and dips for everyone. It was a sho nuff party going on up in here," he said and sighed. "I'm going to miss this place."

Verenda was laughing, but stopped. "What do you mean you are going to miss this place?"

Bruce frowned. He hadn't meant to break it to her like that. "I'm retiring too, Verenda."

"What?"

"Vicky is leaving, and so am I."

"Why?"

"We are leaving, together," he informed her.

Verenda stared at him. "What?"

"We thought you knew we were a couple, everyone else does; even the children."

How did she not know that? Where in the world had she been? "What! How long has this been going on?"

Bruce laughed. "For the last ten years, Verenda."

"You have been dating Vicky for *ten* years!"

"I would have married her years ago, but she wouldn't marry me. She was holding on to her past, like a talisman. It took me ten years to get that woman to see I wasn't her ex-husband."

Verenda knew Vicky had been an abused woman. She'd been forced to kill her husband, in front of the police. The man just wouldn't stop attacking her, even though the police were watching. They hadn't been powerful enough to keep him off of her. He overpowered them, and took *their* guns. One of the guns flew out of his hand and landed at Vicky's feet. She picked it up, pointed and shot! He died instantly.

She never forgave herself for taking a life. Like Akibeel, Georgia House was her self-imposed penance. They both had a desire to give back to society, as payment for their sins. The gesture was nice, and she appreciated the help, but the concept was all wrong. Jesus had already *paid* the ransom, and purchased their sins.

She was thrown aback that Bruce had eased his way into Vicky's heart; right under her nose. "You both can still live here, Bruce."

"We have purchased a home in the country," he replied. "We'll be leaving as soon as you get replacements for both of us."

Before she could respond the front door buzzer went off. She and Bruce both looked up. Bruce smiled and unlocked the door.

~

The little 'spirit' mates ran to her. "Ms. Verenda!" they all shouted.

It was so good to see the children. She leaned down and opened her arms. "Hey, babies!" she replied.

It took her a minute to finish hugging all of the little ones, and their mothers. They were all telling her about all the new and exciting things they'd done, while she was away. Evidently they'd spent a lot of time at Seraphiel's estate.

She'd never heard so much excitement in the mothers' voices. They were going on and on about the spa. All of them had had a makeover and they looked *wonderful*.

"We can't wait to go back," Karen told her.

"What?" Verenda asked. "Not *you?*"

"Yes me!" Karen replied and batted her eyes.

Verenda raised her brows. "What in the world happened to you, while I was gone?" she asked. Karen had been living at the House for the last ten years.

She'd arrived late one night with her four year old daughter, in tow. Her daughter had a lot of cuts and bruises, all over her little body; but she only had bruises on her knuckles. Karen had shoved Lynne in her arms and said, *"I understand you are a shelter?"*

"That's right," Verenda replied. She hadn't asked how she knew about the House, because she was dressed in her police uniform.

"My name is Karen Davenport. This is my baby Lynne. I don't need shelter. I just need a babysitter for a couple of hours."

"For what?"

"My neighbor called nine-one-one, because there was a disturbance at my house. I intercepted the call and rushed home. You see my baby's face? Her father did that to her. I need you to watch her, while I go beat his ass!"

"What!" Verenda had asked.

"I don't want my baby to see me kill her useless, good-for-nothing punk ass, daddy!" Karen replied and stormed out the door. Verenda ran out the door and tried to stop her, but that woman was fast. She'd already taken

off in her cruiser with the lights on, and siren blaring.

She was gone for more than a few hours. Verenda thought for sure she was dead, but she wasn't. She was in jail. She had beaten that man, damn near to death, with her police baton.

She broke both of his knee caps, and one arm. Then she stood over him and beat his ass, with maternal vengeance. She didn't stop until her baton broke. Then she kicked him, over and over. That same neighbor called the police again! When they got there, she was still kicking his worthless ass.

Verenda posted her bail, so that she could be with her daughter. She also took pictures of Lynne to present as evidence, in court. Once the judge saw the pictures, he asked the father why he'd beaten his daughter like that. He said, *'The devil made me do it. He said she had to die, Your Honor.'*

The judge ordered the man to have a psychiatric evaluation. Karen shouted, *"Ain't nothin' wrong with that bastard, that my foot up his ass won't cure!"* They had to hold her back, in the courtroom. She was aiming to kill him, in front of the judge.

She was given probation, forced to take anger management classes, and community service. She'd snarled at the judge, *"I ain't got no damned anger problems, so long as you don't mess with my baby, Your Honor."*

The judge laughed.

Her husband went to jail for child abuse. He also lost all visitation, and custodial, rights.

By law she could have left years ago, but the House

was home. She worked as security during the day, and Bruce was night security. She and her daughter were both happy here, and had no use for the outside world. Verenda was grateful, because Lynne was a 'spirit' mate. She had no doubt Lucifer had indeed told the man to kill the child.

She asked again, "What happened while I was gone?"

Lynne laughed. "Momma got a boyfriend!!"

"Say what?"

Karen blushed. "Shush, Lynne."

All the other mothers laughed, but no one said anything.

The Walker children laughed too, and then they started hugging her; and welcoming her home. While hugging Desiree, Verenda noticed that Maria, Faith and Charity were not in the crowd. Her heart sank. She was looking forward to a few stolen moments with them. But, that was her doing. She had told them they couldn't come back. She was going to fix that.

~

She sent a shout out, *"Hello, girls."*

"Hey, Verenda!!" they all replied.

She could hear the joy in their voices, and see the smiles on their faces. It did her heart good. *"I was wrong when I told your girls don't come to the House. I'm dying to see you."*

"We can't wait to see you, either," Maria replied. *"But you weren't wrong."*

"I wasn't?"

"It's not just Momma's feelings we have to take into consideration," Charity responded.

"I know. We have to consider your father's feelings too."

Charity grunted. *"He's not who I'm talking about."*
"Who?"

"Your other daughter," Maria replied.

Faith laughed. *"That girl has been real snippy, toward us, this last week."*

"Oh Lord," Verenda replied. Ester was right, she'd spoiled Desiree senseless. From the time they'd met each other they were mother and daughter. Even though she was a psychologist, she still had 'left behind' issues. Her response to Ester's planned departure had proven that.

Desiree didn't mind sharing her with the little 'spirit' mates, because they had their own mothers. Not to mention once they found their mates, they moved on.

If they could get cooperation from Leevearne, and Smittie, these three young ladies would *never* leave. Her baby must be about to have an emotional meltdown. *"I'll speak with her about it."*

"Not today. Let her enjoy having you all to herself, right now," Charity told her.

"Call us when everyone leaves. We'll get Arak and Akibeel to bring us to you," Maria informed her.

"Okay, but Michael and I are going back to the island this evening."

"We'll come there," Faith replied.

Verenda laughed, and not in a comical way. *"It feels like we are sneaking around."*

"We are," Charity replied, and laughed.

~

Chapter XXXI

The week had been too hectic for Verenda, and Michael. Shuffling between her chosen daughter and her forsaken daughters, took some maneuvering.

Desiree had showed up at the House, every single day. That wouldn't have been a problem if she'd done her job, but she hadn't. The woman stayed on her heels, like her shadow.

Maria, Faith and Charity had showed up at the Palace, every single night. They had Arakiel, and Akibeel, teleport them to the island, after everyone at the estate was asleep. They stayed late into the night...every night.

They were all vying for her time. It would've been sweet, except Michael did not appreciate them taking up all of her time.

"Those young ladies are infringing on our time," he complained. "I do not intend for the island to have a revolving door policy."

I know, Michael," she replied.

This was their spot. She wanted her children's visits to be often, but not every day. Not only that, but she didn't like sneaking around lying to everybody, especially Desiree. "I'm going to put an end to it, tonight."

"Thank you," he replied, and kissed her. "My brothers would still like to visit."

"I'm sorry we had to put them off. I was looking forward to theirs, and the twins, visit." She stroked his cheek. "Do you want some coffee?"

He lifted her off the floor. "I *want* my wife."

"The girls will be here in less than an hour, hon."

"We have time," he replied and teleported them to their room.

~

They were still lying in the bed when they heard Donnell's shout out. *"We will be there in just a few minutes."*

"Give us fifteen minutes, Donnell,*"* Michael replied, and nibbled Verenda's neck. *"Maybe thirty."*

Donnell chuckled. *"Just let us know when we can come."*

~

Verenda had invited all four of her girls to dinner. Before they arrived, Michael informed her that he would not be joining them. "This issue was between you and your daughters, not me."

"I could use your support," she replied.

"I am not going to be a mediator, Ruby. Desiree's behavior is being driven by the spirit of Selfishness. If I attend I will snatch that spirit out of her."

Verenda laughed. "It's not selfishness, Michael. She's afraid of losing me."

"Selfishness or Fear; they both are negative spirits. She let them in and now they have taken control."

~

Cook was preparing shrimp kabobs, wrapped in bacon. They were skewered with the special apples, from the island, and brushed with a sweet and spicy glaze. They were being served over a bed of wild rice, and a wild green salad. The salad was filled with dried fruits, from the garden; and drenched with pomegranate dressing.

~

Faith, and her sisters, wanted to eat on the patio, in Verenda's bedroom. They were going on and on about how nice it was.

That offended Desiree, because she hadn't seen it. "Michael wouldn't let me come upstairs," she complained. "He told me you needed to talk with *your* daughters."

Verenda sighed. "He was right, baby. It was a conversation I needed to have with them. He didn't mean that you are not my daughter," she replied. Then she reached for her hand. "Our relationship is set in granite, and it is impenetrable, baby. No one will ever take your place, in my heart."

Then she reached for Charity's, Faith's and Maria's hands. "They are the daughters I chose not to give birth to. I love them, just as much as I love you; and I want to be in their lives. My heart is big enough to love four daughters, Desiree."

"You'll forget about me, eventually," Desiree replied. "You just don't know it yet."

"That is not true, lil girl!" Verenda replied. "Your natural mother didn't love your brothers any less when you came along, did she?"

"No, but that's different."

"How?"

"All of us were her *natural* children."

"Do you think Hope loves Jon and Jas less than she does Ruth and Ruben? Has Brock ignored Aurellia, since he has biological children?"

"No, but you feel guilty, Verenda."

"I hope she doesn't," Faith said. "We don't want that. We just want to get to know her."

Maria frowned. "When did you start acting like Lillian? You helped her overcome her selfishness. What did that spirit do, leave her and get into you?"

Desiree didn't respond. Maria was right; she was acting just like Lillian. She shook her head.

"Tell me something," Charity said and reached for Desiree's hand. She squeezed it. "If it were possible for your birthmother to come back would you discard Verenda?"

"Of course not," she replied.

"Why not? I mean after all she's your real mother."

"So is Verenda. She's all I've had for over twenty-four years. I could never stop loving her."

"And you are all she's had for that same amount of time, Desiree," Charity said. "She could no more stop loving you, than we could stop loving Leevearne. One relationship doesn't negate the other."

"Leevearne is our mother. Nothing will ever change that," Maria added. "We just want to know the woman that *should* have been."

"Besides don't think of it as losing your mother. Think of it as gaining three little sisters," Faith added.

"It will be refreshing not being the oldest," Charity added. "You used to *be* a big sister to me, Desiree."

"We've always been family. Our entire family thinks of you, and Donnell, as family members," Maria reminded her. "Your father and Daddy were best friends. Daddy has always felt like you were another one of his daughters."

"That's true," Charity added. "And you know it. I don't remember a single time in our lives that you've been this selfish. What happened to you?"

Faith took up for her. "Some of it is just her hormones. She knows we're family. What did your mother tell you before she died?"

"Find the Walker brothers," Desiree replied. Her eyes watered, because everything they said was true. Her mother had told her that they knew what to do. She'd said *'they will see after you.'* And they had.

Their families had always been close, even when they all lived in Chicago. Once she lost her parents they became hers and Donnell's extended family. All of the Walker brothers became surrogate fathers to her, especially Smith. He felt duty bound to her, because of his close relationship with her father.

They were so accommodating that on holidays they would bar-b-que at *night,* so that Donnell could attend. Of course back then they thought he had the skin disease Polymorphous Light Eruption.

She knew she still had underlying issues. She still remembered the night her mother died. She'd been so young when she experienced all of her immediate family's death. Her biggest fear had been that she was all alone, in this big ole world. She'd been so afraid that she'd resigned herself to letting Rondell kill her. Even though it had only been a nanosecond, that fear took up residency in her heart.

She clung to Verenda, Ester and Dena with every thread of her being. She'd almost lost her mind when Ester tried to leave. It appeared that after twenty-four years, the wounded healer was *still* wounded.

She wiped her eyes. "I'm sorry. You all are right,"

she said. "I just can't handle losing another mother."

"That won't happen, baby," Verenda hugged her. "Your momma will always be here, for you."

~

They were eating dinner, on Verenda's patio. Desiree agreed that it was a good spot. She loved how the butterflies hovered over the plants. "My mother had these plants, when I was a little girl," she told them. "I'd spend hours chasing butterflies."

"That's so cool," Maria replied.

"I put some in a mason jar once, so I could keep them in my room. Madea opened the jar and set them free. They all flew back to the plants. She said, *'Love is not about bondage, Desiree. See what happened when I opened the lid? They flew back to the place that lets them be free to be themselves, didn't they? You have to provide a setting that makes them, and people, want to stay.'* I didn't understand what she meant, until I was bound by Rondell."

"Your mother was very wise," Verenda replied.

"Have you and Donnell decided on a name for your baby?"

"If it's a boy, his name will be William Curtis; after my father and brothers. If it's a girl, her name will be Donna; after *her* father."

"What do you want?"

"A boy. So does Donnell."

"All men want sons," Charity replied. "Sal is still beside himself, over our triplets."

"But he is smitten with Dee," Desiree replied.

"He loves our daughter, for sure. But have you ever

noticed how he looks at Eugene?"

"He swoons, over that clown," Maria replied and laughed.

They all laughed. Sal looked at Eugene like the sun was set on his face.

~

Verenda took them on a tour of the house. Even though Charity, and her sisters, had come every night, they hadn't seen it.

Desiree flipped out over her and Donnell's bedroom. It even had a baby bed for when the baby came. "I love it, Verenda."

When Charity questioned Verenda about her and her sisters, sometimes spending the night, she frowned. Michael had told her only their children would be allowed to spend the night at their home. Yet, there were just enough extra bedrooms, and baby beds galore. That sneak! She loved herself some Michael.

"Michael made sure there were guestrooms for all of our children, and grandchildren. That includes you girls, too," she informed them. "Plus there are rooms for Dee and Aden, and Eugene and Nantan."

All their faces lit up, even Desiree's.

"He did?" Maria asked.

"Yes," Verenda replied. "But it is only for when you *visit*."

Charity laughed. "I guess last week was too much for him."

"Child, that man was pouting," Verenda replied.

"What happened last week?" Desiree asked.

All of their eyes bucked. Faith sheepishly said, "We

were here every night to talk with Verenda."

Desiree pouted her bottom lip. "Now see; y'all ain't right."

They laughed at her.

~

Chapter XXXII

The sun had just gone down below the horizon. The moon was in its new phase, and darkness covered the sky. A breeze swept across the landscape that was so stifling, it hindered one's breath. But the ambience was not one of imminent dread, but exuberance.

The yard was hooded by crystal lights, draped from post to post. They served as awnings, over the meet and greet reception, taking place.

A spotlight shined down, from the main building. A large banner was strung high between two lampposts, in front of the building, at the end of the drive. It read: "THE WAY WE WERE."

~

Men and women from all walks of life had dressed in formal wear, for this affair. They were mingling in the courtyard, of the country club; getting reacquainted. Doctors, Lawyers, School Teachers, Ministers, Small Business owners, Steel workers; and even the unemployed, and retired, had gathered.

Some had come by bus, others by plane. Then there were those that had driven thousands of miles…just for this special occasion. They drove up in their leased Cadillacs, Porches, and other fancy cars.

~

Dozens of valets were on hand. They hustled and bustled about, swiftly moving cars to the parking area at the back of the building. Others stood with flashlights and directed traffic to the garage, for the self-parking drivers.

~

The planning committee had done a spectacular job,

organizing this gala. They'd announced this event in every newspaper, every radio station, and social media, across the country. It was announced from every pulpit, and scrolled across every Christian broadcast network.

They'd even secured a fund for those who weren't in a financial position to attend. They wanted everybody to participate. The lofty and the lowly...the haves and the have nots, had all come. Black, White, Spanish, Jewish, and all other races were in attendance. Liberals, and conservatives, put their political views aside, for this celebration. Even those who had been racist, and militant, back in the day were in the yard.

The committee had spent hours creating and mailing name tags to the expected attendees. And their labor had not been in vain. There were thousands of people present, and everyone was having a grand ole time. The conversations and joyous laughter was deafening, until...

~

The black stretch limo slowly cruised down the cobble driveway. When it pulled up in front of the country club, a resounding hush fell over the courtyard. The men and women that were socializing on all sides of the circular drive stopped, and stared. They all wondered who was behind the tinted glass.

As far as they knew, only one celebrity had emerged from their close knit community; and she was in the crowd. The local political dignitaries had other engagements, and couldn't attend. So who *was* this?

They watched, with anxious curiosity, as the chauffeur walked around the limo; and opened the door...

~

Michael stepped out of the black stretch, with his dark shades on. He was dressed in a black Italian silk tux, with matching bowtie and cummerbund. His classic pleated shirt was a silvery gray, and matched the strap that held his thick mane in place.

He heard the thoughts of everyone in the crowd.

"Who is that?"

"WOW!"

"Do you know him?"

"What class was he in?"

"Did he go to this school?"

"Is he at the right place?"

"Is he black?"

"That's a big dude!"

"He fine!"

"Sweet Chocolate!"

"He could eat crackers in my bed anytime!"

"If he was in my bed he'd be nibbling on more than crackers!"

"Ain't that the truth!"

~

He removed his shades, and handed them to the driver. *"Are you going to hang around?"* he asked.

"If you want me to," Cook replied.

"Please do. Keep an eye out for that weasel's vassals," he instructed.

"No prob," Cook replied. *"You know at an event like this Drunkard is bound to appear."*

"I am aware of that, but these people have free will."

"So you don't want me to hinder him?"

"No. Not him." If he monitored Drunkard, these humans would have no alarm bells. They'd drink until they eventually died of alcohol poisoning.

"Very well," Cook replied. Then he returned to the driver's seat.

~

Michael slid his hands in his pants pockets, and gazed over the top of the limo, at the crowd. He didn't smile, or frown, as he turned completely around, and perused the ones behind him. These were *them*. The heartless men, and women, who had systematically made Ruby's youth unbearable.

Fortunately for them there wasn't a malevolent spirit willing to embody him. However, he hoped they put on their best behavior tonight.

Reap, and his team, were also in the crowd. He invited them to join the party. They all were waiting to reward Sow.

~

All eyes were on Michael. Notwithstanding his mode of transportation, he *looked* like he came from nobility.

He wore privilege, and arrogance, as well as he wore that tailored suit. Charisma *and* ruthlessness snuggled up against him, like kidskin. Although his face was expressionless, he had an old world aura; that exuded supremacy.

None of them recognized him. They all wondered what a man of his distinction was doing at this combined, Hoosier High Schools, Class Reunion.

The men wondered who amongst their classmates

had snagged this caliber of wealth. The women wondered which one of their old classmates snuggled up next to this mysteriously exotic specimen...*every single night!*

He was standing in the gap of the open door, so none of them could see inside. That, of course, was by design...

~

When Michael finished scrutinizing the crowd, he took his hands out of his pockets and buttoned his jacket. Then he stepped back, out of the jamb, stretched his hand forward; inside the limo. "Allow me, Ruby," he offered.

Those standing close by were hypnotized by his suave demeanor, and authoritative voice. Others moved closer, on impulse, to get a glimpse of his companion. They lined the sides of the circular drive, like it was a night at the Oscars.

One group did not advance. They already knew who he was, *and* who was in that limo. They had no idea that they would be here tonight.

~

Verenda accepted Michael's hand, and gracefully exited the limo. She was dressed in a black taffeta formal. The top half had three quarter length sleeves, and was studded with black, and silver, beads. It melded to the smooth surface of her exquisite waist. Then it ever so slightly flared, just below her decadently curved hips.

She wasn't trying to entice anybody, and had dressed down as much as she could. There wasn't a split in the dress to expose her shapely legs, and even the neckline was high; and non-revealing.

She didn't realize that imaginations run wild, when

left to their own devices. She did not know that although the dress exposed nothing, it revealed *everything!*

It heightened the imagination of every single one of those onlookers, men and women alike. It hugged her slender, and splendid tapestry; like the men *wished* they could! They could only imagine what her luscious form looked like, beneath the garment.

Even the women noticed that the dress emphasized her full breasts, tiny waist and perfectly round hips.

There was nothing pretentious about her. She was *simply* elegant.

~

In all of their gawking none of them had looked at her face. When they did they were confused. This vision of loveliness could not be Verenda *Strong!!* She was too refined! She was too damn young! But that mole above her lip said it was indeed her.

All of her old classmates felt *their age.* Their hair was gray, thin or thinning; from constant dying. Hers was thick, black, and richly flowing.

Some had walking canes, or were in wheelchairs. Some of those who were on their own two feet were in flat comfortable, old people, sandals. Others were in orthopedic shoes, designed to ease their corns and bunions. She, on the other hand, had on *four inch heels.*

All of them had telltale signs of age, by the wrinkles, arthritic fingers, and liver spots that plagued their exposed flesh. She was sixty-five, but didn't look a day over thirty-five.

~

Some started to whisper, amongst themselves. "She

must have spent a lot of money on plastic surgery," one whispered.

"That's easy to do if you marry rich," another replied.

"Maybe so, but I ain't mad at her," another one added. "As a matter of fact, I'm happy for her. We were awful to that woman! Every single one of us."

"You're right," someone said, from behind them. They all turned around. "It looks like she got the last laugh, didn't she? She is stunningly beautiful!"

"She always was. That's why we picked on her," another one whispered.

"When I think of the things we did to that girl, I still feel guilty."

"The worst was the swimming pool," someone else reminded them.

"I had no idea that ammonia and chlorine was deadly," yet another voiced. "We almost killed her that day."

"We didn't throw her in," one said defensively.

"True, but we didn't stop it, either," the first one replied. "And we ran out and left her to drown. We were just as guilty."

"But she wouldn't tell the principal that it was us. The meaner we were the nicer she was," one said. "We were wretched teenagers!"

They all nodded.

~

Even the men were whispering.

Link stared at her, while his mind tripped back to yesteryear. He'd had a real thing for that girl. He'd wanted to ask her to go steady, but couldn't. He was the star player, and captain, of the football team. He was too popular to tarnish his rep, by dating only a black girl. So he slept with other girls, and pretended they were her.

Then when she married her *white* husband, he realized he was a coward. He should have stood his ground, and claimed that girl! He'd married, and divorced, five times. None of his marriages worked, because he couldn't get beyond his feelings for that black beauty...Verenda!

The only reason he came to this reunion, and all of the past ones, was to see if she would show. Each time he came he hoped, beyond hope, that she would. He prayed she was divorced, or widowed; so he could finally claim the woman, he'd *always* loved. He shook his head and whispered, "Damn!"

~

"Damn is right," Vaughn replied and rubbed his chin. "She was a foxy chick, back in the day, but who knew she'd blossom into this goddess."

It amazed him that she'd allowed all of them to take advantage of her. They'd all wanted her...and got her. It still bothered him that they walked around with unblemished reputations, while she bore the scarlet letter. Back in those days, double standards was a bitch.

What bothered him more was that she wasn't the only girl that was supposedly easy. Most of the women here had had their share of under-aged sex. Those same girls had labeled Verenda a 'ho', 'tramp', slut; even though they were doing the *same damn thing*. Some of them were pregnant – father unknown – yet, they called Verenda the tramp!

He wasn't in love with her, back then, he just liked her. But, he had no doubt, if given the chance; he could've fallen for her. Now he wished, like nobody's business, he'd taken that chance.

~

Jared was gazing at her with longing. Like all the others standing around, he'd slept with her, too. Her reputation was well known, and they all took advantage of it.

But, she was playful and fun to be around; and he'd really liked that girl. A lot!

He'd had such a strong crush on her, that whenever she came into the lunchroom, or out in the courtyard, he'd leave. He never looked her way, when he exited, because everyone would have known *why* he was leaving.

But, he wasn't the only one that did that. All of the guys she ever slept with would get up and leave. They all wanted that girl, and not as a plaything! They were just immature kids, who cared too much about what others thought of them. That is all except Smith Walker.

That boy was a breed apart. He didn't bow to any trend, or other people's opinions. He would've bet money that Smith and Verenda were soul mates. Even now he still believed they should have been.

He folded his arms across his groin, because she provoked that same old sinful feeling, in him. After all of these years, that was amazing. "I knew," he replied.

"How?" Vaughn asked.

"I've seen her from time to time over the years. She hasn't changed in the last thirty years, man."

"She still *lives* here?" Percy asked. He liked that girl so much, he still had wet dreams about their times together. They were all mean to her, but she was the sweetest girl, in their class. She never had a bad word to say about any of them.

He married his wife because she was the spitting of Verenda. They divorced after a couple years of marriage, because she was like Splenda...an artificial substitute, for the real thing.

Jared nodded. "She runs a women's shelter, called Georgia House."

"Where is it located?" Link asked.

"Downtown."

"Who is that gentlemen with her," Link asked.

"That's her husband," Jared replied. Then he grunted. "They've been together for more than forty years, but just got married, a few weeks ago."

~

None of them had taken their eyes off of her, from the moment she stepped out of the limo. But they turned and stared at him. "How do you know so much?" Link asked. He was a private investigator. She was the only person that neither he nor his team could find. And he'd looked...for years.

Jared never diverted his gaze, from Verenda. He adjusted the collar on his shirt and replied, "Floyd just told me."

~

Reverend Al Green started jacking with Smittie's mind, the minute Verenda stepped out of the limo. *"Hear the whispers of the rain drops, blowing softly...*" He shook his head, and looked away. "*...against my window.*"

~

"I didn't know Michael and Verenda were coming," H said.

"Neither did I," Howard replied.

"None of us knew," Clyde added, and looked sideways at Smith. That boy was torn.

Smittie had told him he thought Verenda was his children's mother. He'd laughed his ass off, and told him he needed some *serious* help. They all were there when the girls were born.

"You mean that's *thee* Michael?" Brown asked.

"Yeah," Floyd replied. "And you know what? I've had *enough* of this mess!!" He stared at his wife, and then his brothers' wives. Then he stared at his brothers. "You guys can keep putting up with foolishness, all you want. I'm going to go speak to my friend, and introduce myself to his wife," he told them, and walked off.

"Wait, Floyd," MeiLi called after him. "I'm going with you."

Her sisters-in-law had been pissed with her ever since she went off on Dee. Floyd hadn't been much better. She knew she was wrong to say it aloud, *before* she said it; but it was in the heat of the moment.

The truth of the matter was she *did* have hard feelings towards Dee. The woman had come to attack her beautiful daughter. What mother wouldn't have a problem with that? Her daughter had been beat on enough to rip a mother's heart to pieces. Why couldn't any of them understand how she felt?

It was going to take a minute for her to embrace Dee, but Verenda hadn't done a thing to her; or her children. "Wait, Floyd," she shouted behind him, again.

"C'mon, Randolph," Betty said and pulled his arm. "I want to meet both of them."

~

"Floyd is right," H agreed. "This nonsense has got to stop. What has Verenda done to you, Snow? Give me one good reason that you have helped tear this family up, over that woman."

SnowAnna bowed her head. The woman hadn't done a thing to her. She'd never even met her. Wolf was right. If she didn't get her act together, she was going to lose her grandchildren.

Elizabeth and Hannah had come back bragging about the fun they'd had with their *E-li-si*, and Grandpa Michael. They were going back to Michael's island, over the weekend. Neither she, nor H was happy about that. Not only was she about to lose them, she was about to make H lose them, as well.

She didn't respond to H. She just reached for his hand and started walking toward the limo.

~

All of the Walker wives did the same thing. H was right. The woman hadn't done a thing to any of them. And what she'd done to Leevearne was over forty years ago. In fact, it was more like fifty years.

Not only that, but all of their children loved that woman. They'd gone to Georgia House every day, this past week. Next week they were going to start taking their children. They were not going to have their babies liking Verenda, more than they liked them!

They also realized something else. There had to be an endearing quality about the woman, for her to have captured Michael's heart.

~

Leevearne reached for Smith's hand. She'd taken to nagging him day and night, about the woman. He'd taken to standing up for Verenda. He claimed none of their problems were Verenda's fault. She didn't see it that way. In her mind, Verenda was the third person in their marriage. If she didn't straighten up she was going to lose him.

Her daughters were infatuated, and obsessed, with Verenda. They hounded her every day about the woman.

They wanted Verenda in their lives, but wouldn't tell her why. They kept saying they'd give her time to adjust, but it was going to happen.

In one of their heated discussions, Faith had almost slipped and told her; but she stopped. Then she said, *"One day you are going to find out what Verenda did for you, Momma! When you do, you are going to regret how mean you've been to her! Mark my words!"*

What did that mean?

~

Smittie didn't take Leevearne's hand. Instead he wrapped his arm around her waist, and kissed her temple. He was trying to reassure her, but *damn* that Al Green. *"Make believe you love me, one more time...for the good times."*

Clyde was right. His sick ass needed some damn help!!

~

Chapter XXXIII

It had been years, but Verenda never forgot a face; especially a hateful one. She couldn't believe the class reunion was not for the school she graduated from. The people in this courtyard went to the school she left, after her fight with Leevearne.

They were gray or graying, bald or balding. Some had so many wrinkles they looked like Shar-Pei puppies. Some had gained a ton. Others had aged gracefully, and really looked good.

But she didn't see any of their aging, or obese, bodies. All she saw was the faces of the boys and girls who *still* taunted her, in her dreams.

For a minute she was that bullied child again. The one who'd wanted Death to help her escape her tormented life. She turned her gaze back toward Michael, and looked up at him, nervously. "This isn't my class reunion."

"Yes, it is, Ruby," he replied.

She shook her head. "No, it is not. Why am I at this reunion, Michael?"

"They combined the two schools' reunions, because the other school was demolished last year. This one will be torn down next week. It is the end of an era."

"Good riddance," she replied. "I really don't want to be here, hon. Why have you done this to me?"

He stepped up and blocked her in the doorjamb, of the limo. Then wrapped his arm around her waist, and kissed her temple. "You have old ghosts that you need to put to rest, Ruby. I hear them while you sleep. You are still tormented."

"You don't mean Smith?" she asked. She was so far past him. She thought Michael knew that.

"Not Smith," he replied, and squeezed her waist. "All of the others. All of the ones that hurt you; male and female."

Her eyes teared, because those ghosts were perpetual. They'd all gone on with their lives, and forgotten what they'd put her through. Only the wounded remembered. Only the wounded carried the scars. She'd never forget them, but she didn't want to see any of them, either.

Michael stroked her cheek. "Trust me, Ruby. You look exquisite. You are the belle of the ball."

She sighed, and laid her head on his chest. He evidently wanted to confront her tormentors. "Please tell me Smith and Leevearne aren't here."

"All of the Walker brothers, and their wives, are here."

Her heart dropped. Those people did not like her, and she could care less; with the exception of Leevearne. The last thing she wanted was to come face to face with any of them. "Why are they all here?"

"The reunion is for ten graduating classes. That includes all of the Walker brothers," he replied.

She looked at him, again. "Did you arrange this, Michael?"

"Of course not, Ruby," he replied. "But, I did not want to miss the opportunity."

"You just better hope none of these people make me cut them. I ain't got no pro-"

He robustly laughed, and caressed her cheek. Then

he tilted her head back, and gazed into her eyes. His Ruby! She was the key that unlocked the deadbolt to his emotions. Her love allowed him to commune with all the *good* spirits. "I love you, woman. Please behave yourself. I will make it up to you tonight," he promised.

She stroked his waist. "You'd better."

His stomach bunched. He leaned down to kiss her, but was interrupted.

~

"Excuse us."

Michael and Verenda paused and glanced toward the voice. He closed the car door, but kept his arm around Verenda's waist. "Good evening," he replied.

"Good evening," Verenda echoed.

"I'm Betty Jean Brown, and this is my husband, Randolph."

Michael extended his hand. "Good to meet you, Mr. and Mrs. Brown. I am Michael, and this is my wife, Verenda."

"Oh, we know who you are," Brown replied. "It is a privilege to meet *you!*" He was holding Michael's hand with both of his, and rapidly shaking it. "My wife and I would love for you, and your wife, to share a table with us."

Michael stilled his hand. "Are you not sitting with Floyd, and his brothers?" Michael asked.

"There's not enough room," Betty Jean replied. "We'd much rather sit with *you,* anyway."

Verenda wrapped her arm around Michael's stomach, and laughed. Mrs. Brown was acting like she was standing in the presence of God. Greatness perhaps, but not God. Her fingers were tee-peed, and she was on the verge of bowing. Her reaction was what Michael has had to deal with from everyone, but her, Donnell…and Desiree.

Michael stopped her before she actually bowed down. That would have been grossly inappropriate, especially with of all these nosey people staring.

Mrs. Brown looped her arm in Michael's free arm. She was giddy! She smiled and asked Verenda, "Do you mind if I escort your husband to the table?"

Verenda smiled. Michael was letting her hear Mrs. Brown's thoughts. The woman wanted to jump in Michael's arms, but held back out of respect. It had nothing to do with how handsome and debonair he was, either. The woman just wanted to *touch* the Archangel. She stroked Michael's stomach. "Of course not."

Brown smiled. "Thank you, for that. All my wife talks about is meeting Michael. Brock promised he'd introduce her to him, but you guys were out of town," he informed them. Then he extended his elbow. "Allow me to escort you," he offered.

He felt sorry for Smittie, because if it were him, he would have chosen this *fine* woman. Betty Boop would have been a distant memory!! But then, Michael might have killed him.

He jumped when he heard Michael's voice in his head…

"You are correct, Mr. Brown. I would have. She has always been my bride."

The only response he had was *"My bad."*

He heard Michael chuckle. He liked the Archangel.

There was definitely a human component to the man.

~

Before they took a step they saw the Walker brothers, and their wives, walking toward them. Verenda and Michael reached for each other, at the same time. He wrapped both arms around her, and she squeezed his stomach. She did not like drama, and especially not in front of this gawking crowd. Man, she hated nosey people.

"Don't think I won't cut them, Michael. I am not in the mood for their mess. I told you I didn't want to be here, in the first place!!"

He rubbed her waist reassuringly. *"Be easy, Ruby."*

"Oh I'm easy alright! I'm so easy that I'm going to bitch slap the first one who says something smart! Watch my word!"

He chuckled because Ruby never used foul language. *"Behave, woman!"*

~

Floyd huffed. "I started this way before you, Brown. How did you beat me here, man?"

"Betty Jean was damn near running, man," Brown replied and laughed.

"With my brand new legs," Betty Jean added, proudly.

They all laughed.

Floyd shook Michael's hand. "Hey, man."

Michael smiled. "Good to see you, Floyd."

"I'm sorry I missed your send off."

"I understood," Michael replied. Floyd had given him the courtesy of reaching out and explaining the situation. He assured him that he was going to put an end to this discord. In fact, Floyd was the one who told him about the reunion. They both agreed that now was the time.

He'd promised to bring Ruby to the reunion. Floyd promised to work on the women, at the estate. He heard Floyd when he declared he was done with this mess.

At that point, he reached out and initiated a come to Jesus moment. He put the fear of losing their children on all of those women's hearts.

The Master was tired of their pettiness, too. He had gently whispered, *"What they do to the least of my children, they do to me, Michael."* Then He commanded him to get it handled. His command had been, *"Do not tarry."*

Of course the Master knew, like he did, that Lucifer was trying to destroy Smith's marriage.

~

"I am Floyd Walker," Floyd said and hugged Verenda. "You look lovely tonight. Congratulations."

Verenda knew Floyd was going to catch hell for speaking to her, not to mention touching her. She went formal. "Thank you, Reverend Walker."

Floyd shook his head. "No, ma'am. I insist that you call me Floyd. Michael is my dearest friend. I hope and pray one day you will be too."

~

She was downright speechless when all the Walker brothers, including Smittie, hugged her. She felt Smith's hand tremble, and linger a moment too long. She patted his back and pulled away.

Then, one by one, *all* their wives apologized, and

welcomed her to their family.

"I know you must hate us," SnowAnna said. Then she hugged her. "I am sorry for the cruel things we said."

MeiLi hugged her and said, "Let us make it up to you."

Lucinda hugged her and said, "We'd like to get to know you, Verenda."

Sasha hugged her and added, "We'd like for you to get to know *the real* us."

Earlie hugged her and added, "We're really not like that."

Rebecca laughed and said, "Normally." Then she hugged her.

~

Verenda felt their sincerity and there was no strain, in their voices; or their embraces. She didn't know what had happened, but she suspected Michael was behind it. That's why he insisted she come to this god awful reunion. She was gon' cut him!

"You said you would never go to the estate, and they were not welcome on our island, Ruby. This was neutral ground," Michael responded to her thoughts.

~

Leevearne was the last one to hug Verenda. She squeezed her tight, and wouldn't let go. "I'm sorry. I made all of my sisters-in-law not like you, for no reason," she whispered. "I'm so sorry, Verenda."

Verenda's eyes crested, and she hugged Leevearne, just as forcefully. She didn't care, a thing, about those other Walker women, but she did Leevearne. She always had. She just forgot.

They both sobbed and started crying.

~

The crowd watched as these two women cried in each other's arms. Everybody there knew about the fight that took place, over forty years ago. They all thought that rivalry had died years ago! Some of them wondered if Smith had gotten involved with Verenda again, over the years. They wouldn't have been surprised if he *had*.

The women in the crowd shook their heads, out of guilt and remorse. They were old now, and could be honest with themselves. They'd made fun of her and told her that Smith Walker would never settle for a tramp, like her. They all knew that was a lie, when they said it.

They were jealous because he never paid them any attention. They were jealous because of the way he looked at her. They were jealous because there was no doubt in any of their minds, that Smith *loved* Verenda.

And from the look in his eyes...he still did!

The men in the crowd of onlookers, thought about that old school song by William Bell. Those old timers started crooning, in their heads, "Trying to Love Two Ain't Easy to Do..." They all felt sorry for Smith Walker, because they saw it in his eyes. "He needed to be three men in one, to get the job done. A man to go to work. A man to stay at home. A man on the outside, to keep that woman strong. Trying to love two..."

That brotha was grappling!

~

Michael gazed at the banner that floated overhead. How apropos that the theme of this combined reunion was, "THE WAY WE WERE!" Indeed.

It was time to bring order to this chaos.

~

He opened the car door, and gently ushered Verenda and Leevearne inside. Then he looked at Smittie, and commanded, "You too."

He gazed at the Walker family. "We will join you inside, shortly." Then he leaned down and kissed Mrs. Brown's cheek and said, "Save a seat for me."

She swayed. Her husband had to catch her, to keep her from hitting the ground.

~

Michael got in the car, and closed the door.

~

Chapter XXXIV

"Leave us, Cook," Michael commanded.

"Do you want me to hang around?" he replied.

"Yes. Keep an eye out. Call your brothers in, too. Lucifer is about to get started, and I cannot be distracted by his foolish games, right now."

"What is he up to now?"

"What is the one act that requires my undivided attention?"

"That weasel never gives up, does he?"

"No. But he has gone too far, this time."

"Okay; we'll be in the garage."

"No. Cloak yourselves, and go inside. The Walkers are in there, unguarded."

"Very well," Cook replied, and vanished.

~

Leevearne and Verenda were sitting across from Michael and Smith. They both were still hugging each other, and crying. Leevearne kept reciting, "I'm sorry, Verenda. I'm so sorry."

Her mind swept back to how everybody always picked on Verenda, when she was a girl. She'd always been the underdog. People had *always* been mean to her; and even back then, she held her peace. She hadn't known how to defend herself physically, or verbally.

Just like they'd done in high school, her and her sisters-in-law didn't blame their husbands. It had to be *Verenda's* fault, not Smittie's!!

It wasn't like the woman told Smittie 'you better love me'. It wasn't even like she'd flaunted herself in his face, and enticed him. In fact, she'd done quite the contrary.

Georgia House wasn't five miles from where they used to live, yet they'd never once crossed paths. Not at the gas station. Not at the drycleaners. Not even at the grocery store.

They'd spent countless hours at Desiree's and Donnell's house, but never once saw her. She'd even demanded that Desiree never tell them that they knew her. Donnell had told them that Verenda wanted no part of either of them.

Verenda had deliberately kept a low profile, for well over forty years; yet Smith *still* carried a torch for her. That wasn't *her!* That was *him!*

She finally got it. Smith's love for Verenda had nothing to do with his love for her. He'd always been a devoted husband, and doting father. Her girls lacked for nothing, from him. She hadn't been denied one ounce of devotion. If all she had to share was a minute piece of his heart, she could do that.

In the end her daughter, Maria, was right. Smittie's heart won't *let* him forget.

She squeezed Verenda harder. "I'm so sorry."

~

Michael reached out and eased their spirits; and Smittie's too. The man was falling apart on the inside. Then he opened his arms and beckoned, with both hands, for Ruby to join him.

Verenda traded places with Smith, and slid into Michael's open arms. He cupped her cheek and wiped her tears with his thumb. "It is time," he said.

She nodded, and kissed the palm of his hand. "Okay."

~

"There has been a lot of unfounded resentment, and cruel accusations, since Ruby came back into your lives. It was offensive to me, but it did not bother her. That is the only reason I have not previously acted on her behalf," Michael informed them.

~

Smittie reached for Leevearne's hand, and squeezed it. Leevearne squeezed his hand, with both of hers; and looked down. They both thought he was getting ready to chew on her, for her blatant disrespect.

And rightly so...

~

"However, it pleases me greatly, Leevearne, that you and your sisters-in-law have apologized to my wife."

He stroked Verenda's side. "After Ruby and I got married, I revealed a truth to her. Because of Faith's ability to see beyond the veil; she is also aware of this truth. A couple of weeks ago Faith shared what she knew, with her sisters; and their husbands. This truth is why they cling to my wife. They need her to be a part of their lives; and she needs them, in hers. Since I do not intend for Ruby to want for anything, it is time I disclose that same truth to you."

"What truth?" Smittie asked.

"What?" Leevearne echoed. She remembered what Faith had said. "Tell me."

~

Michael did not respond. Instead he took the liberty

of drawing the curtains, to their memories…

~

"I don't want to be a nun, Verenda."

"I don't blame you, Leevearne. I don't want to be one, either."

"You're not slated to be one. The Master has given you Smith. He hasn't given me anyone."

"I know. Smith is nice, but he wants you, not me."

"He does?"

"Yes, and stop acting like you are surprised. It's me you are talking to, girl. I know that you want him too. So, don't pretend like you don't."

"He wants you too, Verenda."

"Not as much as he wants you."

"Does that hurt your feelings?"

"No. I love Smith, but not as much as I love the Archangel."

"My goodness, Verenda. Are you still infatuated with Michael?"

"I'm not infatuated, Leevearne. You know no false feeling can be felt, in Heaven. I'm desperately in love with Michael."

"What are you going to do?"

"There is nothing I can do. I hope I don't get a human body for a long…long time. That way I can still be with him."

~

Michael stopped to let them absorb what they'd just heard. He kissed Ruby's temple, and smiled. She smiled back at him. A conversation between her and Leevearne was the perfect place for him to start.

She stroked his stomach, and whispered to his mind, *"I still am."*

He lifted her hand, and kissed it. *"Temptress."*

"Stallion."

~

Smith was frowning. What the what! They were openly discussing him, in Heaven.

Leevearne was staring at Verenda. "We were friends," she stated, more so than asked.

Verenda nodded and stroked Michael's stomach. "Best friends. All three of us."

Michael started again:

~

"Verenda knows how we feel about each other, Smith."

"She does?"

"Yes. The thing is she doesn't want you, either."

"I know that. I'm not blind. I see the way she looks at that Archangel. She's always with him."

"Does that bother you?"

"It does, but only because she is my soul mate."

"But she does love you, Smith."

"I love her, too. I always will, because we are soul mates. But neither of us will be enough for each other. I can't compete with Michael. She can't compete with you. I imagine our union will be a happy one, because we are soul mates. But, I will always be longing for you. And Verenda will always long for Michael."

"I hope when we finally get our human bodies we get to at least remain friends, Smith."

"Me too, Leevearne. I can't imagine not knowing

you on earth. I'll always be missing you, if we aren't."

~

Michael brought them out, again. Smith stared at Verenda, for the longest time. His eyes glazed. "That's why I can't get you out of my mind. *You* are my soul mate, not Leevearne. That's why I've *never* been able to let go," he said, and palmed his mouth. "I've *always* loved you, Verenda!"

Verenda nodded. "But not enough. Not as much as you have always loved Leevearne, Smith."

"Oh God!" Smith replied. "I didn't see you, Verenda! When my mother told me to imagine who my future was with, I only saw Leevearne. She's the only one I saw! What the *hell* happened?"

"You did not see Verenda because Providence blocked your view," Michael informed him.

"How did this happen, Michael?" Leevearne asked. "How did I end up with Smith; if it was ordained that he and Verenda were soul mates? Have we been wrong all of these years? Is our marriage out of order?" She was almost hysterical. "I'm supposed to be a dad-blasted *nun?* What the hell? I'm not even Catholic, for God's sake! A *nun!* You gotta be kidding me!"

~

Michael opened up their memories again. First he let them see Verenda asking the Father for him. Afterward they heard Verenda pleading Leevearne's case, about being a celibate nun...

~

"If you give me Michael, my friend doesn't have to be a God awful nun!"

"A what kind of nun?"

"Sorry, Father, I don't mean to take your name in vain. But, Leevearne is too beautiful to hide herself in a convent."

Then they heard her beg for her children. They heard her say...

"If I can't have them, give them to Leevearne. I wouldn't trust anybody else to love them better."

Then they heard her one more time beg for her children. *Her* children...

"But can I please have my children?"

They heard the Master deny her *'her'* children, but grant His blessings over her and Michael's union; as well as theirs...

"So be it. What you have bound in Heaven, shall be bound on earth."

They heard her plead one more time for the children. They saw her stomp her feet, in tantrum...

"I don't want Smith!"

Her tantrum reminded them of how Faith had a tantrum in heaven, over Arakiel.

~

Michael jumped them to another scene. Smith and Leevearne were leaning against the balcony with their backs to the whole of Heaven. They were lamenting over what their future would be like, without each other.

~

"I'll always feel the void, Leevearne. I'll always be missing you."

"And I'll be stuck never knowing what it feels like to be a wife, or mother. It's not fair, Smith. I hope I never

see you on earth."

"What? Why not?"

"I don't think I could stand to see you with Verenda, and your children. It would break my heart."

"Oh hush, you guys."

"You were eavesdropping on us, Verenda? That's rude."

"Hush, Smith. Besides, I got a surprise for both of you."

"What?"

"I had a meeting with the Father."

"Was He mad at you for touching that dreadful Barren?"

"Yes, but that's not the surprise, Leevearne."

"What is?"

"I asked Father to let me have the big Archangel."

"You didn't."

"What about me?"

"You don't want me any more than I want you, Smith. Let me finish. Father agreed to let me have my Michael."

"He did?"

"He did?"

"Yes! Then He asked me about the children."

"Oh God, Verenda. You are barren. Does that mean they won't be born?"

"Father said that the children could born, without me. I was only the vessel. They can be born through another womb."

"They can?"

"Yes. And I suggested your womb, Leevearne."

"That won't happen. I'm destined to be a nun."

"Not anymore. He agreed to let you and Smith be mates. He also agreed to let you carry the children."

"What?"

"I told him that I didn't believe anybody could love my children, as much as I would've, but you. I told him you were too beautiful to be stuck behind a baggie nun outfit. I begged him to let you have Smith, and the children."

"You did that for me, Verenda?"

"Of course I did. You and Smith are my best friends, Leevearne."

"But, you are giving me your family!"

"Yes, I am; in exchange for the big Archangel. But, you both have to promise me that I can be in their lives."

"You are my best friend, Verenda; and I love you."

"I love you too, Leevearne. That's why I'm entrusting my children to you."

"We will share them. I promise. Our children will love you on earth, as much as they do here in Heaven."

"Since Leevearne is going to be my children's mother; you have to be their godmother, Verenda."

"Okay!! The Master said I could tell the children. Do you guys want to tell them together?"

"Yes! Yes!"

~

Michael brought them out of the memory. "Leevearne and I are the Master's permissive will. We are the Rams in the bush," he informed them.

~

Leevearne and Smittie stared at Verenda.

Leevearne's tears started flowing again.

She and Smith both were remembering more than what Michael had just shown them. They were *feeling* how close the three of them had been. Leevearne was feeling how much she *loved* Verenda.

In *Heaven* all of their hearts were pure, without the stain of sin. In *Heaven* there had been no jealousy; even though it was a three-way love.

In *Heaven* Verenda could have gotten what she wanted, and been done with it. But, she didn't leave it at that. She made sure that not only would she be happy, but her friends would be too. What an honor for her to testify that Leevearne would be a good mother. How amazing that Verenda had *sway* with the Master.

It was abundantly clear why their children, and all of their nieces and nephews, gravitated to this woman. Everyone called Michael "saint", but Verenda was the *true* 'saint'.

Smittie thought that he was crazy before, but he was about to lose it for sure. "You made sure I ended up with Leevearne. Oh God, Verenda! How could you do that for Leevearne, and me?"

Verenda stroked Michael's stomach, again. "You were my friends. I wanted all of us to be happy."

"I've been torn for weeks. My mind kept telling me that you were my children's mother. I thought I was going crazy, Verenda. You gave up your children, for us."

"No, I didn't," she replied. She looked up at Michael, and smiled. She still had no regrets. "I gave them up for *my* Michael."

Michael rubbed her waist and smiled.

~

Leevearne wiped at her tears, and pushed her hair out of her face. Faith had warned her that she'd regret her behavior, and she was right. She was ashamed of what she'd done to this woman. "You did that for me?" she said, just above a whisper. "You pleaded my case, before God. You gave me *your* children."

Verenda nodded, and wipes her eyes. "I knew you'd love them, and be good to them; because you loved their father," she said and pouted her lips. "And in Heaven, you loved me, too."

"I remember," Leevearne whimpered, and shook her head. "I'm sorry, Verenda."

"I don't want Smittie, Leevearne; and he doesn't want me. I just want to know the girls. You promised me you'd allow me to be a part of their lives."

Smittie squeezed Leevearne's hand. "You will be a part of our daughters', and grandchildren's lives, Verenda." He was eternally grateful, because without Leevearne there was no him.

"Smith is right. You were God's choice to be their mother. You are their *Madrina* - "God" mother."

Verenda laid her head on Michael's chest. "Thank you."

He squeezed her, and kissed the crown of her head. Then he gazed at Smith. "Thank you."

~

When they finally exited the car, Leevearne had her arm looped in Verenda's. She was telling her things about their grandchildren, that Verenda was not aware of. She wanted her to know all their little habits. She was also telling her about *their* daughters.

Verenda patted her hand. "They are lovely young ladies, Leevearne. You and Smith did an excellent job raising them. They told me that you have always been a good mother. They said you never once hit them. I knew you were the right choice."

"When did they tell you that?"

"They've been sneaking to my home, every night. Hopefully, they will no longer have to do that."

"They won't," Leevearne replied. "I promise."

"Maybe you and Smith can come with them sometime," Verenda added, and then stipulated, "But just the two of you. I'm not ready to deal with your sisters-in-law."

"That's my fault," Leevearne said and squeezed her arm. "They really are decent women."

"It's not that. They were not my friends, in Heaven. You were. I didn't even know them."

To be truthful, she didn't want to get to know them. She understood Leevearne's issue with her. She couldn't deal with Michael loving another woman, either. But, they had judged her on supposition, and they'd never even met her.

"I feel like I owe you an apology, girl," she said, and laughed.

"Why?" Leevearne asked.

"You got stuck with *them!*"

They both cracked up.

~

They were laughing and talking, like they used to do, in Heaven. Then Leevearne said, "I'm going to introduce you to waterproof makeup, girl. You looked Goth, in that car."

Verenda laughed. "I always do, when I cry. I didn't know they came up with waterproof."

"Girl, yeah. Where have you been?"

Verenda laughed. "Hiding out."

~

Smith and Michael were walking behind them. Smith whispered, "Thank you for sharing with us, Michael. I feel a whole lot better, about everything. But, can you get Al Green out of my head, man?"

"No. But, it will be to your detriment if *you* do not," he replied.

That was a threat, if Smith ever heard one. Michael hadn't chuckled or cracked a smile. "I've tried."

"If you resist that gutless wonder, he will flee from you," Michael replied.

~

Chapter XXXV

A soft instrumental was playing, when they entered the hall. Everyone was standing around, and still fellowshipping. All eyes fell on them. The crowd fanned out, to let them through.

Leevearne felt Verenda's arm tremble, and squeezed it. She knew it had taken a lot for Verenda to show up to this reunion. She wished she had a link to her.

Verenda responded to her thoughts, *"You do."*

"Oh," Leevearne replied. *"Don't let these stares bother you. I've talked with most of these people, over the years. They feel bad about the way they treated you, Verenda."*

"They should," she replied dryly. *"They broke my spirit, Leevearne."*

"I know. I'm sorry. But, a couple of the guys have been looking for you for years."

"For what?"

"To apologize, I imagine."

"I don't want their apologies. All I've ever wanted was to be left alone."

"Michael evidently knew that. I hear your palace is on an island, inside the Triangle."

"Can you imagine my surprise?" she replied and laughed. *"But I love it."*

"There's our table," Leevearne said, and headed toward the Walker table.

"Michael and I are sitting with the Browns," Verenda informed her. *"Will you and Smittie sit with us?"*

"I'd really like that."

~

Leevearne's sisters-in-law nodded their approval and understanding; when she sat with Verenda. Although they wanted to join them, they refrained. But, their tables were right next to each other anyway.

~

Michael was sitting between Verenda and Mrs. Brown. That woman was holding his hand and swooning. Leevearne was sitting between Verenda and Smittie. The three of them were chatting, like there had never been discord between them.

They were telling Verenda about Faith, and how everyone had thought she was mentally challenged. Smith laughed. "Our daughter had a tantrum in Heaven, just like you did."

Verenda laughed. "She did?"

"That girl stomped her foot, just like you did," Smith replied. "God laughed at her, too."

"Your *ahijada* – goddaughter - still has some of you in her, Verenda," Leevearne told her. "She doesn't like a crowd, either."

They all realized that Verenda must have spent a lot of time with the girls, in Heaven. They imagined it was before, and after, she gave them to Leevearne.

~

Verenda looked across the table and got an idea. "Are you going to continue to work, as Police Chief, Mr. Brown?"

"No. I'm going to retire, and help build the subdivision, at the estate. And please call me Randolph."

"Okay, Randolph. Would you consider coming to

work at Georgia House, as head of security?"

"Really?" he replied.

"My security guard is retiring. You would be a perfect replacement, since you already know about the Watchers."

Brown looked at his wife. He never made a move without discussing it with her, first. But, he sure did want to.

Betty Jean could see it in his eyes. He wanted to do it. He agreed to help build the subdivision because Brock gave them more money for their house, than it was worth. He was going to make up the difference, in trade. But, he wasn't very good at construction, or any other physical labor. She was not going to let her husband be a joke, at the estate. She answered for him, "He'd love to help protect those little children, Verenda. Is there anything I can do?"

"I'm going to be cutting my hours down. The lady that is taking over will need some help."

"I'm her girl," Betty Jean replied. "My daughters and I used to have a catering business, before my illness. They are now beauticians."

"Can I help too?" Leevearne asked.

"Yes," Verenda replied. "Deborah Dunson is taking over."

"Really?" Leevearne replied. "I haven't seen her in years."

"Me either, not since we graduated. She was supposed to be here tonight," Verenda told her. "I can't wait to see her."

~

Things were going so well, Michael invited Floyd and MeiLi to join them. It was appropriate because Floyd was closest to Smith, Brown...and him.

He chuckled when Verenda threatened to cut him. She did not want MeiLi at her table. MeiLi had called her a tramp! *"Behave, woman,"* he replied to her rant.

He was grateful that MeiLi was sitting between Mr. Brown and Floyd. She was far enough away from Verenda to keep from getting cut.

Before Verenda could respond, the master of ceremony came across the microphone.

~

"Can everyone take their seats?"

It took a minute for those who were still standing to even find their appointed seats. Once they did, a hush fell over the banquet hall.

"For those of you too young to know me, I am Nelson Allen; Chairman of the planning committee. I'd like to welcome everybody. I'd also like to thank those of you who live out of town for finding your way back to Indiana. It has been too many years, and you all look wonderful."

He paused and took a drink of water. "I want to thank the planning committee, for their unyielding labor. The records show that the only ones not here are the ones who have left this earth. Let's take a moment of silence to recognize them. They are gone, but not forgotten."

Behind him was a flat screen that floated one picture after another, of their classmates who had died. Chatter started again. Some were discussions of old memories. Others were because they didn't know certain ones had died.

Leevearne's eyes teared when her ne'er-do-well brother's face, flashed across the screen. She still missed him. Verenda and Smittie both squeezed her hand.

The Walker brothers looked at each other when Blue's face showed up on that screen. He was not worth the memory, or the acknowledgement. But, they were curious how they knew he was dead. Brock had taken him straight to hell.

~

Nelson started talking again. "I'm not going to take up a lot of time. At other reunions we took the time to see if everyone accomplished what we thought they would, when we graduated. We are not doing that his year. The *person mostly likely to* will not be discussed. We most likely got it wrong anyway."

The crowd laughed.

"We also will not acknowledge king and queen, because there are twenty couples," he said and laughed. "Most of whom are married to someone else."

The crowd roared!!

Nelson kept talking. "As you know we established a scholarship fund for those who were not financially able to attend."

Everybody nodded. That fund had secured plane tickets, hotels, and clothing for a lot of them.

"A few weeks ago I received a call from a very generous philanthropist. He offered to sponsor anyone who was unable to attend, due to finances. Imagine my surprise when he provided me with a gold card, with *no* limit. When we tallied up the cost it was astronomical. I immediately called him; because I was sure he had no idea how expensive it was. I was stressed out, but he was unfazed by it. I asked him if he wanted to adopt me."

Everybody laughed.

"Even while I was spending his money, I had no idea who he was; or his connection to our reunion. I invited him to come. He advised me that he and his wife planned to attend. I still don't know what his connection is, but it is good to see him and his wife here."

He walked over and handed the gold card back to Michael. Michael stood up and shook his hand. "Michael Strong, ladies and gentlemen."

~

Everyone gasped. Floyd smiled, one sided. Nelson graduated with H and E. He really *didn't* know who Verenda was. Or all the hell her classmates had put her through.

He assumed the minute he told Michael about the reunion, he'd reached out. Michael wanted to get a glimpse of everyone who had hurt his wife. He also wanted them to get a glimpse of her. He wanted to flaunt her youthful beauty, and success, in their faces. It was working too, because the men were drooling.

The Walker brothers stared at Michael. He was a trip. He deliberately took ownership of the sir name they'd saddled Verenda with. Her classmates meant it for evil. Michael's physique, and powerful persona, changed the dynamics of the meaning. Strong indeed!!

They weren't the only ones who realized that. Many wondered what his *real* last name was.

Verenda frowned. Michael had set the stage for this

entire event. *"I'm gon' cut you!"*

Michael lifted her to her feet, stroked her hair behind her ear; and kissed her. *"Behave, Ruby."*

~

One by one all those who had received a free ride stood up, and clapped. Half the room had made it to this event, on Michael's dime.

Their free ride wasn't limited to this one night. He'd paid for them to have a week's vacation. That allowed them to see family, they hadn't seen in years. They all thought *'this man has more money than God!'*

Not only that but, they all realized none of them would have voted Verenda as *'most likely anything.'*

~

As clueless as he were, Nelson started talking again. "In addition; Mr. Strong has also purchased the property that our old high school sits on. I just got word today, that the school will not be torn down. It will be turned into a women's shelter."

Everyone started clapping and whistling.

"I'm not running it, Michael," Verenda said.

"Of course you will not," he replied.

Nelson started talking again. "One of our school's alumni, Deborah Dunson, will run the new shelter; and the one called Georgia House."

Verenda stared up at Michael. *"You already talked with her?"*

"Yes, Ruby," he replied. *"That is the reason she came back."*

"You lied to me."

"I had to say something to get you here, woman."

"Just wait!"
He chuckled.

~

Nelson continued. "I'd like for Pastor Walker to bless the food, before we eat." Then he handed the microphone to Floyd.

Floyd stood up and said grace. In his mind he also thanked God for the ties that bound him and Michael. And for the peace between Leevearne and Verenda.

~

Everyone had finished eating. Some were dancing, others fellowshipping. Quite a few came to the table to thank Michael, personally.

Some of those who had tormented Verenda asked her forgiveness. Link wanted to at least say hello. But a fear ripped through him; the likes of which he'd *never* experienced. He swore he heard a voice, in his head, warning him to keep his distance. Unbeknown to him, all of those jocks had received the same warning.

~

Michael felt it the minute Drunkard appeared in the room; and he wasn't alone. No matter how much planning was done to make the event a success there was always one...

~

Everybody jumped when they heard the pounding, and loud sharp screeching coming from the mic. They grabbed their ears, and looked toward the podium.

~

Chapter XXXVI

Thad shouted in the mic, "Can y'all hear me, out there?"

Everyone frowned and nodded. He was the class alcoholic. And he was drunk now!!

"Who believes this joker's name is Strong? They show up, in a fancy limo, flaunting all their money. It is a slap in us poor people's faces. Well, you know what? I got news for ya, Ms. Verenda! You still ain't..."

He lost his breath. He started choking and gasping for air. He dropped the mic, and grabbed his throat. He looked like he was choking to death.

~

Smith stood up the minute he said *'flaunting all their money.'* Every jock who loved Verenda stood up! They were all going to beat his ass tonight. He was the cruelest of them all, to her. None of them knew why, but for some reason he *hated* her!

All of the Walker brothers, and Brown, stood up too. They were all going to handle this clown.

Once he started choking they all paused.

~

Michael froze Verenda, in her seat. Her face was on fire, and her eyes watered. Everybody in that room knew he was getting ready to attack her...*again.* He reached over and grabbed her trembling hand. The one that was now holding her switchblade! *"I will never let that happen, Ruby."*

Leevearne was holding onto her other one hand. "Don't stoop to his level, Verenda," she whispered. She couldn't believe how fast Verenda had flipped that knife out. Where the hell was she hiding that thing?

Yesterday she wouldn't have cared if Thad hurt Verenda. But, today was a different story. She remembered how much she loved the woman. She wanted Smittie to handle it, like he had when they were teenagers. "Kick his ass, Smith!!" she demanded, way too loudly.

Smittie glanced at Leevearne, and then Verenda. His heart broke to see their tears. Everyone knew Thad was the bastard who threw Verenda in the swimming pool. His sister was the one who poured the ammonia. She was on the big screen, with the dead.

Verenda wouldn't let him tell the principal who had pushed her in the pool. He hadn't told, but he'd beat Thad's ass, for almost killing her. He wanted to beat his ass now.

~

"Sit down, Smith," Michael commanded. *"I will handle Thad."*

"It appears you already have," Smittie replied, and took his seat.

"Not even close," Michael replied.

~

Michael was the only one who saw those demons, who had possessed Thad, cut and run. He was also the only one who saw Cook, and his brothers, grab them both; and hand them over to Reap! Lucifer had also sent Gossip to do his dirty deed. They'd both live to regret it.

There was another secret that weasel wanted to reveal.

~

Someone shouted, "Call nine-one-one."

One of the doctors ran up on the platform, and performed the Heimlich maneuver on him. It did not work. Thad still could not breathe. The doctor shouted, "Get me a knife and a straw!"

Another doctor ran up on the podium, to assist him. They performed an emergency tracheostomy, right there on the floor. They both were concerned, because an odd liquid was seeping from the hole, in his trachea. It had a strong odor that smelled like ammonia, and chlorine.

~

Thad never lost consciousness, which was unfortunate; because he was in excruciating pain. It felt like there were nettles in his throat. Even though he was conscious, his life flashed before his eyes. He saw all the terrible things he, and his sister, had done to Verenda. Then he saw something else...or *someone* else.

In his mind's eye he saw Michael, hovering over him. He was no longer in a suit, but ancient battle regalia. His massive arms were folded, and he had large wings. His eyes twirled, as he glared back at him.

Even though Michael's lips weren't moving, he heard him speaking to his mind, *"The bread you casted on the water has returned to you."*

His eyes leaked, and he begged God to just let him die. He heard Michael again, *"You will have no escape from me. You will not die tonight; or any other night."*

Thad was so terrified, he forgot about his pain. He was immediately reminded of it, when he tried to scream. He lost control of his bodily fluids. The smell of chlorine and ammonia permeated his, and the doctors', nostrils.

What in the world kind of creature did that stank ho' bring to the reunion?

He heard Michael again, *"I am Michael, the Archangel. That stank ho' is my wife. Her name is Verenda. Of course you know that already. You made it your mission to make her life miserable; and for that you will pay. There will be no letup. When I deem the time is right, you will join the others, who tormented my wife."*

~

Several of the men helped the doctors carry him out the ballroom. His eyes fell on Michael. He was sitting at the table, in his suit. He thought maybe it had just been a hallucination; then Michael's eyes twirled. Only he could see it.

~

Verenda was humiliated. How long was Thad going to hold a grudge against her? She hadn't done a thing to him. She never even told what *he'd* done to *her*.

It wasn't her fault that his father went to jail for raping her. She was just a child when the man raped her, and beat her to a bloody pulp. Thad and his entire family blamed her.

Last she'd heard the man, and her other foster father, had escaped from prison. No one knew where they were, or had seen them since. She had her suspicions, though; and she was alright with it.

"I want to go home, hon," she whispered.

Michael stood up. "Allow me to escort you."

As he was escorting her across the dance floor, someone else came over the intercom.

~

"Don't go, Verenda. Don't let Thad win...*again!* You are better than that. You are better than him. You are better than most of us, in this room. You always were."

Verenda looked back, and saw it was Jared. He was one of the jocks who'd taken advantage of her. She frowned. He had on the same shirt Floyd had on. A clergy shirt!

"Don't go," he repeated. "Don't allow his behavior to order your steps. God has prepared a table for you, in the presence of your old enemies. It is so obvious, to all of us, that God has blessed you *immensely*. It is abundantly clear that God has found favor in *you*, Verenda. If God is for you what does it matter who's against you?"

Floyd was about to get wound up. He'd just learned, earlier tonight, that Jared was the new pastor; of his old church. That pleased him because, even though he was younger, he had always been Jared's mentor. He was the new pastor's pastor. His old congregation was still being taught the sufficiency of grace.

He stood up. "Preach Pastor!!"

Jared kept talking...or preaching. "Having done all else...you *stand,* woman!! Let the light of His love lift you up, *elect* of God! Rise above the pettiness that has always plagued your life. Don't surrender to the fiery darts of Satan! Don't give him a stronghold on you! Don't let him, or Thad, control your comings and goings! Rebuke him, Verenda! He that is in you is greater than he that is in the world, and Thad! If you trust him he'll give his angels charge over you. I'm a witness they'll keep you, sistah!"

"Won't he do it?" Floyd shouted. He looked at

Michael and laughed. If Jared only knew. "Yes sah, he'll do it alright!"

~

The crowd started chanting, "Don't go! Don't go! Don't go!"

They all came to their feet and started clapping; while they continued to chant, "Don't go! Don't go!"

Michael turned her around, to face him. "What would you like to do, Ruby?"

~

He'd stopped in front of Link's table. Link still had the feeling of doom, if he approached her; but he took a chance. "We were wrong, Verenda," he stated. "Everyone in this room knows that. We knew it back then. We made you think we thought you were worthless, when in truth we felt just the opposite. You were kind, and sweet; and you left your mark on *my* heart. We were just immature kids, who didn't know how to express what we *really* felt for you. If I could turn back the hands of time," he said and stopped. The truth was if he could he'd still be that cowardly jock. Like a fine wine, his courage had only come with age. "I'm sorry I didn't have the courage to tell you how I really felt. How I still feel."

Verenda was blown away. She could see it in his eyes. He wasn't just spouting words. Link loved her. And he apparently always did. She frowned and said, "What?"

He extended his hand to Michael. "Allow me to redeem myself, Mr. Strong. Whatever your plans are for the high school; I'd like to help."

All the doctors, lawyers and other professionals in

the crowd, joined in.

"So would I."

"Me, too."

"I'm in."

All the jocks that had taken advantage of her also joined in. And she saw the same look, in their eyes that she saw in Link's. She was speechless.

They all offered their time, and financial support. Some offered to give it a fresh paint job. Others offered to handle the landscaping. One of the jocks owned a roofing company and offered to replace the roof, for free.

They were going on and on, about what they would contribute.

~

The women that had been mean to her joined in. "Our lives are aimless," one said. "We are old, but not dead. We need a purpose. We can be mentors for those young ladies."

"We should name it Verenda's House," another one said. "We owe Verenda that much."

And the crowd went crazy. They were coming up with one name after another. All of which had Verenda in it.

~

Michael heard their hearts. This would be penance for all of them. In their old age they wanted to work on their heavenly mansion. They all wanted to reap a good harvest, a good reward. "Thank you for your generous offers. You will have to discuss them with Deborah Dunson. She will be running the center."

Then he beckoned for the Walker brothers to come

over. When they got there, Michael said, "Howard, and Smith's, children own a construction and landscaping company. All of the Walker brothers' sons, and daughters, work with them. You gentlemen get with these men. They will setup a meeting with you guys and their sons. I'm sure there will be plenty of work to go around. However, I insist on paying you for your labor."

The Walker brothers were grinning from ear to ear. They would roll up their sleeves and work with their sons, and these men.

Jared walked in the middle of the dance floor and shook Floyd's hand. "We will call ourselves 'Nehemiah'."

Floyd smiled. Nehemiah's spirit was troubled over Jerusalem falling apart. He requested the king let him go and rebuild the wall. "That's right, Pastor. We can start with the school. Once that's done we can take on helping all those who need repairs, but can't afford it."

Those old men were excited. Who knew they'd find purpose at a class reunion. There was something about Verenda's husband that invoked their need to be better. Do better. There was something about Verenda!!

~

Michael lifted Verenda's chin. "What do you want to do, Ruby?"

She was torn. Physical scars healed, but Thad had just painfully scraped the scabs off the emotional ones. She wanted no part of any of them. She never did. That is with the exception of Smith and Leevearne.

However, this was her opportunity to lay her ghosts to rest. The only way she was going to do that was to forgive these people. But, how do you forgive a room full of people whose mission in life was to devalue your worth?

How do you forgive the people who pushed you over the cliff? How was she supposed to forgive the people who chiseled in her brain "YOU! ARE! NOT! LOVABLE!!"

She didn't answer...

~

Michael reached out and started the music. Then he walked her, through the crowd, to the center of the dance floor. This time the guitar was being strummed by Johnny Guitar Washington. And Johnny was making those strings talk!

Michael pulled her into his embrace. He stroked his hand up and down her back, and started to serenade her...

"Thinkin' bout the first time, I saw you, baby..."

~

He showed her the vision she had not seen. The vision when their eyes locked for the first time...in Heaven.

"Fell in love, so fast. Anyone could tell this kind of love has gotta last...last."

He leaned in, kissed her ear, and sang, "Ta Ta Ya Baby...Thank you. For bein' mine, mine, all mine."

~

The old school boys, in the crowd, smiled. Every one of them remembered where they were when that song came out. Back in the day, that song helped them improve their rap, by a playa's mile. It gave them some smooth moves, too.

All the jocks that still loved her looked down,

including Pastor Jared.

~

Smittie chuckled. That angel was singing to Verenda, but he was speaking for all the men in the house. All of them had wives they should be thanking, for putting up with them; especially him.

But, by God, he *finally* got it. He still believed that Verenda was the cream of the crop, but she wasn't *his*. And no matter what he felt for her, he felt *infinitely* more for Leevearne.

He could stand to see Verenda with another man, but not Leevearne. He could *never* tolerate that! And if Providence blocked his view of Verenda, he thanked him for doing so. Because, although Verenda was his *soul mate*; Leevearne was his *life mate*. Leevearne gave his life meaning, and purpose. She made his life worth living.

In the end, it was okay that he loved Verenda. He always had, and always would. But, from the rising of the sun, unto the going down of the same, he was *in love* with his wife. He always had been!!

Not only that, but he didn't mind Leevearne being the ram in the bush. That analogy made Verenda the modern day 'Isaac'. That meant, like Isaac, Verenda was *never* his intended mate. She was his *test*, and he was *hers*. Up until the truth was revealed they were both still being tested, most notably him!

He drew on his knowledge of God's word. *"It is not good for man to be alone."*

God sat on His throne, and made provisions for *all* of His creation. He gave man woman. He gave the stallion the filly. He gave the bull the cow. He gave the alpha the dam. He gave the tom the molly. He gave the cock the hen. He gave the drone the queen. And even in plant life, He gave the stamen the pistil.

God had even gone one further. He had compassion on the *Nephilim*. He gave the offspring of His disobedient fallen sons a 'spirit' mate; even though they were an abomination.

Howbeit then that He would leave His angels out of the equation. He wouldn't! It only stood to reason that He would give His *faithful* angel a mate. After all, wasn't Michael a man? Weren't all the angels? He had no doubt that Michael wasn't the only angel with a 'sanctioned' mate.

He truly believed that God was a rewarder of those who diligently sought Him. God was a rewarder of the faithful, and there was none more faithful than *Michael*.

And for his faithfulness, He gave Michael the cream of the crop...*Verenda!*

His heart gladdened because oh, what a mighty God he served.

Now that he knew the reason he felt what he felt, he could deal with ole Al. Get thee behind me Satan! I rebuke you, in the name of Jesus!

~

He left the dance floor, and strolled over to the woman he'd seen, in his vision, over fifty years ago. The one who had helped him survive *all* of life's storms. The woman that had willingly, and without hesitation, bore all of his children. The woman who'd walked by his side, for more than fifty years; and made that mannish boy a better man.

When he reached her side, he smiled down at her. His entire body responded when she gazed in his eyes, and smiled. They both knew that the storm, that threatened to ruin their marriage, was over!!

He extended his open palm to the only woman he truly loved...more than enough! When she accepted it, he pulled her to her feet; and passionately kissed her. Then he wrapped his arms around her, and crooned, "Ta ta ya baby. Thank you..."

~

When Clyde spotted Smith and Leevearne dancing, he sighed. Smittie was holding Leevearne, like the jewel they *all* knew she was. His boy's shoulders were relaxed. The scowl that had made itself at home, from all the tension, was gone. He didn't know what was said, in that car, but he knew things were back to normal. He was grateful for his brother's peace.

He walked toward his table; to the cantankerous woman he loved...*Rebecca.*

All the other Walker brothers followed suit; Brown did too. Couples all over the ballroom made their way to the dance floor. The men wrapped their arms around their women, and serenaded them...

"Ta ta ya baby. Thank you..."

~

While Johnny crooned to the crowd, Michael crooned, in Ruby's mind, *"Remembering when I first saw you, baby. How I wished, that you were mine! Had a little talk with the man upstairs, I said Daddy, would you please make her mine."*

~

Verenda saw the vision of him, bowing before the Master's throne. It was astonishing to see the big angel kneeling, in submission. He let her hear his plea for a special dispensation.

"I did not mean to, but I have fallen in love with Verenda, Father."

"How did this happen, Michael?"

"I do not know, but it is the truth. I know that we do not have mates, but I love her, Abba - Daddy. If it be your will, let her womb remain barren; so that I may have her."

She saw God place His hand on Michael's bowed, and humbled, head. *"You are my most faithful servant, Michael."*

"I always will be, Father."

"I know. If she will have you, so be it."

~

Verenda smiled up at him. He was the only man she needed to love her. She reached up and caressed his cheek. God didn't tell him that she'd already solidified their relationship. Michael had actually looked surprised, disbelieving even, that God said yes.

She had known all along the big Archangel wanted her, as much as she wanted him. Her Michael!! *"Let me see your eyes, hon,"* she whispered to his mind.

He smiled down at her, and his eyes twirled; but only she could see them. Then he leaned down and passionately kissed her. At first contact, both of them moaned.

Once again, they zoned everyone else out. Couples were dancing all around them, but it was just the two of them in that room.

He let her see and hear the question she asked him, in Heaven: *"What if you find someone else, before I'm born?"*

He kissed her forehead, and crooned, *"Ain't no girl in the whole round world, for me but you! Don't you understand I'm your only man, baby. My love is so true. It's true, baby! Ta ta ya baby. Thank you, for being mine..."*

Then he did something he'd never done before. He hoisted his wings, and possessively wrapped them around *his* Ruby. *"All mine,"* he crooned.

No one else in the room could see the wings.

~

Link stood on the sideline and watched them. It was abundantly clear that he never had a chance with Verenda. Even if he'd manned up years ago, he would have lost her; in the end. To Michael!!

~

Deborah Dunson never showed up.

~

Chapter XXXVII

Lucifer was sitting on his pathetic throne chair. He'd seen Michael and his wife in the car; with Smith and Leevearne. Michael had preempted him, and told the truth. He could not believe those three were actually happy about it. They were too stupid to realize they'd all been manipulated!!

But Michael was keeping more than one secret from that woman. He switched gears. He sent Drunkard and Gossip with another message.

He knew Michael's mind was somewhere else. He'd deliberately created a scenario where Michael's mind would have to be undivided.

He was sitting in that ballroom, acting like nothing was wrong. But he was also contending with Doom, and Spite.

Those two powerful brothers of his were the best he'd sent so far. *"Keep him occupied!"* he shouted at them.

That human, Thad was about to complete the deed. He'd used Thad years ago to throw her in the swimming pool. He knew Smith Walker would rescue her. He'd counted on it.

Smith kept saying *"I never should have touched that woman."* No truer statement was ever said. They'd been in each other's presence, all long. But unlike the Watchers, and their mates, no sparks were ignited. That was because of his stand-in, Leevearne.

He worked on Leevearne's parents, for years. He sent Liar to them and whispered in their ears, *"Smith is a thug. He will get your daughter killed."* He made sure they didn't accept Smith, but Leevearne and Smith kept seeing each other.

Then he realized Smith had to *touch* Verenda, to ignite the spark. That's when he devised his next scheme. He made sure Smith was in the locker room. Then he hit Thad, and his sister, with all he had. He didn't whisper, he shouted, "DROWN THAT TRAMP!"

He knew that Smith would jump in the ammonia laced water, and save her. Fighting for the underdog was in his DNA. His Nephilim DNA!

Once Smith *touched* her...*shazam!!* They gravitated toward each other, like vines. It was all over.

He made sure Leevearne never saw them together. He made sure nobody told her, about their relationship. He wanted them entwined to the point they couldn't be unraveled. He was so sure he had covered every angle; he took his eyes off of them.

He realized his mistake, but it was too late. He forgot to make sure no one told *Verenda* about Leevearne!

If Smith had been with Verenda for another month, or so; he would've chosen her. He'd kept doing the test in his mind, over and over again. That was because he was hoping to see Verenda! He wanted to choose her!

That's when he realized he'd underestimated that spirit, Providence.

Damn!

~

He heard Thad say, "You ain't-!" And that was all he said. He watched as he hit the floor, gasping for air.

"Get up!" he shouted. "Tell her!"

He saw the doctors cut Thad's throat. And he also saw what had obstructed his breathing! Damn! He'd underestimated Michael. He should've taken into consideration that puppet had the hots for his wife. He would never leave her unprotected.

Thad's throat, and esophagus, were both lined with that bastard's eyes. No one could see them but him.

Human doctors would label them as cancer. They were going to radiate the hell out of Thad's throat, in an effort to destroy the growths. Then they were going to poison that man, with chemo; for months. He wished he could tell them that nothing they did would destroy Michael's eyes. As long as Thad lived, he would struggle to swallow; and he would never speak another word.

He saw Drunkard and Gossip jump out, but they were captured. Shit!! He hadn't seen those Watchers standing in the room. If he had, he would have warned them.

Tempest's grandsons were beating the hell out of them. Evidently they were protective of Michael's woman too!

Then he saw Reap. Oh shit!! Ain't no telling what Reap had in store, for them.

Finally, he saw Michael standing over Thad, but he was also sitting with his wife. Not to mention he was still contending with Doom and Spite.

It finally hit him that Michael had split himself! No one knew he could do that shit! He thought only Samjaza had that power.

Michael was keeping a *lot* of secrets.

~

Doom and Spite appeared in his throne room. He stared at them. They looked no worse for wear. "What happened?"

"Michael's brothers showed up," Spite replied.

"Raphael and Gabriel?"

"Them, Araciel and the other six," Doom replied.

"They didn't touch you guys?" Lucifer asked. None of them looked like they'd been in a fight.

"No, they just surrounded Moses' bones," Doom replied. "Then Michael left."

"But, we still couldn't get near them," Spite added.

"Michael has a message for you, though," Doom told him.

"What message?" Lucifer asked.

~

They all heard Michael…

~

"Every knee shall bow."

They couldn't tell if Lucifer jumped out of his throne seat; or if Michael yanked him out. But he was on his knees. He tried to get up, but his hands were covered in Michael's eyes. He couldn't brace himself, because the shit hurt!

He teleported to a standing position. "I will never bow!" he declared and sat back down in his throne chair.

He flew straight up again. Back on the floor he went, on his knees.

"And every tongue will confess!" Michael roared.

Lucifer teleported again. When he went to sit down, his chair was covered in Michael's eyes. He screamed, "Get those out of my chair!"

"Bow down to the one true God, and I will," Michael replied.

"Hell no!" he replied. He went to step away, but found himself barefooted, surrounded by a patch of Michael's eyes. He tried to teleport, but was locked in place.

Demons started filing into the throne room. They lined the walls, on all four sides, three deep.

~

It was clear that Michael always followed orders. God said Lucifer was untouchable. Well so be it. He was not going to touch him. He was going to humiliate him, in front of all of his followers.

They could see Michael dancing with his woman. He was crooning to her, while jacking with Lucifer.

She could not see, because of his tux, but his glyphs were glowing. He was serious. As long as Lucifer didn't comply, he would stand in that one spot.

"Bow, Morning Star. Declare YHWH is the Lord of Lord," Michael commanded.

Lucifer actually trembled; so did the other demons. Michael had pronounced His name, without the vowels. No human had ever learned how to pronounce it that way. It was way too holy for human utterance. They needed vowels, to form a word. Pronounced this way carried a lot of unseen power.

"I WON'T EVER BOW!" Lucifer screamed.

"Very well," Michael replied.

Lucifer felt a sharp pain under his right foot. He yelped, and lifted it off the floor. Michael's eyes immediately rolled, like marbles, and covered the spot.

"Then, you will stand there, on one foot; until I feel you have learned your lesson," Michael said, and closed the link.

~

Lucifer's followers wondered how long Michael was going to make him stand there. He looked like a kid being punished, for misbehaving. The only thing missing was the corner. Every time he tried to put his foot down, Michael's eyes twirled.

To top it off, Tempest and Taz came into the throne room, relieved of Michael's eyes. Tempest was smiling from ear to ear, while inspecting his body. "I FEEL GOOD ALL OVER!" he shouted.

"How did you get rid of his eyes?" Lucifer asked.

"I didn't," Tempest replied. "Michael agreed to release me."

"What's the catch?"

"I agreed to never come near his woman, or his granddaughters, ever again."

"You agreed to that!"

"You damn skippin' I did! I don't give a damn what he did, or didn't do, to his woman! I don't care what he does to her, in the future, either. He can lie to her, and keep any damn secret he wants!" he replied, while rubbing his arm. "Not my problem!"

"You damn coward!" Lucifer shouted at him.

"Well yeah, I guess I am," he replied. Then he reached down and groped his groin. "But my plums don't hurt!"

He turned and walked out of the room. Then he peeked around the doorjamb. "Hey, Lucifer?"

"What?"

"Who you gon' call?" he asked, and laughed. Then he raised his hands and shouted, "I FEEL GOOD ALL OVER!"

Lucifer screamed, "You bastard!"

~

The demons, standing around the walls, frowned. What was Lucifer going to do? Tempest had asked a legitimate question. Who *was* he going to call? If it had been Seraphiel who'd jacked him he would call Michael, to get his boy in order. But, it was Michael who was giving him the business. There was only one person who could get Michael in line. Michael knew that, and so did Lucifer.

Michael was cold!!

It was Lucifer's pride that caused them all to fall, in the first place. Now it would be his pride that would keep him from yielding to Michael's demand.

Lucifer called Michael 'the puppet', but he was wrong. Michael was anything but a puppet. In fact, he was the best, and the baddest, God had ever called. He'd made Michael physically, and intellectually, superior to all of the other 'called into existence' beings. He gave Michael *unlimited* authority, over the Fallen, the Nephilim, *and* humanity! Not to mention he was over all of the called into existence beings: Archangels, Cherubim, and Seraphim. He even gave Michael authority over every spirit, except Holy. But that didn't matter, because Holy was *always* willing to assist him.

Michael was more notorious than all of them, put together. But he did his deed under the pretext of spiritual warfare. Never once in his existence had he done anything that was displeasing to his Master.

He didn't demand Lucifer do anything for *him*. Or even acknowledge *him*. He didn't demand Lucifer leave his woman, and grandchildren, alone; like he had Tempest. He went one step beyond. He knew how to torment Lucifer, without irritating his Master.

He demanded Lucifer acknowledge the one true God. Yahweh! He knew that would please his Master, immensely. He knew God would not stay his hand.

He'd called all of the demons, in the room, to come and bear witness to Lucifer's shame. Either he would acknowledge Yahweh, or he'd stand in that one spot; until he did.

Either option was evidently good for Michael.

~

Lucifer screamed, "ARACIEL!"
No answer...
"ARACIEL!!"
Still no answer...
"RAPHAEL!"
No answer...
"GABRIEL!"
No answer...
"I KNOW YOU BASTARDS HEAR ME!"
Laughter...

~

Chapter XXXVIII

Michael reached over and brushed Ruby's hair, out of her face. Then he kissed her cheek. She was sleeping peacefully, for the first time since he found her.

She tossed and turned, for years; and struggled with the memories. There had been no demons bothering her, or he would have dealt with them.

Her tormentor was Memory. And as powerful as he was, he could not conquer that spirit. Well that was not exactly true. He could banish Memory, like he had done with Brock and Jodi.

However, in Ruby's case, she would have known he had done it. Had it been one or two incidents he could wipe them away, no problem. But, her entire childhood had been a horror show. She would not know *what* he took, but she would know he removed something. As a matter of fact, she would know he removed *everything!!*

~

If he would have removed her memories, he would have had to wipe out years. She would have memories no further back than Cappy. And since Cappy knew about Smith, he would have had to wipe Cappy's memories, also.

Of course she would have remembered *him*, but not how they met. If she remembered how they met she would want to know why she killed herself. She would go on to ask questions about her parents. Where were they? Who were they? She would want to know what school she went to. Did she have any childhood friends? How it was that she became friends, with an angel. How did she lose her memories? Was she in an accident?

Of course he would not tell her anything, because it would defeat the purpose of wiping her memories. And his silence would have led to her not trusting him. It would have driven a wedge between them. He would never chance anything coming between him, and his Ruby.

There was one more truth he had to tell her. Lucifer was never going to stop; and in this instance, the little weasel was right. You cannot have lies and untold truths in a marriage. Sins of omission were sins, nonetheless.

~

He was not going to wake her up to tell her, but he would tell her today. Right now he was going to work on building their swimming pool. Or rather he was going to supervise the building of their swimming pool.

After the reunion, he brought the twins to the island. They were tickled that they were coming back, for an entire week. They had no idea it was the start of his training them.

He kissed Ruby's cheek again and vanished.

~

The twins were with Cook, eating their breakfast. They were excited about the plans for today; all they wanted was cold cereal.

The minute Michael walked in the room they ran and jumped in his arms.

"Grandpa!"

"Grandpa!"

"Good morning, Little Ones," he replied and kissed their cheeks.

"Where is E-li-si?" Hannah asked.

"She is sleeping in this morning. So we have to be really quiet, okay?"

"Okay. She gon' help me build a sandcastle, Grandpa," Elizabeth whispered.

"Me too!" Hannah added.

"Okay, but I thought you girls would like to build a swimming pool, with Grandpa."

"A swimming pool?"

"Yes. In the backyard."

"There is a lot of trees back there," Elizabeth said, and frowned.

"I know. But maybe you can help me uproot them."

"By hand?" Hannah asked and frowned. "We too little!"

Elizabeth was nodding. "Yep. Too little."

Michael and Cook laughed.

"C'mon, let's give it a try," Michael replied and vanished with them.

~

There was a ground level patio, just outside the back door. It was as large as the one off their bedroom. It also had the customary patio dressings, including a large stainless steel bar-b-q pit.

Beyond the patio was a vast terrain of various tropical trees, and low lying greenery. Cook and his brothers' houses sat on the other side of the terrain.

~

Michael walked them through the forestry. They were surprised it was so big. "I didn' know all this was back here, Grandpa," Hannah said.

"Me neither," Elizabeth added. "This look like my

daddy's preserve."

"It's pretty," Hannah added.

Michael smiled. "Yes, it is. But we are going to tear these trees down."

"We too little, Grandpa," Hannah replied. Then she looked up to see how tall the trees were. She lost her balance, and plopped down on her butt. She looked up and pointed her finger. "See!"

Michael and Elizabeth laughed.

He picked them both up and said, "I bet you girls can do it." Then he used his mind and blasted a clearing through the trees.

"You gon' let us do that?" Hannah asked.

"Yes."

"Daddy don't like it when we do things like that," Elizabeth told him.

"Shut up, Lizzie!" Hannah shouted. "How you know? We never did nothin' like that, anyway!"

"I know but Daddy not gon' like it," Lizzie replied.

"I wanna do it, Grandpa," Hannah said. "It look like fun."

Michael laughed. "You father said it was okay if you girls help me, today. That is why I came to get you."

"For real?" Elizabeth asked.

"Yes."

"Let me try!" Hannah shouted. She was excited. "I can do it better than Lizzie, Grandpa."

Elizabeth smirked.

"Okay but first look into my eyes, girls. You cannot just blast things away, without sending them somewhere."

"Okay!" Hannah replied and turned his head toward

hers. "Show me first!"

"No, you girls look at the same time. No matter which way I'm looking, you should be able to see my eyes."

He put them down, and turned his back to them. "Can you see my eyes?"

"I can't see them, Grandpa!" Hannah said.

Elizabeth didn't respond, because she didn't want Hannah to feel bad.

Michael smiled. Elizabeth's eyes were right in front of his, but Hannah's were wandering. She really could not see. That was not surprising to him. He knew that Elizabeth was stronger with her mind, than Hannah. This was just a small test to see what levels of mind power they had. He would have to train them, in the future, at different times. He sensed Elizabeth did not want Hannah to know she was stronger. She was more compassionate than Seraphiel had ever been.

He turned around and lifted them both in his arms. "Okay, look in my eyes." He looked at Hannah first. Then he looked at Elizabeth. She smiled in his mind. She knew he knew.

Somehow he knew that when their ages caught up to Adam's, she would return to being the big sister.

"I will," she said. *"I'll be a good big sister, Grandpa."*

He frowned. *"You read my mind, Elizabeth?"* That freaked him out. No one could read his mind, unless he allowed it. Not even Gabriel, Raphael *or* Araciel.

"Yep," she replied, and laughed at the expression on his face. *"Don't tell nobody, Grandpa."*

He shook his head. This child was too powerful! He definitely needed to get her off by herself. He needed to know the magnitude of her power.

"Okay, you girls got it?" he asked.

"Yes!"

"Yep!"

"Do it," he instructed.

Although she didn't need to, Hannah was animated. She waved her arms, like a magician. Elizabeth, on the other hand, just looked at the trees. The trees, the roots and all, vanished.

"Yea!" Hannah shouted. "We did it, Grandpa. That was fun!"

"You girls did very well," he replied.

"That's a deep hole, Grandpa," Elizabeth replied.

"I know. Now comes the swimming pool. Look in my eyes again," he said and looked at Hannah.

"That's pretty," Hannah replied. "How we gon' get that in the ground?"

"You and Elizabeth are going to materialize it," he replied.

"What's that?" Hannah asked.

"You are going to make it appear," Michael replied.

"We don't know how to do that," Hannah said and frowned. "Where we gon' get it from?"

"*I do,*" Elizabeth replied to Michael's mind. She really didn't want Hannah to feel bad.

Michael smiled. Elizabeth was a kind, and considerate, child. She would rather pretend she did not know how to do it, instead of making Hannah feel bad. As powerful as she was, that was refreshing.

In conjunction with nurturing her gifts he would also nurture her compassion. That was the only mistake he made in training her father. Seraphiel had come out the gate a raging egotistical bully. That attitude did more damage than good.

He would get it right with Elizabeth.

He was going to have to work with Hannah, because she should be able to do it, too. All Nephilim could materialize things, but at the present her mind was thinking like a *human*. Or it could be that she didn't understand what materialize means.

"Okay, Elizabeth; you do it but we will allow Hannah think I did it."

Elizabeth smiled. *"Okay!"*

~

The pool was shaped like Ruby...a perfect figure eight. The middle of the pool had a jasper stone waterfall that separated it from the Jacuzzi. Like a water faucet, cold water flowed on the pool side; warm water on the Jacuzzi side. Both the pool and Jacuzzi border was made of jasper and marble stones. The bottom of the pool was sky blue and engraved with the words "Michael and Ruby Strong." Above and below their name were "Lizzie" and "Hans".

~

Michael looked at Elizabeth and smiled. *"I did not tell you to put names in there."*

She giggled. *"I know, Grandpa."*

"How did you know to use the name Strong, Elizabeth?"

"I snooped," she said and giggled again.

"We need to talk about that, young lady."

"Okay," she replied, but kept laughing.

~

The patio around the pool was also jasper, but had diamond shaped rubies, throughout.

Large jasper boulders were strategically placed on both sides. Large planters, with palm trees, and patio furniture were also staged.

Elizabeth had an eye for detail. In some ways she reminded Michael of Faith. She took it upon herself to add another setting to the pool area.

On the far end of the pool she placed a large U-shaped crystal cabana, with a mini bar. It served as a privacy wall, against the backdrop of the Watchers' homes. It was surrounded by a large, red and white, rose garden.

"That was a good idea, Elizabeth," Michael told her. *"It is very nice."*

"Thank you," she replied and kissed his cheek.

~

Michael put the girls down. Hannah took off toward the pool. "I like it! I like it! I want to get in!"

"No, Hannah! Stop!" Michael commanded. "You do not yet know how to swim."

Hannah stopped. "Oh. It's so pretty, Grandpa."

"I will teach you both how to swim, okay?"

"Okay."

"You both must promise me that you will never go near the pool, or the ocean, without an adult present."

"I promise," Hannah replied.

"Yep," Elizabeth added.

"If you disobey me I will take you home, and you can *never* come back," he threatened. "You *understand?*" His voice was so forceful and stern, it scared them.

They started crying, because their grandpa was mad at them. Elizabeth grabbed Hannah's hand and they vanished...

~

Michael appeared in his bedroom. Verenda was comforting the girls. She looked up at him and frowned. "You just a big ole meanie!"

"What did I do?" Michael asked. The girls were really crying.

"You yelled at us," Hannah sobbed. She was crying up a storm. So was Elizabeth.

He looked at Verenda and hunched his shoulders. *"What?"*

"It was your tone, hon," she replied. *"You frightened them. You have to speak gentler, to the children. We have a lot of little grandbabies. You can't talk to them like that."*

Michael sat down on the bed and pulled them into his arms. "I am sorry," he said, and kissed their cheeks. "Grandpa just does not want anything to happen to you girls. I did not mean to be mean to you. I love you girls."

"Love you too, Grandpa," they replied, but kept crying.

"How about I teach you how to swim, today? E-li-si does not know how to swim, either. You girls can help me keep her from drowning."

They wiped their eyes and sniffled. "Okay."

"You girls want to show E-li-si the pool now?"

They both nodded.

~

Verenda loved the swimming pool *area.* The girls took to swimming much easier than she did. They were splashing around, and having a ball.

It took her more than three hours to get comfortable. When she was finally able to do it, on her own, she felt a sense of great accomplishment. She'd beat down her greatest fear.

She climbed out of the pool and sat in the lawn chair, next to Michael. "That was relaxing," she said.

"I told you it would be," he replied.

She laughed. "And you were right."

When he didn't respond, she looked over at him. He had the same expression he'd had when he revealed how they met. "What's wrong, hon?"

He glanced at her and then back at the children. Then he sent a shout out for Cook. *"Come and get the girls, Cook. Let them help you prepare lunch."*

~

Cook appeared on the patio, and squatted by the pool. "You girls want to help me prepare lunch?"

"Yes!" they replied and swam toward him.

He smiled. They were so cute. "Okay, let's go inside," he said and lifted them out of the pool. Then he wrapped a Disney World towel around them, and picked them up.

"What we havin'?" Hannah asked.

"What would you like?"

"Ummmm...hotdogs!"

"Yep!" Elizabeth agreed. "And french fries."

"Hotdogs, and french fries, it is," he replied.
They waved at Michael and Verenda. "Bye!"

~

Chapter XXXIX

Michael put up a cone of silence, and a mind block, so that Elizabeth would not be able to hear. "You are aware that Lucifer sent Thad to attack you."

She frowned. Why was he bringing that up now? "Yes. Thad has always hated me, and Lucifer capitalizes on that hate."

"That is true. That is why I allowed Link to admit how he felt about you."

"Why?"

"To even the scale, Ruby," he replied.

"I didn't need to hear that. All I've ever needed is for you to love me, Michael."

"It was important for you to hear it. Your spirit needed to know that none of those guys used you, Ruby. They all loved you, including Pastor Jared. They were just immature boys."

"Perhaps you are right."

"I know that I am right. You did not wrestle in your sleep, last night. Your spirit was finally able to have a good night's rest."

She smiled. That is why he always said, *'have a good night's rest.'* Her body slept, but there had never been rest for her weary spirit.

Memory wasn't an evil spirit, but it was relentless and truthful. It hid in the corridors of her mind, during the day; overshadowed by her busyness. But at night it eased out of the peripheral, and took control of her idle mind.

Like the little children she grew up with, Memory innocently tormented her...all night long. That is up until last night.

When she woke up this morning she felt different, but hadn't known why. Now she did. Her spirit finally had recuperative rest. It wasn't weary.

Michael knew her struggles. That's why he insisted she go to the reunion. He'd said, *"They torment you while you sleep."* He was right.

She squeezed his hand. "Thank you for insisting I go to the reunion."

"Lucifer sent Thad to deliver a message to you," Michael informed her.

She frowned. She'd just thought he was going to light into her, like he did when they were kids. "What message?"

"There is another truth that I have kept from you. Lucifer is aware and he will not quit until you know. He believes it will be the final blow; that will make you leave me."

Her heart stopped. How bad could it be? She would love to cut that bastard. "It doesn't matter what the secret is, I am never going to leave you, Michael."

"You say that now, but you are unaware of the secret."

She felt the good spirits leave him, again. "If it is that bad, I don't want to know."

"For once in his life Lucifer is right, Ruby," he replied. "Relationships cannot survive with untold truths. You saw how it affected Smith and Leevearne. They were at the end of their marriage."

"What?"

"They would not have lasted another month. All of

the families on Seraphiel's estate were suffering, because of that untold truth. The daughters were fighting their mothers. None of the brothers, and their wives, were getting along. Even the Watchers had aught against their mothers-in-law. The only person happy was Lucifer."

Her heart hurt. She wished she'd remembered earlier. She wished they'd all remembered. "I'm glad you told them the truth."

"That one truth reaffirmed Smith's and Leevearne's commitment to each other," he replied and looked in her eyes. "If I do not tell you this truth, Lucifer will continue to send his vassals after you. If you decide to leave me, it will be because I was honest with you. Not because Lucifer twisted the truth, for his insidious purposes."

She reached for his hand. "Nothing will make me leave you, Michael, but tell me."

~

He opened up a link so that Lucifer could bear witness. He let Ruby see the weasel standing on one foot. She also saw that he had the little pest trapped in that one spot. She laughed. She wondered when Michael had done that. He let her hear his words, *You think that you can win, but you never will, Morning Star. However, you are right. I do need to be truthful with my wife.*

"You bastard!" Lucifer shouted. *"Release me!"*

~

Michael muted him, so that they could not be interrupted by his rants. Then he looked in Ruby's eyes, and said, "Your parents are not dead."

"What?"

"They did not die in prison," he replied.

~

Just like that, she was that scared little abused, six year old girl. Everything they did to her accosted all of her senses. The filth, the degradation, the hunger, the pain, their hands, their mouths! Oh God! They were clawing at her! She screamed, "They're hurting me!"

Michael eased her spirit, and brought her mind back to the present. "They can no longer hurt you, Ruby."

Her heart was racing. After all of this time, she was still afraid of them. "Where are they?"

"I was filled with rage, the day I found you. When I put your spirit back in your body, I commanded Slumber keep you under, until I returned."

"You went looking for them?"

"I did indeed. I snatched them, and your two foster fathers, out of Time."

~

She knew about his private torture dungeon. That was the place he took Carl, for what he'd done to Symphony.

She'd suspected, all along, that that was where her foster fathers were. They'd disappeared from behind prison walls. No one had seen them since. But, she remembered someone had told her that her parents died in prison.

She frowned and looked at Michael. "You told me they were dead."

"Yes."

"Why?"

"It was best, at the time. They were released from prison, the day you killed yourself. They claimed that it was the drugs that made them behave the way they did. They had gone through rehabilitation, while in prison. They would have looked for you, Ruby. I could not allow that."

She trembled. That was a scary thought. Back then she would not have been able to handle seeing them. In truth, she couldn't handle seeing them now.

Seraphiel was wrong in one instance. Even if children stand up to their parents, underneath they still feared them.

Those people would be in their eighties by now. But she knew, like her, they hadn't aged. Humans only aged on earth, inside the sphere of *Time*. Michael's dungeon, like heaven and hell, was out of Time's reach.

She didn't buy into pedophiles being rehabilitated. She didn't believe that the drugs made those people rape her, either. She believed pedophiles thought about molesting a child, long before they acted on their depravity.

She believed drugs gave them the courage to throw caution to the wind. The drugs allowed them to do what they wanted to do, in the first place.

She couldn't imagine those two pedophiles being unleased into the world. Her innocent little 'spirit' mates, and her grandbabies, would be at their mercy. She couldn't handle the thought of her babies being hurt.

She shook her head. Michael could never allow that to happen. "They are not my parents, Michael. They are my rapists. You made the right choice, hon; and I love you for that." She leaned over and kissed him. "Thank you. The world is a safer place without them."

~

Once again, Michael was relieved. Once again, Lucifer had underestimated the power of Love; he had too. He kissed her hand. "I can release them into hell, if you like."

She wrapped her fingers around his. "I don't care. Whatever you feel is best, hon."

"If I release them, they will be at Lucifer's disposal," he informed her.

She frowned. She could see Lucifer plotting with them against her. She could envision them...

She shut her own mind down. "Let them stay where they are, until that Great Day of Judgment."

~

She glared in Lucifer's face. *"You meant it for bad, but you have no idea the peace this information affords me. I'm still abiding, you pathetic weasel. You and no one else will ever come between me and my Michael. And you'd better leave my friends, Smith and Leevearne, alone too!"*

Michael chuckled. Lucifer was cursing up a storm, but Ruby could not hear him. He closed the link. Then he leaned over and kissed her. "I love you, Ruby."

"I love you too, hon," she replied. Then she stroked his cheek. "I do have one question."

"What is that?"

"You knew all along that I was your mate. Why did you let me marry Cappy?"

Michael's eyes twirled. Everyone, including his brothers, had asked him that question. He could have told her that they were mates, the day he found her. But, she was not in the right mind to hear that. And it was not a part of their agreement.

He leaned over and kissed her. Then he spoke to her mind. *"Listen."*

~

"I will come for you when you reach age thirty-five, in human years."

"Why so long, Michael?"

"If I come sooner, you will be too young for me. By then you will have lived, Verenda."

"I'm always going to be too young for you, Michael," she replied and laughed.

"You will be the right age, by human standards. At that point you will never age another day."

~

He brought her out and they both laughed. "You were way too young, Ruby."

"And now?"

He kissed her again. "Just right!"

~

Lucifer was still cursing and shouting, "Michael is manipulating you, Verenda! Can't you see that! You can't be that stupid! You are Smith's woman!"

Man, he hated humans!

~

Chapter XL

Verenda decided to take a swim, before her company arrived. She still could not believe she *could* swim. And she could not believe she loved it. Michael was right; the water was holding her up. She flipped over, and just floated on the water. Elizabeth and Hannah were floating, on each side of her. Michael had patiently spent the week teaching all of them how to swim.

~

In the beginning her grandbabies were more confident than she was. She was scared to let them swim, by themselves too. They told her they could teleport out, before drowning.

However, she agreed with Michael. "Do not get in this pool without me, or Grandpa."

"Okay," they both replied.

~

She stood up. Bless Michael's heart, the water was only three feet deep. If she drowned in that shallow of water, she should. "C'mon, girls, time to get out of the pool. We have to get dressed, for our company."

"Who comin' over, E-li-si?" Hannah asked.

"Some of Grandpa's brothers," Verenda replied.

"I didn't know Grandpa had brothas," Elizabeth said.

"He got a lot?" Hannah asked.

"Yes. He has a whole lot."

"They not bad, like my daddy brothers, are they?" Elizabeth asked.

"No, baby," she replied, and squatted in front of

them. They looked concerned. "Grandpa's brothers are good, like him."

"Do my daddy know them?" Elizabeth asked.

"No," Verenda replied. "He hasn't met them yet."

"Then we can't meet them," Elizabeth replied. She reached for Hannah's hand.

Hannah was vigorously shaking her head. "We gotta go home," she said and pointed her finger. *"Right now!!"*

"Why?" Verenda asked.

"My daddy has to snoop on anybody who gon' bring they ass up in here," Hannah replied.

"What?"

"That's how he roll," Hannah added.

~

Michael was sitting in a lawn chair, holding Smittie and Abraham. They had all four of them, for the week. Abraham was older, but Smittie was much bigger.

He heard what Hannah said, and howled. "Hannah!" he shouted. He wanted to reprimand her for her language, but he couldn't stop laughing. That nosey little girl was a trip. She reminded him so much of Floyd, when he was her age.

"That's what he say, Grandpa," she replied.

Elizabeth was nodding her head. "Yep!"

Michael was still laughing. "Okay."

The last thing he was going to do was change the rules. They were Seraphiel's children, and he had set guidelines that the girls understood. He was not about to tell them that this one time would be okay.

He spoke to Verenda's mind. *"Do you mind if*

Seraphiel joins us? Or would you rather send the children home?"

"What I'd like is for your brothers to meet all of our children, and grandchildren."

Michael arched his brows. *"I thought you did not want the two worlds to collide?"*

"You and Seraphiel have different teams, but it won't hurt for them to know your brothers."

"Very well," he replied. *"But just him, for right now. We will introduce the others, as time permits."*

"Okay."

He sent a shout out to Seraphiel, and told him what Hannah and Elizabeth had just said. He and Seraphiel both cracked up laughing. *"You are going to have to watch your language, son."*

"Their nosey little butts got the message, though," Seraphiel replied. *"Who are these brothers?"*

"Come by and meet them."

~

Brock appeared by the pool. He had a big smile on his face. His babies looked so cute in their little Princess Ariel swimsuits. He bent down and opened his arms. "Hey, girls."

"Daddy! Hi, Daddy!" they shouted, and jumped in his arms.

He kissed their cheeks. "That's my Cute Girl and Pretty Girl. Always let Daddy check the strangers out first."

"See, Grandpa," Hannah said. "We told you."

Michael and Brock both laughed. "Where are Abe and Smittie?" Brock asked.

"They wore themselves out, playing," Michael replied. "They are taking a nap."

Brock leaned down and kissed Verenda's cheek. "Hey, lady." She'd wrapped a beach towel around her waist, to cover herself; but she was still stunning. "You look good."

"Thanks, hon," she replied, and reached for the twins. "C'mon, girls, let's get dressed."

~

Ariel, Chamuel, Jeremiel, Jophiel, Raguel, and Zadkiel all appeared in the foyer. Like Michael they claimed no race, but they were all exotic, and dark. None of them were as big as Michael, but their size was impressive, nonetheless.

They were all accompanied by their 'sanctioned' mates. Ariel's mate, Erica George, was tall, dark, and slender. Jeremiel's mate, Anita Foster, was choco chocolate, medium height, and slender. Jophiel's mate, Wanda Williams, was tall, a little heavier but slender. She was a smooth milk chocolate. Raguel's mate, Brandi Williams, was Wanda's twin, and they were identical in every way. Zadkiel's mate, Charlotte Green, was light chocolate, with cat eyes. Chamuel's mate was Kay Young. She was tall, full figured, and extremely fair.

None of them had consummated their union. Like Verenda, their women had been a victim of society. And like Verenda, they didn't remember what had happened, in heaven.

His brothers were waiting to see how his relationship blossomed. In every sense of the word, Michael and Verenda were the test subjects.

All of heaven was watching; to see how the most powerful Archangel handled having a mate. Would it interfere with his responsibilities? Would his attention be split? Would he step outside the Master's will, while dealing with Lucifer?

Thank the Master it had not. That was encouraging to not only his brothers, but their mates as well.

They immediately noticed the change in Michael, and not just his size. Marrying Verenda had done wonders for his personality. Even his aura changed.

~

Michael smiled and shook their hands. "It is good to see you boys," he told them.

Zadkiel laughed. "Man, when are you going to give Lucifer a break?"

Michael cracked up. It had been over a week and Lucifer was still standing on one foot. "When it suits me."

Chamuel grunted. "Y'all know big brother believes in longsuffering."

They all laughed.

"You need to do something, Michael," Ariel said. "Gabriel, Raphael and Araciel are getting tired of him screaming for them to come help him."

Michael cracked up. He'd tuned Lucifer's voice out the first night. "Why do they not mute him?"

Chamuel clapped his hands and rolled. "You know your sidekicks are a little slow."

~

Raphael and Gabriel appeared in front of him. "What did you say?" Gabriel asked.

"You heard me," Chamuel replied.

"Don't make us hurt you, boy," Raphael replied.

They started playfully boxing each other.

~

Brock was amazed at the bantering between his uncles. They all were Archangels, but they had a human side to them. Or maybe it was the humans that mimicked them. After all they were here *first*. He wondered when God said, *"Let us make man in our image and after our likeness"* if the Archangels were a part of *'our image'*.

He felt privileged to be in their midst.

~

Michael introduced his brothers to Brock. "This is my son, Seraphiel. And these are his twin daughters: Elizabeth and Hannah."

Brock was blown away. He didn't know any of the Archangels, except Michael, Raphael, Gabriel and Araciel. That was no big deal, seeing that he hadn't been a citizen of heaven; before his redemption. What got his attention was their companions.

He thought it was only Michael. He could not believe that all of these birds had stolen some poor sap's woman. He was showing his pearlies, and thinking *'you dogs!'*

~

Michael's brothers were all well aware of Seraphiel. Even though not an Archangel, he was more powerful than they were. That was because of who his father was.

However, he would never be an Archangel because of his human DNA. He was born in, and through sin; shaped in, and by, iniquity. Negative spirits, like rage and wrath, embraced him at every turn; but he was a good man.

They were glad to finally meet their oldest, and most powerful, nephew.

They burst out laughing. "Your son is tripping, Mike," Chamuel said and continued to laugh.

Brock was showing all of his pearlies. He was on the other end of the spectrum, because now these birds were reading *his* mind. He wished Jodi was here, she'd get a kick out of this scenario. But, he felt very comfortable with them.

They all looked *much* younger than Michael, but bore a striking resemblance. As exotic as these birds, and Michael, were he wondered where that redhead weasel came from.

They all laughed again.

"Get out of my head, and introduce me to your women," he said and laughed.

They introduced him to their 'sanctioned' mates. None of these women knew anything about Seraphiel. Zadkiel took the liberty to bring them up to date. "Seraphiel is the first born Nephilim. He is more powerful than most Archangels."

"What?" Erica asked.

"How is that possible?" Kay asked.

"It's a long story," Brock replied and shook all of their hands. He was not going to let the conversation be about him. This was Michael's party. "It's nice to meet you young ladies," he added.

They were all beautiful, and pore-less. He wondered if Barren had affected more than their wombs. Maybe he closed their wombs and the sweat glands in their faces. That had to be it, because like Verenda, their faces were devoid of spots or blemishes. And even though they were way too thin for his liking, they were gorgeous.

~

Speaking of which, Brock frowned. "Where is Verenda?" he asked.

Michael smirked. "She will be down shortly." Then he sent a shout out, *"Ruby, what is taking you so long?"*

"Don't act like you don't know, Michael."

"Hurry up, woman!"

"I will be down in a minute."

~

Verenda finally came down the stairs, to greet her guests, and she was stunning. Michael always complained about how long it took her to get dressed, but he always appreciated the end results.

She was dressed in a white sundress, with eyelets trimmed in red thread. It didn't flare, but hugged her form decadently. She had on three inch ankle strap sandals that emphasized her shapely legs.

His eyes twirled. *"Temptress."*

She smiled, and perused his form. He was dressed in a black quarter sleeve muscle shirt, with black dress slacks. Her heart stuttered. *"Stallion."*

~

Hannah and Elizabeth got to her, before Michael. "You look pretty, E-li-si," Hannah told her.

"I like your dress," Elizabeth said. They both had on little red and white sundresses. They had on cute little flip flops, and Verenda had polished their toenails.

"Thank you, babies. Y'all look pretty, too."

~

Michael stroked her waist. *"You look scrumptious, Ruby."*

"Thank you, hon. You look..."

They were about to get lost in each other's stares, again. His brothers, and Brock, smacked their lips. "Don't start that!" Jophiel said, and distracted them.

Verenda blushed. "Hush, Jophiel, and get yourself some business."

"My E-li-si ain't got no problem cuttin' a brotha!" Hannah said, and shook her finger at Jophiel.

Brock's eyes bucked. "Hannah!"

They all cracked up laughing. Brock didn't laugh, and neither did Michael. It was one thing to repeat his words about meeting strangers. His words were the authority they lived by. It said 'we can't meet strangers without Daddy checking them out'. Even though colorful, Hannah was right.

This was something else. This was disrespectful, and sassing. And it was *not* cute!! He was not going to tolerate that. He picked her up. "What have I told you about respecting your elders, Hannah? Now apologize to your Uncle Jophiel."

"Sorree," she replied. Her little feelings were hurt. She laid her head on his shoulder, and pouted.

He kissed her cheek. Then he reached down and picked Elizabeth up. They were supposed to stay through the weekend, but he was going to take them home for a while. This was a grownup party, anyway. "It was nice to finally meet you guys. I need to get back to the estate," he informed them.

"You're taking the girls?" Verenda asked.

"Yes, just for a couple of hours. Their mother misses them. I'll bring them back later this evening."

She knew better. He was upset that Hannah repeated *her* words. "I'm sorry, Seraphiel."

He kissed her cheek. "No worries. Hannah is a very impressionable four year old. She doesn't know when to speak, and when not to. I can't let them get comfortable disrespecting their elders. I'll bring them back once your party is over."

Verenda kissed them. "Okay. See you later, okay. E-li-si loves her babies."

"Love you, E-li-si. Love you, Grandpa." they both said and waved.

Michael totally agreed with Seraphiel. Her pointing her finger at Tempest was funny, because she didn't know he was there. If he and Ruby were going to be spending time with their grandchildren Ruby would have to watch her language too. Although truthfully; that little nosey girl had snooped on Ruby, months ago.

"Why don't you take the girls home, and come back with Jodi, Seraphiel," Michael said.

Brock squinted. "Are you sure?"

"Man, c'mon back," Gabriel replied. "I wasn't invited, but I'm here, ain't I," he added and laughed.

"You know you want to," Raphael added. "C'mon back, and hang out with us."

"Hold on," Michael commanded. "I will have Cook and Saul escort Smith and Abe back home too. Tell their parents I will get them all back later tonight."

"Alright," Brock replied, and smiled. He'd love to

get to know his uncles. He'd love for them to get to know his 'spirit' mate.

The minute Cook and Saul appeared with the boys, they all vanished.

~

Chapter XLI

Michael, his brothers and Brock were in the caverns, performing a hallowing ceremony. Michael had told them that Lucifer kept sending his vassals to mess with Ruby. They all knew there'd be times when Michael would have to leave her alone. Plus, Michael couldn't keep fighting petty battles.

His brothers were rolling when he told them about Elizabeth beating up Tempest.

"Seriously?" Jophiel asked.

Michael was boxing around shouting, "She gave him a one-two punch to the face. Then she hit him in the gut. Then she slammed him into the table!" He jibbed and jabbed his fist. "My granddaughter smacked him upside his head." He was having a ball, giving them blow by blow details.

Brock was laughing too. He heard the pride in Michael's voice. He was proud too! "That's my baby," he bragged.

Michael stopped and raised his eyebrows. "Let me tell you something else about Elizabeth."

"What?" Brock asked.

"She materialized that entire swimming pool area."

"What!"

"The swimming pool, the patio around it, the flower pots, and the lawn chairs. The cabana!"

"The little quiet one?" Raguel asked.

Michael nodded. "The quiet one. Both girls vanquished all the trees. Hannah couldn't materialize the pool. She doesn't have that concept down yet. But

Elizabeth was on it. And I tell you something else. She is so sensitive she did not want Hannah to know she had done it."

"Why?" Brock asked.

"She was concerned about her sister's feelings. She is precocious, and has a kind heart, Seraphiel."

Brock's eyes watered.

Michael kept talking. "She told me that when she gets older she was going to reclaim her role as the oldest. She is just letting Adam have his fun for now," Michael said and cracked up laughing. "Poor Adam."

Brock hadn't even thought about Adam. When he finds out how powerful his 'squirt' is he is going to go into shock. "Oh man," he replied. "That boy is gon' be screaming for his diaper!"

"And Elizabeth will give it to him," Michael replied and fell out laughing.

They all were laughing at how much fun he was having over his grandchildren.

"Do you know that your daughter read my mind," Michael informed him.

Brock and all the Archangels said, "WHAT!"

"I am telling you; that is a powerful little girl you have."

Brock couldn't speak. No one could read an Archangel's mind. "What?" That was all he could say.

"I know Jodi misses them, but I would like to keep them for a few weeks."

"Hell nawl!" Brock replied. "I've missed my babies all week. We need to set up a schedule, but it won't be weeks on end, man. That's for damn sure!"

Michael laughed. "That is where Hannah gets her colorful language, Seraphiel."

"May be, but you still ain't stealing my children."

"Alright, we will discuss a schedule."

~

Verenda, her future sisters-in-law, and Jodi were lounging, around the pool. There was a cool breeze blowing off the ocean, and it felt wonderful.

The women were asking Verenda a boatload of questions, including Jodi.

"How does it feel being married, to Michael," Erica asked her.

Verenda laughed. She knew they all thought Michael had no personality. And without the spirits, he didn't. "My Michael is a wonderful husband," she bragged. "Everything you ladies think he's not, he is. He is romantic, sensitive and compassionate. And Lord, that man makes my toes curl so far back, they cramp."

"Damn," Jodi said and laughed. "That's vivid."

They all laughed when Jodi and Verenda started comparing techniques.

"I can't wait," Kay said. "I've been holding out for so long, I wouldn't know what to do."

Verenda's heart leaped when she gazed at Kay. She didn't know how she'd never seen it before. "Who was your father, Kay?"

"His name was Damon," she replied. "Why?"

"Because you and I are sisters," Verenda replied.

"What?"

"You are my sister."

"How do you know?"

The Archangel...MICHAEL

"I just do," she replied. Michael had told her she couldn't tell what she'd seen in the vision. And what she'd seen was Kay was destined to be her sister. "You look just like the man," Verenda replied.

"I never met him," Kay replied. "My mother said he was married to another woman. When she realized she was pregnant she moved back to New Orleans. She said he and his wife ended up in prison, for molesting their daughter."

"That would be me," Verenda replied.

They got together once or twice a year, but they never discussed their personal lives. It was apparent that they each had their own shame.

But, that's what she liked about these women. They...were...not...nosey! Maybe they learned a lesson, in Heaven, like she had. All of them had touched Barren. What still baffled her was they were not her best friends, in Heaven. Leevearne was. Why hadn't she been on that balcony?

She laughed when she heard Michael. *"Leevearne was not there because she was sneaking around with Smith."*

"You are probably right, hon."

~

Kay grabbed her chest. "You!"

"Yes," Verenda replied. "I was the child they raped."

"Oh Verenda," Wanda added, and reached for her hand. "I'm so sorry."

Kay reached for her other hand. "I'm so sorry, dear."

"Just be glad your mother was smart enough to get away," Verenda replied.

Kay turned red. "She may have been smart about that, but not other things." She wasn't ready to tell her story. "One day I'll tell you guys about it."

"I think we all have a sad story," Brandi said. "I know Wanda and I did."

"Yeah, but I'm not ready to talk about it, either," Wanda said.

"You are sisters too?" Jodi asked.

"Twins," Brandi said and smiled. "Like your daughters."

"They are so cute!" Wanda said and laughed. "That Hannah is something else."

"Oh God," Jodi sighed. "What did she do?"

Verenda told her what had happened. "It was my fault."

Jodi shook her head. "That little girl is a parrot. No wonder Brock sent her to her room."

"He didn't!" Verenda replied.

"Yes, he did. He told her she had to sit in there by herself, until she learned to behave."

"Poor baby," Verenda replied. "I love her so much. She's just doing what four year olds do. She's right, Seraphiel is just a big ole meanie!"

"She told you that?" Jodi asked, and laughed.

Verenda chuckled. "Yes, and she is right."

~

"How many children do you and Seraphiel have, Jodi?" Erica asked.

"Including the two brothers he adopted, we have

eight."

"Eight!" Erica replied.

Jodi smiled. "We have four sons and four daughters."

"Are Elizabeth and Hannah the youngest?" Charlotte asked.

"No, we have another set of twins that are just a couple of weeks old. Hezekiah and Eunice."

"You have a lot of grandchildren, Verenda," Charlotte said.

Verenda smiled. She had to keep quiet because Jodi didn't know about her relationship to Smith's children. "I am a blessed woman, for sure."

~

Just as the men walked back out on the patio, Araciel appeared. "Gentlemen," he said and smiled. He had his arm around his 'sanctioned' mate.

"It is about time you got here," Michael replied.

~

Verenda jumped up. "Deborah Dunson!" she shouted and hugged her old friend. "I have missed you, girl."

"And I you," Deborah replied. "I came to Georgia House to see you, but you were out of town. On your honeymoon, I understand. It is so good to see you, Verenda."

Verenda looked Deborah up and down. She only looked slightly older than her. She wondered if Michael had held her youthful looks, like he'd done hers. Now that she thought about it all of the 'sanctioned' mates looked as young, or even younger, than her. "I thought you were coming to the class reunion."

Deborah looked at Araciel, and blushed. Then she smiled. "I was otherwise engaged."

"C'mon, let me introduce you to our sisters, and my daughter-in-law," she said and pulled her away from Araciel.

~

Michael nodded. "So your sons' mothers were okay with this?"

Araciel never took his eyes off Deborah, but nodded. "Yeah, they were okay."

"Batariel and Jehoel?" Michael asked.

Araciel smiled. "My sons are fine, Mike."

"You?"

Araciel looked at Michael. "Do not worry about me, big brother. Everything is as it should be."

Michael nodded.

~

Brock put two and two together. That is why Michael wanted Batman at Georgia House. Deborah Dunson had been there the week Verenda was gone. He wanted Batman to get to know his new stepmother.

He looked at Michael and thought, *the Watchman!* He took care of everybody. He looked out for him, the Watchers, Ester, the 'spirit' mates, Floyd, Verenda, his brothers, and now the twins.

In addition, Michael was Chief Archangel. That meant every other angel yielded to his command. Evil spirits ran from him. Good spirits lined-up to embrace him. That sniveling weasel, Lucifer, antagonized him day and night.

His dad had a lot on his plate, but he handled his responsibilities seamlessly.

He was grateful the Master had compassion on him and gave him a mate. At the end of the day everybody needs someone to come home to. Verenda was perfect because, like Michael, she was a breed apart.

He thought about what Raphael said, and realized something else. Raphael had said he had not been invited to this get-together, either. He realized Michael had his *own* inner circle. Those brothers he was closest to. That circle did not include Raphael and Gabriel.

He wondered if Michael *had* been trying to break all ties, when he met with the Watchers. He hoped not, because that would've broken his heart. Just as he planned to always be there for his sons and daughters, he needed Michael to always be there for him. Even five thousand year old men need their fathers.

~

Michael smiled. He was talking with his brothers, but listening to Seraphiel's thoughts. Because of the way he was fashioned he would *never* have a 'begotten' son. And he was okay with that.

When the Master sent him to recruit or execute Seraphiel He had said something else. *"You will never be able to father children, Michael. Seraphiel will be your son, and you will be his father. Teach him well."*

He would forever be grateful that the boy chose his side. He could not imagine killing him. He could not imagine an earth without him. But, he realized the Master *knew* all along that Seraphiel would accept.

With all these spirits embracing him, he could

actually feel the emotions that accompanied Love. And he *loved* his son, greatly. He imagined he should, one day, thank Samjaza for making that possible.

He may have wanted to break his ties with the Watchers, but never with his son.

He turned and looked at Seraphiel, and spoke to his mind, *"Nothing will ever compel me to walk away from you, Seraphiel. You are my son, and I love you."*

Brock looked up and their eyes locked. That was the first time Michael *ever* said those three words to him. His heart quickened, and he smiled. *"I love you too, Dad."*

Michael placed his hand over his heart, and spoke out loud, "Blessed be the ties that bind."

~

Epilogue

"ARACIEL!"
No answer...
"ARACIEL!!"
Still no answer...
"RAPHAEL!"
No answer...
"GABRIEL!"
No answer...
"SOMEBODY ANSWER ME!"
No answer...
"I NEED SOMEBODY TO HELP ME!"
No answer...
"I KNOW YOU BASTARDS HEAR ME!"

~

"MICHAEL!"
"What do you want, Lucifer?"
"YOU KNOW DAMN WELL WHAT I WANT!"
"Are you ready to bow down to Yahweh?"
"NEVER!"
Silence...

~

Stay tuned for Book #2

THE ARCHANGEL

ARACIEL

(Coming early winter, 2014)

ARTHOR'S BOOK RECOMMENDATION

While waiting on my next book, check out these books by one of my favorite authors, Melinda Michelle.

<u>Spiritual Warfare</u>

Surviving *Sunday*
Monday Madness
Temptation *Tuesday*

<u>Romance</u>

Color Me Blind

BOOKS BY THE AUTHOR

A "SPIRIT MATE" SERIES:

BROCK'S REDEMPTION #1
RAMIEL'S SYMPHONY #2
DENEL'S LILIA #3
CHAZIEL'S HOPE #4
BATARIEL'S ROBYN #5
BEZALIEL'S DESTINY #6
ARAKIEL'S FAITH #7
WEDDINGS & BIRTHS #8
BARAQIEL'S DAWN #9
HENRY'S PIA #10
THE BROTHAS #11
SEPARATE VACATIONS #12
YOMIEL #13
ADAM #14
THE PROMISE #15
THE WRATH OF SERAPHIEL #16
THE WALKER BROTHERS #17

"A SANCTIONED MATE"

THE ARCHANGEL, MICHAEL #1

LF

Made in the USA
Charleston, SC
09 April 2016